SOMETHING IN THE WATERS

A BEAUFORT SCALES MYSTERY – BOOK 9

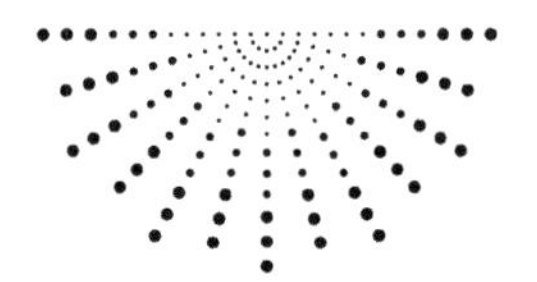

KIM M. WATT

Seriously, don't steal books. Share them. Talk about them. Review them. Tell your friends about them. Writers *love* that. But book thieves will be thrown to the geese, if Nellie doesn't get them first.

For further information contact: www.kmwatt.com

Cover design: Monika McFarland, www.ampersandbookcovers.com

Editor: Lynda Dietz, www.easyreaderediting.com

Logo design by www.imaginarybeast.com

ISBN (ebook): 978-1-067011-66-6

ISBN (print): 978-1-067011-67-3

First Edition: December 2024

10 9 8 7 6 5 4 3 2 1

CONTENTS

1. Miriam 1
2. Alice 11
3. Mortimer 23
4. DI Adams 33
5. Miriam 45
6. Alice 55
7. Mortimer 67
8. DI Adams 77
9. Miriam 89
10. Alice 101
11. Mortimer 111
12. DI Adams 123
13. Miriam 135
14. Alice 145
15. Mortimer 157
16. DI Adams 167
17. Miriam 179
18. Alice 191
19. Mortimer 203
20. DI Adams 215
21. Miriam 227
22. Alice 241
23. Mortimer 253
24. DI Adams 265
25. Miriam 277

Thank You 289
Beware the snap-snap-snap ... 291
Treats to tame the cold 293
About the Author 295
Acknowledgements 297
Also by Kim M. Watt 299

To my lovely friends,
online and off, who have been
endlessly patient with me this year.
And to you as well,
lovely reader.
Thank you.

1

MIRIAM

Miriam stood in the main doorway of the village hall, partially protected from the persistent rain by the little shelter over the door. Water dripped from the hood of her waterproof jacket and somehow aimed directly into her wellies, making her think flip-flops would have been a better choice. But winter had wrapped Toot Hansell in a firm, cold-fingered grip, the last of the leaves long gone from the deciduous trees, gardens sunk deep and quiet into the gentle dreams of hibernation, and the rain had a chill she could feel even through her trousers, which she'd donned in place of her usual long skirts as a nod to the weather. She was regretting it now. The rain never got into her wellies when she had a skirt on.

She plucked at the front of her jacket, shaking her arms and trying to get the worst of the rain off before she ventured inside, and Priya shouted, "You're letting all the warm out, Miriam."

"Sorry." She hurried in, pulling the door closed behind her, and set her large (and distinctly damp) hessian carrier bag down on the floor so she could struggle out of her wellies, placing them on the mat and frowning at her sodden socks.

"You didn't *walk*, did you?" Pearl said, pausing as she unpacked bundles of soft willow twigs from a cardboard box onto one of the tables, four of which had been pushed together in the centre of the hall to form a large square. It was already scattered with scissors and glue guns and some alarmingly large hammers to go with disproportionately small nails. "It's not really the day for it."

"It never seems like the day for it at the moment," Miriam said, taking a couple of Tupperware containers from her bag and carrying them to the tables, socks squishing unpleasantly.

"Rubbish," Rose said cheerfully. She was already seated, and attempting to untangle a cat's cradle of ribbons in various pinks and pastels and other gentle colours. They looked as if some small creature had been nesting in them since last year, and with Rose that was always a possibility. Miriam had discovered a hibernating dormouse in the older woman's linen cupboard when she'd been looking for a hand towel once. She still wasn't sure if it had been invited or not, but given the fact they were endangered she rather supposed it had been there for safekeeping. Now Rose said, "No such thing as bad weather. Only the wrong clothes." She gave Miriam a critical look. "Waterproof trousers, Miriam."

"Far too hot." Miriam replied. "Plus they're only good when one's outside. I can't stand sitting around in them after."

"Just take them off when you get where you're going," Rose said, twisting in her seat and kicking out a leg to demonstrate the fact she'd evidently been wearing luminous green leggings (they matched her short hair) and knee-high, dinosaur-print socks under her own. Her Great Dane, Angelus, looked at her in alarm, as if he thought she might need saving from the dinosaurs.

"If this rain keeps up, I'll consider it," Miriam said truthfully, and went through to the hall's compact, slightly shabby kitchen, where Jasmine was filling the kettle from a large glass bottle of water. Her Pomeranian, Primrose, was lying in the corner with a dog chew between her paws, and she broke off her gnawing to bare her teeth at Miriam. Miriam ignored her, in the hope the horrible dog would return the favour. She never liked to think the worst of anyone, but she was certain Primrose spent all her free time plotting the downfall of the human race. "Hello Jasmine, love. Have we got enough water? I brought some extra." She set a matching bottle down on the worktop, next to the one Jasmine had just emptied.

"I think we're okay," Jasmine said, flicking the kettle on. "We've still got half a crate left from yesterday's delivery. The toilet's making dreadful noises, though. I don't think we should use it."

Miriam tried the tap, and frowned at the water that gurgled into the sink. It wasn't *too* bad, she supposed, not when one considered what people dealt with in other parts of the world. It didn't smell, and it was only barely discoloured when one ran it into a glass, milky with trapped air and suspended grit, but she didn't fancy drinking it, boiled or not. And it was most out of the ordinary for Toot Hansell. She'd never known the village to have trouble with the water before.

"It's got to be this rain," Gert announced, collecting glasses to take through to the hall. "Playing havoc with the springs. I had a bath last night and when I got out it looked like I'd been rolling in chalk or something."

"Mine's exactly the same," Miriam said, picking up an array of mismatched mugs. "It is odd, though. It's not like we haven't had rain before."

"Not like this," Jasmine said. "It feels like it's never going to stop."

Miriam couldn't argue with that. The Yorkshire Dales were hardly known for being arid, of course, but this was excessive. She felt as if she could barely remember their last sunny day, and her garden was rapidly becoming a swamp. Despite this, though, the levels of the waterways that encircled and cradled Toot Hansell were oddly low. It was as if the rain was building up in the land rather than making its way to the proper places, and the water that was still in the wells and springs that supplied the houses was distinctly unpleasant.

As the entire village's water supply was private, the county water board wanted nothing to do with the problems, and several calls to the Environment Agency had resulted in nothing more than an assurance that it was likely just the rain and would go away on its own. After some enthusiastic complaining, though, Skipton council had sent someone out to take a look. They'd snapped some photos and siphoned some water into a few sample jars but pointed out that it wasn't *their* responsibility either, and now any sort of progress on a solution was somewhat stalled.

Meanwhile, a spate of stomach upsets and some rather nasty fevers had led to a general agreement on the village Facebook group that no one should drink the water. Connor at the deli had taken it on himself to create a very official-looking graphic to make everyone pay attention, but Miriam doubted anyone had really needed telling. Some of the descriptions of the aftermath of drinking it had veered into the unpleasantly graphic.

But a bit of rain and some technical difficulties weren't the sort of thing that could slow down the Toot Hansell Women's Institute. They had a Valentine's Day market to prepare for, after all, gifts to make and schedules to plan and tasks to allocate, and one couldn't make a fuss about a little inclement weather or water shortages. So Miriam went back into the hall with the mugs, setting them on the table among the steadily growing collection of cakes and slices and biscuits, glue guns and ribbons and tiny heart-shaped baubles, as the remaining ladies of the W.I. emerged out of the rain, damp but good-humoured.

MIRIAM SQUINTED at the tangle of willow, dried flowers, and ribbon on the table in front of her, put an extra blob of glue onto a clump of pink feathers to fix them in place a bit more securely, then nodded in satisfaction. She got up and carried her wreath to the little stage at the front of the hall, where a dozen others were already laid out neatly, waiting for the glue to set. They ranged from classically pink-themed creations, crowded with hearts and glittery spangles (Gert), to a cheery flow of rainbow colours (Pearl), to minimalist and natural-looking (Alice), and … well, interesting. Miriam set hers (lots of dried flowers and feathers, with a dusky pink theme) down in a spare patch of space next to Jasmine's, which featured a smothering of red ribbons that were already slowly unravelling.

Miriam surveyed the others, then said, "Rose, have you put *skulls* on yours?"

"Just a couple of bird ones I picked up," Rose said. "Plus some feathers. Adds a bit of interest."

"I put extra hearts on mine," Carlotta said. "And some of those little adult dice. *That's* interesting."

Miriam made a face. She thought she preferred Rose's sort of interesting. "More tea?" she asked the hall at large, and was rewarded with a chorus of acceptance. She took the two big teapots from the tables and wandered into the kitchen, the door swinging shut behind her. The kitchen was low-ceilinged, a lean-to that had been added onto the back of the hall as a much later afterthought, and the rain was a ceaseless monotone on the roof, splashing from the overflowing gutter and painting the windows in a shifting flood that distorted the slumbering garden beyond. It should've been soothing, but the long days – weeks, even – of rain had her unsettled. She felt like the village was slowly sinking under the weight of it all.

A crate of glass bottles of water sat on the worktop, half of them empty, and Miriam pulled her attention off the garden, scolding herself for being silly. It was just *rain*. She filled the kettle from one of the bottles, then examined the label to distract herself. The bottle was heavy and square-shouldered, and the label was minimalist in the way only very expensive things are. A swirling logo decorated the front, and small print ran up one side, both on translucent backgrounds. *Sourced: better than water*. On the other side, similarly small, was *100% Toot Hansell, refined, purified, and bottled at the source*. She sniffed, and looked around as Alice came into the kitchen to wash her hands.

"Utter tosh," Miriam said, showing her the bottle.

Alice barely glanced at it. "All the *better than water* nonsense? I'm not even sure what that means."

"I know. It *is* water, so how's it supposed to be better than itself?"

"I imagine they simply think it sounds impressive. Although we do have very good water." Alice turned the tap on, and it spat angrily, gurgled, banged about in the pipes, then disgorged a trickle of milky liquid into the sink. Alice grimaced, but washed her hands in it anyway and added, "Usually."

"I suppose we should be grateful Lachlan's giving us all this," Miriam observed, meaning the owner of the bottling company.

"I suppose we should," Alice said, her tone non-committal. "I don't imagine one gets as rich as him by giving things away, though."

Lachlan was new to the village, and Miriam was fairly sure the water donations were a ploy to get everyone to like him, but it was also desperately handy. He'd turned up as soon as the complaints about the supply being undrinkable had appeared on the Facebook group, handing out crates of bottles and waving off thanks, talking about being "all in this together" in the manner of someone who'd never been in *this* at all. But one couldn't deny the fact it was helpful.

She offered the bottle to Alice, tipping a little over her hands to rinse them, and was about to point out that, so far, Lachlan hadn't asked for anything in return, and it would be quite a hassle if the whole village had to trek all the way to Skipton to buy water, but movement through the window distracted her. She leaned over the sink, peering out into the sodden garden. Nothing. It must've been a combination of the endless rain and the low afternoon light.

She started to turn away, then caught that same fleeting glimpse, stolen through a momentary gap in the rain on the window, revealing a slight figure in a calf-length dress, a cardigan, and slippers, mired in the garden.

"What on earth—" she started, then the figure was gone again. Not just lost in the rain, *gone*, as if a curtain had been pulled over them. She blinked, and set the bottle down to hurry to the door.

"What is it?" Alice asked.

"There's someone out there." Miriam opened the door onto the rustling, grey-hued dampness, hesitating on the threshold as she strained to see over the low drystone wall at the bottom of the hall's garden into the churchyard that adjoined it. Alice joined her, peering dubiously at the dull afternoon.

"Who was it?"

"I don't know. But they were in slippers." Miriam frowned. No one would be out here in slippers on a day like this. But she was sure that was exactly what she'd seen. *And* a cardigan, not a waterproof jacket. She couldn't see them now, but she had done, she was sure of it, and she couldn't just leave them out there. Not dressed like that. She pulled her socks off, keeping her eyes on the garden.

"Miriam, wait," Alice said, but Miriam had already stepped out into the grey afternoon, the grass soft and slick under her bare feet, water squishing between her toes and rain chilling her face.

"Hello?" she called, hurrying to the wall and leaning over the stile. "Is someone there?"

"Miriam!" Alice called after her. "Come back and get your coat. You'll catch your death."

Miriam ignored her, peering into the skeletal stands of trees in the churchyard, then checking each way along the wall, as if someone might be crouched there waiting to jump out at her in some strange prank. But the trim grass among the gravestones was empty, the bare trunks of the trees too slim to hide anyone other than a child. Miriam was sure she hadn't seen a child, not with those slippers and that cardigan. She turned away from the wall and trekked around the hall, paying no attention to the steadily increasing weight of her sodden jumper and the chilly trails the rain was plotting down her neck.

At the front of the hall the road was empty in both directions, no one out walking on such a miserable day, not even dragging a reluctant dog along. The only cars were the ones parked at the kerb, all of them belonging to the W.I. She stood there frowning at the deepening afternoon, aware of a chill collecting on her arms that was nothing to do with the cold January rain. She could taste something oddly brackish at the back of her throat, as if she'd been drinking the stale tap water, and the day seemed dimmer than it had a moment ago. She took a shivering breath, hugging herself tightly, then looked around as an umbrella swung over her.

Teresa looked down at her, her face serious. "Are you alright, Miriam?"

Miriam looked back at the hall, finding the front door wide open and the W.I. packed into the gap, all of them watching her with worried faces.

"I saw someone," she said. "I'm sure I did. In slippers. They can't be well, dressed like that in this weather."

No one answered for a moment, then Alice stepped out into the rain, her wellies on and the hood of her sky-blue coat pulled up over her silver hair. "Then I think we'd best find them, don't you?"

"I'm ready!" Jasmine called, pushing out after her and struggling on her luminous yellow Police Community Support Officer jacket as she came. "I can coordinate!"

"Joy," Gert said, but Jasmine barely glanced at her.

"Miriam, come in and dry off," Priya said, waving at her. "I've turned the heating all the way up. It's ever so efficient since Amelia fixed it. It won't take a moment, then you can go out again."

Efficient was an understatement when it came to the hall's old boiler, which was what one got when a dragon put themself in charge of repairs. But as tempting as it was (she was already shivering, and had lost feeling in her toes somewhat), Miriam abandoned the shelter of Teresa's umbrella to continue her circumnavigation of the hall. "There's no time. They can't have gone far – perhaps they got over the wall and into the church before I got there?"

Teresa hurried after her, trying to keep the umbrella over them both, her running shoes squelching in the wet grass. "Did you recognise them?"

"I only saw them through the window. It was too far away to tell."

There was no one on the other side of the hall either, and Alice caught up to them as they reached the garden to the rear again. "Teresa, you go back," she said, handing Miriam her jacket as the younger woman climbed over the stile into the churchyard. Miriam took it, pulling it on without taking her eyes from the dripping trees and damp gravestones. That brackish taste at the back of her throat seemed to have intensified.

"Are you sure?" Teresa asked. She was shivering in her koi-print leggings and light jumper.

"Yes, no point all of us getting pneumonia," Alice said, giving Miriam a pointed look.

Miriam looked away from the churchyard finally, her cheeks flaring with heat. "I'm sorry. But I really did see someone. And we can't just leave them."

"Of course not," Teresa said. "You go on. I'll get the kettle on again for when you find them." She headed back to the hall with her trainers squidging audibly.

"Sorry," Miriam said again.

"Not at all," Alice said. "Enough of us have decent clothing to be out in. Shall we check the church?"

"It's the only possibility I can think of," Miriam said. "They'd have had to run, though." And the person she'd seen didn't look like much of a runner. But she fell into step with Alice as they headed for the graceful old building, small but crowned with an impressive spire.

They were barely halfway to it when Carlotta shouted from the hall garden. Miriam spun around, almost slipping in her bare feet, and Alice turned a little more circumspectly.

"There!" Carlotta shouted, standing at the corner of the hall and pointing urgently toward the road and the green beyond it. "I saw someone there!" Pearl was on the road itself, peering in the direction Carlotta was pointing while her old Labrador, Martha, splashed in the overflowing drains.

Miriam ran back to the stile, scrambling over it and rushing to join Carlotta. "Who was it?"

"I couldn't tell," she said, trying to stop her hood falling over her eyes. "But they looked like they were in a dressing gown."

"I saw someone in a cardigan," Miriam said, frowning.

"I hope there's not two of them out here," Pearl said as Alice joined them, and another shout went up from the green. Miriam caught a glimpse of Jasmine's bright yellow jacket in the shadows among the trees that edged its far side, then the younger woman emerged, sprinting across the grass with Primrose in her arms and half a dozen geese in fierce pursuit.

"There's someone in there!" Rose yelled from the edge of the green, pointing at the duck pond.

"You get them, then," Jasmine shouted back. The geese had stopped but she was still running, and the women at the church gate looked at each other.

"If they're in there with the geese, good luck to them," Carlotta said.

"Yes, but ... a dressing gown? Slippers?" Miriam said. "We can't just leave them."

"Running around in all directions isn't getting us anywhere," Alice said, then raised her voice. "Ladies, regroup!" The words rang sharp and clear across the road and around the hall, and Miriam half expected the geese to come to attention along with the W.I. All the birds did was glower from the edge of the pond, though.

The ladies filed back into the cake-scented, welcoming heat of the hall, but Miriam lingered on the edge of the road, scanning the green with its flat, lurking pond, and the empty streets stretching to either side of the hall. Chimneys puffed smoke and windows glittered with leftover Christmas lights, but she couldn't shake the feeling that it was all a façade, an illusion projected on a cold and dreadful reality, one that tasted of muddy, brackish water and cold silences. She really wanted to be wrong, for there to be no one out here in their slippers or their dressing gown, lost and wandering. Wanted to just be seeing ghosts and mirages brought on by the long cold of the winter and the dreadful, endless rain.

But she didn't think so. She thought the day was just as it felt. The sort of day that could swallow one whole, never to be seen again.

Unless they did something about it, of course.

2
ALICE

Alice often thought that, if she'd had access to the Toot Hansell W.I. in her Air Force days, many operations would have gone altogether faster and more smoothly, even if lacking somewhat in the usual level of discipline. The ladies regrouped and organised themselves swiftly, and five minutes later Alice was driving around the green, Miriam in the passenger seat. They were both perched on bin bags to protect the seats from the worst of the wet, and Alice could see Miriam shivering slightly despite the fact she'd turned the heat all the way up. The car hadn't had a chance to warm up yet.

On the side facing the village hall, the green flowed smoothly to meet the street with barely the blip of the pavement to show its boundary, but on the far side, where the duck pond nestled among trees and looming water plants, a bank reared up to protect it from the road. A guardrail stopped small children on trikes and overeager dogs towing hapless owners from plunging to the smooth green water below, and Alice parked at the closest point to the pond.

She and Miriam peered out at the deep shadows between the wet tree trunks and dripping bushes, looking for movement. Teresa and Pearl had taken their car to check the church, while Carlotta and Rosemary were driving around the green from the opposite side to

Alice and Miriam. Rose and Jasmine, fully kitted up in their waterproofs (with Primrose in a matching yellow jacket and Angelus mournful and drenched) were marching down the street in one direction, checking in neighbouring gardens, while Priya and Gert went the other way. There had been a general consensus that braving the geese was unnecessary, as if anyone had ventured close enough to the pond they'd have been chased out just as quickly as Jasmine had been.

Miriam got out and went to lean over the guardrail, frowning at the bank below. Her hood was still down, and her curly hair was damp and dark. Alice joined her, and they examined the low undergrowth and the dimpled, murky water visible beyond.

"Should we go down?" Miriam asked. "See if we can talk to Nellie, perhaps? She might've seen something." Nellie was the village water sprite, and the geese were, if not her pets, certainly her bloody-minded companions. Their aggressive mood didn't bode well for Nellie's own.

"I'm sure Nellie would have seen off anyone who came close," Alice said, looking along the bank. "I was more interested to see if anyone climbed up this way." *Or fell down it,* she thought.

"If they got that far. The geese have been worse than ever recently."

Alice made a small noise of agreement. The Toot Hansell Facebook group had been host to a steadily increasing flow of complaints regarding the hostility of the birds, and demands that Someone Sort It Out. As most people outside the W.I. didn't know about the sprite, or dragons, or any of the other, rather less ordinary aspects of the world, the general expectation seemed to be that the council should get involved, but the council seemed even less concerned about problematic geese than they did about the steadily worsening water quality.

"I don't see anything," Alice said, finishing her survey of the banks. "Maybe you saw Nellie."

"It wasn't her," Miriam said. "And if someone's out in this ..." She trailed off, spreading her hands wide. "I mean, it's easy enough to get hypothermia."

Alice nodded. It was. Far *too* easy in this incessant damp, and Toot

Hansell had its fair share of frail residents, in both mind and body. It didn't bear thinking about. "Come on. We'll keep looking."

They climbed back into the car and headed off again, expanding their search by a block, as much as Toot Hansell could be said to have *blocks*. Which was not at all, really, favouring meandering lanes and unexpected side streets instead. The headlights fractured on the raindrops and painted the tarmac in glossy streaks, but all was quiet. Alice didn't doubt that Miriam had seen something. Miriam often saw – or *sensed,* more accurately – things that Alice missed. Alice rather prided herself on her ability to see what was in front of her, and not be swayed or deceived by any sort of fanciful thinking, but she had to admit that, since meeting dragons and discovering a whole hidden world that existed around them, it had become rather the norm to assume fanciful things were quite as concrete as council taxes and power bills. And more pleasant most of the time. So long as one discounted goblins and faeries and the like, of course.

Now she slowed the car even further as they crept through the rain-smothered village, checking the gardens as well as they could between the murky visibility and deepening shadows of the late afternoon. Toot Hansell had never felt dull or oppressive, but today, for some reason, it seemed unfriendly, as if it had turned its back on the human world, curling protectively around its disturbed waters like a cat hiding its wounds.

"We should have checked the pond better," Miriam said. "What if they fell somewhere? Or fell *in?*"

"The geese wouldn't let anyone get close enough," Alice pointed out.

"Unless the geese *made* them fall in," Miriam said darkly. "And what if ..." She trailed off, swallowing audibly. "It's bottomless sometimes. What if they sank?"

"I doubt it. The last thing Nellie wants is humans in her pond." Nellie was, if not anti-human exactly, certainly antisocial.

Miriam nodded slowly. Her fingers were twisted into her sodden jumper, fidgeting with the hem persistently. "Unless Nellie was the one who pulled them in."

Alice gave her a startled look. "Why on earth would she do that?"

"She's been very odd lately. She was in my garden pond a week or so ago, shouting about humans making a mess of things. She didn't even want any Welsh rarebit."

Alice doubted Welsh rarebit was a sprite's natural diet, but scones and mince pies were hardly a dragon's, and they had certainly adapted to them rather well. "What exactly did she say?"

"She accused me of poisoning her water, which is so unfair. I did say I'd be the least likely person to do that." Miriam sounded mortally offended. "I don't even rake my leaves!"

"But why would she think it was you?" Alice asked.

"I'm not sure she really did. She was just *so* upset, and kept saying someone had done something, and she was going to get to the bottom of it. The next time I saw her she was in the village square, sitting in the well bucket with a bottle of whisky, hissing at everyone who asked her if she was a performance artist. Apparently people can see her very easily when she's tipsy." Miriam thought about it. "Drunk, really."

"Oh dear," Alice said. "That doesn't seem like very sensible behaviour." The magical Folk of the world were mostly unknown to humans, and in general Folk wanted to keep it that way. They'd gone into hiding centuries earlier, becoming myth to protect themselves against the endless expansion of humanity and their horror of the unfamiliar. While some still lived among humans, they went unnoticed, protected by the simple fact that they weren't meant to exist. It was quite likely that people really had thought Nellie was a performance artist. Humans are terribly good at self-deception.

"I'm not sure Nellie is exactly sensible," Miriam said. "Not the way she sets those geese on people."

"She is rather too keen on that." Alice thought about it. "Did you suggest she talk to the dragons about the water issue?"

"She said they were too soft on humans, and she wasn't going to be hanging about asking nicely if she found anyone damaging her springs."

"Oh dear," Alice said again, keeping her voice neutral.

"She *can* make the pond bottomless, can't she?" Miriam almost whispered.

Alice checked her mirrors, then swung the car into a U-turn. "I don't know. But let's see if we can find her."

She drove back to the same spot where they'd parked before, pulling her hood up before she climbed out of the car, and bracing herself against the complaint of her hip. The colder weather always brought out the worst in it, and it annoyed her how handy her cane had become with the slick streets.

Miriam was already out, leaning over the guardrail again. Beyond it, the bank was coated with a slippery hide of old leaves and muddy, lichen-crusted roots as it slid down to the pond below. Nothing looked different to when they'd left, the ground undisturbed. The water was still and sleek, dimpled lightly by the raindrops and decorated with the flat green swathes of lilies. "Nellie?" Miriam called.

There was no response, just the persistent patter of rain on the trees and the car roof, and the low grumble and swish of a vehicle approaching on the wet road. It stopped, and Alice turned to see Carlotta lowering the driver's window.

"Anything?" she called.

"Nothing," Alice replied. "You?"

Carlotta shook her head. "No. What's the plan?"

Alice looked down at her damp trousers, then checked her watch. "It's going to get dark soon, and we don't know that anyone's out here—"

"I saw them," Miriam protested.

"But we haven't found anything, dear. And we're all wet and cold. There's no point getting pneumonia over this."

"*They'll* be getting pneumonia."

"Someone's probably already seen them and taken them inside," Carlotta said. "No one would leave anyone out in this."

"That does seem likely," Alice agreed. Miriam still looked dubious.

"We'll take another turn around the green before we go home," Rosemary called from the passenger seat. She waved her phone. "No one's come up with anything in the WhatsApp group. No sign at all."

Alice took her own phone out, shading it from the rain with one hand while she checked the W.I. chat. Everyone reporting in, all with the same answer. Nothing other than more rain and drenched streets. "We can't just wander around all night, hunting for ghosts."

Miriam made a frustrated noise, looking back at the pond. "I suppose."

"I'm telling you, someone's found them already," Carlotta said. "Don't be out in the cold too long, you two." She pulled away, already rolling the window back up, and Alice looked at the pond, sinking deeper into shadow as the light faded, night coming early in the dull stretches of winter. She didn't know what she was expecting to see. A soft rush of bubbles breaking on the surface, perhaps, followed by the dreadful flash of pale skin as a corpse rose?

For a moment she almost thought she did see something, a glimmer of creatures passing swift and sure under the surface, then the pond was empty again. No Nellie emerging with a fish between her teeth, no slipper-clad wanderer appearing between the trees. A goose waddled across the green, though, beady eyes fixed on them and neck snaking with fury. It hissed, shuffling its wings, and more answered from the cover of the trees.

"We'd best go," Alice said.

"Alright," Miriam said with a sigh. "I know what I saw, though."

"I believe you. But there's nothing we can do if we can't even find a trail." Alice took a final look at the smooth, placid surface of the pond, then turned back to the car, the soft damp scent of the old earth rising around them, cold and comforting all at once.

In the warm cocoon of the little 4x4, Alice examined Miriam as she did up her seatbelt. There were unfamiliar frown lines digging into the corners of the younger woman's mouth and dividing her forehead. "We can keep looking if you want."

"No, I'm sure you're right. It's not that. Or not *just* that. It's the water, and Nellie being so upset, and *everything*. It all feels *off*, and I can't stand it. I've lived in this village forever, and it's never felt so ..." She searched for the words, lifting her hands and letting them drop back in her lap. "Lost, perhaps?"

Alice nodded. "The water's been troubling me, to be honest. I thought it was just the rain, but ..."

"But it's not. Not with Nellie and everything else."

Alice turned the car to head toward Miriam's house. "We need to spend some time looking into it. This has been going on far too long, and the council isn't doing anything."

Miriam sighed softly, and when Alice glanced at her she was smiling. It was only a small smile, but it looked more natural on her than those frown lines. "I was hoping you'd say that. I thought maybe I was being silly and overreacting."

"Not at all. This is our village, and we need to look after it. And that means more than just jams and market stalls." She indicated, pulling smoothly into the next street, the wet tarmac purring under the wheels. "I'm dropping you off. Have a shower and warm up, and I'll come by a little later. We can make a plan."

"But we were in the middle of the wreaths," Miriam said. "Everything's still out at the hall."

"I'll deal with it," Alice said. "You need to dry off."

Miriam looked down at herself, then back at Alice. "So do you."

"My top half is dry, at least." Alice pulled into Miriam's road and headed down it toward where an ancient VW Beetle huddled sadly by the kerb. "You're entirely soaked. Get the fire on before you get a chill."

"At least I can," Miriam said. "Those poor people. Our poor springs." Her smile had faded, and there was a dejected note to her voice that squeezed Alice's chest.

"Off you go," she said as she stopped the car, and patted Miriam's shoulder, wishing she could pull her into a hug, but that just felt so terribly *personal*. "I'll pop back soon and we can decide what to do tomorrow."

Miriam nodded and climbed out, walking slowly down the garden path in her bare feet with her head bowed. She'd left her wellies at the hall, evidently.

Alice didn't watch her go, just turned the car around, keeping half an eye out for underdressed walkers, but without much hope. The night was already swallowing the day.

AT THE HALL, Alice found Carlotta, Rosemary, Pearl, and Teresa already packing away the wreath supplies and stacking the Tupperware, the room warm but subdued.

"Any luck?" Teresa asked as Alice pulled her muddy boots off.

"None at all. Anyone else?"

"Nothing."

"The others have gone home to change," Rosemary added. "Gert said her nephew's niece's cousin's god-daughter is a plumber and might be able to help."

"Her niece's sister-in-law's god-daughter," Carlotta said.

"No, that wasn't it." Pearl was curling ribbons into a box while Martha sneakily licked a couple of plates clean behind her. "Nephew's cousin's god-daughter's niece, I think."

"They're a plumber, anyway," Teresa said to Alice. "Not that it'll help the town, but it might sort the toilet out."

"That would be something," Alice said, stacking baubles in a bin. "We can't spend too long here without one."

A murmur of agreement greeted that, broken by Pearl exclaiming, "*Martha!* Bad girl! Drop it!"

Martha gulped the sausage roll she'd just stolen and fled at a surprising pace, given her creaky joints. The ladies kept packing up while Pearl tried to figure out if the old Labrador had managed to get into any of the Tupperware, or only the plate of sausage rolls. Alice thought that, given the water they were currently washing their dishes in, a little Labrador slobber might be undesirable, but it was hardly the end of the world.

The craft boxes were organised, the contents of the Tupperware deemed edible and returned to the kitchen for the next day, the tables folded and stacked to one side of the room, and Teresa was sweeping scraps of twigs and straw off the floor when the front door swung open, revealing a tall, lean man clad in the sort of waterproof gear that came with its own pedigree. He had two crates of glass *Sourced* water bottles clutched to his chest, and judging by the grimace on his face he was trying to pretend they weren't heavy.

"Oh, hello," he said, peering at them. "I saw the lights on. Should I bring them in?"

"Just leave them outside the door," Alice said, and he started to bend down.

"Use your legs," Teresa called.

"Mind your back," Carlotta said at the same time, and he froze, then awkwardly crouched to set the crates just outside the door.

"Are you sure you don't want them inside?" he asked, stepping onto the mat and pushing his hood back. He had thick brown hair with suspiciously well-placed streaks of blonde, and his face was pale and barely lined above a weathered, gently creased neck, giving him an oddly patchwork appearance.

"Easier for people to grab them from outside," Alice said. "If they're coming and going from the hall itself, someone will only leave the door open and let the geese in."

"Those geese are a menace," he said, flashing her a white-toothed grin that didn't crinkle his face in the right places. "They're everywhere. It's an infestation."

"Awful," Carlotta agreed, loosening her scarf and adjusting the neckline of her jumper.

"Tea?" Rosemary offered. "You must be parched, running about the place with all those crates."

He waved dismissively. "No, thanks. I'm a bit particular about my tea."

"We have Yorkshire," Pearl said, looking scandalised.

"I'm sure," he said, turning his smile on her. "But I prefer green."

Pearl made a face.

"Mr Jameson, isn't it?" Alice asked.

"Lachlan." He offered her a hand, the skin smooth under her fingers as they shook. "And it's Alice, right? Head of the W.I."

"Yes. How are your water supplies holding out? You've been bringing a lot to town."

"Fine," he said. "Happy to help until this is all sorted out. Can always bottle more, after all."

"You still have good water?" Teresa asked.

He shrugged. "Well, I'm outside the village."

"It's *so* nice of you to help," Carlotta said, extending her hand. "Carlotta."

"Hi," he said, shaking her hand and pointedly not looking at her neckline.

"Very nice," Alice agreed. "You're not on the same waterway as Toot Hansell, then? I thought you marketed it as being from here."

"It is," he said immediately. "I imagine the problem's downstream from me, is all."

"That makes perfect sense," Rosemary said. She'd retrieved a Tupperware from the kitchen, and offered it to him. "Coconut slice?"

He peered at them. "Sugar-free?"

Teresa snorted so loudly he gave her a startled look.

"No," Rosemary said, sounding faintly bewildered.

"Then no thanks." He disentangled himself from Carlotta, who somehow still had hold of his hand. "Let me know if you need more water." He vanished hurriedly back out into the evening, Carlotta and Rosemary peering after him.

"He has very nice arms," Carlotta observed.

"And hair," Rosemary agreed, taking a bite of coconut slice.

"*Sugar-free,*" Pearl sniffed. "And no Yorkshire Tea!"

"Interesting his water's still fine," Alice said.

Teresa *hmm*ed. "If the problem's downstream, it makes sense."

"True," Alice said. "All these issues started after he set up his water business, didn't they?"

Carlotta frowned at her. "And after an awful amount of rain. How could him bottling some water affect our supply?"

"I'm not sure. Seems odd, is all."

"Didn't Dom sell him the bottling plant?" Rosemary asked. "Wasn't it already in place?"

"No," Pearl said. "Dom sold Lachlan some of his land, but Lachlan set up his own bottling thing. Dom's quite upset, apparently. He didn't expect the competition."

"Can't trust anyone who doesn't eat sugar," Teresa observed.

"How upset?" Alice asked, and Carlotta pointed at her.

"This isn't a case, Alice. It's *rain*."

"You're probably right," Alice said, and brought a couple of water bottles inside for the next day. "Come on. It's too cold and wet to be out all night."

The women left the hall in a final, cheerfully efficient sweep, shutting off lights and locking the door in their wake. Alice glanced at the crates of water as she headed for her own car. They *were* lucky he was being so generous, she supposed.

In fact, they should go and thank him in person.

And maybe say hi to Dom at the same time. Just to cover all bases.

3

MORTIMER

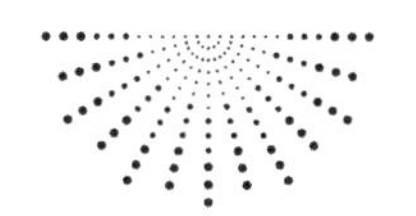

Mortimer stood at the edge of the woods, where the trees were lean and young, looking doubtfully at the stream that divided them from the village. Miriam's garden was just on the other side, shadowed and sleepy, and a curl of smoke drifted from her chimney up into the gloaming sky. Somewhere the early winter sunset had come and gone, but all that had happened in Toot Hansell was the grey had deepened to darkness.

"Are you alright, lad?" Beaufort asked, joining him on the bank.

"I am. The waters aren't, though." They were worse than not alright, really. Normally the stream carried a crisp, pale non-scent, sprinkled with the whiff of drifting reeds and smooth stone, the memory of mossy glades and hidden, unpeopled spaces deep underground. Now it smelled like something abandoned, forgotten and lost by those who once cherished it, struggling to keep flowing but sliding further into stagnation every day, while the plants died and rotted, and the fish fled. The water level was low despite the rain, the stream muddy and shrunken in its bed.

"No," Beaufort agreed. "These water issues are concerning. Even the tarn doesn't smell right. We should have a word with Nellie.

Maybe she's fallen out with the tiddy 'uns and they've stopped cleaning."

Mortimer made a doubtful sound. Tiddy 'uns were small residents of ponds and streams, little scaled guardians who worked tirelessly to keep their waterways free of muck and debris, but this seemed rather more than simple neglect. "It feels more like something's *happened*."

"Run-off from all the rain affecting it, perhaps," Beaufort suggested. "Come on. We shall think about it more clearly with a cup of tea." The High Lord of the Cloverly dragons, older than the village and the largest of his clan, almost the size of a Newfoundland dog if one discounted the wings and tail, splashed cheerily through the mud and up the opposite bank, in pursuit of cake. Mortimer, altogether smaller and finding it very easy to hold onto his gloomy camouflage colours of greys and deep greens, gave the stream a final, dubious look, then followed. He *would* feel better with a cup of tea, and, more to the point, a mince pie while they lasted. He still couldn't understand why they were limited to Christmas. In his mind, if something was as delicious as a mince pie, one should eat them year-round. But it was hardly the biggest idiosyncrasy he'd encountered in dealing with humans. He did find it one of the more inexplicable ones, though.

Beaufort knocked on Miriam's kitchen door gently, the garden slumbering in the dark around them, rich with the scents of leaf mould and deep earth and hibernating creatures. Mortimer hoped none of them were being flooded out by the rain, and had to restrain himself from suggesting they check on the hedgehogs. He was spending too much time around young Gilbert. He'd be catching vegetarianism and some sort of predilection for activism if he wasn't careful.

Miriam opened the door in a pair of fluffy, deep purple trousers with white stars on them, which she'd paired with even fluffier pink boots and a large green jumper that reached her mid-thighs, her nose pink and her hair in disarray. Mortimer caught the anxious orange threads snaking around her immediately, like the scent of hot metal in the rain, even though she smiled as soon as she saw them.

"Hello, you two. Come in." She stepped back from the door, and the dragons trailed awkwardly in onto the old stone flags of the floor, Beaufort trying to wipe his paws thoroughly on the mat on the way. Unfortunately, that didn't do an awful lot for his tail, and he left a wet sweep of muddy water behind him as he went to sit by the AGA stove, basking in its heat.

"Sorry about the mess," Mortimer said, inspecting his paws.

"Not at all," Miriam replied, finding an old towel by the door and giving the floor a quick wipe. "No harm done."

Mortimer could still smell that anxiety rising from her, acrid as metal filings, and he said, "What is it? What's happened?"

Miriam took a deep breath, twisting the towel in her hands, not even noticing water squeezing out of it to drip back to the floor. She hesitated, then, as if she'd just been waiting for someone to ask, she burst out, "Oh, Mortimer. I don't even know. Maybe it's simply the weather."

"You don't think it is, though."

She shook her head, curls bouncing. "Something's *off.* All these problems with the water, and Nellie's geese are being awful, and I'm sure – or I think I'm sure – I saw someone wandering around in the rain, but there was no one there when I went to look, and ..." She trailed off, pressing one hand to her chest, and took another deep breath, swallowing hard before continuing a little more calmly. "But it feels like something's terribly wrong. Not just with the water, or all this awful rain, but something *more.* Don't you think?"

Mortimer found his talons scratching the stone flags, and forced himself to relax his paws. He'd been trying not to think the exact same thing, trying, like Miriam, to believe it was nothing more than the inclement weather, but now she'd suddenly pulled everything out in the open, and it made his chest feel both tighter and much, much better. "They've got worse," he said. "The waters, I mean. And it *does* feel off. I just don't know why." He looked at Beaufort.

"If you say so," Beaufort said. "All I know is the water's a bit unpleasant, but you two are the most perceptive creatures I know. If you think something's really wrong, I believe you." He looked at

Miriam, who'd gone very pink. "What did you mean, though – you saw someone but couldn't find them? I take it you don't simply mean you lost sight of them."

"No, they were out in the rain in their slippers and a skirt. Nightclothes, really. I saw them through the window at the village hall, then when I went outside they were gone. Carlotta thought she saw someone on the green, but we couldn't get close enough to take a look, what with the geese. We couldn't even see Nellie." She hesitated, looking from one dragon to the other. "She wouldn't … she wouldn't *do* something, would she? If she was angry about the water, perhaps?"

"That's unlikely," Beaufort said.

"What about the geese?"

"Well, they answer to her, so I don't think they'd really hurt anyone."

Miriam looked doubtful, which Mortimer thought was more about the geese than Nellie. And he agreed with her. Geese were terrifying, and there were the swans, too. Swans always seemed somewhat untrustworthy to him. So pretty and serene-looking, then they'd go for your tail. At least a goose always *looked* like it was up to something.

"I just don't understand how they could simply vanish," Miriam said. "And I definitely saw *someone*." She almost sounded as if she were trying to convince herself, and Mortimer gave the kettle a longing look.

"We could go and have a look," he said. "Maybe I can catch some trace of them."

"Would you?" Miriam asked. "Really?"

"Of course. It's dark and rainy. It'll be safe." He could feel the colours draining from his scales at the thought of facing swans in the dark, but Miriam's normal peaceful, deep green scent was so twisted with worry and anxiety he couldn't bear it. If he had to face swans to change that, he would.

"We'll have a word with Nellie at the same time," Beaufort said, abandoning the AGA and heading for the door. "See what she has to say about these waters."

"I'll put some more wood on the fire for when you get back," Miriam said. "Do be careful."

"Will do," Mortimer said, as cheerily as he could, and walked out of Miriam's warm, brightly-lit kitchen into the dull cold rain once again. At least he'd spotted the mince pies on the table. Although they were bought ones, which said something worrying about Miriam's state of mind.

❧

IT DIDN'T TAKE them long to get to the green, heading back across the murky stream to follow the heavily shadowed path on the edge of the woods. The scent of old leaf matter and wet earth was almost swallowed by the persistent reek of the water, seeming even stronger and more intense than it had such a short time earlier, as if in recognising it they'd somehow enhanced it. Mortimer found himself wondering if the waters were carrying some infection, delivering it into the heart of the village, eating it up from the inside like a worm at the centre of an apple.

He was glad to leave the stream behind as they slipped into the still, reflective dark of the churchyard, going straight across it to the stile by the village hall. He caught, very dimly, Miriam's lingering scent as they climbed over the wall and into the garden. The rain was washing everything away so quickly, leaving only shadows behind, and even though he padded one way and then the other across the grass, searching for traces, he couldn't come up with very much at all. Dragons didn't smell the way other creatures did. Rather than physical scents, they picked up the emotional traces of events imprinted on the world around them, explosions of joy or fright, trails of happiness and sorrow. They were fickle and hard to catch, but unmistakable once found. Not in this everlasting wetness, though. Not with the overwhelming scent of the waterways bubbling up from the very ground, by the feel of things.

"Nothing?" Beaufort asked quietly.

"Nothing," Mortimer agreed, and followed the High Lord around to the front of the hall, both of them keeping to the shadows of the wall until they were sure the road and the green beyond were empty. The faint, familiar traces of the W.I. persisted on the gate as they padded past it, and a whisper of something else too, sharp and inquisitive, but not clear enough to tell anything. It smelled like toothpaste dried and forgotten in an unused bathroom, fresh and not all at once.

The dragons were all but invisible, their scales matching the shadows of the night as they headed for the pond. The green was as free of scents as the hall garden had been, other than the reek of the pond that crept toward them, squishing out of the ground like the mud between Mortimer's talons. By the time they were halfway across the grass it was so strong that he sneezed, wrinkling his snout.

"Yes, even I can smell that," Beaufort said, leading the way cautiously to the edge of the pond. "Nellie?" he called.

There was no answer, just the whisper of rain on the winter-drab trees. No glooping from the reeds, no splash in the centre. Mortimer edged up to the water's edge and touched it with one paw, almost expecting it to sting with whatever nastiness was causing that terrible cold scent. The water shivered, and gave him back a fractured image of a puzzled, bespectacled woman. He jerked back, staring around, but there was no one there, and nothing in the pond when he looked again.

"Beaufort," he started.

"I see them, lad."

"Them?" Mortimer followed the High Lord's gaze, but the older dragon's attention wasn't on the water. He was looking across it at six geese and four swans, who were returning his stare with unmistakable belligerence. "*Oh.*"

"Nellie?" Beaufort tried again. "We're just here to help."

One of the geese hissed, and the horde shook their wings out, necks snaking and big webbed feet padding the soft ground like bulls preparing to charge. The pond gave a sudden surge, and the edge gave way under Mortimer's paws, vanishing into the depths. He squawked, plunging snout-first into the icy water, eyes stinging and nostrils filled with the awful, stale stink, and the birds erupted toward them in honking fury.

"Mortimer, run!" Beaufort shouted, and the younger dragon flung himself out of the pond, wings beating wildly and paws tangled with water plants and weeds. The High Lord of the Cloverly dragons, veteran of crusading knights and thoughtless wars and fire-fuelled airborne battles, bolted, leading a panicked retreat across the green and over the road, the birds charging after them in a furious comet tail. The dragons didn't stop running until they were safely back in the woods beyond the stream and the pursuit had stopped, the birds lining the churchyard wall and hissing balefully at them.

"That was so unnecessary," Mortimer panted, his snout still itching from the plunge into the pond. "What's Nellie *doing?*"

Beaufort looked at the birds, then at the rusty, grumbling waterway, and said, "I'm not sure, lad. But this isn't like her. She wasn't even there, and normally she only sets the birds on people so she can laugh at them. It's very worrying."

Mortimer wiped his snout with a paw, finding a grimy piece of water lily clinging to it, and thought of that infection creeping through the heart of the village again. It was seeming less fanciful all the time.

❧

WHEN THEY GOT BACK to Miriam's, Alice was sitting at the kitchen table, two generous glasses of red wine set out along with a large, bright orange packet of cheesy puffs. The scent of actual, melted cheese and baking bread filled the kitchen, banishing the chill of the night, and plates sat warming on the AGA. Miriam let them in, a little pink-cheeked and with cheesy puff crumbs still on her fingers.

"Hello, Alice," Beaufort said, padding through the door. Mortimer followed, trying to get the worst of the muck off his paws and tail. The plunge into the pond had resulted in him wearing an awful lot of mud on his belly, and he sat back on his haunches to wipe it off.

"Don't worry about that," Miriam said, waving at him. "I think I walked half the garden in with me earlier."

Mortimer looked around dubiously. Miriam's place was gently worn, with the comfortable, slightly threadbare patches of a place well-loved and well lived-in, but it was always clean. The only mud he could see on the stone flags was what he and Beaufort had brought in with them.

Alice got up, taking a large, softly bubbling pan of cauliflower cheese out of the oven, along with a fat, rounded loaf of bread. She tapped the bottom and made a satisfied sound. "Perfect timing," she said.

"Mince pie to start?" Miriam asked Mortimer.

"Please," he said. If any evening called for a mince pie, this one did. He joined Beaufort in front of the AGA, soaking up the old cooker's heat and trying not to get in the way too much.

"Did you find anything?" Alice asked, spooning cauliflower cheese onto the plates.

"No," Beaufort said. "And no Nellie, just her birds. When was the last time anyone saw her?"

The two women and the dragons looked at each other doubtfully. "I saw her about a week ago," Miriam said finally. "She was very upset."

"This is most out of character," Beaufort said. "I can understand her being upset about the waters, but I rather thought she'd be here trying to sort it out."

"The waters are *terrible,*" Mortimer whispered. "Maybe she can't." It was a horrifying thought, that it might be beyond even the sprite's help.

"She must be able to," Beaufort said. "If the waters die, the village dies with them."

There was a long silence following that horrifying statement, broken only by Miriam taking a handful of cheesy puffs and crunching on them disconsolately.

"I have an idea," Alice said, setting plates on the table. "About the water, I mean."

"Shouldn't we be concentrating on the disappearing person?" Miriam asked, and Mortimer thought of the half-seen glimpse of the woman in the water. He shivered.

Alice frowned. "Are you sure it wasn't Nellie you saw?"

"In slippers?"

"The light wasn't that good," Alice pointed out, and Miriam huffed.

"I can tell the difference between a sprite and a human."

"Well, perhaps it's all connected," Alice said, her tone brisk. "The water problems and Nellie's absence, and maybe your vanishing person, too. We need to get to the bottom of it."

"But *how* do we get to the bottom of it?" Miriam asked, staring at the bread as if waiting for it to offer an answer. "We're not water experts."

"No," Alice agreed. "But the water issues started when Lachlan Jameson set up his water bottling plant and whatever else he's doing out there."

"It's a retreat," Miriam said. "Some sort of very fancy, very exclusive retreat, I heard."

"Retreat from what?" Beaufort asked.

"Life, I suppose," Miriam said after a moment's consideration. Mortimer thought that sounded rather good.

Alice nodded. "Well, there's certainly been plenty of construction going on. I saw him tonight, and he says his water's still fine, but he also mentioned the geese being everywhere. Maybe Nellie's gone up there, either to get to cleaner water or to find out what's going on."

Miriam narrowed her eyes at Alice. "You're suggesting we go and poke around a billionaire's house, aren't you?"

"Multimillionaire, I believe, and I'm merely suggesting we have a little chat with him, and while we're there we see if we can spot Nellie, or some blockage he may have caused to the waters."

"So we're just forgetting about the woman I saw?"

"Not at all. It's quite possible someone did find them and help them, as Carlotta said. But we have nothing solid to go on right now as far as that goes, while we can look into the water issues. And I think we should. We could start flooding at any point, all while not even having water to drink. The council's not doing anything, and it's not going to fix itself."

Miriam made a dubious noise. "Is going to see Lachlan really going to tell us anything?"

"Only one way to find out. Maybe there'll be something quite clearly wrong when we get there. Earthworks, or something like that. And we'll ask Rose to test the water, to see if that gives us some ideas. It's a start, at least."

"And we'll look for Nellie," Beaufort said. "See what she knows, maybe help with cleaning up if we can."

"Excellent," Alice said. "We have a plan."

Beaufort gave a sudden, huge grin. "Are we investigating, then?"

"Quite possibly," Alice said, smiling, and Miriam gave Mortimer a slightly despairing look.

"Maybe two mince pies," he said.

"Good idea," Miriam said, and had another cheesy puff as she got up.

4
DI ADAMS

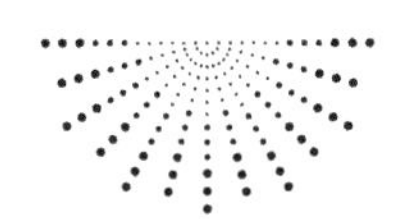

"It's *hooliganism,*" the man insisted, his face red and round, and what DI Adams sincerely hoped was brown sauce decorating his finger as he jabbed it at her. "Arrest her!"

DI Adams looked at the small woman standing in the middle of the man's shop, arms folded over her chest. She had wispy, greying hair and a frayed, canary-yellow cardigan that was almost certainly crocheted. DI Adams had been into Vera Hampton's tea-shop once, and she had an idea that if the mugs themselves could've been crocheted, they would've been.

"The prices you're charging are *terrorism,*" the woman snapped. "You're the one should be arrested!"

It wasn't even ten a.m. and the inspector was already wishing the day was over, having fielded three calls from her mum, one from a woman whose goldfish had vanished (DI Adams suspected the cat, and had said as much, which had not been well-received), and another from a man whose girlfriend had driven over his golf clubs. As far as the inspector could tell, he deserved to have his golf clubs driven over, and while that time she'd managed not to say what she was thinking, she wasn't in any rush to get to work on that particular case.

She was also struggling through the tail end of a nasty cold, which she was sure had been brought on by a recent stakeout on a sheep farm. She and a couple of other officers had spent half the night hiding in the damn bushes waiting for what they suspected were a bunch of teenagers to turn up, spray-paint the sheep with mildly rude (and, she had to unofficially admit, kind of hilarious) slogans, then release them in unlikely yet pointed places, such as the local head-quarters of an unpleasant political party, or the show home of an unsympathetic new development. They'd intercepted the culprits, discovering not a bunch of rebellious and socially conscious teenagers, but instead a local book club, tipsy on white wine spritzers and rebellion. They'd been astonishingly uncooperative, and DI Adams had ended up in a water trough in the subsequent tussle. She was considering suing for the cost of all the decongestants she was going through.

And now she was in Toot Hansell, which was never a recipe for a calm day, but instead of the usual upheavals caused by the W.I., she was moderating a dispute over bottled water. None of this was what she'd trained for, but she had resigned herself to the fact that country policing – and particularly anything involving Toot Hansell – was almost entirely nothing to do with policing as she knew it from her London days.

"Ms Hampton," she started.

"Vera."

"Vera, did you steal two six-packs of bottled water from this shop?"

"Yes. But he was charging ten quid a pack! Even five would be a disgrace. It's price-gouging, that."

DI Adams stifled a sneeze, startling Dandy, who'd been skulking around an automated coffee machine at the back of the shop. He gave her a reproachful look from behind a screen of heavy grey dreadlocks, and went back to investigating.

"It's supply and demand," the shopkeeper was saying, glaring at Vera.

"It's not when you nick all the water from everyone's doorsteps, Ed!" Vera slid her handbag off her shoulder, and DI Adams held up her hands. The original report had involved assault by handbag, and she didn't need a repeat.

"What water's this?" she asked.

"I didn't *nick* it," Ed said, but he wasn't quite looking at her.

"We've been getting free water deliveries from Lachlan Jameson. He's that billionaire, you know?" Vera said.

DI Adams did not know, but she was more interested in the deliveries. "Why's he giving you water?"

"Our water supply's *awful.* Undrinkable. It was making people sick, and Lachlan stepped in to help." Vera had gone a little wide-eyed and breathy. "It's *so* lovely of him."

"Oh, sure," Ed said. "Except if your business is, you know, *selling* things like water. Did me over, he did. And Dom."

"He *didn't,*" Vera insisted. "Dom got a *huge* sum for selling Lachlan that land!"

"But Dom had a water business too, didn't he?" Ed said, jabbing a finger at a jumble of plastic bottles in one corner. They had slightly wonky labels on them that read, *THE Water* in blurred ink. "Now no one's buying it."

"But Lachlan's water's better!"

"It's the *same,* just in fancy bottles!"

DI Adams fumbled some paracetamol out of her pocket, and Dandy padded back to her with a paper coffee cup in his mouth. He tried to give it to her, and she nudged him away with her knee. The cup was as invisible as he was right now, but if she took it from him, it'd be very visible, and that raised a lot of questions, as she'd discovered early on in their relationship, when she'd wrestled a stolen pack of sausages off him in the supermarket, only to turn around and find a shop worker staring at her in bewilderment. She didn't think her explanation that they'd been wedged on the shelf and she'd pulled them off had been exactly believable.

"Alright, alright," she said, dry-swallowing the paracetamol and wishing DI Colin Collins was there. Not only was he the only other copper who knew about the peculiar qualities of Toot Hansell, he was also much better at people than she was. But he was off on one of his endless continuing education courses, something about forensic data in cattle farming or something, so she was just going to have to handle it. "Mr Wiggan, did you get your water back?"

"Ed, and no."

"Vera, replace the water."

"I can't. I used it, and now I've just got what Lachlan's delivered. And that's only because I make sure they don't stay on my doorstep for a *second* after they're dropped off!"

"So give Ed some of that."

"It's my water! Tell him to give back all the water he stole!"

DI Adams took a deep breath as Dandy tried to give her the cup again. "Look, I have a cold. I don't even know why I'm investigating a *water theft*—"

"Don't forget the assault," Ed said.

"*Assault*. It was barely a tap!"

"It—"

"*Stop,*" DI Adams snapped. "I swear I'll arrest both of you just so I don't have to hear about any more bloody water, alright?"

They both stared at her, and Dandy dropped the paper cup, which rolled past her feet, spilling a trickle of coffee across the floor. Which probably improved the cleanliness, if she were honest.

"Where—" Ed started.

"Vera, split the difference and give him six bottles of water. Ed, stop price-gouging. Don't make me come back here." She turned on her heel and marched out of the shop, not bothering to see if Dandy followed. He had his own way of navigating the world, including walls and doors. He'd catch up.

Outside, she sneezed again, and fished her tissues out of her pocket as she headed to the car to retrieve her travel mug. The deli had decent coffee, and she needed a top-up after that. She'd parked in the village's central square, cobbled and compact, and currently still occupied by the Christmas tree, which was looking a little dull and sorry for itself. It seemed to have been half-dismantled, the decorations and lights gone, but maybe the weather had delayed getting the tree itself removed.

The rain was persistent, slicking the cobbles, and the well in the centre of the square glooped as she walked past, as if deep currents were moving within it. She paused, peering into it with a frown. It had a rather twee little tiled roof, and a bucket hung from a beam inside, the handle for cranking it up poking out of the shelter. She couldn't see anything, not even the glimmer of water, but she could hear splashing. Wells didn't usually splash, did they?

She patted her pockets, finding her keyring with a little rubber duck rendered in brass hanging from it, as well as a mini-Maglite. She used that, rather than the duck, although the duck had a built-in torch. That wasn't really for everyday use, though.

The beam of the Maglite illuminated smooth stone walls stretching down to the surface of the water, which was surprisingly close. It was choppy and uneasy, sloshing from one side of the well to the other, and there was an odd, metallic smell rising from it that made her nose wrinkle. She looked up as Dandy put his paws up on the other side, his mouth dropping open as he peered at the water. Then he backed away, shaking his head and huffing, giving her a reproachful look from LED-red eyes that were almost invisible behind his hair.

"That's a bit unpleasant," she said.

"All the water's like that," someone said, and she turned to find Teresa looking at her, an umbrella over one shoulder and some very unfamiliar waterproof trousers and boots on in place of her usual sportswear. "All disturbed and horrible."

DI Adams sighed. Couldn't go five minutes in this place without running into the W.I. "Hello, Teresa. I suppose you have a theory?" She nodded at Pearl as she joined them, coaxing her old Labrador along with her. Martha looked less put out by the rain than by the fact that she wanted to investigate the puddles and Pearl was dragging her away.

"I think Alice does," Pearl said.

"Of course she does," DI Adams said. But, outside of assault by handbag, water problems were hardly her territory. It shouldn't matter what Alice's theory was.

"I just want to know how it ties in with the missing person," Teresa said. "That's *very* intriguing."

DI Adams looked at the well, rubbing the back of her neck as the rain trickled into her collar along with a rather familiar sinking feeling. "The what?"

"Miriam saw someone out in their nightclothes."

"Carlotta did too," Pearl added. "But we couldn't find them."

"Really?"

"Yes, yesterday afternoon," Teresa said. "You haven't had any missing people reports, have you?"

"I can't discuss cases with you," DI Adams said automatically, already pulling her phone from her pocket. "They're *sure* they saw someone?"

"Maybe two different someones," Pearl said. "Miriam's was in a cardigan and Carlotta's was in a dressing gown." She shivered. "I hope they're alright. Imagine being out in this all night!"

There were no alerts on her phone, which was something. She looked longingly at the deli, then said, "What's all this about water deliveries and so on? I thought you had good water here."

"The best," Teresa said. "Usually, anyway. But it's all gone nasty. Completely undrinkable, and all the council and the water people do is say it's the other's problem."

"I heard there's some rich bloke supplying bottles?"

"Oh, *him,*" Pearl said. "He doesn't even drink Yorkshire Tea!"

"Or eat sugar," Teresa added, and DI Adams looked at them blankly.

"Damning, I'm sure," she said finally, when the two women offered nothing else. "Why's he giving you water?"

"Probably to make nice," Teresa said. "He bought part of Dominic Blackwood's farm. Dom already had planning permission for a spa-type thing, but couldn't afford to build it. Lachlan Jameson bought the land, threw up a fancy retreat in no time, then went on and set up a water bottling plant in direct competition with Dom. Now he's handing water out for free like some sort of water fairy."

"Dom could've done quite well out of the water shortage if it weren't for that," Pearl said.

DI Adams frowned. "Thought there'd usually be an anti-competition clause in the contract stopping that sort of thing."

Teresa shrugged. "I don't think Dom was looking at the details too closely. Word has it Lachlan made him a *very* generous offer, and he snatched it up."

"Plus I don't think Dom's set-up was *exactly* official," Pearl added.

DI Adams wiped her nose with her tissue, snuffling. "Well, that doesn't sound—"

"Do you have a cold?" Pearl asked.

"Yes, it's fine—"

"Lemon and honey," Teresa said.

Pearl nodded. "And a little whisky."

"Probably not best form for me to be sipping whisky at work."

"Purely medicinal," Teresa said, grinning, and the inspector found herself smiling back.

"Right, well, if you hear anything else—"

"DI Adams! *DI Adams!*"

DI Adams turned, the sinking feeling turning into a swooping dive as Jasmine ran across the square to join them, water splashing from her boots at every step. She had Primrose in her arms, both of them in matching high-vis jackets, and the inspector wondered vaguely if Jasmine had made up a *Police Community Support Dog* one. It wouldn't surprise her. "Hello, Jasmine."

"The missing person! It's Esther Williams! Her carer's been looking for her, and she stopped me because of my being the village PCSO, and—"

"Slow down," DI Adams said, her voice clipped. "Who's Esther Williams?"

Jasmine took a gulping breath, then said a little more calmly, "Seventy-eight, lives alone but has a carer come in to help daily. Not dotty, but not quite right." She stopped. "I shouldn't say dotty, should I? Impaired?"

"It's fine, I get the picture. Where's her carer now?"

"I told her to call the police and to go back to the house in case Esther comes back. I was just about to call the W.I. so we can organise a proper search."

DI Adams raised a hand. "You're not in charge of this, Jasmine."

"Well, no, but we do have local knowledge," she pointed out.

"And we can start now," Teresa put in. "Pearl and I can head to the hall, start getting organised. Time is of the essence, after all."

"Plus Miriam might've seen Esther last night," Jasmine said.

"The vanishing person?" DI Adams asked.

"Yes, exactly."

"I hope she didn't fall in the duck pond," Teresa said, almost to herself. "I'm sure it's growing."

DI Adams swallowed a sigh. "It's what?"

"Growing," Teresa said patiently.

"So it's of indeterminate size as well as indeterminate depth now?"

"All part of the water problems, I imagine."

"It really is getting bad," Pearl said. "Our neighbour's koi pond vanished. There's just a great big hole left, and his trellis fell in."

DI Adams nodded resignedly, watching Dandy – who was also of indeterminate size, although he favoured his current Labrador dimensions most of the time – touch noses with Martha, who wagged her tail gently. Primrose tried to lunge out of Jasmine's arms, and she gave a little yelp, tugging the dog closer.

"Alright," the inspector said aloud. "Jasmine, you're in charge *only* until I can get some more bodies out here. Just no one do anything silly, like getting lost in the woods or falling into ponds, got it?"

"We're not *silly,*" Jasmine said, then grimaced slightly as DI Adams raised her eyebrows. "I mean, yes."

"Good. What's Esther's address?"

TEN MINUTES later DI Adams was heading to Esther's house, her mug topped up with coffee and Dandy panting at it hopefully from the passenger seat. She'd already tried calling Miriam, with no luck, and now she tried Alice. The phone rang a couple of times before the line clicked open, filled with the telltale background hiss of a car.

"Hello, Alice," DI Adams said. "Have you overthrown the government yet?"

"Never on a Wednesday."

"Good to know. Where are you?"

"Taking a cake to a new arrival."

Of course she was. "Lachlan Jameson?"

"However did you guess?"

DI Adams could hear the smile in Alice's voice. "Why?"

"To say thank you for supplying the village with water, of course."

DI Adams doubted very much it was that simple, but she could worry about that later. "Is Miriam with you?"

"Hello, DI Adams," came Miriam's voice, a little reluctantly.

"Hi. I heard you saw someone out in the rain last night?"

"Yes! I did – in their *slippers*. Why, what's happened?"

Well, Jasmine would tell them soon enough. "There's a woman missing from the village. Esther Williams."

"Oh, no! Oh, poor Esther. It must've been her!"

"Where, exactly?"

"At the back of the hall. But they vanished before I could get to them."

"Vanished how?"

"Well, *vanished*. There, then not. I don't see how they could've moved so fast," Miriam said.

"Did anyone else see them?"

There was a pause, then Alice said, "Carlotta said she saw someone in a dressing gown."

"The same person?"

"No," Miriam said. "Mine was in a cardigan. And a nightie, I think."

"*Two* vanishing people?"

"Apparently."

"Apparently." DI Adams took a sip of coffee, wishing she could take Pearl's whisky suggestion. "And no one saw where they could've gone?"

"No," Alice said. "We went out and had a good look, but there was no one we could see."

"Any strange cars around, anything like that?"

"Nothing at all, Inspector. But it was late afternoon, and the rain was bad, so it's possible we missed something."

"Plus there were geese," Miriam added.

"Geese?"

"We're becoming somewhat overrun," Alice said. "They're a bit of a problem."

DI Adams sighed. "Well, I'm not getting involved with geese. I'll only end up with Nellie in my bathtub insisting I bring them back."

"If you can find her," Alice said.

"I'm sorry?"

"She seems to be missing too."

DI Adams pulled into the kerb outside a trim little bungalow that her GPS indicated was Esther's house. She didn't move to get out, just had another sip of coffee and ignored Dandy's plaintive whine, the fingers of her free hand tapping her thigh restlessly. She'd been around Toot Hansell long enough to know that things intersected in improbable ways, and that there was no point ignoring the stranger aspects of the world.

"The waters are contaminated, Nellie's missing, and now a woman's gone too?"

"And maybe the person in the dressing gown," Miriam said.

"Plus don't forget the geese issue," Alice added. "They've gone somewhat feral."

"What do the dragons say?"

"They don't know. They're trying to find Nellie, I believe."

"And you're off to visit Lachlan Jameson. Why?"

There was a pause, then Alice said, "Well, the water issues seem to be at the heart of things. And they started after he set up his bottling plant."

"How would water issues be behind a missing woman?"

"I'm sure I don't know, DI Adams. But I'm not much of a one for coincidences."

DI Adams wasn't either. But it still felt like a stretch, unless one took into account the expanding, bottomless duck pond that might or might not be affecting koi ponds, among other things. Which she supposed she needed to. "Jasmine's organising a search party."

"Oh, good. We'll join as soon as we get back."

"You're still going to see Lachlan first?"

"We're just popping in for a neighbourly chat, Inspector. We'll be back in no time."

DI Adams couldn't think of a single reason to tell the women not to do it, and she doubted it would've made any difference anyway, so she just said, "Well, tell me what the neighbourly chat turns up," then hit disconnect. Dandy nudged her arm, staring at her mug expectantly. "No. Caffeine is not for dogs." He huffed, and she scrolled through her phone. She needed to call this in to her DCI, get some more bodies out to help with the search, but she had a niggling, uneasy feeling that they weren't going to find anything. Not with a traditional search, anyway. This had Toot Hansell written all over it.

Although, it was January, so at least there should be no hungry Santas involved. She'd almost tackled some old boy in a red suit who'd *ho-ho-ho*-ed at her outside Morrison's before Christmas. This place was giving her some interesting phobias.

5
MIRIAM

Miriam hadn't expected to sleep as well as she did, not with vanishing women and missing sprites and the terrible feel of the fading waters. Plus there had been Alice's declaration that she had an *idea*, one concerning not geese or monsters but the horribly confident Lachlan Jameson, which was much worse. Miriam had never met him properly, but even at a distance he made her very uncomfortable. She had an idea it was the teeth, or possibly the face. He was unnervingly smooth, as if someone had been photoshopping him in real life, and she was never sure what to do with people who exuded confidence in such an aggressively nonchalant manner.

But her personal feelings regarding dubiously motivated multimillionaires were far less concerning than the fact they were going to be poking into things that didn't concern them again, and she'd already seen someone vanish. What if someone vanished *them?* She should have known it was all going to end badly when Alice had turned up carrying both wine and cheesy puffs. No one arrived bearing wine and cheesy puffs unless they were up to something.

But despite having all these things rushing around her head when she went to bed (and possibly aided by two larger-than-normal glasses of Alice's good red wine), she woke up feeling rested and marginally less panicked. If she were to try to put her Alice head on and think about it logically, she was worrying for no reason. After all, the dragons were sure to be able to track down Nellie, and as soon as the sprite was back she could sort out the waters, and the geese and swans would calm down.

And, in those blissful early morning moments, there hadn't been anything in the village Facebook group about anyone being missing, so she had presumed Carlotta was right and someone had helped the person she'd seen get home safely, and there was nothing wrong with taking Lachlan a cake to say thank you for the water. It was only common courtesy.

And now, of course, barely three hours later, everything was already going horribly wrong. Esther was missing, they had a detective inspector on the phone, Alice was talking about everything starting with Lachlan's water exploits, the W.I. were launching a search party, and she and Alice were heading out of the village in entirely the wrong direction. She looked at the bag on her lap. "I'm not sure I've brought the right cake for this."

"For what?" Alice asked.

"A multimillionaire."

"I imagine they like the same cakes as the rest of us."

"I'm probably not even dressed right." Miriam regarded her patchwork skirt and teal jumper dubiously. She'd attached a large, crocheted flower in violet wool to one shoulder, as a nod to formal dressing, but she had an idea that her wellies and pink coat printed with yellow rubber ducks was spoiling the effect somewhat. "The butler might not let me in. Or they might be sniffy at me." She wasn't sure which would be worse.

"We're just popping in to say thank you, not having a business meeting. And I'm not sure he's the sort of multimillionaire who has a butler."

"We don't know he's not. He's bought a country estate, hasn't he?"

"I don't think butlers are compulsory even on country estates," Alice said. She was dressed as normal, in well-cut trousers and a smart jumper, her silver hair annoyingly smooth despite the damp. Alice's normal was rather more suited to visiting multimillionaires than Miriam's, so it didn't help her feel any more at ease.

"Do you really think Lachlan could be sabotaging our water?" Miriam asked. "I mean, he's giving his away. Surely if it was some sort of money-making scheme he'd be making us buy it."

"True," Alice said. "And I think such a thing would be rather small-scale for his interests. But he was very eager to help out. The problems had barely started before he and his workers were dropping bottles off all over the village. As if it's a way to keep us all quiet and happy."

"Or maybe just because he's new and wants to make a good impression?"

"It's possible."

"You don't think so, though."

"No. The timing's very suspect. Plus he still has good water when no one in the village does. That hardly seems coincidental."

"But what would he gain from messing up our water supply?"

"Probably nothing. It may have been accidental. Some side effect from his building, perhaps, that he wants to keep covered up."

Miriam nodded, looking out the side window at a skinny woman in a red jacket walking a rotund spaniel in a green one. They were both peering doubtfully into a large puddle that was swelling across the footpath, probably wondering how deep it was. "I can see why Nellie's upset. The waters really are a mess."

"They are," Alice agreed. "It can't carry on."

Miriam turned in her seat to keep watching the woman and her dog as they drove past. The pair backed rapidly away from the puddle and walked urgently the other way up the street. A swan emerged from the bushes and beat its wings furiously, and the woman and her dog broke into a run, swerving as three ducks launched themselves off a garden wall at them. "Maybe she's decided the *village* is the problem, and she kidnapped Esther as punishment. Or set the birds on her."

"I doubt that," Alice said.

"With the water being so awful, she might not be herself."

Although Miriam was of the opinion that Nellie was quite grumpy enough when she *was* herself.

"I suppose it's possible, but I would have thought she'd just want to fix things. They are her waters, after all."

Miriam watched the street for a moment, then said, "I hope the dragons find her."

"I'm sure they will. And in the meantime, we shall see if we can spot the problem from a human angle."

"Are you sure we shouldn't go back and help with the search?"

"This won't take long. Besides, the water situation may be the key to everything. Esther isn't *that* dotty. Not to be suddenly wandering around in the rain in her slippers."

Miriam frowned. "Do you think she was still drinking the water?"

"Maybe. Or maybe it's getting so bad that showering in it is having a similar effect. We can't rule anything out at this stage."

"I suppose not." Miriam settled herself more securely in her seat and surreptitiously checked her seatbelt as Alice skirted the last of the surface flooding on the narrow streets and accelerated out of the village. It seemed to her that a multimillionaire would have better things to do than destroy the water supplies of a small village, even by accident. In fact, wouldn't he avoid it? Surely it'd just be bad publicity.

Then again, there was no telling what rich people got up to. Maybe he was simply bored.

THE NEWLY BUILT retreat was on the north side of the village, down a tangle of smoothly paved single-track lanes that snaked between drystone walls and broad fields, wildly green even in the dull light. The rain seemed a little lighter beyond the borders of Toot Hansell, but a steady drizzle persisted nonetheless, and the trees beyond the farmland to the west, where the old forest tumbled toward the dragons' mount, were deep and moody, holding their secrets close. Still further north the fells climbed out of the valley in heavy slabs toward the sky, their peaks lost in cloud.

Miriam was watching the fields thoughtfully, wondering where all the extra birds had come from, as there had seemed to be a lot more stalking Toot Hansell than was usual of late, when Alice pulled off the road into a gateway. Miriam looked around, puzzled.

"This isn't the retreat."

"No," Alice agreed, rattling gently over a cattle grid and onto a muddy track, the ruts deep and lost in puddles. "I thought we'd pop in and see Dom first."

"You didn't mention that," Miriam said accusingly. "I only brought one cake!"

"I wasn't suggesting we stop for tea," Alice said.

"Still. It seems rude to turn up empty-handed." Miriam peered through the windscreen, then undid her seatbelt as Alice stopped in front of a gate. She got out, opened the gate to let Alice through, then shut it behind them and hurried to the car again. "What're we doing here, then?"

"Asking if he's seen anything untoward at the retreat," Alice said, pulling into the farmyard. It was muddy and potholed, with a large barn and a couple of smaller outbuildings off to one side, and the house itself crouched at the end, looking over the fields with a certain attitude of weariness in the grey day. No one came out to meet them, no dogs barked, and there was only the endless sound of rain on wet ground when they got out.

"Hello?" Alice called, but the word fell flat. She led the way to the house and knocked briskly, Miriam standing back a little. The stillness was making her uneasy. It felt like a ghost town, hollowed out and abandoned. "Nothing," Alice said, and headed for the barn.

"Where are you *going?*" Miriam hissed, hurrying after her. "We can't just poke around. Farmers have *guns!*"

Alice gave her a look that was far too amused for Miriam's liking. "He's not going to shoot at us."

"He will if he thinks we're trespassing."

"We're trying to find him." The barn was divided into sections with moveable metal fencing, and held only half a dozen goats, cuddled down in some hay. They jumped up as the women entered, bleating hopefully. Alice ignored them, heading deeper into the building, toward where a tractor was parked facing one of the doors.

Miriam was more concerned by the goats. They were crowding the fence, lifting up on their hind legs, and she wasn't sure how well they could jump. The last thing they wanted was to inadvertently instigate a goat escape. "Stay," she said to them, backing away carefully, but they just bleated more loudly, and one of them tried to jump onto another's back. It fell off again, but that seemed like a bad development. She rushed after Alice.

"Look at this," Alice said. She'd circled the tractor, and was frowning at some equipment piled up behind it. Miriam had almost reached her when someone shoved her legs from behind, and she yelped, staggering. She spun around to find a goat staring at her. It bleated, a loud, imperious demand.

"Shoo!" she said, waving at it. "Go back!"

"*Meeeehhhhh!*"

"Miriam, what are you doing?" Alice asked.

"I'm not doing anything! It got out." She jumped back as the goat lowered its head and feinted toward her. "No! Bad goat!" Another bleat caught her attention, and she looked up to see a second goat had made it over the fence, apparently using its siblings as a step. "Oh, Alice, there's more!"

Alice joined her, and the two goats glared at them.

"*Meeehh-ehhhh!*" the first one declared.

"Off you go," Alice said, shaking her cane at them, and the second goat promptly put down its head and charged at her.

"*No!*" Miriam flung herself at the goat, suddenly certain it'd knock Alice to the ground, doing terrible things to her bad hip, or, worse, damaging the other. She managed to snare it around the neck and it bleated in alarm, bucking wildly as it tried to throw her off. "Alice, run!"

"Miriam, what are you *doing?*"

"*Oi!*" someone yelled from the door, and two dogs shot inside, flanking the women with their teeth bared and their hackles up. "Bloody thieves!"

"We're not!" Miriam exclaimed. "Your goats attacked us!"

"You're the one tackling it!"

Miriam barely had time to react before someone had hold of her arm, hauling her roughly away from the goat. She squawked, more in surprise than pain, and Alice snapped, *"Let her go,* Dominic."

Dom didn't, clutching Miriam's arm tightly as he glared at Alice. "What the hell are you doing in my barn?"

"Looking for you," Alice said. She had a firm grip on her cane, and not in a manner that suggested she needed it for walking. "Let Miriam go."

Dom pushed Miriam away from him, and she stumbled a couple of steps, almost bumping into one of the dogs, which backed away with a growl. "Ow," she said, more for effect than anything else.

"What were you doing to my goats?" Dom demanded. He was a big man with sloping shoulders, looming over both of them. "And snooping in my bloody barn?"

"I told you. Looking for you," Alice said calmly. "We wanted to ask if you knew anything about the water."

"Out," Dom said, his voice barely below a shout as he pointed at the door. "Get *out.*"

"Sorry," Miriam whispered, mostly to the goat. It bleated at her.

"We're trying to find out where the problem is," Alice continued, as if he hadn't spoken. "What's your water supply like?"

Dom gave a low, sharp whistle, and the dogs stepped forward in perfect unison, heads low and eyes on the women. "Out," he repeated.

Between the dogs and Dom they were pinned in on three sides, and Miriam gave Alice a pleading look. She nodded slightly. "Of course," she said, and walked to the door with her head high and her back straight. Dom followed them all the way to the car, the dogs keeping pace with him, and Miriam scrambled in as quickly as she could. Alice paused with one hand on the door. "If you are having trouble with the water, perhaps we can help," she said. "I understand Lachlan hasn't necessarily been fair to you in his business dealings."

"I'll do the gate for you," Dom said, and walked off. Alice watched him for a moment, then climbed in.

"Well," she said, as she turned the car to follow him. "That was interesting."

Miriam stared at her. "That was *terrifying.* Those dogs looked like they wanted to eat us!"

"But no one shot at us," Alice pointed out.

"I don't think that's the sort of criteria one should base things on."

Alice didn't answer, nodding at Dom as she drove through the gate, and then they were bumping back up the drive, Miriam checking behind them as if the goats or the dogs might be in pursuit. Only once they were on the road again did Alice say, "Did you see what was behind the tractor?"

"No."

"Concrete pipes and auger drills."

"Auger ... like for drilling wells?"

"Possibly," Alice said. "I think Dom might be doing some earthworks of his own."

Miriam stared at her. "So you think *he's* messing up the water?"

"Or trying to find a solution to it. That was what I would have liked to find out, but he really was rather unreasonable. We'll have to try again later."

Miriam made an uncertain noise. She wasn't sure Dom *had* been unreasonable, considering they'd been trespassing. But there was no point saying that to Alice, so she went back to fretting about meeting Lachlan Jameson. This really was too much for one morning.

THE RETREAT WAS a low-slung building set behind an open metal gate and a parking area of pale, unused gravel, all light modern wood and glass. It looked like it belonged on an episode of *Grand Designs,* but was surprisingly well-suited to the folds of green land and spans of grey stone wall around it, looking as if it had grown like an alien yet entrancing bloom among the fields.

Alice pulled up to the front of the building, which was bordered by a small wooden deck and flower-beds full of herbs and local plants. It had an odd shape, with one wall facing them and the adjoining ones to either side veering off at a wide angle, as if the place had more than four sides. Each wall held a big wooden door with dark metal fittings, framed by huge floor-to-ceiling windows that offered glimpses of soft, natural-coloured furniture inside, along with more expanses of pale wood and gauzy white curtains. An overhanging roof protected the decking, and Miriam and Alice hurried into its shelter, heading for the nearest door. There were no signs to suggest whether this was the main entrance, or where to find it, and no one emerged to greet them, even when Alice knocked.

"Are we sure this is it?" Miriam asked, peeking in one of the windows at a scattering of metal and beige cloth chairs clustered around low wooden tables. There hadn't even been a sign on the gate to identify the place as the retreat. "This looks more like a fancy house."

"We shall soon find out," Alice said, adjusting her hood. "Come on." Rather than continuing around the deck, she stepped out of the shelter of the overhang and went back down onto the gravel, following the drive as it continued deeper into the property.

"Where are you going?" Miriam hissed, hurrying after her.

"To see if there's anyone out the back."

"What if there's security?"

"Then we can ask them where Lachlan is." Alice didn't slow, swinging her cane lightly in one hand as she walked. Miriam had no intention of waiting around on her own, especially not after the goats, so she followed as they crunched over the gravel, passing more big windows, some with tinted glass, around the wide corners of the building.

The decks and flower-beds continued along the drive, which was hemmed in by a drystone wall to one side and the retreat to the other, until the gravel expanded into a wider circle, held back from the main building by a large swathe of freshly laid turf with a water feature of local stone in its centre. An old two-storey barn flanked the other side of the circle, with *Sourced* on a large sign over its garage doors, and a second, smaller door marked *Private* to the side of it. The original stone looked desperately old, and instead of rebuilding it entirely, a newer building had been constructed within it, wearing the grey stone like a patchy shell. More drystone walls beyond the buildings held back the fields, and off to the right, further around the retreat, the turf flowed into a large garden. Miriam could see the woods looming in the distance, past the garden, and somewhere was the low rumble of machinery, indistinct but persistent.

There was still no one in sight, and Alice paused on the edge of the grass, surveying the area curiously. Miriam hurried to the fountain, putting one hand in the chilly water and letting it run over her fingers. "It's clear!"

"Interesting," Alice started, and was cut off by the unmistakable sound of a shot ringing out across the empty yard, setting off a cacophony of honking and hissing from somewhere in the garden.

Miriam squeaked, dropping into a crouch. "Alice, get down! They're shooting at us!"

"Of course they're not," Alice said, although Miriam was sure she'd seen her flinch.

Another shot went off, the sound a punch to the instincts, and the two women looked at each other.

"We need to go," Miriam said, with more insistence than was usual.

"We need to find out what they're shooting at," Alice replied, and Miriam wondered if she should rethink her friendship with the older woman. Cheesy puffs or not, it wasn't good for her nerves.

6
ALICE

Alice was poised for a third shot, the skin on the back of her neck crawling slightly despite the fact she was sure no one was aiming at them, when someone called, "Are you alright there?"

She turned to see a barrel-chested man with a big beard crunching across the gravel toward them, a black jacket zipped to his chin. A leaner man in a matching jacket walked a step behind him, saying something apparently to midair. Alice assumed he was wearing an earpiece of some sort.

"We were looking for Lachlan," she said.

"He's on the way," the lean man said, looking at Miriam. She was still crouched behind the fountain. "Do you need help?"

"*No,*" she said and stood up, smoothing her skirt with both hands.

A shout of greeting went up from the garden. Lachlan was striding toward them in a waxed jacket and Hunter wellies, a young man hurrying behind him with a shotgun broken over his arm.

"Dreadfully sorry, ladies. I wasn't expecting anyone."

"An impromptu visit," Alice said.

"Always welcome. I hope we didn't alarm you too much." Lachlan gave her that unnaturally bright smile. "Lovely to see you again so soon, Alice. And this is?"

"Miriam," Alice said, when Miriam didn't answer. She was inspecting her carrier bag dubiously.

"Pleased to meet you," Lachlan said, nodding at Miriam. "You should have told me you were coming by. I could have arranged some classes or a spa session for you."

"It seems very quiet. You don't have anyone staying at the moment?" Alice asked.

"No, we're not fully open just yet. Still getting all the kinks ironed out."

"Well, it looks very nice."

"Good to hear. Other than Dom, you're our first locals. I was starting to think you didn't like me."

Alice gave him a small smile. "It takes people time to warm up to new arrivals."

"Supplying the whole village with free water isn't enough?" He looked as if he were trying to raise an eyebrow, but his face remained smooth and unresponsive until he grinned. "I get it. Everyone's probably worried I'm going to put in a five-storey hotel or something, but I promise this is it." He gave an expansive wave, encompassing the fields and the forest lurking beyond.

"Good to know," Alice said.

Miriam spoke up, somewhat unevenly. "What were you shooting at?"

"Damn birds. They keep getting in and ripping up the garden, and we've only just planted it." He looked from her to Alice. "Would you like a tour?"

"That would be lovely."

Miriam handed Lachlan a Tupperware container, and he took it with a blank look. "Ah …"

"Lemon drizzle cake, with no sugar or gluten. Alice said you don't eat it."

His grin resurfaced. "How considerate!"

Miriam made a face. "My kitchen's not exactly … I mean, there might've been normal flour around. There is, even."

"Oh, I'm not intolerant of either," he said, his smile widening. "I just try to avoid inflammatory foods. Is it vegan?"

"Um, no—"

"Good. Love some butter, me." He winked at her, and extended a hand toward the main building. "Let's have a cuppa first, then we can do the tour. Honestly, this is lovely. No one ever brings me cake."

Miriam looked at Alice, who simply nodded politely at Lachlan and headed for the door. She doubted the tour would show them much, but it was worth doing anyway. And they might find some answers about Dom and his auger.

They stepped into a generous room with low pouffes and bolsters in beige covers set against one wall, rolled, neutral-toned mats on shelves above them, and yoga straps hanging from hooks on the walls. Bottles of *Sourced* water were displayed on another shelf, and the back wall was narrower than the front, the lines of the wooden flooring running toward it, wide panels to skinny ones. Everything was rendered in the same muted tones, the ceilings high and open-raftered, the pale walls pocked with recesses for salt lamps, interestingly-shaped branches, and well-worn stones. The only colour came from lush green plants in big pots in the corners, and vines tumbling from the shelves. Miriam's waterproof jacket was a joyful shout of pink and yellow in the midst of it all, and Alice found herself looking at it almost for relief.

"This is the yoga and meditation room," Lachlan said, peeking inside the Tupperware. "Every room has an external door and an internal one that leads into the transition room."

"The what?" Miriam asked.

Lachlan shut the lid quickly, as if caught doing something forbidden. "One can't just go from the peace of this room to beast mode in the gym without a shift in mindset. There needs to be a transitional space."

"A what?" Miriam said, looking even more bewildered.

"I'll show you." Lachlan led the way to the featureless back wall and prodded it, seemingly at random. A section popped out of alignment, silent and smooth, then slid sideways out of sight.

"*Ooh*," Miriam said, and Lachlan flashed his over-white grin at her.

"Nice, isn't it? The architects won a best design award last year. They're Danish."

"Like IKEA?" Miriam said innocently, and Lachlan's grin became slightly stiffer than it had been already.

"That's Sweden, dear," Alice said, following Lachlan into another smooth, well-designed, and personality-free space. There was more colour here, at least, even if the walls were as bereft of pictures and interest as previously. The room stretched out to either side of them, flowing in a sharp-edged curve that followed the same angles as the outside of the building and enclosing an inner courtyard that was open to the sky. Rather than walls, floor-to-ceiling glass panels gave an uninterrupted view of a large, grass-edged pool that took up the majority of the open-air space. There was just enough room for some benches and chairs, and a well-trimmed jungle of potted plants.

Inside, the transition room held chunky armchairs and sofas, low tables, taller bar stools and matching benches, and hanging, bare bulbs in dark metal cages. A small coffee trailer that wouldn't have looked out of place at an artisan market huddled against one wall, as well as a juice stand with a grass roof. The other men had stayed outside and the place was empty, giving Alice a faint feeling of dislocation, as if in an airport departure lounge in the very early morning, where one couldn't help but feel abandoned by a world moving on. She half expected an announcement for final boarding to ring out, but instead there was only the sound of the rain in the courtyard.

"How unusual," she said.

"The building's a hexagon," Lachlan said, leading the way to the glass walls so they could look out at the pool, its surface dimpled with rain and scattered with water plants. "The pool's fed directly from the spring, and having it at the centre means energy flows from it to every part of the retreat. The transition room is where we'll serve all the meals, and it acts as both a common area and a decompression space between the treatment rooms, the gym, the yoga area, and the guest quarters."

"It looks like a pond rather than a pool," Miriam said. "There's plants in it."

"Yes, they purify it. We'll be encouraging our guests to experience it as often as possible."

"People *swim* in it?"

"They will. It's Toot Hansell spring water."

"It's *winter,*" Miriam said, still looking unconvinced.

"Cold water is revolutionary," Lachlan said, which Alice felt was overstating things somewhat. People had been taking cold baths for all of human history, after all. Normally because they had no other choice. "We have a sauna in the treatment rooms, and of course anyone can have a hot shower whenever they want, but the pool is the most important aspect of our proposed regime. It's very healing."

"I rather like a hot tub," Miriam mumbled.

"You've done this very quickly," Alice said, before the conversation could get too derailed. "The construction, I mean."

"All pre-designed, pre-cut, then built on site. I just had to find the right spot and put the foundations down." Lachlan tapped his watch, then looked at the two women as he led the way to a cluster of fat red armchairs and set the Tupperware on the table in front of them. "Can I interest anyone in a green tea?"

"I'd rather regular," Alice said, and Miriam nodded her agreement.

"Any particular milk?"

"Regular on that, too."

"Of course." Lachlan took his jacket off, revealing a tight white T-shirt with *Sourced* printed on the chest as a door popped open further down the room. The young man who'd been carrying the gun hurried to join them, his hair still damp from the rain.

"Niall," he said, nodding at Alice and Miriam.

"Can you print up some spa and class passes for the ladies?" Lachlan asked, before either of them could respond. "For when we're open."

"Be right back." Niall rushed off again.

"May as well get you set up," Lachlan said, climbing into the coffee truck, which bounced gently on three wheels.

Alice watched him set a kettle boiling and take two cheery yellow polka dot teapots from under the counter. "How's the water business going?"

"Mostly to the village at the moment. Hardly profitable." Lachlan took three mugs and a small glass bottle of milk to the table. "But I'm happy to help, obviously."

"Very generous of you," Alice said, looking around for Miriam. She'd found her way through the glass wall panels and was crouched by the pool, trailing her hand in it. "You seem to have rather driven Dom out of the market, though."

"These things happen."

"Was it really necessary to set up in competition?"

Lachlan frowned slightly, as if the thought hadn't occurred to him. "Competition's healthy."

"He can hardly compete with your resources."

"He charged me enough for this land. And I'm not having Toot Hansell spring water associated with cheap plastic bottles and homemade labels. I needed something more in alignment with *Sourced*."

"So you created a monopoly on Toot Hansell spring water?" Alice asked, sitting down at the table. The chairs were soft and deep, and still smelled faintly of shops and packaging.

Miriam had come in from the pool, wiping her hands on her skirt and struggling to close the wall panel. Lachlan set the teapots on the table and went to join her, pointing at a small remote attached to the glass.

"Oh, thank you," she said. "Um ... I thought Dom was rather clever, bottling local water. And the labels had character."

"It was bringing the tone of the village down, and by extension *Sourced*," Lachlan said, returning to the table. "If his product was that good, he'd have nothing to worry about." He opened the Tupperware container and took a large sniff. "Come on, then, Miriam. How did you make this? It smells fantastic!"

"Oh, it was nothing," she said, colour climbing in her cheeks.

"It's not nothing at all. You made this for me. What an incredible thing to do!" He looked at Niall as the young man re-emerged into the transition room, clutching some sheets of paper. "Isn't it incredible?"

"Yes?" Niall offered, although he couldn't have heard what Lachlan was saying.

"It's very normal. We make cakes for every W.I. meeting," Miriam said.

"Really? How delightful." Lachlan checked the teapots. "It's very sweet how you keep all these old traditions alive."

Miriam looked torn between being complimented and insulted, and Alice poured a little milk into two of the mugs. "You haven't had any problems with the water here?"

"No," Lachlan said, sniffing his green tea appreciatively. "But Dom did tell me we're right at the primary source of the village's waters."

"So the problem's downstream from you?" Miriam asked, taking her mug from Alice.

"I imagine so. Don't you, Niall?"

"Yes," Niall said, with more confidence, and handed Alice and Miriam each a sheet of paper. "We don't have gift cards set up yet, I'm afraid."

"Of course. Thank you." Alice scanned the printout, which had the *Sourced* logo at the top – she was starting to get quite sick of the sight of it, Niall had it on his fleece as well – and simply said, *We are delighted to gift you five free classes and five spa sessions at Sourced. Prepare to be renewed!* "Lovely," she said, and set the paper down, picking up her mug. "Odd timing, of course."

"Timing?" Lachlan asked. "The classes? We don't have times for them yet."

"No, the water issues starting right after you finished construction. During would have made more sense, after all."

Lachlan took a sip of green tea. "I'm sorry, are you accusing me of something?"

"Is there something to accuse you of?" Alice asked.

"Only helping out a village in need. Pouring money into the local economy. Building a whole new avenue of tourism. That sort of thing." His tone was amused rather than offended, and he took a piece of cake, biting into it with a sigh and closing his eyes. "Oh, that is *wonderful*." He held the Tupperware out to Niall. "Try it."

"Thanks," Niall said, taking a piece and perching on the edge of a seat. He stared at the cake as if he wasn't sure what to do with it.

"You don't think it's unusual, then?" Alice asked.

"All the construction was signed off by the relevant authorities, as was the plant. It's just one of those unfortunate things."

"It's more than *unfortunate*," Miriam said. "And what about the birds?"

Lachlan looked at Niall. "What was your theory on the birds?"

"It's the new plantings," the young man said, still cradling his untouched cake. "They're looking for worms and things."

"And you're shooting at them," Miriam said, frowning.

"*Over* them," Lachlan said. "Not *at* them."

Miriam looked unconvinced, but she didn't say anything else, so Alice said, "I do hope you tell us if you notice anything unusual with the water."

"Local environmental patrol, are you?" Lachlan asked, grinning, and nodded at Niall. "Eat it! It's good!"

Niall took a very small nibble of cake.

Alice smiled slightly, and said, "We all look out for our village. And we seem to be struggling to get any help from the authorities regarding the water problems."

"I suppose you think I've paid them off?" Lachlan was still smiling, but Alice was fairly sure it wasn't whatever cosmetic work he'd had done that was stopping it reaching his eyes.

"That had not occurred to me," she said, not entirely honestly. "But you can't supply the village with water for ever."

Lachlan nodded, taking another piece of cake. Given the ribs Alice could see outlined under his tight T-shirt, she hoped he ate all of it. "Have you been speaking to Dom?"

"Why?"

"I thought he might've been pointing the finger at me."

"For what reason?" Alice asked.

"Jealousy, perhaps. He had the planning permission for this place, after all, but couldn't afford to build it. Seller's regret's a real thing."

"I suppose that's possible," Alice said, trying the tea. It wasn't Yorkshire, but it was rather good. "Could you show us around the bottling plant?"

"Sorry, no. Health and safety. I'll show you the rest of this building, though." Lachlan took a third piece of cake. "Take this away! Miriam, you are a *temptress.*"

"Um," Miriam said, and concentrated on her tea.

THEY DIDN'T LINGER over their tea, and while Lachlan showed them around the rest of the hexagonal building afterward, it revealed no secrets. There were half a dozen still, airy guest rooms, a gym full of free weights and squat racks and rings suspended from the ceiling, a sleek stainless-steel kitchen, and pale, immaculately equipped rooms for spa treatments. Nothing interested Alice particularly, and there was no chance of poking around with Lachlan escorting them like a estate agent, extolling the virtues of ginger shots and the joys of having no mobile reception. When he offered to show them the medicinal herb garden she interrupted before Miriam could agree. The younger woman looked faintly disappointed as they walked to the car, Lachlan waving from the door with the Tupperware clutched in one hand. He'd offered it back, but hadn't hesitated when Miriam said he could return it with the next water delivery.

"What an odd place," Miriam said as she closed her door. "I couldn't get a feel on it at all."

"Or him," Alice agreed, taking her phone out to check on the WhatsApp group. "He's right about the signal. Nothing at all."

"I thought he'd want to be all connected. He seems that sort."

"I'm sure he has satellite or something." Alice put the car into reverse and backed away from the front of the building while Miriam stared out at the rain, frowning.

"Did you believe that stuff about Dom and seller's regret?"

"Hard to say. And it doesn't mean he did anything." Although the digging equipment still intrigued her. "You made quite an impression with your cake."

"Mmm."

Alice paused at the gate, looking at her. "Miriam?"

"It was bought," she burst out. "The cake. Gluten-free's one thing, but sugar-free as well is *so* difficult, and I was trying to make something for my cousin at Christmas, and nothing would work, so I *bought* some. I still had one in the freezer. I did make some sugar-free lemon syrup for the top, though. So I wasn't *entirely* lying."

Alice checked the road, a smile twitching the corners of her mouth. "It was a very small lie."

"I don't like it. I shouldn't be good at lying."

"Oh, it can be handy," Alice said. "It's just another skill." She started to pull onto the road, but as she did so Miriam shouted, *"Stop!"*

Alice slammed the brakes on. "Miriam?"

The younger woman was already scrambling out of the car, the door yawning behind her as she ran down the front of the retreat, heading for the garden.

"Miriam!"

Miriam didn't turn around, and Alice had to get out of her seatbelt to close the passenger side door. A moment later she was reversing rapidly back onto the gravel, jerking the handbrake on as soon as she was clear of the gate. She climbed out and hurried after Miriam, who'd already vanished into the garden.

"Miriam, wait!" Alice paused at the edge of the trees, frowning, then caught a flash of blue among the foliage. She headed toward it, using her cane to steady herself. *"Miriam!"*

The garden was still and peaceful-feeling, the flower-beds and trees planted in clumps that allowed a gentle flow of grass between them, the varied heights of the herbs and bushes offering private spaces and benches which would have views of the fells in better weather. Alice didn't bother to appreciate it, just chased after that glimpse of blue jacket. She came around a carefully layered rock garden looking a little soggy in the rain, and found herself at one of the garden walls. It looked over the fields that ran toward Dom's farm, and she could see the woods to her right, the retreat's outbuildings and yard to her left. Everywhere was still, and she turned, puzzled, trying to see where Miriam had gone.

"Alice!" The shout came from behind a rather startled-looking apple tree that didn't seem to have taken to its new home just yet, and a moment later Miriam ran toward her. She rushed to the wall, peering over it. "Did you see her?"

"I saw something—" Alice stopped, looking at Miriam's pink and yellow jacket. She had it zipped up to her neck, not a glimpse of her jumper visible. "Has your jacket been done up the whole time?"

"Yes," Miriam said, giving up on the field and looking back at the garden. "I'm sure it was Esther. But how did she get away so quickly? She was in the garden, then the field, then she was just *gone*. Again!"

"Was she wearing a blue cardigan?" Alice asked.

"Yes! You did see her!"

"Alice? Miriam? Are you alright?" Lachlan strode down the garden toward them, rain beading his blond-streaked hair.

"What did you do to her?" Miriam demanded, taking a step forward. "Where is she?"

"Who?"

"I saw her! I know she's here!"

"Who are you talking about?" he asked.

"Esther! Esther was *here!*"

Lachlan spread his hands. "I'm sure I don't—"

"She's a missing person," Niall said from behind him. He held up his phone. "It's on the Facebook group."

"But why would she be here?" Lachlan asked, sounding genuinely puzzled.

"I don't know," Alice said. "But we need to call the police."

"Of course," Lachlan said. "Niall?"

"Already on it," he said, poking his phone.

Alice took out her own mobile, and Lachlan frowned. "You won't have signal."

"I happen to know an inspector's already in the village," she said, scrolling through her phone. “Let me give you the number. We may as well speed things along, hadn’t we?”

“Of course,” Lachlan replied, but Alice thought he looked unsettled for the first time, and that was oddly reassuring.

7
MORTIMER

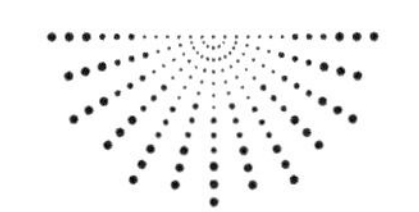

The morning was dull and damp, the clouds pressing low to the dragons' mount and rendering everything several shades darker than seemed necessary, including Mortimer's mood. He'd tried to distract himself by experimenting with some small amulets that bloomed into ladybirds when heated, but by the time Beaufort came to find him he'd been chased out of his workshop cavern twice by an infuriated, oversized, dragon-scale insect, and it was having rather the opposite effect to what he'd hoped.

"Fancy a little excursion, lad?" the High Lord asked from the tunnel that led to the cavern, ducking as the ladybird zoomed past.

Mortimer wasn't sure he liked the sound of an *excursion*. An *excursion* sounded like the sort of thing that was going to end with them hiding under tables or running from large, probably very official men with nets and Tasers. On the other paw, at the rate he was going, he'd end up with the ladybird wedged in his ear before long. "Where to?"

"I've had a little ask around, and no one's seen Nellie recently. I think we need to start searching a little more seriously."

"Alright." Mortimer took a large piece of wood from under his workbench, watching the ladybird, then as it zipped closer he swung at it wildly. It swerved, but he caught it with the edge of the plank and sent it slamming into the wall, where it bounced down to the workbench. He upended a pot over it and set a large rock on top to contain the furiously buzzing trinket, which was hitting the inside so hard the pot was wobbling. "Is anyone else worried?"

Beaufort had been watching with interest, and now he said, "About your ladybirds?"

"No, Nellie."

"Ah. Of course. Well, let's just say there's a certain sentiment floating about which suggests Nellie may have finally taken action against humanity, and good for her."

Mortimer sighed. "Lord Margery?"

"However did you guess?"

"Oh, just a hunch." Lord Margery was younger than Beaufort, but more than old enough that she would be the natural choice for the next High Lord, a position she was clearly eager to step into sooner rather than later. Unfortunately for her, Beaufort showed no indication of rolling over and giving up, and while Margery had initially been very resistant to the High Lord's push for modernisation, she seemed to have embraced the concept of politics by strategy rather than force quite enthusiastically. She was unlikely to agree to anything Beaufort suggested, especially if it involved their connections to the village.

"She feels we should just stay out of things, as if we're not all bound to the same waters." Beaufort huffed, steam drifting from his snout to collect on the cavern ceiling.

Mortimer sighed inwardly. He did understand Margery's inclination toward secretiveness, and he'd really rather not be hunting about in the middle of the day, but they couldn't continue with the waters as they were. "Where do we start?"

"The woods," Beaufort said. "Come on, lad." He turned and led the way out of the cavern, and Mortimer followed. It was better than the ladybirds, anyway.

The dragons' mount grew gaunt and forbidding from a sea of trees, the opalescent tarn at its foot offering a final barrier to anyone who ventured past the forest. Not that anyone ever did. The woods that surrounded it were deep and old, and while their edges were wound through with a filigree of trails, further in the trees thickened, and charms set into the very bones of the land closed the way to outsiders. Old growth clung grimly to life, the trunks grew heavier and closer, and the paths dwindled to wildlife trails and unmarked ways frequented only by four-legged beasts. Faced with that, even the most intrepid of explorers found their feet veering off, leaving the wild places to their ancient magic.

Rain spackled Mortimer's scales as they passed the tarn, which had taken on an uneasy green stain, and swung over the heavy canopy of the old forest. It was glossy with damp where the leaves still clung on, while the branches of the deciduous trees were painted stark and dark among the evergreens. Rather than heading for the village, they spiralled toward the dense heart of the woods, coming down to land in a clearing before the growth got too thick for dragon wings. The trees swallowed them, and where they landed the soil was soft with patchy grass and leaf mulch. Mortimer dug his talons into it, catching the whiff of the sleeping forest falling deeper and deeper into hibernation as winter ground on. Everything was quiet other than the patter of rain on the leaves, punctuated by the occasional calls of the birds, unalarmed by the dragons' presence.

They passed unchallenged but not unnoticed. It had been a long time since a dragon had laid waste to a forest, and now there were too few of both for the woods' inhabitants to consider them a threat. Still, small creatures marked their passing as they wound their way into the ever-thickening undergrowth, following unseen paths until they came to a quiet clearing where moss carpeted the ground. Roots sank deep into the earth, the trunks of the trees were twisted and knotted with age as they curved over the dragons, and all was deep, cool scents and stillness. A little spring jumped through green banks, the water chuckling softly to itself. It was as low as the village's waterways, and not as clear as it could be, and Mortimer snuffled it cautiously.

"Anything, lad?" Beaufort asked.

"It doesn't smell right," he said.

"Not right how?" Beaufort asked.

"I can't quite tell. There's just something missing, or there's something there that shouldn't be. It's hard to say."

"It's humans," a new voice said, and they both looked around. They didn't see the dryad at first, not until she stepped away from one of the trees, lean and gnarled and the same mottled browns as the wood behind her.

"Hello, Daphne," Beaufort said. "Are you well?"

"Not really," Daphne replied, nodding at the spring. "Have you two been hanging around having tea parties so long you can't smell when something's got a human stink on it?"

"It's not polluted," Mortimer said. "I know that smell. This is different."

"Maybe. But it's always something, some new way to destroy things. It's only going to get worse."

"Not necessarily. There's not been bad run-off from the farms for years. The humans are a lot better than they used to be."

Daphne snorted, but Beaufort said, "It's true. For a while there, I thought we were all going to choke. But they learned. The air's better. The water's improved."

"Not by much," Daphne replied. "And *our* waters always stayed clean at their heart. Now look at it. It's deliberate, that is. Someone's poisoning it."

"It can't be deliberate," Mortimer said. "What would be the point?"

Daphne shrugged. "Water's not my department. It's started affecting my trees, though. I'm not best pleased."

"Terrible," Beaufort said. "We need to put a stop to it."

"We do," Daphne agreed, flexing her knotted fingers. "Didn't think you'd be thinking that way though, with your little human buddies."

"What way?" Mortimer asked, his throat suddenly tight.

"That we need to put a stop to things. Like the sprite's doing."

"What's that?" Beaufort asked. "What's Nellie doing?"

Daphne shrugged. "I'm just assuming, to be honest. Haven't seen her for ages. We had a bit of a falling out last time I saw her. Her bloody birds tried to steal my hair for their nests and we had words."

"What do you think she's doing, then?" Mortimer asked.

The dryad waved vaguely in the direction of the village. "Isn't it obvious?"

"Oh dear," Beaufort said, almost to himself. "I was hoping not."

"I thought you said you wanted to put a stop to things?"

Mortimer's throat felt tighter than ever, and he tried to cough, producing a little burp of flame instead. "What *things* do you mean?"

"The humans and all their horrible messes, obviously," Daphne said.

"The *humans?*"

"Well, not all of them, but definitely the ones responsible for this. Word is someone's been helping themselves to the water at the Source itself, and making a mess of it. One step too far, isn't it? Nellie's evidently serving up some repercussions."

"Making a mess of the Source?" Mortimer whispered. The Source was the origin of all Toot Hansell's waters, all the *valley's* waters. Only the sprite knew for certain where it was, and if it failed … Well, he didn't even know what that would mean. Didn't *want* to know.

Beaufort regarded Daphne with a level gaze. "You think Nellie's drowning Toot Hansell? That's rather extreme. Even dragons gave up on razing villages centuries ago."

"Maybe that was your mistake."

"Daphne, we can't take a battle to the humans. It's not the village's fault, and we can't win even if it is. There are too many of them. We'll just expose ourselves."

She shrugged. "Maybe the problem is we've been thinking like that for far too long. Maybe we need to *do* something rather than just let them keep pulling the world down around us. Besides, you've been *exposing* yourselves plenty."

Mortimer looked at his talons. His scales had gone a terrible, blotchy grey, and there was a hot, tickling shame at the back of his neck. This was his fault. *His.* He'd come up with the barbecues as dragon beds idea, and set up the scale trade to make it happen, and got them all tangled up with the W.I. Admittedly, he wasn't the one who kept pulling them into *investigations,* but it had certainly all started with him and his baubles.

"We're coexisting," Beaufort said, his voice calm and deep. "It's the best option for everyone."

"Not everyone agrees."

"So what's your solution? To join forces with Nellie? Take the village down by root and stream?"

Daphne didn't answer straight away, inspecting a raw patch on one arm, where the bark was curling away from smooth tan skin. Neither dragon spoke to fill the silence, and eventually she said, "Not yet. I'm waiting to see what Nellie does. But I'm withdrawing from the borders. Some bloody humans have been poking around in it."

"Past the charms?" Beaufort asked. "Were they down?"

"No. But someone got in anyway, so I've moved the charms deeper. It's unacceptable, Beaufort. We've got little enough left for us as it is." For a moment the anger in her voice slipped, revealing something rawer and more fragile beneath, like the glimpse of soft skin under her bark.

Beaufort nodded gravely. "It is. But the answer isn't to attack."

"It is if it's the only choice they leave us."

"We're not at that point yet."

"No? If the Source is corrupted, none of us will survive. The waters will poison everything. The forest will die. Your tarn will turn rancid. Even your precious bloody village will crumble."

Mortimer shivered, trying not to imagine the rot spreading out from the springs' heart, infecting everything it touched, a blight on the skin of the Dales even as it leached deeper and deeper into the earth, festering and merciless.

"Well, we shall just have to make sure it doesn't get that far," Beaufort said. "Nellie may be upset, but I'm sure we can sort this out if we just find her."

Daphne shrugged. "Good luck, then. But sprites are so *dramatic*. Lolling about in ponds, handing people swords just to stir things up. She might drown the whole valley just to see what it looks like."

Beaufort made a thoughtful noise, then said, "Thank you, Daphne. I do understand your concerns. We'll fix this."

"Maybe you will, maybe you won't. Maybe Nellie will start something new. The humans have got away with too much, for too long, after all."

"We don't want to draw attention to ourselves. It's not worth it."

"You don't speak for all Folk, Beaufort," Daphne said, and flicked a hand at them. "Go on. Get out. Try your little fixes, then we'll see what happens."

Mortimer waited for Beaufort to order the dryad to leave the investigations to them, or to remind her that the Watch looked unfavourably on any Folk who called attention to themselves, but he only inclined his head slightly. "We'll do what we can," he said, and turned away, slipping out of the clearing into the thick trees. Mortimer looked at Daphne, who stared back at him blankly.

"Um. Bye," he said, and hurried after the High Lord before she tweaked his tail. She looked like she wanted to.

THEY WORKED their way slowly back to a gap large enough to take off from, their wingtips scraping the thin branches and dislodging the last of the leaves. Beaufort angled toward the north, keeping low over the canopy. In this weather, this deep into the forest, there should've been no one about to see them, but Mortimer felt far too exposed. Knowing some unknown human had been past the boundary charms made the whole world feel suddenly untrustworthy. There were few enough places where Folk were safe these days, and particularly dragons. They couldn't pass for human the way some Folk could, such as dryads and faeries and sprites. And passing for dogs hadn't gone well for them so far. If the safety of the forest and the mount beyond it were lost, he didn't know where they'd go. He didn't know where they *could* go.

"Chin up, lad," Beaufort called to him.

"People in the forest is really bad," Mortimer said.

"It may be nothing. Entirely unrelated to the waters, even."

"But it's us, isn't it? It's us being around humans so much that's causing problems. Weakening the charms, or making us all more visible or something."

"Perhaps," he said. "But we can't know that, and we can't undo it."

"We can stop."

"I'm not sure we can. Not unless we want to go backward."

They were quiet for the rest of the way, not speaking until they came down to land close to the northern border of the forest, where the trees thinned out and the charms weakened. The woods were separated from undulating green fields by a high drystone wall, well maintained on this side, likely by the dryad. Mortimer could smell the charms on it as they approached, old, well-trodden things that were as much in the soil as they were in the stone. There was no way a human could have just wandered past them.

He looked at Beaufort. "Do you think this is where the humans were?"

"I'm not sure. But I know the waters run from here to the village, so it seems like a good place to start looking for Nellie, at least."

Mortimer put his paws on top of the wall and peered over, spotting sheep in the field beyond.

"Catch anything, lad?" Beaufort asked.

"Not so far. It all smells normal." Well, normal except for that odd whiff of loss, the scent of the dying water. It seemed to linger everywhere.

"Well, we'll just have to poke around and see if we can find any sign of her," Beaufort said, and slipped up and over the wall.

"*Beaufort,*" Mortimer hissed. "What're you *doing?*"

"There's no one around, lad. And we're not going to get anything on that side, are we?"

"We might," Mortimer protested.

"Unlikely. On this side the charms aren't as strong, so you'll be more likely to sniff out any traces."

"Maybe," Mortimer said. "But what if someone sees us?"

"There's only sheep. I think we're pretty safe with the sheep."

Mortimer took a deep breath and followed the High Lord up and over the wall, eyeing the sheep clustered across the field, who stared back at them with wide yellow eyes.

"I'm not sure," he said. "I don't think I trust the sheep."

"You are a dragon. Don't forget that, lad."

Mortimer didn't reply, but instead just set off along the wall, having no problems at all keeping himself as grey as the shadows. He didn't feel much like a dragon. He felt like a betrayer of Folk.

They didn't have to go far before they found something. Or, rather, before something found them. Mortimer was still keeping a wary eye on the sheep, who were accompanying them in their trek along the wall, not making much noise, just jostling each other and watching the dragons with their strange yellow eyes. He hadn't found anything much of interest, just the usual scents of cold dawns and old mud, and was about to declare as much to Beaufort, in the hopes that they could get out of the field before they got any closer to the buildings he could see beyond the next wall.

But even as he turned to say so, the sheep started shuffling around, bleating uneasily. Mortimer froze, staring around the field, but there were no large men with nets striding toward them, not even any cryptid journalists with cameras, or hostile members of unfamiliar W.I.s, or anyone wielding Tasers (he had plenty of possibilities to worry about after the last year or so).

"What is it?" Beaufort asked. The High Lord had been ambling behind him, looking about with interest.

"The sheep see something," Mortimer said, and both dragons stared at the animals, who stared back at them. Mortimer still didn't like their eyes much, but he had to admit that all that fluffy wool, even wet and grey with rain, wasn't *that* intimidating.

"I'm not sure," Beaufort started, then a thundering rush of feathery wings and paddling, furious feet swept toward them from the direction of the buildings in a cacophony of honking and hissing.

Mortimer yelped and spun around, flinging himself up and over the wall, where he crashed to the muddy ground. Beaufort was right behind him, and they struggled out of a shallow bog into the cover of the trees, splattering mud and stagnant water all over themselves and each other while the geese and swans lined the wall, blaring their displeasure.

"*What?*" Mortimer shouted at them, the worry of the day and the clinging stink of the water suddenly too much. "What do you *want?*"

To his astonishment, the birds quieted, still watching the dragons with glassy, unreadable eyes, shifting slightly on the wall. In the stillness that followed, Mortimer became aware of two things: he could hear Miriam shouting somewhere in the area the birds had come from, and, faint as melting ice in the spring, a scaly, furious trace ran through the muddy ground, all old stone and fresh moss.

He looked at Beaufort. "Nellie's been here."

Beaufort put a paw into the mud, and they both felt the delicate tremor that ran beneath them, shaking the very bones of the earth. A little more dank and rotting water vomited out of the ground, and both dragons drew back. The birds shivered, shifting their wings, then took off again, vanishing back into the fields.

"Oh, Nellie," the High Lord said softly. "What have you done?"

8
DI ADAMS

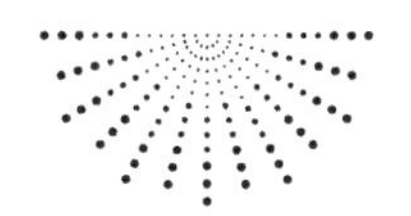

Dandy sprinted down the street, casting so many anxious glances behind him that he stumbled, almost smacking his snout on the kerb. He swerved, vanishing into a garden, and the five geese that had been in furious pursuit came to a halt, hissing in satisfaction, fluffing their wings out and glaring about in a manner that seemed desperately familiar to DI Adams. She'd normally seen it with a bunch of lads who felt they'd come off best in a showdown, however, and those at least she'd been able to arrest.

She was still considering how one might arrest a goose when a woman opened a low gate across the road, a small girl trotting after her with a toy lizard hugged to her chest. The birds wheeled toward them instantly, eyes bright with interest.

"Watch out!" DI Adams shouted, waving urgently.

"What?" the woman asked, looking at the geese with a bemused expression.

"Big birdies, Mummy!" the little girl yelled, trying to get past her mother. "Look, they're coming to say hello!"

They were, rapidly.

"Go back inside," DI Adams yelled, intensifying her waving as she hurried across the road, trying to distract the birds. "Hey! Hey, over here!"

"Shoo!" the woman shouted, pushing the girl behind her. The geese went from a trot to a charge, and she grabbed her daughter and bolted back to the house. DI Adams stopped short, backing up to the opposite kerb as the birds' heads snaked toward her, disgruntled.

"Easy," she told them, without much confidence, and looked for Dandy. He wasn't much good at seeing them off, but he'd been doing well at distraction. "Stay?" she offered, taking her baton slowly from the pocket of her coat. A yelp attracted both her attention and that of the birds, and she risked a look around, spotting Police Sergeant Graham Harrison retreating out of a small footpath that ran between the houses, fending off a swan with his baton as he went.

"Get off," he snarled at the bird, poking the baton at it. The swan hissed, rearing back and beating its wings threateningly. Graham stumbled backward, feinting at the bird to keep some space between them. It seemed to have realised he wasn't going to actually hit it, and for a moment she thought it might get the best of him, then a dog leaped up at the nearest fence, barking hysterically, and the swan hesitated, torn between two targets. Graham took his chance and fled to join DI Adams, his normally jovial face flushed with exertion.

"Bloody overgrown chickens," he said. "Ideas above their damn station."

"They're a nightmare," she agreed.

"Bit late for Christmas, but I wouldn't say no to some roast goose."

"Pretty sure you can't eat the swans."

"Then the geese can serve as a lesson to them." He shook his baton at the gaggle, which was still watching them from across the road. "They're not normally this bad, are they?"

DI Adams wished she hadn't somehow become the Toot Hansell expert, but said, "It must have something to do with the water problems. Disturbing their habitat, maybe."

"They're disturbing *my* habitat."

"And everyone else's." The marauding packs of birds consisted of geese for the most part, but also swans and ducks. The latter seemed fairly unthreatening until one was being mobbed by about eight of them, all quacking wildly and pecking anything they could reach, as she'd found out firsthand earlier. They'd barely started the search for Esther, but it was already clear the birds were going to make it all but impossible. "We need to get bird protection out."

"More like the bloody army," Graham said, rubbing the back of his thigh. "It *pecked* me."

"Horrors," DI Adams said, then when he gave her an offended look she said hurriedly, "Is it bad?"

"I bet it bruises."

She made a noise she hoped hit the right sympathetic note, but Graham still looked put out, so she said, "Right, well, we need to move this on. Give the RSPB a call, will you?"

He grunted in agreement. "Not liking the way these waters are coming up." He pointed into one of the gardens, where the front yard was awash, flooding from what was probably a pretty little water feature in more usual times. For a moment she thought she saw motion in it, the reflection of a bird passing overhead or the dance of dragonflies, but there was nothing around. She frowned, and glanced at Graham, but he didn't seem to have seen anything. He was still talking. "I'm going back to the car to call. I'm going to end up piebald at this rate."

"Sure," she said, trying to watch the water and the birds at the same time, and wondering if Nellie was sneaking about the place. That would solve at least one problem, if she could get the sprite to call off the birds. Movement caught the corner of her eye, and she glanced around to see the swan doing a not particularly subtle job of sneaking up on them from the side.

Graham growled. "How come they're not going for you?"

"They are."

"They're not. Those geese are just hanging about watching you, while that swan tried to *disembowel* me."

"Maybe you're more threatening," she said, although she was pretty sure it was Dandy keeping the birds somewhat at bay. He was out of sight now, and the geese were starting to advance across the road.

"Great. Sexist birds," Graham muttered. "You coming?"

"No, I'll keep looking."

"Suit yourself." He hurried off toward the centre of town, the swan and four of the ducks waddling off in pursuit. He kept spinning around and walking backward to brandish his baton at them, and was halfway down the block when the first swan charged him from over a garden wall. He yelped and took off at a sprint, the birds honking eagerly as they gave chase.

DI Adams eyed the two closest geese, who glared back at her. "Behave," she said, shaking her keys at them. The little brass duck clattered against the keys warningly, and the geese shuffled their big feet, settling their wings. She and the birds stared at each other, and she checked the street. Graham had vanished, and there was no one in sight other than a platoon of ducks pattering busily across the road a few houses down. She looked back at the birds.

"What've you done with Esther?" she asked them, her voice low. They didn't answer, obviously, but they didn't attack her either. "Have you chased her into the nearest garden shed?" she suggested hopefully.

The geese turned and fled, and she stared after them, wondering if she should be following. Then someone said from behind her, "You getting anywhere with your interviews, Inspector?"

DI Adams turned to look at Rose, who was kitted out in muddied black waterproof trousers, a too-large, multipocketed camouflage jacket with the hood pulled over her head, and a mysteriously large pack with a waterproof cover tucked neatly around it. "What've you got in there?" she asked.

"Supplies," Rose said cheerfully, tugging Angelus' leash. Evidently the geese weren't fans of the big dog, as they'd stopped a little further down the road and were peering at him with nervous belligerence. Angelus, for his part, was hiding behind Rose's legs, but given their relative sizes that wasn't going well. "No sign of Esther?"

"Not yet," DI Adams said. "The birds are making things difficult."

Rose nodded. "They're behaving very oddly. No explanation for it."

DI Adams adjusted her hood, rain dribbling onto her cheeks. "If it really was Esther that Miriam saw last night …" She trailed off, then shook her head. She should be discussing this with colleagues, not the bloody W.I.

"No one just vanishes," Rose said. "It's not possible."

"Not even in Toot Hansell?"

"I don't think so," Rose said, apparently giving it due consideration. "And I'm still not sure who I saw last night, either."

"Sorry, what?"

"Well, it wasn't Esther. It was some old boy in a dressing gown."

DI Adams found herself, not for the first time in the vicinity of the W.I., wanting to slap a hand to her forehead. "You saw someone too?"

"Yes, when we were looking for Esther."

"Why am I only just hearing about this now?"

Rose shrugged. "Carlotta already said she saw someone in a dressing gown. I assume it was the same person."

"Right. Did they look like someone who could've caused Esther harm?"

"Hard to tell, given the visibility."

DI Adams pulled her phone from her pocket and hit dial. "Graham," she said as he answered. "A second witness saw someone else on the green around the time Esther was last seen. Unidentified male, possibly older, in a dressing gown. Likely the same person Carlotta saw."

"Anything more on them?" Graham asked. "Are we looking for an attacker or another victim?"

"Not sure yet. But brief everyone. We may have someone else out here."

"On it." The phone disconnected, and DI Adams put it back in her pocket, checking on the birds again.

"I don't think he'd have attacked her," Rose said.

"Why not?"

"Well, like I say, he was an old boy in a dressing gown. It seems more likely that wherever Esther vanished to, he did as well."

DI Adams nodded. "Anyone seen Nellie yet?"

"Not that I know of." Rose took her phone out and checked it. "Um ... Gert's asking for votes on whether she can serve her elder-flower cordial to the searchers, because Jasmine's saying it's not appropriate. Pearl wants to know how many sandwiches we need. Teresa and Priya think there's quicksand near the school and are taping it off—"

"Quicksand?"

"Probably not really," Rose said. "But the ground's extremely waterlogged. Some of the ditches are collapsing, and Nicola Peabody's nymph statue fell into a sinkhole."

"Unfortunate," DI Adams said, thinking of the tunnels that riddled the foundations of the town, secret byways and escape routes that were as old as the village itself. The ground couldn't be that stable with all those down there, even before the flooding started.

"Not so much. It was a really ugly statue." Rose took a final look at her phone before stashing it back in a cavernous pocket. "Carlotta and Rosemary have been trapped in Bryan's pub by a bunch of geese."

"How distressing for them."

Rose snorted. "That's all we have so far."

DI Adams watched Dandy re-emerge from around the side of the flooded garden, a squeaky toy in his mouth. He stared down into the water, and she tried to see what he'd spotted, but at this angle there was only the reflection of the heavy grey sky. Dandy squeezed his stolen toy a couple of times, making it squawk, and Angelus whined.

Rose looked around. "Is that your critter?"

"Yes, thief that he is."

"Is he being helpful?"

"Keeping the geese at bay, but that's it," DI Adams said, crossing the road to peer at the water more closely. Rose followed, and they stood side by side, examining the short grass drifting beneath the surface. There was nothing, no movement, no suggestion of anything untoward.

"Are you alright there?" a man called from the house. He was leaning out a window, frowning at them.

"You haven't seen anyone out in inappropriate clothes?" DI Adams asked. "A man in a dressing gown, a woman in slippers?"

"I saw Esther was missing on the Facebook group," he said. "But she's not in my flower-beds."

"Right," DI Adams said. "Thanks." She turned away, and glanced at Rose. "No sign of Nellie either?"

"No. Is that who you were looking for in the water?"

"Not sure. I thought I saw something earlier."

Rose nodded, and took her phone out again, swiping it open and handing it to the inspector. "Read that thread."

DI Adams took the phone with a frown.

- Anyone else see the faces in the water?

- No, but I heard them.

- Heard who?

- The people in the water.

- Are they ghosts?

- I think they're aliens.

The thread continued, people talking about movement in the flood-waters, or in the many fishponds and water features around the village, or in the drains (that set off a whole subthread to do with clowns and sewers). No one had answers, and no one was too clear about what they'd seen or heard, but they all agreed something was there. Even for Toot Hansell, the apparitions were unnerving, and the fact that they were almost immediately followed by invasions of large aggressive birds meant no one was investigating too much.

She handed the phone back to Rose. "I need to get more bodies on the search."

"You've got the W.I.," Rose said, falling into step with the inspector as she turned toward the centre of town. Dandy cruised around them, keeping the birds at bay.

"You're not police."

"You think vanishing people are a police matter? Apparitions in the water? The birds, even?"

DI Adams growled, and took her phone out as it vibrated,

checking the screen. She didn't recognise the number, and she hit answer with a frown. "DI Adams."

"Hello, inspector. It's Alice."

"Alice? Are you alright?"

Alice *hmm*ed. "I am, yes. But we may have seen Esther at Lachlan Jameson's retreat."

"*May* have?"

"We've lost her again. But we're looking."

"We? Whose number is this?"

"There's no signal here, so I'm using Niall's."

"Who's— never mind. No one go poking around and destroying evidence, alright? And send me a pin drop." She hung up, shoving the phone back into her pocket.

"Where are they?" Rose asked, and DI Adams waved her away.

"Keep looking. I'm not sure if this is solid or not." She broke into a jog, leaving Rose behind. Maybe it was nothing, Miriam chasing ghosts again. But it was the best lead she had to find one vulnerable woman, out here in the cold, confused and alone. The apparitions in the water could wait.

DI ADAMS LEFT Graham to coordinate the search in town, which he seemed less than happy about. She had an idea that wasn't so much to do with the job itself than it was the fact Jasmine and Ben were arguing loudly in front of a large village map over whether Jasmine was in charge of the volunteers or if everyone answered to the police; Gert was handing out her alarmingly potent elderflower cordial with an air of innocence; Pearl had commandeered a confused-looking PC to serve sandwiches; and Primrose was attempting to bite anyone who walked through the door. DI Adams left before anyone could drag her into the confusion and headed for the coordinates Alice had sent her, driving at a frustratingly sedate pace through the flooded streets. The puddles by the kerbs were spreading across the roads to meet in the middle, but when she eased across the bridge that crossed the stream, the water was low and dirty in its bed. She wasn't here to investigate waterways, though, so she just accelerated into the drier roads beyond the village, flipping the windscreen wipers down a speed.

She almost overshot the gate to the retreat and had to brake hard, pulling into the gravelled gateway as she did so. Dandy tumbled off the front seat into the footwell with an offended yelp, and she said, "Sorry."

He huffed, climbing back onto the seat. She'd given up on trying to keep him off it and had invested in a seat cover, but it wasn't helping with the paw prints on the door and dashboard.

There was no one at the front of the building, just Alice's car abandoned in the middle of the gravel, so she pulled up to what looked like the main door and swung out, still in her high-vis jacket. She ran up to the door and knocked, then when no one answered she stepped back and shouted, "Hello?" Still nothing, and she said quietly to Dandy, "See what you can find, can't you?"

He tipped his head to one side, giving the squeaky toy a squeeze, and she sighed.

"Please stop stealing things." She jogged around the building, following the gravel drive with her footsteps loud in the damp silence, broken only by a hint of machinery running somewhere, probably in the big outbuilding that faced the retreat.

"Alice?" she called, taking her phone from her pocket. The back of the retreat was immaculately clean, with none of the jumble of old equipment and potholes and collapsing sheds that she'd found to be characteristic of the farms she'd been to. She hesitated, wondering whether to check the buildings or the grounds first, then Dandy loped past her, squeaking his toy as he went. "Alright, then," she said, and ran after him.

Dandy led the way across the grass and past the retreat, into an artful garden with luminous green grass and an attractive assortment of shrubs and trees, flowering plants and rock gardens. The ground was soft and treacherous, even the decent tread of her boots threatening to slip, and Dandy didn't stop until they reached a large wooden gate in the wall to the left that opened onto fields. The garden looked as though it continued straight ahead all the way to the woods, and she was fairly sure the road must lie beyond the wall to the right, although she couldn't see it from here.

She didn't have time to explore, though, as Dandy hurdled the gate into the field effortlessly. DI Adams followed him over it into a wide sweep of green field dotted with sheep, their black legs and faces turning them into disembodied white clouds, sunk too low and fragmented in the grass. The dark loom of the forest curved around to border one side of the field, and in front of that wall were a huddle of people, one in a bright pink and yellow jacket and another in a sky-blue one with her hands folded over a cane in front of her. The others were dressed rather more soberly, and they all turned to look at her.

"Hello," a tall, lean man called out as she jogged toward them. "Are you the police?"

"I am," she said. "DI Adams. Lachlan Jameson?"

"That's me."

"What's happened?"

"Well, the ladies thought they saw something," he said.

"We didn't *think* anything," Miriam snapped, turning away from the trees. "She was here!"

Lachlan nodded mildly. "I fully believe *you* believe that." He looked at the three men with him, two in matching black jackets and the other shivering in a fleece, his hair slowly drooping over his forehead. "We didn't see anyone, though."

"Alice?" DI Adams asked.

"I saw *something*," she said, sounding unconvinced.

"I just don't see how some elderly lady from the village can be here," Lachlan said, gesturing broadly at the world. "But of course, you're free to look."

DI Adams looked across the field, empty except for the sheep. "You're sure it was Esther, Miriam?" she asked her.

"*Yes*," she said, her cheeks pink in the cold. "She was here, I'm sure of it." She pointed at Lachlan. "He *did* something!"

Lachlan spread his hands apologetically. "I don't even know who Esther is."

"You do. You delivered water to her!"

"My team and I have delivered water to half of Toot Hansell. All of it, in fact. I can't remember every single person."

Miriam looked at DI Adams. "I did see her. Slippers and a blue cardigan, just like yesterday."

DI Adams swallowed a sigh. She couldn't risk the possibility Esther *had* been here, not when they were finding no trace of her in the village. She looked at Lachlan. "Do I have permission to search your premises?"

He shrugged. "Of course. Within reason. The bottling plant's running and it's not safe, but you can look from the door. You'd be better asking Dom, though."

"Why?"

"This is his field," Lachlan said, and pointed across it, away from the retreat, to a gate. Just beyond it was someone on a quad bike, watching them. "Why would I be abducting anyone?"

"Why would he?"

"Stirring trouble," Lachlan said. "He's been digging up his fields too. Wouldn't surprise me if the water problems are starting from his place."

"You didn't mention that before," Alice said.

"I didn't realise you were about to accuse me of kidnapping."

"No one's accusing anyone of anything," DI Adams said, pointing everyone back toward the retreat. "Let's go." She let them go ahead of her, looking at the figure on the quad bike as they backed away and vanished again. She wasn't narrowing the search down. It was expanding by the minute, and all they had to go on was another apparition. It was starting to feel like a ghost hunt, which was a bit much even for Toot Hansell.

9
MIRIAM

Miriam might have been intimidated by DI Adams before, but she'd never seen anything quite like the efficiency with which the inspector had them bundled into Alice's car and pointed back along the road toward the village. It seemed to take no time at all for her to quiz them, scribbling things quickly in her notebook as they stood under the overhang on the retreat's little deck, then she was shepherding them out to the car, Lachlan looking on with interest.

"Do you have all you need, Inspector?" Alice asked, tapping her keys against her leg.

"Yes. I might have more questions for you later, but for now just head back to the village. Graham's running the search, so don't let Jasmine stage a mutiny, alright?"

"Of course," Alice said, smiling slightly.

"No detours." The inspector opened Alice's door pointedly.

Alice didn't move. "Did you believe him about Dom?"

"What I believe is irrelevant. And you're not to talk to Dom. We appreciate the help with the search, but that's as far as you go."

"Well," Alice said, and DI Adams looked at the sky.

"You've already spoken to him."

"He wasn't best pleased to see us. We did spot some digging equipment in his barn, though."

"Good to know. Please stick to the search."

Alice nodded and got in the car, and DI Adams looked from her to Miriam, then pushed the door shut, turning back to the retreat as Alice started the engine and headed for the gate.

Alice didn't turn toward the village, though, choosing instead the opposite direction. Past the retreat's garden, the forest took over, trees pressing up to the moss-encrusted stone wall that bordered the lane, promising the deep green scents of old, lost places. Across the road was a different world entirely, the foliage thinning as it slouched up toward the fells, lay-bys and stiles pointing invitingly to walking trails for the adventurous.

"Are we going to pick up the dragons?" Miriam asked. She'd seen them straight away, of course, peering over the wall into the field, and had tried as subtly as she could to wave them off. Although she evidently hadn't been *that* subtle, as Lachlan had given her a couple of funny looks. He'd even peeked over the wall himself, but hadn't seen anything, the dragons faded into the mud among the trees like so many old tree stumps.

Alice nodded. "Hopefully they'll be watching for us, and we can see if they sniffed anything out about Nellie. Or Dom."

Miriam gave her a worried look. "We are going to listen, aren't we? About sticking to the search?"

"Of course," Alice said, pulling into a lay-by not far from where the retreat's gardens met the woods, but distant enough to be unseen. The ground was patchy with puddles and mud and fallen leaves, and there were no cars or walkers around. It hadn't exactly been the weather for it, not for a couple of weeks at least. "But we can't help where the search takes us, can we?"

"Alice."

"Imagine if Graham stumbled over Nellie? Or anyone else?"

Miriam very much wanted to argue, but she couldn't. They had a responsibility to keep the dragons secret and the Folk safe, after all. But she didn't have to like it.

It wasn't long before the top of a scaly head lifted itself slowly over the forest wall, the same deep greys as the stone, and revealed large eyes of old, hazed gold. Miriam waved cheerily, getting out to open the back door and check the tarp was tucked tightly over the seats. Beaufort slipped up and over the wall, Mortimer following, and Alice wound her window down.

"What are you doing flying about in the middle of the day?"

"Oh, we were over the forest," Beaufort said, clambering into the car. "Plus with this cloud cover, even if anyone was looking up, they'd barely be able to see us."

Miriam gave Mortimer a sympathetic look. He was definitely the right colour for the clouds. "Did you find anything?" she asked.

"Nellie's been here," he said, climbing in after the High Lord. "We couldn't find her, though."

"And things are rather unsettled," Beaufort added, as Miriam closed the door and got back in the front. "There's been a human in the woods, apparently. Past the charms, which indicates an extremely high degree of determination. Even on the edges, the woods here are very well guarded."

"Why would someone be in there?" Alice asked.

"I'm not sure, but Nellie was in the woods too," Mortimer said. "It must all be to do with the water."

"I wonder if it was Lachlan," Miriam said.

Alice glanced at her, smiling slightly. "Not Dom?"

"Or him," Miriam admitted. "Esther was in his fields, I suppose."

"Is Esther the missing woman?" Beaufort asked.

"Yes," Miriam said. "Whom nobody believed I saw." She couldn't help feeling a little bit vindicated.

"Of course we believed you, dear," Alice said, checking the road before pulling into a U-turn to head back toward the village. "It's just the visibility was very bad yesterday."

Miriam huffed slightly. "But you believed me this time."

"Yes," Alice said, her tone careful. "But I do wonder how she got out here."

"Maybe Lachlan kidnapped her," Miriam said.

"Why would he do that?" Beaufort asked.

"I don't know. Perhaps she was at the retreat for a treatment and saw something she shouldn't have."

"I rather doubt she was visiting the retreat," Alice said. "It's not even open."

"Then he kidnapped her to frame Dom, to draw attention away from himself. No one's that …" She waved one hand in front of her, looking for the words. "*Smooth.*"

"Or Dom kidnapped her himself," Alice pointed out.

"Or Nellie did," Beaufort said, and Miriam twisted in her seat to stare at him.

"Surely not."

"Her traces were very upset," Mortimer whispered. He was still a dejected grey, although Beaufort's scales were warming up to fainter shades of his usual greens and golds. "And then there's the birds."

"The birds are awful at the moment," Miriam agreed. She'd been chased into her own garden gate by a swan when she'd put the bin out that morning. "But that's just usual Nellie, really."

"Did you notice anything about the water in there?" Beaufort asked. "Even in the woods, it's smelling rather unpleasant."

"There's a fountain and a pool," Alice said. "Both very clean, as far as I could tell."

Miriam nodded. "They did seem clean. I checked both." Although she was still trying to decide if the water felt the same as it usually did in the village or if it was slightly *off,* as if it were sickening but not as quickly.

"The only clean water anywhere," Alice said. "Except possibly for Dom's." She tapped her fingers on the steering wheel thoughtfully.

"No," Miriam said. "I don't want dogs set on me again."

"Of course. But if Nellie's looking for clean water—"

"Or sabotaging it," Beaufort said, his voice serious.

"Sabotaging and kidnapping?" Alice asked. "Do you really think so?"

The High Lord sighed. "This is not something I want to believe, but there is a certain theory she may be so upset that someone's being so dreadfully careless with her waters – especially someone from the outside, not even from the village – that she's decided to take action. That she's making things worse, not better."

"Oh dear," Alice said, and Miriam covered her mouth with one hand.

"But what would she want with Esther? She didn't do anything!"

"No," Beaufort agreed. "I rather think that could be accidental. Wrong place, wrong time."

"This is *awful,*" Miriam said. "And the flooding? Do you really think she'd do that?"

"It's hard to say. But I think we have to consider it a very real possibility. She is capable of it, after all, and if the Source – the heart of the waters – is at risk, who knows what she might do."

There was a long silence, then Miriam said, "What do we do?"

"We go back to the hall and regroup," Alice said. "DI Adams is covering Lachlan, and presumably Dom. We'll join the search and make sure Esther isn't in the village. You dragons can't be searching in the daylight, so there's nothing more we can do right now."

No one answered, and Miriam watched the fields pass with a terrible tightness in her chest, hoping for a glimpse of blue cardigan. She hated that Nellie having Esther was even possible, but how else was the woman vanishing and reappearing? That wasn't any sort of human kidnapping, after all. But Esther hadn't *done* anything, which was just so awful. The thought of her trapped in some underwater hollow somewhere, or abandoned in a swamp, all because some rich person had got too greedy over the water and upset the sprite, was unbearable. "Poor Esther," she whispered.

❧

THE VILLAGE WAS under siege when they got back. Rather than a few rogue birds, packs of geese and swans patrolled the streets and gardens resolutely, and had been joined by platoons of ducks and, curiously, a couple of suspicious-looking herons. Other waterfowl that Miriam couldn't identify at a glance paddled in the overflowing gutters, looking put out.

"We can't take much more rain," she said.

"No, the drains aren't meant to handle all this water," Alice replied. "All the silt and debris must be building up terribly."

"The waterways are still low, though," Beaufort said. "It's the same all around the village."

Miriam pressed a hand to her chest, her heart suddenly hurting at the thought of Toot Hansell drowning in the stale, dying waters, sinking beneath the weight of the rain to be swallowed by the earth, as if it had never been. "Oh, it's terrible," she whispered, spotting a couple in matching anoraks peering at a yawning chasm that had appeared in their front garden. "Everything's going so wrong."

Mortimer put his snout between the seats, still deeply grey, and looked up at her with warm amber eyes. "We'll find Nellie," he said. "We'll stop this."

"We really must," Alice said, her voice serious. "Things are deteriorating rather rapidly." Ahead of them, a dog barked hysterically at a bubbling drain, while a small boy tried to pull him away, and just down the street a man frantically tried to sweep water away from his front door.

Alice turned into the churchyard, stopping in the shelter of the trees to let the dragons out. "We'll let you know when it's safe to come into the hall."

"Of course," Beaufort said, and he and Mortimer slipped out into the shadows, leaving Miriam abruptly bereft. She was quiet as Alice drove back to park just down the road from the village hall, behind a line of other cars, some belonging to the W.I. and others that were less familiar. They hurried through the rain to the door, the creaking agitation of Toot Hansell like a storm pressing down around them, heavy and suffocating. Someone was shouting on the other side of the green, a dog barking, and a horn went off, punctuating the day, while under it all ran a dislocated sense of loss from the troubled waters.

Alice opened the door onto a ragged little crowd. There were no police officers inside, but Gareth from the dodgy pub, Ed from the village store, Rita who owned the deli, and a dozen more were milling around, clutching mugs of coffee or tea and helping themselves to the cakes and sandwiches, which were disappearing at a rapid rate.

"There you are," Jasmine said, hurrying up to them. Her hair was somehow both plastered limply to her head and also sticking out in various directions. "We have a problem, and they're not listening to me."

"What sort of problem?" Alice asked.

"You!" Gareth shouted, pushing past a few people and hurrying over to them with a mug clutched in one hand. All heads turned their way, and Miriam had to stop herself from retreating out the door in the face of the stares.

"This is your fault," Gareth said, jabbing a Scotch egg at them.

"I'm sorry?" Alice said.

"We're not getting any more water."

"I'm not sure what you mean."

"Look!" He wedged the egg in his mouth and shook the phone at her. Miriam leaned over to squint at it. It was open to the Toot Hansell Facebook group, and at the top of the page was an update from Lachlan.

Terribly sorry, no water deliveries today. A couple of ladies have set the police on me. 😉

A photo of Alice and Miriam standing in the middle of the garden, evidently taken from a security camera, accompanied the text, and Miriam tugged at the front of her jacket. She didn't think it looked half as bad as the picture seemed to indicate. Part of the problem was likely the fact that the still had caught her waving wildly, both hands in the air, as if she was at an Ibiza rave.

"What the hell are you doing setting the police on him?" Gareth demanded. "He's the only thing stopping us all having to drive to bloody Skipton every day to get water. *And* pay a fortune for it."

"We didn't set the police on him," Alice replied. "We saw Esther in the field, so of course we reported it."

"But why were you there in the first place?" Vera asked.

"Bloody harassment is what it is," Ed said. "Always poking your noses into everything, aren't you?"

"I've already used all my water," Vera added. "I don't have a car. How am I meant to get more?"

"He doesn't say he's stopping it completely," Alice replied, handing the phone back to Gareth. "He merely says there's none today. A little bit of restraint and I'm sure we'll all be fine."

A ripple of disagreement went through the room.

"We shouldn't be relying on him to supply us anyway," Gert added, her heavy forearms crossed and her feet planted wide. "My niece's god-daughter's brother—"

"Oh, so *you* get to cash in?" Ed asked, and Vera scoffed.

"You would think that." They glared at each other, and Alice turned to hang her jacket up, leaving room for Miriam to step inside. She wasn't sure she wanted to.

"We had *free* water," Rita complained.

"Which you were selling," Teresa said.

"I have a business to run," Rita said. "At least I wasn't price-gouging like Ed."

"You were selling water you were *given.*"

"This is hardly important right now," Alice said, her voice calm. "Is there any news on Esther?"

"No," Jasmine said. "No sign."

"You still haven't explained why you were at Lachlan's," Janine from the butcher's said. "I bet you were just poking around, weren't you?"

"We weren't *poking around,*" Miriam said. "We took him a lemon drizzle cake." She wasn't sure it added much to the argument, but she felt she needed to say something to support Alice.

"A lemon drizzle cake," Rita said. "The man's a bloody billionaire, and you took him a *lemon drizzle cake?*"

Miriam flushed. "He said it was very nice."

"And how rich he is is hardly relevant," Rose said. "Everyone likes lemon drizzle cake."

"Besides," Priya said, pointing a teaspoon at Rita, "he's not a billionaire, he's a multimillionaire."

"Oh, that makes all the difference," she snapped.

"Well, he *liked* it," Miriam insisted, glad she'd bought the thing in Skipton and not at the deli.

"Never mind that. You have to stop this," Gareth said, shaking his phone at Alice. "We need that water. He's been nothing but generous."

"And yet all these problems started when he arrived," Teresa pointed out.

Gareth turned to look at her. "What, you think *he's* ruined the water supply?"

"Can't trust anyone who doesn't drink decent tea," Pearl said, before Teresa could reply.

"And he's still got clean water," Gert agreed.

"That's not a reason!" Ed said, his voice too loud.

"This is *enough*!" Jasmine said, the words squeaking at the edges. "I'm the police community support officer—"

"Oh, shut up about your police community supporting," Gareth snapped, and Jasmine looked like she'd been slapped.

"Don't be so rude, Gareth Mullins," Carlotta said, moving a plate of sandwiches out of his reach. "You're only miffed because she busted your lock-in a week ago."

"And I only gave you a warning," Jasmine said. Her nose was very pink.

"You didn't stop Esther from vanishing, though, did you?" Rita demanded.

"How was I meant to stop that? And who's been organising everything, and making sure we're covering the right areas, and—"

"We can't cover anything," Gareth said. "All these damn birds, they should be rounded up and *shot!*"

"*Hey!*" Rose jumped to her feet. "We're the ones affecting *their* environment, you know!"

Everyone was talking at once now, demanding to know where they were going to get water from, and how to deal with the birds, and Miriam was deeply tempted to simply walk straight back out into the rain and find some cheesy puffs, or even join the dragons hiding in the churchyard. Anything seemed better than to have everyone fighting so horribly, and the waters dying and the birds rioting, and Esther still missing. It was all so *awful*—

A piercing whistle rang through the hall, making Miriam flinch and Pearl clap both hands over Martha's ears. Angelus set up a wobbly howl, and Primrose started yapping, dancing in circles.

"Excuse *me,*" Jasmine said, her voice very nearly steady. She had a small black whistle in one hand. "This isn't helping anyone. Our key objective is finding Esther, so I suggest we all get back to it."

"You can't—" Gareth started, and Rita jabbed him in the ribs with one bony elbow. "Hey!"

"Shut up, Gareth. She's right."

"But—"

"I'm very sorry about the water," Alice said, raising her voice slightly to carry through the hall. "But we need to listen to Jasmine. Esther is the most important thing. And I'm sure Lachlan will be back tomorrow."

"I think you should apologise," someone said, his voice mild, and Miriam saw Bryan, the owner of the decent pub, sitting in one of the chairs with half a scone on a napkin in front of him. He flushed. "I don't mean to be rude. But we really do need that water. And maybe if you apologise to him, he'll bring it back a little sooner."

Alice inclined her head, and Miriam thought she was going to protest, then she nodded. "Very well. I shall do that."

"Bloody better," Ed said.

"You can shut up too," Vera said. "*You* can afford to buy water."

Gert clapped her hands together, the sound sharp and hard. "Come on, then. Move! We'll lose the light before we know it."

"Does everyone know where they're searching?" Jasmine asked, her voice almost completely steady now. "I have a map—"

"No, you're right, love," Janine said. "Come on. Let's get on." She led the way out the door, the rest of the crowd filing out with sausage rolls and sandwiches still in their hands, leaving behind a litter of empty mugs and crumb-strewn plates. Gareth tried to stop and say something else to Alice, but Rita and Janine pushed him out, and Alice shut the door in their wake.

She turned to look at the W.I. and the suddenly empty hall. "Well," she said. "That was a little bit of a to-do, wasn't it?"

Miriam thought that might be the understatement of the year, even if it was only January.

10

ALICE

"Locusts," Carlotta said with a sniff, regarding the mess the searchers had left behind.

"Ungrateful ones, at that," Rosemary said, taking a sausage roll from one of the plates. "Not a thank you among them."

"They might have a little point about the water, though," Teresa said. "We were somewhat relying on Lachlan."

The ladies looked at Alice and Miriam, and Alice shook her head. "We didn't go out there to upset him."

"And I did see Esther," Miriam put in.

"Was she alright?" Jasmine asked.

"I don't know. She vanished again."

"That's impossible," Priya said, looking at Alice, who spread her hands. It should be impossible, of course, but many unexpected things had been proven possible over the past few years, so who could say?

"The dragons might be able to tell us more," she said aloud. "Once we're sure everyone's gone, we can get them in." She started collecting plates and cups to carry through to the kitchen, where Pearl stacked them in the ancient dishwasher. It was quicker to wash by hand, but at least the machine had filters for the unpleasant water.

It didn't take long to put the hall back to its usual tidy state, the dishwasher grinding and sloshing its way through a first load, the extra chairs folded and leaned against the walls, the tea station wiped down and new mugs put out, awaiting the next round of refreshments.

Only then, with no indication that anyone was coming back to the hall, did Miriam open the back door and call Beaufort and Mortimer in from the churchyard. The High Lord shook himself off in the kitchen, then looked apologetically at Priya as she jumped back, brushing off the front of her trousers.

"Sorry," he said.

"That's all right," she replied. "I just hadn't thought I'd need waterproof trousers inside."

Alice picked up one of the big catering teapots and said, "Come on. Before any of the search party turn up again." She led the way into the main hall, setting the teapot on the table among the ladies' mugs and the remains of the cakes and biscuits.

"That's the last of the bottled water," Pearl said, tipping it into the hot water urn.

Alice frowned. "Lachlan dropped off rather a lot last night."

"I think people might be stockpiling," Teresa said.

Rose put two mince pies on a plate and handed it to Mortimer. "Eat up. You look peaky."

"It's the stress."

"So rude, taking all the water," Carlotta said. "That's not the way a proper community behaves. In the old country—"

"In Manchester, they'd mug you for half a cup of tea," Rosemary said, and Carlotta frowned at her.

"I wasn't talking about Manchester, but I still take offence to that."

"Of course you do," Rosemary said. "You take offence to everything."

"I do not!"

"You shouldn't," Priya said. "Given how offensive your parrot is, you should be immune."

"Bertie's not offensive. He's spirited."

"He was talking about my baps when I popped in the other day."

Carlotta wrinkled her nose. "Well. Yes, he does do that."

Alice tapped her fingers on the table, watching Miriam pouring large soup mugs of tea for the dragons. They were sitting on the floor, scales slick with rain.

"You said there had been a human in the forest," she said to them. "Could you tell who?"

Beaufort shook his head. "Perhaps it was Esther. Through the forest is the shortest route from the village to the retreat."

"How ever did she find her way up there?" Teresa asked. "Pearl and I have walked Martha all around the paths in the woods, and it doesn't matter what way you turn, you just end up back at the village. There's no way through them."

"That's the charms," Beaufort said. "It's concerning, the fact she got past them."

"She does keep vanishing," Miriam pointed out. "Maybe it's like the cats. Shifting, or whatever it is they do."

Beaufort made a thoughtful noise. "That's a very cat-specific thing. It takes a lot of cats to move one human, and they only do it in dire circumstances."

"What about the birds?" Rosemary asked. "What's happening with them?"

"It'll be something to do with Nellie, but we can't find her."

"The birds are terrible," Jasmine said. "Primrose and I got chased by a bunch of those decorative ducks this morning."

Rose looked at her. "Decorative ducks?"

"You know, the ones with the bits on their heads?"

"Mandarin ducks?"

"Well they weren't orange," Jasmine said, and Rose snorted.

"Do you really think Nellie's behind all this?" Alice asked Beaufort, as Pearl started to say something about snipe. The other women looked at her, startled.

"You mean more than just the birds?" Gert asked.

"It's possible," Beaufort said. "Sprites accept that others use their water, but they don't necessarily like it. Excessive use – such as the water bottling, and building a pool, redirecting so much of her stream – might've really upset her. And if he has been affecting the Source itself, that would be even worse."

"Would she really start kidnapping people, though?" Pearl asked.

"That bit I don't understand," he admitted.

"It would explain the vanishing," Priya said.

Beaufort made a doubtful noise. "I've never heard of a sprite being able to do that."

"Well, it's more likely than a human," Gert said, pouring a little more cordial into their glasses. "If your average criminal could just vanish people, we'd have some problems."

There was a murmur of agreement, then Miriam said, "But she's not making the water horrible. That happened first."

Rose inspected an egg sandwich, pulling a chunk of onion out of it. "The way the streams are low yet the ground's flooding doesn't happen naturally, though."

"Perhaps the polluted water was the catalyst," Beaufort said. "And rather than clean it, she's making it worse. Nature spirits are not always predictable."

Alice thought that could apply to humans just as well. Everyone was quiet, and she listened to the whisper of the rain on the windows and the quiet ticking of the radiators for a moment, then said, "Whether the water issues are caused by Nellie, or if they've started elsewhere and she's merely reacting, we need to handle this. Other than DI Adams, no one else knows about Folk. We have a responsibility here."

"And we could use your help," Beaufort added. "We can search for Nellie, of course, but where there's crossover with the human world, we're somewhat constrained."

"You hardly have to convince us," Teresa said. "Of course we're going to help, aren't we?"

A murmur of agreement went around the table, and Priya said, "What do we do?"

Alice smiled. It wasn't as though she'd expected anything else, really, but it still never failed to astonish her just how quick the W.I. were to step in when needed, whether it was for one of their own or someone else entirely. Aloud, she said, "I take it the village hasn't been fully searched?"

"No," Jasmine said. "The birds are making things really difficult."

"Then we begin by narrowing things down. We keep looking for Esther here and in the woods for as long as we have light. We let DI Adams carry on at the retreat, as I doubt she'll welcome our help, then tomorrow we shall go back to apologise to Lachlan and try having another word with Dom."

Miriam sighed deeply. "*We* means you and me, doesn't it?"

"You are the one who keeps seeing Esther. It may be to do with your ..." Alice searched for the word. "*Perceptiveness*."

"Alright."

"Rose, can you test the water?" Alice asked. "See if there's anything odd in it that might give us some clue as to where the problem's coming from?"

"I already did a home test when we couldn't get anyone out to help. None of the usual suspects like pesticides, fertiliser, or effluent."

"*Urk*," Teresa said.

"Are there any other tests you could do?" Alice asked.

"Sure." Rose looked at her watch. "I've got a friend who'll let me use a lab. I can go now."

"Perfect," Alice said. "The rest of us, Esther is our main concern."

"And we shall make ourselves scarce while the village is so busy," Beaufort said, inspecting his empty plate. "We'll resume the hunt for Nellie in the forest, and see if we can find any traces of Esther."

Carlotta tipped the last of the sausage rolls onto the High Lord's plate. "We'd better restock for the searchers, as well."

IT WAS dark by the time Alice got home, still mostly dry in the waterproof gear she'd changed into before rejoining the search, but with her hip aching from the damp and the cold. She was almost certain they'd covered every piece of ground in the village and the land that bordered it, probably twice over, and knocked on so many doors that at least one house had put a note in the front window reading, *No, we haven't seen Esther. Yes, we will look out for her. No, we don't know anything about the birds.* And the searchers could've written the same notes themselves. The only thing the search had revealed was that the flooding was getting worse. Garden sheds were developing precarious tilts as the ground softened under them, drains were rebelling, spilling more water over the streets, and fishponds were sinking away to leave mysteriously slopping pools in place of pretty backyards.

Alice had the uneasy feeling that Nellie's sometimes-bottomless pond was being a bad influence on every scrap of water in the area, and she'd spent the last hour, once it was too dark to search effectively, organising sandbags. The main bulk would be delivered in the morning, and meanwhile Gert's second cousin's son-in-law's something-or-other had turned up with a couple of sturdy young people in a nondescript truck, and were already stacking bags in the most affected areas. Alice hadn't asked where any of it had come from, or who was paying for it. Such details mattered rather less than the fact that it was here.

She let herself into the kitchen, easing her boots off with a sigh and hanging her coat on the hooks by the door. It was warm inside, and she stood where she was for a moment, massaging her hip, before walking slowly upstairs and putting the shower on. Her knuckles were sore too, with the creeping insistence of arthritis, light but present. She sighed slightly, clasping her hands gently together in front of her chest, then straightened up, pulling her shoulders back and adjusting her hair as she frowned at herself in the mirror.

"Silly woman," she muttered. "Feeling sorry for yourself over a little damp." Then she checked over her shoulder into the bedroom for the cat. It'd be just like him to turn up and find her talking to herself. But the room was empty, leaving her feeling oddly lonely. Only for a moment though. She didn't have time for such things.

Showered and warm, Alice went back downstairs in sheepskin slippers and a cosy jumper, and filled the kettle from a bottle of Lachlan's water, checking her supplies as she did so. In addition to two more of the *Sourced* bottles, she had a couple of large six-packs of one-and-a-half litre bottles which always lived in her pantry in case of emergencies. She never quite understood people who didn't have such things laid in, or torches kept handy in the event of power cuts, or a basic tool kit on an easily accessible shelf. One just never knew when they might be needed.

She slipped her reading glasses on so she could examine the *Sourced* bottle a little bit more closely, but it revealed nothing she hadn't seen before. Expensive, heavy glass, a slightly squat body with right angled shoulders, and a short neck. A mostly transparent label, which she could barely read even with her glasses. She huffed slightly, then finished making her tea, taking it through to her reading room. The heating was on, and she settled into her favourite chair, pulling a blanket over her legs as she picked up her tablet.

Alice wasn't a huge fan of technology, but she could use it efficiently enough for her own ends. It was the work of a moment to look up Lachlan Jameson. A rush of articles filled the screen, mostly from tech or business websites that all had an awed, admiring tone to them.

She didn't bother trying to understand the details of how he'd made his money, although it seemed to be something to do with a dating site that used some specific algorithm to match people rather effectively. He was also credited for various other tech breakthroughs, all of which sounded highly far-fetched and not particularly practical, but then it wasn't her area of expertise. His latest venture seemed to involve electric cars and the hunt for lithium sources that were less environmentally damaging, which she supposed was respectable at least. And no doubt highly profitable.

Lachlan Jameson wellness, she tried, and a new set of articles popped up, most of them still from the tech and money sites, talking about his optimal productivity routine and other such things. One article was from a fairly reputable news site, though, titled *Lachlan Jameson and the Rise of Biohacking*. It was headed by a photo of Lachlan in a tight T-shirt and jeans that hung from his skinny hips, arms crossed over his chest in a manner that accentuated his biceps dramatically.

Lachlan Jameson, a British multimillionaire, intends to live forever, the article exclaimed breathlessly. *He plans to accomplish this through a strictly controlled diet, mindfulness, intense and rigorous exercise, and now the acquisition of what he believes to be the water of life itself.*

Alice grimaced, deciding she needed to reevaluate her assessment of the reliability of that particular website. A video accompanied the article, and she clicked on it. Jameson's unnaturally smooth face filled the screen.

"So what is this water of life?" the interviewer asked in the same breathless tone as the article.

"Well, it's not the fountain of eternal youth," he said with a chuckle. He seemed to be having trouble with his expressions again, and Alice thought he might be best to ease off the Botox. "But there is a village in the Yorkshire Dales where it seems the locals are particularly healthy. They don't even have a pharmacy."

"Really?" the interviewer gasped. "No pharmacy?"

"No pharmacy, no doctor, no dentist. Nothing at all."

"Amazing."

Alice thought it was rather less amazing than it was an indication of how local services had declined, since everyone now had to go to Skipton.

"They're also a very long-lived population," Lachlan was continuing, "and the only possible reason I could pinpoint – all other things being equal, as far as I could tell – was the fact the village has its own water source. Which indicated to me that this water must be truly exceptional. I confirmed that on testing. It's very pure. So I bought some land to create a retreat, and share this part of my journey of wellness with everyone."

"Everyone in a higher tax bracket," Alice murmured. *Journey of wellness*, indeed. She got up to pour herself a whisky while on the screen Lachlan expounded on the virtues of ice baths, hydroponic greens, and sensory deprivation tanks, all of which were best conducted or grown in Toot Hansell's spring waters. She noticed he didn't mention anything about putting local farmers out of business. Not as good for the brand, she imagined.

She skipped the video forward a little, bored of the detailed inventory of herbs and tailored supplements Lachlan seemed to survive on rather than actual food (although it did explain why he'd been so taken by Miriam's shop-bought cake). There were no great revelations to be discovered. Lachlan was on a quest to extend his lifespan by the greatest degree possible, which Alice thought he might rethink once his own joints started revolting against him. Staying healthy as long as possible she could understand. Wanting to live on and on, while those around you faded and crumbled? She couldn't imagine why anyone would want that at all.

She stopped, thinking about it. He was *saying* it was the water that had special properties, but how long did a sprite live? The way the dragons talked, she could be as old as they were. What if he somehow knew about Folk, and Esther was the casualty of an entirely different trap? Perhaps it was Nellie he'd been after from the start, in search of the secret to her longevity. He wouldn't be the first person they'd come across who did know about Folk, or the first to have their own designs for them. It was an awful thought, but it had a certain ring of possibility to it.

She went back to her tablet, searching for anything that would suggest Lachlan had any particularly esoteric beliefs, but other than an intense meditation practise there was nothing. The rest of her poking around didn't reveal anything more that might shed light on either the water issues or Nellie, and she gave up, calling Miriam instead.

"Alice?" Miriam said as soon as she answered. "Are you alright?"

"Just checking in for tomorrow morning. We'll head out and give our apologies to Lachlan first thing, then talk to Dom."

There was the rustle of a bag of cheesy puffs at the other end of the line. "Alright," Miriam said, slightly indistinctly. "Shall I bring a cake?"

"That's a good idea," Alice said.

"I don't have anything gluten-free or sugar-free, though, and the shop's closed."

"Well, maybe just something for Dom, then. Is your house alright?"

"So far." Miriam's house was so close to the waterways that Alice was surprised she wasn't flooded, but that didn't seem to be the way things were working. "My pond's sunk, though."

"Sunk?"

"Like a sinkhole. My apricot tree fell in."

"Oh dear."

"Yes." Miriam didn't continue, and Alice listened to her chewing, waiting. There was something else on the younger woman's mind, she was sure of it. "Did you see anything ... *odd* in the water?"

"I assume you don't mean birds."

"No. More like ... people."

Alice made an interested noise. "Such as Nellie?"

"No, it wasn't her. But I kept thinking I heard someone calling out, and then I'd see movement, like a reflection, but there was no one to cast it. Other people have been mentioning it, too."

"How odd."

"Yes." Miriam crunched on another cheesy puff, then said, "Sirens are only in the sea, aren't they?"

"To my knowledge. But I have to admit that I haven't found mythology books to be terribly accurate or helpful so far."

"I'm just wondering ... maybe Esther followed the voices or something?"

"Perhaps," Alice agreed.

Miriam sighed, a great gust down the line. "I really hope she's okay."

"We shall do our very best to find out," Alice replied. They talked for a little longer, and when she hung up she put a heavy fleece on and slipped her feet into her boots, then went out into the back garden. She had no waterways on her own property, but she could hear water running somewhere, and an ominous splashing, as of a fish caught between tides. No one calling out, though, and when she circuited the property there were no lurking ghosts in the heavy puddles on the street, only the shattered reflection of the streetlights. She watched the night for a little while, then went back in before her trousers were too wet, shutting the dark and the rain out.

The village was sinking. But they'd figure this out. They had to.

11
MORTIMER

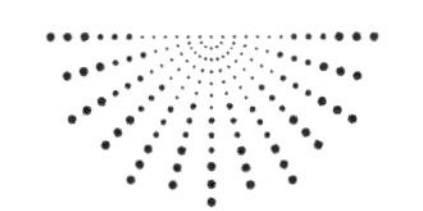

The night was opaquely dark, no moon or stars to break through the clouds. The lights of Toot Hansell were off, as they always were in the deepest stretches of every night, to protect the local wildlife. Only small, localised glows washed across the flooded streets from the shops in the centre and the occasional lights on the outsides of houses. Rain slid off Mortimer's wings and steamed softly on his back, wreathing him in a second camouflage of vapour, and in the sodden darkness he was, for once, not concerned about being spotted as they wheeled over the village.

The dragons stayed high initially, just in case anyone was out on the flooded streets, but there was no one to be seen, everyone huddled away from the night. The state of the village was clear to the dragons' prismed eyes that collected every scrap of light possible, painting the scene below stark and grainy. Gardens had been engulfed by flood-waters. Trees and sheds tilted into crevasses in the earth. Roads had transformed into rivers, and while the streams and waterways remained inexplicably low, the rain was still coming.

"This is terrible," Amelia called. "The whole village's being swallowed up."

Beaufort gave a rumble of agreement. "I know. We really need to find Nellie."

"Damn sprites," Lord Walter muttered. "Can't trust a one of them."

"Can she even fix this?" Lord Margery asked, her wings curving softly through the night.

"If we can find her." But even Beaufort sounded doubtful, and Mortimer didn't blame him. It seemed impossible that one sprite could handle this, no matter how much control she had over the waters. Even if she'd been the one to set it in motion.

Beaufort angled away, barrelling toward the edge of the woods and a handy clearing. They'd found nothing more in the forest during the day, the rain and the stink of the tortured waters swallowing all traces of sprite or human alike. With the majority of the birds still mobbing the village, it was possible Nellie could still be lurking there, watching the chaos unfold in the same way she always did from the pond when she set her geese on visitors.

The earth squished and slid under Mortimer as he landed, the rain so ceaseless he found himself checking for moss growing on his scales. He shuffled out of the way as Amelia and Lord Margery landed, and Lord Walter and Harriet followed. Mortimer still wasn't sure why Beaufort had chosen to include Margery in the search party when she so clearly objected to humans as a whole (whether that was heartfelt or just a way to be against Beaufort was a completely other question), but the High Lord would have his reasons. He always did. Even Walter, who might seem to be a poor choice given not only his general disposition but the distinct possibility he might try to eat anyone who surprised him, was a truly excellent tracker, even better than Mortimer himself.

"Now what?" Walter demanded, as they crowded together in the little space among the trees, shuffling to avoid clashing their wings. Well, everyone except Walter, who was shaking his wings off irritably and forcing everyone else to avoid him. "Humans are a bloody nuisance anyway. Maybe Nellie really has just got sick of them. We all should be."

Margery snorted. "Like you aren't sneaking off to take tea with your little pet. If anyone's a human-lover, it's you."

"I do not have a *pet.* She gives me things. Like tributes."

"Cake's a tribute now?"

"And whisky," he snapped. "The good stuff, too."

"You've gone soft."

"I have not."

Amelia huffed. "Both of you acting like you don't love Mortimer's barbecues, and the blankets, and every other bloody thing those *humans* have helped us get."

Both older dragons glared at her. "The *cheek,"* Margery started.

Walter growled agreement. "No damn respect—"

"Can we just start?" Harriet asked, her voice calm. "We're wasting time."

"Quite right," Beaufort said. "We should be fairly safe in this weather, but the usual precautions apply. We'll split up, start from the border river, and work our way to the centre. We're looking for any hint whatsoever as to where Nellie is, or how to sort out this water problem ourselves. There's also a human missing, a woman, so keep an eye out for her too."

"Always a human in the middle of things," Margery said.

"Probably went off for a spa weekend, like some people we know," Walter said.

"Did they have to come?" Amelia asked Beaufort. "They'll probably shove some humans in the duck pond themselves."

"No one's shoving anyone in any ponds," the High Lord said.

"I might," Amelia muttered, looking at Margery, who arched her eyebrow ridges at the young dragon.

"I'm off," Harriet said, turning away. "If I wait for you lot to stop squabbling, it'll be next week."

"We're not *squabbling,"* Walter said.

"I have two hatchlings. They're more reasonable than you two." Harriet melted into the trees, taloned paws silent on the ground and her tail twitching as it trailed after her, erasing every trace she'd ever been there. Harriet had a dryad's talent for simply vanishing into her surroundings.

The other dragons followed, falling silent as they scattered into the shadows. Mortimer headed toward Miriam's house, wishing he could knock on the door and go inside, to curl up in front of the fire and watch re-runs of the *Great British Bake-Off*. Miriam had strong opinions about the excessive fanciness of the baked goods on the show, but Mortimer was delighted by them. Humans were endlessly inventive, and while he wasn't sure why one *needed* a cake that looked exactly like a handbag, he adored it nevertheless.

However, he couldn't do that tonight. He had a sprite to find, so he stuck to the edge of the woods, following Amelia until she turned off toward the village, then keeping on alone to reach his own section, watching out not just for humans, but for geese and swans. Mortimer didn't need any more help losing scales.

He looked suspiciously at a sodden barn owl perched above him fluffing its feathers out irritably, but it didn't seem inclined to take its frustrations out on him, merely looked on with luminous eyes. It appeared only the water-borne birds were agitated, which was something, at least.

THE VILLAGE WAS restless in sleep. Lights came on periodically over front doors, and torches flooded backyards as people got up to check sandbags at doorways, or to peer at the lapping waters of a swelling, unplanned pond. Rabbit hutches had been moved to higher ground or shifted into garages and sheds, chicken coops were empty, and the roads swirled with stale, muddy water. The trees were heavy with rain, drooping toward the earth as if melting under the deluge. Packs of birds roamed the streets, eyes glittering in the dark, and Mortimer found himself ducking around corners or diving over walls to avoid them. His eyesight was better than theirs, so he was able to escape mostly unmarked, although he did have a close encounter with a pair of herons, stalking through the shallows on their fragile legs. They barely looked at him, though, simply gave him a baleful glare and strolled on, heads twitching from side to side as they searched for prey.

He'd paused to peer into a back garden, paws resting on the low wall that encircled it, when movement caught his eye, a flash of something in the water feature. It was too small to hold a sprite, so maybe it was a fish, swept away from a pond somewhere. It came again, a shimmer of luminosity. He wrinkled his snout. Fish didn't glow. Not unless they were deep sea ones, such as he'd seen on Miriam's nature documentaries.

He checked the house, then bounded lightly over the wall and padded to the water feature. The surface had stilled, showing nothing but murky water and Mortimer's own dim reflection. He wondered if the spring had stolen fancy fish from someone's aquarium or private pond, or if he'd simply seen a sliver of light from a house reflected back at him. There was nothing there now, anyhow, so he started to turn away, then light flared again. He stopped, and for one shimmering moment he saw a woman with a thin face, staring out at him in bewilderment, then she was gone. He blinked, and looked around the garden, as if she might have been standing behind him. There was no one there.

"Right," he said, checking the water again, but it was as empty as it had been when he first looked. He turned and headed on into the heart of the village, hoping he was going to come up with something more than roving birds and hallucinations.

He didn't, though, and after a seemingly endless tour of the sodden streets, during which he wondered if he was going to start developing webbed feet, he hobbled into the village square with his wings drooping and a hedgehog cupped in one paw.

The dragons were assembled in the deep shadows under the still-standing Christmas tree, ominous and forlorn without its lights as it loomed high above the square, smelling of dead foliage and rot.

"Finally," Margery said. "Thought you'd run off for another tea party."

"What is *that?*" Amelia asked, pointing at the hedgehog.

"He was floating down the street on a cushion," Mortimer said, offering the critter to her. "Can you give him to Gilbert?"

"*No.* He doesn't need to know about any of this. He'll be down here trying to rescue everything."

Mortimer sighed, cradling the hedgehog again. "Did anyone find anything?"

"Geese," Walter said, scratching something from between his teeth with a talon.

"I just spent half an hour fishing chickens out of a drain," Amelia admitted. "Their hen house washed away."

Margery huffed. "*Hatchlings.* No sign of Nellie. Not that I blame her. This water's not tolerable."

"Well, at least we can conclude she's not in the village," Beaufort said. "Does anyone have any idea where the Source could be? She could be protecting it, so perhaps if we find that, we'll find her."

No one answered, until Harriet said, "Tiddy 'uns."

"Sorry?" Beaufort said.

"There are none. None at all."

"Water's probably too filthy even for them," Margery said.

"But they'd be trying to clean up, if there was a chance of saving it." Harriet looked around thoughtfully. "If even the tiddy 'uns have given up, these waters are all but dead."

"That's a bit dramatic," Amelia said.

"Good for them, not tidying up after humans anymore," Margery said.

"They wouldn't just quit, would they?" Mortimer asked, thinking of Daphne and her *something new.*

Margery shrugged. "Nellie could've told them to, and I wouldn't blame them if they listened. Give the place a good clean out."

"Hardly, with the quality of this water," Beaufort said, his voice mild. "Anything else?"

"Ghosts in the waters," Walter said, still digging in his teeth.

"Yes!" Mortimer said. "I saw her too!"

"Her? I saw two. A man and a woman."

"Oh. I thought it might be Esther, but maybe not, then."

"Unless someone else has gone missing we don't know about," Amelia pointed out.

They were silent, listening to the rain pattering on the tree and the cobbles, and an ominous gurgling from the well. Finally Beaufort said, "Well, this seems to be all we're going to find out here. But the flooding's clearly getting worse. Margery, you get on well with Daphne. Can you talk to her and see if we can divert some water in her woods, to keep it away from the village?"

"She won't like that."

"We can ask. If not we'll have to do it outside the forest."

Margery bared her teeth, almost in a hiss. "We could be seen."

"We have to do something, or we'll lose Toot Hansell."

"And that's worth being exposed? Losing our home?"

Beaufort just looked at her, and the moment stretch thin and hard, then Walter said, "Yes. Humans are a nuisance, but these are *our* humans. You're not old enough to remember, Margery. Beaufort and I do. This village protected us in the days of the dragon hunts. They were part of why we survived. They turned away the knights, warned us of hunting parties, brought us sheep in the winters so we didn't have to roam. We wouldn't have survived without them."

"I know the history," Margery said sharply. "But that was so far beyond the memory of these humans, they can't even comprehend it. They know *nothing* of us, which is as it should be. Except for your pets." She gave Beaufort a disdainful look. "Not having them here would mean *less* risk, not more."

Mortimer looked at Beaufort, waiting for him to rebuke Margery, but he merely watched her with interest, his eyes gleaming in the shadows.

"They might not remember, but we do," Walter said. "And we don't turn our backs on those who need us." He arched his eyebrow ridges at Margery, his back swayed under the weight of centuries, his skin baggy and patched with loose scales, but his gaze steady.

Margery sighed, looking up at the branches, then at Beaufort. "No point asking what you think about it. You'd take the lot up to the mount and keep them, if you could."

"If it was that or lose them, yes," he said.

She growled. "*Fine.* I'll talk to Daphne. What're you going to do?"

"Ghost hunting," Beaufort replied.

❧

WHICH WAS how Mortimer found himself, with dawn not yet creeping around the edges of the sky, back where the birds had chased them into the woods the day before. He peered over the wall, trying to avoid eye contact with the sheep, which were staring at them with singular intensity. He still had the hedgehog, which had fallen back asleep as soon as he picked it up and was snoring very, very softly.

"Do they usually snore?" he asked Beaufort.

"I'm afraid I'm not sure. Why don't you pop him somewhere dry and leave him, lad? He's in hibernation anyway."

"What if he wakes up and doesn't know where he is? How's he going to get home?"

Beaufort nodded gravely. "Have you been spending a lot of time with Gilbert?"

"A bit," Mortimer admitted.

"Yes." Beaufort looked over the wall. "There's no one about. Shall we go?"

"I suppose," Mortimer said, and followed the High Lord as he slipped up and over the border of the forest. The charms were strong on the woodland side of the wall, but old. The dryad hadn't reinforced them for a long time. He landed with a splash, curling the hedgehog a little closer as he did so. "It's even wetter than yesterday," he said. "It's going to undermine the wall. The whole thing could come down, and the trees."

"We're not at that point yet," Beaufort said, but his eyebrow ridges were pulled together as he looked up at the low sky. "I've never seen anything like this, though. Even the rain feels a little odd, don't you think?"

Mortimer raised his snout to the sky. He hadn't really considered it, and with the stale, choked water rising up around his paws, he couldn't decide what was coming from above and what from below. "It *all* feels wrong," he said. "I can't tell what anything's meant to feel like anymore."

Beaufort made a sympathetic noise. "We'll get to the bottom of this. Come on. We've got time to have a good look around before it gets light."

Mortimer wasn't entirely happy about that, but he hobbled after Beaufort, wondering what exactly he was going to do with the hedgehog. He was still wondering when Beaufort stopped abruptly, and Mortimer stepped on his tail. "Oh! Sorry!"

Beaufort didn't answer, and Mortimer looked up to see a man standing on the grass just in front of them, looking around in bewilderment. He was wearing pale blue pyjama bottoms, slippers that had sunk deep into the mud, and a deep purple dressing gown with gold piping on the edges.

"This isn't my bathroom," he said, and turned, his gaze falling on the dragons. He froze, staring straight at them, his eyes getting wider and wider. He had a toothbrush in one hand, and it slipped from his grip as Beaufort raised one front paw in a gentle wave. The man screamed and clutched his chest, took a stumbling step back, then vanished.

Both dragons yelped, and Mortimer said, "What happened? Who was that? Where did he *go?*"

"I don't know," Beaufort said, and it was the first time Mortimer had ever heard the High Lord sound properly startled.

"But *how?* And where did he come from?"

"His bathroom, evidently," Beaufort said, nodding at the toothbrush.

"But how—"

"I don't know, Mortimer." Beaufort's tone was sharp. "But hurry up and get a whiff of him before the rain washes it away."

Mortimer jumped forward as if the High Lord had jabbed him, casting around for some sense of the man, any clue as to where he had come from. There was nothing, not even a swirl of shock from someone whose world had just shifted in directions they didn't know existed. It was as if they'd imagined him into being. He looked at Beaufort. "Nothing."

"Well, seeing him was something, at least," Beaufort replied. "We know how Esther got here from the village, and how there's been humans in the forest."

"Not really," Mortimer said. "All we know is he vanished. Actually *vanished.* Could it be the Watch?" He looked around warily, as if expecting to find an army of cats watching them from the wall, ready to whisk them away for some mysterious feline punishment for daring to expose humans to the truth of the world. There were only the sheep, though, crowding around them.

"I doubt it," Beaufort said. "But we can ask Thompson."

"I haven't seen him since the rain started." Thompson was the local Watch representative, but, like any cat, he followed his own counsel, and since Beaufort had saved his kitten self from losing a life in the river, he'd developed a large blind spot when it came to the dragons.

"True," Beaufort said. He headed off, leading the way across the field to the wall that divided the farm from the retreat. The sheep followed, a damp and fluffy entourage, and Mortimer gave them an uneasy look over his shoulder. One of them came close enough to nudge his tail.

"*Hey.*" He flicked his tail away, and the sheep bleated at him.

"Are you alright, lad?"

"The sheep are after me. First geese, and now sheep?"

"I think creatures just like you," Beaufort said.

"Well, I don't like them," he replied, picking up the pace and trying to keep his tail out of reach. He passed Beaufort and stopped before they reached the wall, looking up at it distrustfully. "The smell's odd."

"Odd how?"

"There's electricity everywhere." He squinted at the wall. "There might be cameras, or alarms."

"Only one way to know," Beaufort said, and before Mortimer could react he was over the wall and into the garden beyond.

The reaction was instant, light exploding across the night as huge spotlights came on, casting harsh shadows over the wall. Beaufort shot back out of the garden, his wings tight to his body, and they fled across the field, headed for the cover of the woods. Mortimer couldn't move fast enough, not with the hedgehog still cradled in one paw, his heart pounding so hard he kept stumbling, waiting for the crack of a gun or the hiss of a net being thrown, for someone to drag them down like big game hunters.

A searchlight beam swept over him, and he crashed to a halt, freezing as well as he could. Beaufort was already at the wall to the forest, and Mortimer willed him to keep going, to get away. There was no point both of them being caught.

"Mac, you got anything?" someone called.

"Nah," someone else shouted back. "Probably a fox or something. You?"

"I thought I saw something in the field, but it's just sheep."

"Bloody wildlife."

"Pretty sure sheep are livestock, not wildlife."

"Whatever." The light roamed across the field, and Mortimer waited for it to light him up like an actor on a stage, for his shadow to be cast long and unmistakable on the grass in front of him, painting Folk secrets across the dawn. But the only shadows he saw were those of the sheep, and after a moment the spotlight flicked off. A couple of minutes later, while he still hunched there with his muscles twitching, trying not to even breathe, the lights in the garden went off as well, and he slowly relaxed.

Beaufort's head appeared over the forest wall. "Mortimer?"

"Here." Mortimer very slowly unwound himself, turning to look back at the retreat. There was no one in sight but the sheep, packed around him and returning his stare blandly. One bleated. "Thanks," he said.

"See?" Beaufort called. "Told you they liked you."

12
DI ADAMS

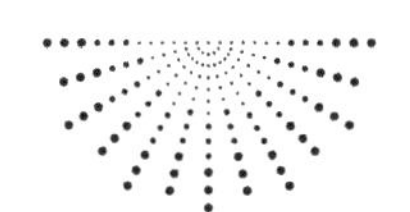

DI Adams had thought that, having been up and on the road well before the long northern night was even thinking about moving on and giving the dark a break, she'd be knocking on Dominic Blackwood's door while he was still in his pyjamas. Instead, by the time she'd bumped down the potholed drive and let herself through the gate into the farmyard, he was already standing in the doorway to the kitchen, light spilling around him to gleam on the slick mud outside.

"Expecting me?" she asked as she swung out of the car. Two lean, scrappy dogs peered around him, ears back and teeth bared as they watched Dandy ambling out into the fields.

"Got cameras, don't I?"

"Why?"

"Livestock theft's a thing," he said, watching her as she walked to the door, the rain sharp on her cheeks. "Plus there's all those posh gits up at Lachlan's place. Don't trust them."

"You think they're going to steal your livestock?"

"No, just trespass and then sue me when they stick their foot in a rabbit hole or get chased by a bull or something."

DI Adams braced herself against a shudder. "You have bulls?"

"Just Highland coos. Thought they'd make a tourist attraction, like."

"Wonderful," she said. "DI Adams, North Yorkshire Police."

"Don't sound Yorkshire."

"No, I suppose not." They looked at each other for a moment, then he stepped back from the door and waved her in.

The kitchen was warm, an ancient potbellied stove in the corner radiating heat. A couple of dog beds were pulled up to it, and a goat with a dressing on one leg glared at her from the corner, giving a threatening bleat.

"Don't mind him. Although, don't turn your back on him, neither." Dom filled the kettle from a plastic bottle next to the sink, a woollen hat pulled down to his ears. "Tea?"

"Coffee if you've got it." DI Adams took a seat at the long, cluttered kitchen table, where she could keep a wary eye on the goat and still see Dom. He wasn't acting like a man with anything to hide, but he hadn't been here when she'd come by yesterday, despite spotting him on the quad bike from the retreat.

She hadn't been able to justify pulling the search out of the village based on Miriam *possibly* seeing someone, but she'd grabbed a couple of officers to help her, and they'd spent a very soggy few hours checking the fields and gardens around Lachlan's property. DI Adams had even ventured into the edge of the forest, warily clambering over the wall to spot dragon tracks in the mud. There were no human tracks, though, and given how muddy it was, there would've been some if anyone had been there. There was no need to go further into the looming, oddly hostile trees, and she'd stuck to the farm side of the wall after that, every now and then popping up on her tiptoes so she could see over it to the soft ground on the other side, and wishing she'd inherited her dad's height rather than her mum's.

They'd found nothing, though, and eventually she'd had to give up. It seemed unlikely Esther had made her way out here, so they needed to concentrate on the village, for all the good it had done so far. Now, as she watched Dom spooning coffee into a cafetière, she said, "Where were you yesterday?"

"Out. I'm not tethered to the farm." He set two mugs on the table, along with a half-full bottle of milk and a bag of sugar, then went back to pour boiling water over the coffee.

"Specifically after you saw us in the field."

"That you, was it? You know you were trespassing?"

"I was looking for a missing person."

He brought the cafetière over to the table and sat down. "Esther?"

"Yes. You know her?"

"I was born here. I know most people in the village."

"Have you seen her recently?"

"No. I was helping look for her yesterday, though. In answer to your question." He slopped some milk into one of the mugs and offered the bottle to her.

She waved it away. "So why didn't you confront us if we were trespassing?"

He shrugged, adding some sugar to his milk. "Bloody Lachlan acts like he bought the whole valley. He's always in my damn fields. I put the bull in the one nearest his retreat at first, but then someone kept *accidentally* leaving the gate open. Wasn't worth the hassle."

"The bull, or confronting us?"

"Any of it." He poked the cafetière, as if that'd make it brew faster.

"Right." DI Adams folded her arms over her chest, wondering where Dandy was. He evidently hadn't smelled the coffee, otherwise he'd be here. "Someone thought they saw Esther on your property."

"Lachlan?"

"No. A witness."

He smiled slightly. "Yeah, didn't think he'd be willingly getting the police in."

"Why's that, then?"

"Bad publicity, isn't it?" He gave up on waiting, and pushed the plunger down on the coffee.

"Can I have a look around your property?"

"Esther's not here." The words were clipped, and in the silence that followed, the goat bleated, sticking its tongue out at DI Adams. She had a sudden urge to stick her own out, but instead just accepted a mug of coffee from Dom.

"I see you're using bottled water."

"Yeah, my supply's as much as mess as anywhere, except golden boy's up there." He jerked his head in the general direction of the retreat.

"Unfortunate."

"You're telling me. The rain's the only reason I'm able to keep the troughs full for my livestock, and I'm rigging bloody tarps for catchment. Have to go to Skipton to buy drinking water."

"He's not supplying you with any?"

"I wouldn't take it if he offered." Dom's voice was level, but his fingers were tight enough around his mug that even his fingertips were white. "He'd probably want the rest of my farm in payment."

"Things go a bit wrong in the sale or something?"

Dom laughed, a despairing sort of sound. "You could say that. He beat me down on the price, but we had a handshake agreement that I'd supply him with bottled water, and he'd help me market it as part of his *Sourced* venture. He made it sound like it was going to be this massive revenue stream, and he also said he'd send people over for animal immersion."

"Animal what, sorry?"

"Part of his wellness stuff – reconnecting to nature by hugging sheep, that sort of thing." He glanced at the goat. "I thought goats might be better, but I suppose it depends on the goat."

"So what happened?"

"For the water, he said he wanted to keep everything under the same brand. I offered to rebrand under his label, but he said my standards were too low, and it was cheaper for him to do it himself. So there went that, and then the next thing my place didn't offer the right atmosphere for animal therapy or whatever. I offered to bring the bloody sheep over to his, but he reckoned they were the wrong sort." He frowned. "They're good Yorkshire sheep."

DI Adams made a sympathetic noise around a sip of coffee. "Must've been a blow."

"It was. And I'd been letting him use the fields for … I forget what he called it. Some other reconnecting to nature thing, anyway. Walking barefoot on the grass and stuff. After that I told him to get the hell back on his own side of the boundary, and I've been keeping an eye on things since."

"Any issues?"

"Oh, he's still in my fields from time to time. I head over there on the quad bike if I see it and give him what-for."

DI Adams folded her hands around the mug, watching him. He was only about her age, but looked older, lines worn around his mouth and bags under his eyes. He didn't seem like he'd be snatching pensioners off the streets, but he did look at the end of his tether. Desperate, even.

"Any ideas on the water issues?" she asked him, and he shook his head.

"He's probably trashed the spring with all his earthworks, building pools and suchlike. Or he's done it on purpose, so everyone gets reliant on his water and has to buy it."

"Well, he is giving it away," DI Adams pointed out.

"*For now,*" Dom replied. "Nothing for free with that one. You can trust me on that."

DI Adams nodded, taking another sip of coffee. It was weak and under-brewed. "Have you got cameras on the retreat?"

"On that field."

"Can I take a look?"

"Sure." He pulled a laptop that was open on the table toward him, the case glossy and free of fingerprints. "Nothing to see but you lot, though."

DI Adams sighed. She'd thought as much, but it was worth checking.

THE CAMERA DIDN'T SHOW much. It was a cheap thing, and zooming in with the dull light just pixellated everything horribly. All DI Adams could see were rain-drenched fields, then Miriam rushing through the retreat's gate, followed by Alice and finally Lachlan and his staff. DI Adams thought there might've been a flicker, barely enough to register, on the grass before they arrived, but it could as well have been static. She asked for a copy of the recording anyway. It was worth having Jules at the station look it over properly.

"Any chance of a look around?" she asked as she gave up on her coffee.

"No," he said. "You've no reason."

"What if Esther's wandered onto your property?"

"The dogs would've sniffed her out."

The dogs in question hadn't moved from his side, their hackles up as they glared at DI Adams. Dandy still hadn't appeared, but she supposed they could smell him on her. "You can't be sure of that."

"I'll look myself," he said. "I'm not having people poking around just because Lachlan's pointing at me. That's what he's done, isn't it?"

"Just doing anything to find Esther, is all."

He snorted, getting up and walking to the kitchen door to open it onto the rain-drenched yard. "Sure."

DI Adams walked past him into the rain, looking at the barn and thinking of Alice's comment about the equipment. "You thought of digging your own water supply, then?"

Dom leaned against the door, crossing his arms. "Bloody W.I. Saw my gear, did they?"

"Just asking."

He grinned. "You should play poker."

DI Adams just raised her eyebrows at him.

"No law against digging my own well, but the kit they saw is for fence posts. Not saying I won't dig one if this keeps up, though." His smile faded. "Good luck finding Esther."

"Thanks," she said, but he'd already turned back inside, slamming the door behind him. She turned on her heel, surveying the yard, but there was nothing to be seen. No wandering ladies, no sulking sprites, nothing. She was wasting her time.

Although, she thought as she climbed into the car, there was the desperation. Desperation was always something. And he was refusing to let her search the place. Perhaps he'd trashed his own water supply and planted Esther near the retreat, all so he could point the finger at Lachlan in revenge for ripping him off. It seemed tenuous, but motives so often did. And it wasn't like she had much else to go on at the moment.

When she got back into the car after closing the gate, Dandy was sitting in the passenger seat. "Hi," she said. "Anything?"

He squeaked his duck at her.

"Great. Thanks." Having an invisible dog should really involve more magical help and less mud, to her mind.

The retreat was only a little further down the road, and a metal gate blocked entry to the yard. The voice that answered the intercom was clipped and generic, a vaguely posh accent she could only place as being public school.

"Yes?"

"DI Adams, North Yorkshire Police."

"Of course."

The gate clicked, and slid back with barely a rattle. DI Adams drove in as the door in the front of the building opened, revealing a young man she recognised from the day before. Niall Moore was slight, but his shoulders were well-shaped under a tight, collared sweatshirt that managed to look like a uniform without actually being one. She parked in front of the door and got out, trotting up the steps in the rain and watching Dandy slipping past Niall into the building. The young man shivered, a barely perceptible movement, and pulled himself up a little straighter.

"Lachlan around?" DI Adams asked.

"He's meditating. He'll be finished soon, though." Niall stepped back from the door. "Come in."

She followed him through a bland room that seemed to function as a lobby of some sort, a little narrow and, despite the big windows and bare walls, faintly claustrophobic. She wasn't sure if that was due to the fat chairs and sofa that took up more room than they needed to, or the fact that everything was so beige and featureless she felt like she'd fallen into a box of tofu. The unseasoned stuff, too.

At least the transition room, for all that it was a ridiculous name for what was essentially a common room, had a bit of colour to it. And the coffee, which Niall produced from a cafe-standard espresso machine in a coffee cart, was excellent.

"Nice," she said, sniffing the mug appreciatively.

"It's a new blend. Organic, obviously, and from Chile. We're creating a *Sourced* blend—"

"You're Lachlan's PA?"

He barely blinked at the interruption. "In a way. He doesn't like the title *assistant.* I'm his logistics manager."

"Fair enough. What sort of logistics do you manage?"

"His schedule. Travel. Organisation."

"Organising what?" She looked around for Dandy, spotting him peering into the pool, his ears perked. He tipped his head, looked at her, then came through the big glass panels of the interior wall, heading for the coffee cart. She wasn't sure how he came *through* the glass, but he did, just moving from one side to the other as if she'd blinked and missed it, even though she hadn't.

Niall shrugged, hands in his pockets. "Everything?"

"The retreat as well?"

"For now. We'll get a manager in once it's up and running properly, but at the moment I'm overseeing setting things up, finding practitioners and so on." He rocked on his heels. "I thought we'd be able to source most people from the village and surrounding area, but they're a bit ..." he hesitated, and DI Adams took a sip of coffee before taking pity on him.

"Odd?"

"Yes." He gave her a grateful look. "One man turned up and offered to do what he called spontaneous therapeutic onsite poetry. Then his sister came in and hit him with a yoga mat."

"Ah," DI Adams said, watching Dandy emerging from the coffee cart, licking his chops. "I think I've met them."

"Really?"

"Yes. No idea about her yoga, but his poetry's terrible."

"It *is*," Niall said with feeling. "And I couldn't give her the job. Not if she's hitting people with mats. There's odd, and then there's ... well, our target market requires a certain *kind* of odd."

"I imagine. And the water bottling? Are you involved in that too?"

He seesawed his hand. "We had someone in to set it up, and now we've got a couple of locals running things. Ex-offenders, actually. We like to give people second chances."

"That's nice. No special expertise needed, then?"

"It's pretty automated. You need to be hands-on at certain points in the process, but we arranged all training."

She nodded. "Must be busy, keeping up with supplying the village."

"It really is. We're running pretty much constantly. Well, in work hours, I mean." The way he added it made DI Adams think work hours weren't his strong suit.

"Is it running now?"

Niall glanced at his watch. "Not yet. Jen and Art'll arrive in about an hour. They come in from Kendal."

Not *that* local, then. She shot a sideways look at Dandy. He'd found a *Sourced* bottle somewhere and walked to the door with it in his mouth, pointing the bottle alternately at her and the back of the building. "Can I take a look at the bottling plant?" she asked.

He hesitated, and she wished again that Collins was with her. He had a knack for talking to people, and then they'd just *do* things when he asked. She was sure he'd have somehow phrased the request differently, or thrown in something *relatable*, and Niall would be just about begging them to come and see the bottling plant.

"I mean, it's just water and bottles," he said. "It's not very exciting. And didn't you see it yesterday?"

"Not properly. It was running," she said, and he nodded, looking around as if hoping Lachlan would appear.

But no one did, so he said, "I think that'd be okay."

"Perfect," DI Adams said, and got up.

Niall led the way to the big outbuilding with the *Sourced* sign, using a keycard to open a side door. It let them into a small, startlingly sleek locker area, where he made DI Adams put blue plastic booties over her own boots and don a hairnet before, similarly garbed, he led the way into the main body of the building. She'd peered in here yesterday while everything grumbled and whined, and the stillness was odd as she stepped over the threshold. The cavernous room was glaringly white and clean under a blaze of overhead lights, the floor smooth, bare concrete, and every piece of metal gleamed. The bottles reflected the light so flawlessly she almost wished she had sunglasses, and she had a moment of disorientation after the drowning fields and muddy waters outside.

"So the filtration process starts here," Niall was saying, indicating one of the machines without touching it. "And we use both mechanical and light-based filtration systems—"

She was less interested in the machines and more interested in Dandy, who was circling the room, his nose low as he inspected the walls. He still had the bottle in his mouth, and finally he walked to the centre of the floor and dropped it with a huff.

"Careful!" Niall said, spinning around as the bottle clattered across the concrete.

She spread her hands. "Not me."

He spotted Dandy's bottle, and went to pick it up with a frown. "That's weird— Oh, *ew*. It's slimy!"

"Must've got away from somewhere," she said, trying not to glare at Dandy, who wagged his tail and sniffed the young man's ear curiously.

Niall jerked away from Dandy, and wiped his free hand on his trousers. "Is there a draught in here?"

"Maybe," she said, and gave the room a last glance. "This is a really big set-up. I hadn't thought you'd need quite so much stuff just for water." The machinery loomed up to the distant ceiling and filled the majority of the floor space, dwarfing the rows of bottles in their crates.

"It's more complex than one might think," he agreed. "We over-specced a bit to allow capacity to expand production, though." He checked his watch. "Come on. Lachlan'll be ready by now."

DI Adams gave Dandy a questioning look, and he trotted out past Niall, making him shiver again, then stopped at one of the sleek locker doors and pressed his snout to it, whining.

"Did you say something?" Niall asked.

"What's in these lockers?"

"Employees' gear."

"Can I take a look in this one?" she asked, indicating the one Dandy was snuffling.

"Sure." He tried the recessed handle and it swung open soundlessly, revealing a coat dangling inside. "People can put their own locks on, but there's not many of us here, so no one really bothers."

DI Adams watched Dandy delicately remove a flapjack from the coat pocket and head back out into the rain, and sighed inwardly. So much for the help of invisible dogs. Although she wasn't sure why he'd needed anyone to open the door for him. Maybe so he didn't have to eat with his head on one side of the door and the rest of him on the other. Perhaps it made swallowing difficult. She took her booties off and dropped them in the bin. "Let's go, then," she said, and followed Niall back across the wet gravel to the main building, where Lachlan was leaning in the doorway, waiting for them.

"Find your missing person trussed up to my bottling machine, DI Adams?" he asked, half-smiling.

"No," she said. "Was I supposed to?"

He laughed. "Only if your little ladies from the village have put her there."

DI Adams winced inwardly at the thought of any one of the W.I. hearing someone refer to them as *little ladies.* "That seems unlikely."

"Maybe, but someone was sneaking around my property last night."

"Really?"

"Yes, they set the alarms off. The cameras didn't catch them for some reason." He frowned. "I thought Alice and Miriam were being *friendly* yesterday, but I think they've got it in for me."

"I doubt they were running around here in the middle of the night." She didn't doubt it that much, to be honest, but she had to try.

He started to answer, then stopped as a car crunched over the gravel, stopping in front of the outbuildings. DI Adams turned to look at it, and behind her Lachlan said, "Are you sure, Inspector?"

She just sighed, as Alice got out of the car, lifting her hood over her hair and swinging her cane in one hand.

"Here we all are again," the chair of the W.I. said. "How fun."

"Quite," Lachlan said.

13
MIRIAM

Miriam's calm of the previous morning was nothing but a memory, what with the unsuccessful search for poor Esther, and her own sinking pond, and now the dragons, who had come splashing through the garden with the first light to report that their search had turned up not Nellie, but ghosts in the water, apparitions in fields, homeless hedgehogs, and a schism in their ranks. Never mind the fact that the dryad wanted to declare war on the village, and the tiddy 'uns had deserted it. She'd abandoned her toast and eaten the last of her emergency cheesy puffs for breakfast while Mortimer inhaled her entire stock of mince pies, and now they were both somewhat bereft.

She looked at the bag by her feet as Alice bumped out of the village, heading once more to *Sourced,* which Miriam was feeling singularly unenthusiastic about. Alice *said* they were going to apologise, but if that were the case they could have just phoned. So *of course* they were going to snoop around, just as they had done yesterday, and Miriam was quite sure she gave away that knowledge with every line of her face. Although hopefully the cake in the bag might make the ruse a tiny bit believable. She intended to hand Lachlan the treat like she were bribing a Labrador, sit down quietly, let Alice do the talking, and try not to make eye contact with anyone.

It wasn't helping her nerves to know Lachlan had not only security cameras and the well-muscled men they'd met yesterday, but also alarms and searchlights, as if the retreat were some sort of secure compound. Mortimer said the guards had been huge, and armed with nets and tranquilliser guns, which Miriam wasn't sure about (he seemed to have overcome his horror of Tasers, but after Gilbert had explained wildlife capture to him in great detail he'd discovered something entirely new to worry about, which wasn't helping his stress-shedding). Beaufort said the guards were of average size and armed with nothing more than torches, which did seem more likely, unless they'd been expecting dragons.

She gasped, covering her mouth with one hand.

"Oh, Miriam. I'm not going *that* fast," Alice said, but she did ease off the accelerator, Miriam noticed.

"It's not that." She twisted in her seat, looking at the dragons in the back. They were covered rather ineffectually by a fireproof blanket, which merely served to make it look as though Alice were transporting sacks of something deeply suspicious. It probably would've been a better idea for them to stay in the woods, or at least at Miriam's, but Beaufort wouldn't countenance them returning to Lachlan's without scaly backup, and not even Alice had protested that strongly. "What if the guards had nets for *Nellie?*" Miriam asked now.

Alice gave her a thoughtful look. "Do you know, I wondered about that. If he's after the sprite, not just the waters."

"Why would he be?" Beaufort asked.

"He practices biohacking," Alice said.

"What's that?" Mortimer asked. "I don't like the sound of it. It sounds messy." He was deeply grey, scratching at his tail.

"It's about trying to ..." Alice paused, evidently trying to recall the exact phrasing. "Optimise the bodily systems for a longer life, I believe. It seems to involve lots of vitamins and very strict diets, and it's why Lachlan says he wanted the waters. But maybe he's looking for more than the water."

"You think he knows about Nellie?" Beaufort asked.

"It's possible. Maybe he thinks he can get some sort of anti-ageing properties from her."

Beaufort made a thoughtful noise. "Sprites are very long-lived. As long as their waters persist, so do they."

"Oh, how *awful,*" Miriam said. She didn't want to think about what terrible things might be done to the sprite to extract the *properties* Alice was talking about, but she doubted it could ever involve a nice chat and a cuppa.

"It would explain the dying waters," Mortimer said, his voice low. "If he's already done something terrible to Nellie. Made her sick or weakened her."

"But why would your men last night have had nets if they've already caught her?" Alice asked.

"Perhaps they don't actually have her," Miriam said hopefully. "Maybe she's hiding." She hesitated, then added reluctantly, "Or they do have her, but don't realise she's the only sprite, and are hunting for others."

"Perhaps," Beaufort said. "I really didn't see any nets, though, and you had your eyes closed, Mortimer."

"I did not. Well, not all the time," he amended.

"Never mind the nets, then," Miriam said. "But what if that *is* what's happened? If he's trapped Nellie somewhere as part of his silly biohacking thing, and now he wants more sprites so he can hack harder or something?"

"It explains the water, Nellie, and the birds," Alice said. "It's a very plausible explanation, Miriam."

Miriam gave Alice a sideways look. The older woman had been very quick to accept the idea, and she suspected Alice might have already come to a similar conclusion. But she was willing to take the praise for putting her Alice head on for a little bit. It was most unfamiliar.

"It would explain why we haven't found any sign of Nellie, too," Beaufort said. "But what about this gentleman in the dressing gown? And Esther?"

Miriam considered it. "Maybe whatever trap Lachlan set for Nellie is catching other people as well. But somehow it's not very stable, and that's why we're getting glimpses of them. Like they're hidden right in front of us, and the camouflage drops now and then or something."

No one spoke for a moment, then Alice said, "Could that be possible, Beaufort? A trap like that?"

"I don't know," he admitted. "It's not something I've heard of, but traps aren't really my territory. Thompson would know more."

"I haven't seen him for a while," Alice said.

"Oh, *no,*" Miriam said, clutching her skirt. "You don't suppose Lachlan got him too?" Honestly, this was becoming *impossible.* Sprites and cats and missing people and furious dryads, and all the while the village was sinking.

"Good luck to him if he did," Alice said, but Miriam didn't miss the frown tugging at the corners of her mouth as she indicated to pull into the retreat. "Now hush, you dragons. If he is running about trapping sprites, we can't have him getting a glimpse of you."

"It'd be scale frenzies all over again," Mortimer said mournfully.

"You're nowhere near old enough to remember those, lad," Beaufort said, pulling the blanket over them a bit more securely.

"I'd like to keep it that way."

The gate was open, and Alice drove straight around to the back of the retreat, Miriam craning to look at the car sitting alone at the front. It was behind them before she recognised it properly, and as they rounded the building she said, "Stop!"

"Ah," Alice said at the same time, bringing the car to a halt next to the turfed area by the fountain.

Miriam didn't really want to look at the three figures by the door, but as Alice switched the engine off she forced herself to anyway, and gave DI Adams a wan wave. Niall lifted his hand in return, looking puzzled, and Miriam sighed. She'd known this was a bad idea, even before she heard about *biohacking.* Alice climbed out, and Miriam fished one of the cakes out of the bag and followed with her pink jacket rustling in the rain.

"Here we all are again," Alice said. "How fun."

"Quite," Lachlan said.

"I brought cake," Miriam offered, holding a Tupperware container out. Some frantic googling last night had resulted in an oat and almond pineapple cake sweetened with dates, which she was somewhat confused by, as that was still sugar, in her mind. But she'd cut the quantities down as much as she dared, so hopefully it'd be alright. The cake looked stodgy, and the mix had tasted a bit bland despite some enthusiastic lacing with ginger and nutmeg, but maybe that was normal for such things.

"Niall, take the cake," DI Adams said. "Then the ladies can head back to the village."

"No rush," Lachlan said, already starting down the steps into the rain. "Let's go in and have a piece of cake and a cuppa, shall we? Then you can all accuse me of kidnapping and environmental terrorism, and we can get it over with."

"Oh …" Miriam said, and hurried across the grass to meet him, just in case he got too close to the car and *could* see dragons. He took the container, giving her a frozen smile.

"A cuppa won't be necessary," Alice said, to Miriam's astonishment. "We'd hate to interfere in anyone's work."

DI Adams snorted so loudly that Niall gave her an alarmed look, and she took a tissue packet from her pocket. "Sorry. Still got a cold."

"I have some excellent ginger shots that'll help that," Lachlan said, prying the corner of the container open. "Do I smell banana?"

"Pineapple."

"I've got Sudafed," DI Adams said, waving a sheet of pills at him.

"Poison," Lachlan declared.

"What, pineapple?" Miriam asked, and grabbed for the container. "Give it back, then! It took me ages!"

"No, no, not pineapple," he said, clutching the tub protectively. "Sudafed. Pharmaceuticals in general."

"Oh. Well, yes. Lemon and whisky," she added to DI Adams.

"That seems impractical at eight a.m. Also likely to get me fired."

"Ginger shots, green juice, and cake," Lachlan announced, having managed to keep hold of the Tupperware. "Do come in, ladies."

"No," DI Adams said.

"No," Alice agreed. "Lachlan, we wanted to extend our apologies for yesterday. We certainly had no intention of harassing you. We're merely worried about Esther."

"Understood," he said, slightly indistinctly. He'd broken off a corner of the cake and was eating it with small noises of enjoyment that Miriam found slightly uncomfortable. She took a step away from him. "This is *wonderful,*" he said to her. "You need to give the recipe to my chef."

"Um. Yes? As an apology?"

"Very much accepted." He turned and headed into the retreat. "Everyone come along who's coming." He vanished inside, and Niall lingered, looking from DI Adams to the ladies. The inspector jabbed a finger rather urgently at the car, then in the direction of the village, looking as if she'd quite like to shout but didn't want to be unprofessional.

"Shall we go?" Alice asked, turning back to the car. Miriam followed, thinking the cake had been a good idea. Everyone always underestimated the importance of cake. It might not be a cure-all, but it was certainly a cure-many-things.

Miriam waited until they were out on the road before she said, "Really? You were happy to just leave?"

"We can't do much with the inspector there."

Miriam found that rather a relief. "So what do we do now?"

"We continue as planned. We'll try Dom again, and see if we can find out what he was doing with that equipment."

"Could he be working with Lachlan?" Beaufort asked.

"Possibly," Alice said. "Or against him. Perhaps you and Mortimer can take a look around and see if there's any indication he's been contaminating the water, or any sign of this trap."

"Eliminating the impossible to find the improbable," Beaufort said, enormous satisfaction in his voice.

Miriam wished she could take as much enjoyment from the idea of facing the goats and dogs again, but at least they were armed this time. She took the second Tupperware from her bag and checked inside it, then frowned. "Oh. Oh *no.*"

"What?"

"I gave Lachlan the wrong cake! This is the free-of-everything one!"

Alice made a non-committal sound. "He did say it was a choice, that he's not actually intolerant or diabetic."

"Yes, but ... but the other one's all regular flour and loads of sugar. Two types of sugar! And chocolate chips! I put *chocolate chips* in it!"

"I'm sure he'll be fine."

"What if he *is* diabetic, though? Or gluten-intolerant?"

"He said he wasn't. And one can't say that then expect people to still make fancy cake," Alice said, pulling into the driveway to Dom's farm.

Miriam looked at the Tupperware doubtfully. "Dom's going to be very disappointed by this one, though."

"That's quite another issue."

Dom was standing in the door of the barn when they stopped in the farmyard, wearing waterproof trousers and a big jacket that made him look even larger than he was already. The dogs came to meet the car, circling it warily, lean sharp-nosed creatures that seemed to Miriam to simply be the essence of dog-ness, with no fuss about them. One barked harshly when Alice opened the door, and Dom whistled. Both retreated to stand next to him, and he watched the two women skirt the worst potholes to meet him.

"Well?" he said, once they were in the barn out of the rain. A dozen chickens clucked around curiously, and Alice led the way a little further inside, so that Dom had to turn his back to the door to face them.

"I brought cake," Miriam said, offering him the tub.

"Oh? Bribe, is it?"

"Not a very good one," she said with a sigh. "I'm experimenting with healthier options, and I don't think I've quite got the hang of it."

He frowned, looking as if he wanted to refuse it, then took the Tupperware and peered inside. "Looks alright. Want a cuppa?" He started to turn toward the door.

"No," Alice said sharply, and Miriam could see the door on the far side of the car was open, the dragons sliding out to investigate. "We just wanted to ask—"

"About my fence-digging kit?"

"If you've seen anyone unusual around. An elderly man in a dressing gown, perhaps."

Dom looked from one of them to the other, and Miriam could feel her cheeks getting hotter and hotter. He had a hard set to his jaw, and his fingers were tight on the Tupperware. "You really think I'm some sort of kidnapper? Or that I'd do *this* to the waters?" He waved urgently at the rain-drenched and thankfully dragon-free fields.

"We're merely trying to get to the bottom of things," Alice said. "There seem to have been a lot of odd happenings since Lachlan arrived, and you are right next door. I tried to catch up with you in the village yesterday, but you seemed rather keen to avoid me."

He sighed. "You ask a lot of questions."

"We're concerned."

Dom was silent for a moment, then he said, "I had to sign an NDA. I probably can't answer half of what you ask, and I'm bloody sick of everyone thinking I sold out. I didn't get a fortune, and he shafted me on half of it, but if I say anything much I can get myself sued."

"Can you tell us if you've seen anything unusual up there?" Alice asked.

"Unusual how?"

"Maybe equipment that doesn't have to do with the plant. Or extra earthworks, things like that."

"Plenty of those. That bloody great pool he put in the middle of the house took some doing, and the size of the plant! That many pipes and bottles and filters, it's madness. Nothing like mine."

"Do you think he could be doing something other than bottling water?"

He shrugged. "Who knows. Maybe he's cooking meth or something."

"I don't think you need lots of equipment for that," Miriam said, and they both gave her startled looks. Her cheeks flared with heat. "I mean, if you did, people wouldn't be able to just make it in their basements, would they?"

"Well, when you put it like that," Dom said, raising his eyebrows.

"So there's nothing you've noticed?" Alice asked.

"No. He's just some businessman I made the mistake of thinking was a decent bloke." Dom peered out at the murky day. "I need to get on, so unless you want a cuppa …"

"No, thank you," Alice said. "We best get back to the search."

Miriam stared at her, thinking that maybe the stress was getting to Alice, given the way she kept walking away from possible snooping opportunities.

"I hope you have some luck," Dom said. "It's no good her being out in this." He waved the Tupperware at Miriam. "Give me a moment and I'll put this on a plate."

"I'll get the car started," Alice said. "You go on with Dom, Miriam."

"Um. Yes?" She followed Dom out into the rain and across the muddy yard to the house. The kitchen was warm and smoky smelling, with the faint whiff of coffee and toast lingering in the air, and she hesitated on the threshold, not wanting to take her boots off. Dom tipped the cake onto a plate and handed the tub back to Miriam.

"Thanks," he said. "Very nice of you."

"I hope it's alright," she said. "I'm not sure free-from cooking is really my forte."

He patted his belly, his jacket tight over it. "It'll be good for me."

Miriam retreated back across the yard to the car. There was no sign of the dragons, and Alice waved at Dom, then drove sedately to the gate. Miriam scrambled out to open it and shut it again behind them, then they continued at the same gentle pace until they were at the road, out of sight of the farmhouse, where Alice stopped again. The dragons still hadn't appeared, and Miriam looked at Alice.

"What?"

Alice reached into the pocket of her coat and took out her phone, turning it so Miriam could see the screen. It was open to a photo of a crumpled hanky lying among the dust and debris of the barn floor. The hanky was pale lavender, and monogrammed with an *E.* Miriam covered her mouth with both hands, and Alice turned the screen so she could look at it again.

"We don't *know* it's Esther's," Miriam said, a little weakly.

"No," Alice agreed. "But it seems like an odd coincidence."

"But *why?* Why would he kidnap Esther?"

Alice shook her head. "The business deals falling through might've been enough for him. He really thought he was coming into a lot of money, and now it seems he's worse off than he was before he sold. He must be furious at Lachlan."

"But enough to hurt Esther?"

"He may not have hurt her at all. It may simply be a way to frame Lachlan."

Miriam thought about it. "And the water? Nellie?"

"Perhaps he sabotaged the water to undermine Lachlan, and Nellie's simply become caught up in it somehow. It does seem more likely than Lachlan hunting Folk. We may be jumping at shadows after Eldmere."

Miriam made a doubtful sound. Eldmere, where Beaufort had been captured by a very hostile W.I. chair, and Dandy, Thompson, Alice, and DI Adams had almost ended up at the bottom of a tarn. It was enough to make anyone jump at shadows. Plus the whole place had been *teeming* with monster hunters. It had been very stressful.

"So what do we do?"

"Tell DI Adams."

"She's going to be furious with us for interfering."

"Not if we've found the kidnapper." Alice turned back toward the retreat, and Miriam stared out at the rain, her stomach tight with misgiving. This didn't feel right, not at all. None of it seemed to *fit.* But Esther was still out there somewhere. They couldn't risk the possibility that it *was* right.

14
ALICE

DI Adams might have been furious, but it didn't show much when she walked out of the retreat to meet them, summoned by Niall. She leaned on Alice's windows, looking from the photo on Alice's phone to the two of them.

"What were you doing there?"

"Taking him cake," Miriam said, and DI Adams looked like she might want to roll her eyes. She didn't, though, and Alice had to admire her restraint.

"*Why* were you taking him cake?"

"Merely expanding our search a little, Inspector," Alice said. "Sometimes people will talk more freely to civilians."

"In exchange for cake."

"It wasn't a bribe!" Miriam yelped.

DI Adams squinted at her. "Maybe it should be. I just about asked Lachlan if he wanted a moment alone with that one you gave him."

"Oh, no," Miriam said, mostly to her hands.

"Anything else?" the inspector asked.

Alice nodded. "We suspect Nellie's behind the flooding, but it's possible it's inadvertent. That perhaps she's been trapped somewhere."

DI Adams frowned. "Deliberately?"

"Possibly. Or maybe she went to fix the water and got stuck somehow."

"Interesting." She looked from one of them to the other. "Can you please just stick to the search party now?"

"We can," Alice said. "But with Nellie involved, it seems this isn't entirely a police case."

DI Adams looked at the ground, shaking her head. "Yes, fine. You have a point. But I'm on it, and you poking around is only unsettling Lachlan and Dom, who are currently the only people who may know what's going on. So, please – enough."

"If you say so," Alice said. "The dragons were checking the farm, though, so they may have something for you."

"Fantastic," the inspector said, and straightened up. "Off you go."

Alice nodded at her, then started the engine and pulled back onto the road. She doubted very much that Dom was guilty of kidnapping, or even of sabotaging the water supply, although that was marginally more likely than him having elderly ladies trussed up in his attic. But having the police focused on Dom meant she was a little freer to investigate Lachlan, and Alice had no intention of stepping back. Nellie being missing meant this was a Folk matter, and that made it a W.I. matter.

"Are we just leaving the dragons?" Miriam asked, peering out the side window as if expecting to see them bounding after the car.

"They were going to see about diverting the waters, so they're better to be out here near the forest than trying to make their way from the village in the day. We'll go back and update everyone."

"Oh, I do hope they can do something about the flooding," Miriam said. "The damage is going to be terrible if it doesn't stop soon."

"It will," Alice agreed. "I think we'll have rather a lot to do once we get back, to be honest."

She accelerated back toward the village, and as they drew closer Miriam's phone dinged. She dug it out of her bag, peering at it a little short-sightedly, and tapped it a couple of times, then gasped.

"Oh no!"

"What is it?"

"Two more people are missing."

"Who?" Alice demanded, her heart giving a little seesaw in her chest. Two more? *How?*

"Ambrose Morton – you know, the one who always wears a smoking jacket and carries around a little pipe?"

"I do know," Alice said. "It's never tobacco he has in that pipe."

"No," Miriam agreed. "I think that probably has something to do with the choice of a smoking jacket, to be honest."

Alice smiled, but it faded quickly. Ambrose was, as far as she knew, rather sharp still – when he wasn't smoking his pipe, anyway – but he wasn't young. Him being missing in the flood-waters was a bad development. "Who else?"

"Vera."

"*Vera?* From the tea-shop?"

"Yes. How can *she* be missing?"

"It rather breaks the pattern, doesn't it?" Vera, despite her rather old-fashioned name, was only around the same age as Alice herself. Which wasn't *old*, certainly not in Alice's view.

Miriam nodded, still scrolling through her phone. "Unless she was with Ambrose? Or saw what happened to him, and whoever took Ambrose grabbed her too?"

"That's entirely possible." Alice accelerated as much as she dared, given the rising waters. It was still nowhere near as bad out here as in the village, but things were definitely getting worse. "Is there anything else?"

Miriam didn't answer straight away, and Alice risked a glance at her.

"Miriam?"

"The well's fallen in," she said, her voice soft. "There's a great big hole in the heart of the village."

Alice didn't answer, but after a moment she took a hand off the wheel to put it on Miriam's, just briefly. That news had put a hole in the heart of her as well.

It didn't take them long to get back to Toot Hansell, and Alice skirted the centre without thinking about it, shying away from the yawning, unseen gap and heading straight for the hall. The streets were even more flooded than when they'd left, everything awash in standing water, and every door was either sandbagged already, or it was in progress, chains of people passing the bags hand to hand across longer gardens, young people with wet hair and sloshing wellies hefting sacks effortlessly from the backs of cars and trucks to the steps of terraced houses and those closer to the road. Alice was grateful there were no basement flats in Toot Hansell. Plenty of basements, but none that anyone lived in, as far as she knew. Although she supposed there were plenty used for offices and suchlike. But that still seemed better than one's whole home being below the level of those menacing waters.

She parked at the end of the row of cars outside the hall, all of which seemed to belong to the W.I. The street was a river flowing downhill as it circled the green and swirled past the hall, but the hall's garden offered a little protection from the fast-moving flood, and while the grass in the front garden was partly underwater, the door was still clear. Sandbags were set in place anyway, waiting for things to deteriorate.

Alice pushed the door open, stepping onto the mat and shaking her jacket off. It was quiet inside, a number of tables pushed together into a long row in front of the stage and packed with cakes and biscuits and sandwiches and sausage rolls, plates and napkins and bottles of water. At a separate table, by the wall, the tea and coffee station waited, along with some glasses and a judicious selection of cordials. None of them seemed to be Gert's, Alice noted with approval. That one was best not left out with the non-alcoholic drinks. The hall was scattered with tables and chairs, set up invitingly.

But despite the banquet that had been laid on, the only people in view were the W.I. Rosemary was sitting at one table picking somewhat disconsolately at a slice of tea cake, while Rose sat at another, rubbing Angelus' belly with one foot. The rest of the W.I. were scattered around the hall, drinking tea and nibbling on biscuits or slices, all of them looking distinctly put out.

"What's happened?" Alice asked, frowning.

"You've not been on the Facebook group, have you?" Gert asked.

"We saw the news about the well," Miriam said. "How awful!"

"It is," Priya said. "We'll never fix it. It's just *gone.*"

"Where were you?" Jasmine asked. Her thin hair was pulled tightly back, and dark shadows lurked under her eyes. "You were at Lachlan's, weren't you?"

"We went to apologise, as agreed," Alice said. "What on earth's going on?"

"We've been fired," Gert said, taking a swig of what was almost certainly not non-alcoholic cordial.

"It's Lachlan," Pearl said. "He was posting first thing this morning about people sneaking around in the night, and Gareth put a response up."

"The actions of the Toot Hansell Women's Institute do not reflect the opinions of the village as a whole," Teresa said, reading aloud from her phone. *"As such, ongoing operations, including coordinating sandbag distribution and planning for further flood defences will be staged from the Golden Hind pub in the village square. Members of the W.I. are uninvited. We entirely disavow any actions they take, and will be reporting them to the national W.I. headquarters for investigation and possible disbanding."*

The room fell silent, and Alice took her jacket off, hanging it by the door, then crossed to the tea station. "Does anyone else want one?"

"Do we want *tea?*" Jasmine demanded. "We've been kicked off *everything!* I'm the village's police community support officer. I'm *meant* to be part of this. I tried to go to their meeting and they pushed me out the door. Rita *literally* pushed me!"

"Oh dear," Miriam said. "Are you alright?"

"*No!* I should be in charge of this!"

"Well, the police should be," Teresa pointed out, then raised her hands as Jasmine glared at her. "Sorry. Sorry, Jasmine. You're quite right. You should be in charge of the civilian side of things, obviously."

"We've been completely cut off," Jasmine said. "Ben said even the police are going to go over there."

Rose *hmm*ed. "That's probably the offer of free pints."

"Not at nine in the morning," Jasmine said.

"Well, you know what they're like," Gert said. "Never turn down a free drink, would they?"

"I certainly hope they would while they're working," Alice replied, topping up two mugs with hot water. "Why are we all sitting around inside when there are two more people missing, then?"

"Well, like Jasmine says, we did try to go to the pub to help out," Priya replied. "Or Jasmine and I did. We thought maybe it was best not to go en masse."

"Very wise," Alice said, taking a flapjack from a plate and setting it on a napkin while she waited for the tea to brew.

"They're too worried about Lachlan and his water," Carlotta said. "They've tagged him in that Facebook post."

"Has it helped?"

"No," Priya said. She was looking through her phone. "He's just posted again. *No water deliveries today. You ladies are persistent!*" She looked up at Alice and Miriam. "He does like taking photos of you two."

"*Again?*" Miriam demanded. "I thought you had to have permission to take photos of someone!"

"We were on his property," Alice said, taking a bite of flapjack. "This is actually quite good."

"Of course it is," Rosemary said. "I made them."

"Not the flapjack. Or rather, as well as the flapjack," she added, as Rosemary folded her arms, scowling. "The situation."

"*Good?*" Jasmine exclaimed. "How is this possibly *good?*"

"Because it gives us freedom to investigate as we like," Alice replied, adding milk to the tea and handing a mug to Miriam before sitting down. "After all, we do have the most information about what's happening, and therefore the greatest chance of getting to the bottom of things. Finding Nellie means resolving all this flooding, and likely locating Esther and the others. We need to take this into our own hands."

"I don't know," Jasmine said. "Everyone's really upset with us."

"People often get upset when they're scared."

"They form lynch mobs when they're scared too," Gert said, and everyone looked at her. "What?"

Carlotta took a sausage roll. "No one's setting a lynch mob on us. We know how to deal with these sorts of things in the old country."

"Horse's head in the bed?" Rosemary suggested, but without much enthusiasm.

"I was thinking more cricket bats to the knees."

"No," Jasmine said. There was an obstinate set to her jaw. "You're all being silly about it, but this is *serious.* It's police business, and we've already made a mess of things. *You've* made a mess of things," she added, looking at Alice. "We have to stop."

Alice sighed inwardly. Of all times for Jasmine to take a stand. "Well, the W.I. is not a dictatorship. Shall we vote on it?"

The ladies looked at each other uneasily, but there was no answer forthcoming, and Alice realised she'd made a misstep. Of course no one wanted to vote on it. No one wanted to see Jasmine defeated, and she had an idea that would be the outcome. The mention of cricket bats already had everyone looking perkier.

"On second thoughts," she said, before anyone else could rush to fill the silence, "Why don't we go over to the pub? We can apologise once again, and offer to help in whatever capacity is needed."

"They won't let us," Jasmine said.

"Sometimes the important thing is to offer."

No one spoke for a moment, then Teresa said, "I don't mind shifting some sandbags."

"We can check on anyone vulnerable," Pearl added. "Even box up some of the food and take it around as well."

"Let's not get too carried away," Alice said. "We'll go to the pub first, and start from there."

Five minutes later they were out of the hall, rain coursing around their wellies as they marched for the centre of the village, a waterproof, multi-hued platoon armed with a motley assortment of mops, brooms, and some wooden swords Priya had found in the costume box. The geese and swans were still patrolling the streets, but whether the ladies were too large a force for them to tackle, or if the swords were an effective deterrent, they kept their distance.

The W.I. sloshed unmolested around the green and headed up the street to the village square, where the leftover Christmas lights glimmered defiantly above a lake of muddy, disturbed water. It lapped up to the walls of the shops, which had sandbags stacked four-deep across the doorways, holding the flood at bay. It was only ankle-deep for now, but faces appeared regularly at the shop windows, staring anxiously out at its advance. In the centre of the square, where the well had been, orange and white barricades had been put in place. There was no sign of the well itself, no remnants of the walls or the little peaked roof visible, but someone had retrieved the bucket and hung it in the lower branches of the Christmas tree, where it swung a little sadly.

"Oh dear," Miriam whispered, one hand pressed to her chest. "Oh, this is awful."

Pearl put an arm around her, hugging her close. "We'll fix it," she said. "Won't we, ladies?"

There was a quiet murmur of agreement, which was broken by a shout.

"Oi!"

They looked around. The door to the Golden Hind pub, the one on the village square with the sticky floors and the scent of cigarette smoke still lingering decades after the ban had come into force, had been pushed open. The pub was raised up off the cobbles, only by a few steps, but it was enough that they had no need of sandbags yet.

Gareth stormed down the steps, stopping just short of the water, and pointed at them furiously. "How *dare* you show your faces around here?"

"Excuse me?" Alice asked.

"You know what you've done!"

Di, his wife, joined him and grabbed his arm. "Easy, love."

He shook her off. "Where's Vera?"

"Why would we know where Vera is?" Gert demanded.

Gareth glared at her. "Sneaking around at night? Sound familiar?"

"We haven't been sneaking around at night," Alice said.

"Lachlan said you were!"

"Lachlan said *someone* was," Teresa said. "It certainly wasn't us."

"What's that got to do with Vera, anyway?" Rose asked.

"She's missing," Di said. "And Ed too."

Alice frowned. "Ed too? When did that happen?"

"You tell *us,*" Gareth snarled. His face was red and hectic, and there were more people hovering just inside the pub doors. It wasn't a mob, but there was an uneasy, nervous energy to them. It might still be morning, but exceptional circumstances often led to a little alcohol-based assistance, Alice supposed.

"You should go," Di said to the ladies. "You can't help here. Not if we want Lachlan to keep supplying us with water."

"He said that?" Priya asked.

"*I* say it," Gareth said, stabbing a finger at them. "You've probably set up this whole mess somehow, just because you don't like Lachlan!"

"You're sabotaging the village!" someone else yelled from the pub door. People were venturing down the steps now, and Alice thought they had a little more pink in their cheeks than the situation required.

"How on *earth* are we sabotaging anything?" Rosemary demanded.

"Just leave it," Di said. "Let it go, can't you?"

"Harassing Lachlan when he was *helping,*" Gareth said. "Word is you set the police on Dom, too."

"No one's harassing anyone, or sabotaging anything," Alice said, keeping her voice level. "We just want to help. When did Vera and Ed go missing?"

Gareth pulled away from Di and splashed onto the flooded cobbles. "Why can't you just leave things alone? Why do you have to always get *involved?* It's always drama with you lot."

"What did you say about no lynch mobs?" Rosemary asked Carlotta.

"I knew we should've got cricket bats," she replied, shifting her grip on her wooden sword.

"Did you use these on Ed?" Gareth asked, grabbing for the broom Jasmine was carrying. Primrose exploded into snarling yaps, trying to reach him, and he jerked back, stumbling. He would've fallen if Gert hadn't caught him. "Get off me," he snarled, pulling away from her and slipping on the cobbles. He almost fell, then swung around to glare at the women. "You pushed me!"

"We're leaving," Alice said, over Primrose's hysterical barking.

"You're not," Gareth said. "Ed's my *friend!* Where is he?"

Di had splashed off the steps to join him. "Gareth, come on," she said, trying to pull him back to the pub.

"No! No, we need to find Ed!" He caught Priya's arm and she promptly smacked him with her mop. "*Ow!*"

"Hands off," she snapped.

He looked as if he was about to try grabbing her again, but a woman with a rough voice shouted from the steps, "The geese! The geese are coming! *The geese are coming!*"

"Gareth, come on!" Di was already splashing back toward the steps, and Gareth rushed after her as a pack of geese came racing across the square, half-flying, flat feet paddling at the water and wings pounding. Their honking battle-cries filled the dreary day, and more birds came charging from the opposite direction. Swans thundered after them, and ducks dive-bombed out of the sky, setting Angelus barking just as frantically as Primrose, but twice as deep. They aimed straight for the pub doors as the patrons tried to jam through them all at once, the air a churning mess of rain and splashing flood-waters and discarded feathers.

The women stared after them for a moment, then Teresa yelped as a duck swooped low over her head before crashing to the water near the lost well. Martha watched it land then gave one thoughtful bark.

"Good girl," Pearl said, patting her head.

"Let's go," Alice said.

They made their way out of the square as quickly as they could, trying to avoid tripping over unseen kerbs or submerged debris. The birds had besieged the pub steps, and watched the ladies pass unmolested, muttering and scuffling among themselves. Only once they were out of sight of the square did Alice stop again, and they clustered together in the middle of the road with the rain pattering on their coats.

"Everyone alright?" Gert asked.

There was a general mumble of agreement, and Rose said, "Unusual behaviour, that."

"The people or the birds?" Miriam asked.

"Both," Rose admitted.

"Well, everyone'll definitely think we're witches now," Priya said.

"Good," Teresa said. "I've been working on that for years."

That raised a small ripple of laughter, and Rosemary said, "What now?"

Alice looked at Jasmine, eyebrows raised. She still had Primrose held close to her, and her hood had fallen back. She relaxed her grip a little, and took a deep breath. "Well, we can't let this go on, can we? Let's fix it."

"Well done, Jasmine," Gert said, patting her shoulder, then snatched her hand away as Primrose growled. "Bloody hell. Can't you let her walk?"

"No. She's too little. She might get washed away."

"And wouldn't that be a shame," Carlotta murmured.

They started back toward the hall, the village fraught and drowning around them. Alice hoped they *could* fix this. Things felt desperately precarious, and they still had no plan, no way forward.

But at least they were united. And that counted for an awful lot.

15
MORTIMER

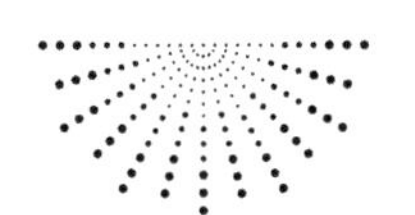

Mortimer didn't know why they hadn't stuck to the plan. He'd have liked to stick to the plan. The plan meant trekking deeper into the woods, away from farms and police and sheep, which were still making him nervous, no matter how helpful they'd been earlier. But one could never actually expect Beaufort to stick to a plan. That was like expecting mince pies in July. It might happen, but it was highly irregular.

So rather than being in the charmed cover of the forest, looking for either the Source or a way to hold back the waters, they were lying in the heavy old rafters of Dom's barn, watching two police officers trying to move the chickens enough that they could check for more evidence without setting the birds fussing so much that they destroyed said evidence.

DI Adams had already taken photos of the hanky before putting it in a little plastic bag, which Mortimer had watched with great interest until he became aware of a soft panting terribly close to his ear. He'd looked up slowly to find Dandy standing on the rafter he was clinging to, the creature's tongue lolling pink and amused between his long teeth. Mortimer swallowed a yelp, and clung a little tighter to the beam, as if he thought Dandy might pick him up by the scruff of the neck and fling him to the floor, then went back to staring at the police, trying to pretend there weren't red eyes burning into him from uncomfortably close quarters. When he finally risked another look Dandy was lying down too, his forepaws almost touching Mortimer's snout. He offered Mortimer something.

"No thanks," Mortimer whispered.

Dandy tipped his head, and tried again.

"No, I'm fine."

This time Dandy chomped down on whatever was in his mouth, and it squeaked loudly.

"What was that?" one of the officers asked, looking around.

"Dog toy, by the sounds," the other said, still poking into the corners of the barn.

Dandy chewed on his toy again.

"*Shhh,*" Mortimer hissed at him.

"There it is again. It sounds like it's coming from up there." The officer craned her neck, playing a torch beam over the rafters, and Mortimer willed himself to the same faded brown colour as the beam, trying desperately to signal to Dandy with a single twitch of his eyebrow ridge that he needed to stay quiet. Evidently it worked, because the creature stayed still, and the light passed over them.

"It'll be acoustics," the other officer said. "Not going to be dogs in the rafters, is there?"

"No," she admitted, but she kept looking, using her torch to illuminate every corner of the barn. "These old places have great beams," she said, bringing the light back onto the one Mortimer was lying on. "Look, the shadow of this looks like a dragon."

Mortimer closed his eyes, trying not to panic. She hadn't said it *was* a dragon. She'd said it *looked* like a dragon, and only the shadow. That was okay. It'd be okay.

Dandy pushed his nose forward, a rubber duck in his mouth.

"*No,*" Mortimer breathed, and watched the dandy fumble the toy onto the beam. It tumbled toward the edge in agonising slow motion, and just as it teetered on the verge of falling DI Adams said, "You think Dom's got people trussed in the rafters?"

"Um, no," the officer said, flicking the torch away, and Mortimer snatched the duck before it could topple. It squeaked, and the officer said, "Did you hear that?"

"Dog toy, sounds like," DI Adams said. "Found anything else?"

"Not so far, no. Did you think that noise came from the rafters somewhere?"

"Not if it was a dog toy."

"No, but—"

"There's nowhere up there to hide anyone. You can see that from here. So whether it's a dog toy or not is irrelevant. We're up to three missing people now, so if you're done faffing about in here, how about we get out in the rain and concentrate on places where they actually could be?"

"Right. Sorry."

Footsteps scuffed across the hard-packed floor, and Mortimer carefully peered over the edge of the beam. DI Adams was at the door, directing the two officers out, and she glanced up, scowling. He raised a paw weakly, and she marched out into the rain.

When no one came back in, Mortimer pushed himself up to sitting, and looked across at the next rafter. Beaufort grinned at him. "You've got another friend there."

Mortimer regarded Dandy, who had sat up too, then examined the duck in his paw. "What am I meant to do with this?"

Dandy huffed and reached forward with his snout to nudge it.

"We should leave before they come back in," Mortimer said to Beaufort. "That was far too close."

"All she saw was a shadow."

"A *dragon-shaped* shadow."

"It's still just a shadow."

Mortimer sighed and offered the duck to Dandy, who snatched it out of his paw. "You could've just kept it," he told him. "It would've saved a lot of trouble."

"Come on," Beaufort said, peering down into the barn. "Let's go and see if we can find anything."

"No! They'll see us!"

"No one's going to see us. Just look at this rain. They can barely see themselves through it."

"They *might*," Mortimer insisted. Police were terribly perceptive. It was basically their job description to be terribly perceptive, and DI Adams certainly hadn't had much trouble seeing them. She'd been somewhat reluctant initially, true, but she'd *seen* them. It had just taken her a little while to accept what she was seeing, and one couldn't hold that against her. He was deeply reluctant to be seen by the police himself.

But Beaufort was already on the ground, and Mortimer glided down after him, landing in the shelter of a tractor and peering around it at the door to the yard. No one was in sight, and Beaufort was sidling up to the door when Dandy suddenly whined and jumped from the top of the tractor, running past the High Lord. DI Adams stepped inside, glaring at them all, then glanced back into the rain before moving away from the door, where she couldn't be seen too easily.

"Give me that," she said, wrestling the duck off Dandy. He resisted, squeaking it a few times, and she said, "I know, I *know*. You can't have all the ducks though, okay? And definitely no squeaky ones."

Dandy whined but relinquished the toy, and she straightened up, looking at the dragons. Mortimer braced himself, expecting her to tell them off for being in the middle of her investigation, but instead she said, "You better have something for me. I just bollocked a more than competent, bloody smart PC because you two decided to play at being bats."

"You don't have anything on the missing people?" Beaufort asked. "We heard you talking about there being more now."

"Three. And not really. We have the handkerchief, but there's nothing else. No witnesses. No real motive. Nothing on Dom's cameras, which is hardly surprising. I've got to work on the assumption that Dom did have something to do with it, but proving all that comes after. We need to find them first."

"We've been seeing faces in the water," Mortimer said, and she gave him a thoughtful look.

"Sprites?"

"No, Nellie's the only sprite in the area. They're quite territorial."

"Also known as anti-social," Beaufort said.

"I wouldn't mind being a sprite," DI Adams muttered, then checked the yard. "So, what – you think these faces belong to the missing people?"

"Possibly," Mortimer said. "Walter saw two different ones."

"So that means ...?"

"We don't know," Beaufort admitted. "But it may well have something to do with Nellie."

DI Adams rubbed a hand over her face. "Great. Of course. We couldn't just have a nice, simple, missing persons case, could we?"

"But you're very good at non-standard cases," the High Lord said. "There's no one else who could handle this."

She gave him an amused look. "Thanks. What's the Nellie situation, then?"

"She's still missing, and there are two options. One is that she's been either deliberately caught or accidentally trapped, and the flooding's from her trying to escape. The other is that she's so angry about the damage to her waters that she's drowning the village as punishment."

DI Adams looked out at the rain, her fingers tapping her thighs. "She'd do that?"

"Sprites can be mercurial."

"Good to know. So we're not going to find anything hunting around here, are we?"

"That depends," Beaufort said. "If she has been trapped, the missing people could've been caught the same way. You might find all of them together."

She scratched her cheek, and nodded. "Well, I'm hoping we find something. I had to lean on Dom pretty hard to get him to let us search at all. I thought he was going to make me get a warrant, and he's likely complaining to my DCI right now."

"If anyone can find—"

"Yes, alright. Do you have anything else?"

"We saw someone in the field by the retreat very early this morning," Beaufort said. "An elderly man in a dressing gown. He dropped his toothbrush."

"Where? Can you show me?"

Beaufort looked at Mortimer. "You can find it again, can't you, lad?"

"At least the general area."

"Alright." The inspector stepped to the door, peering each way. "You're clear. Head into the field and I'll meet you there."

She vanished out into the yard, jogging through the mud toward the farmhouse, and Dandy bounded after her, his dreadlocks seemingly even longer and wilder than usual. Mortimer wondered if it was some sort of defence against the wet, and had a moment of envy. The dandy's fur looked so thick Mortimer couldn't imagine that any of the rain was actually getting through it, unlike his own scales, which he was fairly sure were going to float off at any second.

He followed Beaufort as the High Lord slipped into the yard and around the barn, running for the wall that enclosed the farmyard. A moment later they were in the field, the grass a green sweep crushed beneath the endless cloud. They took shelter in a crumbling shepherd's hut, and before long DI Adams and Dandy came hurrying out to join them, the inspector's high-vis jacket a shout against the grey.

Beaufort didn't wait, just led the way across the field, arrowing toward the retreat and not slowing until they were in the general area where the man had appeared. The sheep came trotting to meet them, bleating eagerly, and Mortimer tried to ignore the animals as he cast around, looking for the toothbrush and hoping that this time he'd find something, some whisper of scent to prove the man had been here. There was nothing, though. The toothbrush was gone, the grass had swallowed the footprints, and the world smelled of damp, grey cold.

DI Adams looked at Dandy, who stared back at her and nudged her pocket. "No," she said, and he looked away with a sigh. "This is it, then?" she asked the dragons.

"This is it," Beaufort agreed. "He just appeared then was gone again."

"And he wasn't one of your reflections?"

Beaufort looked at Mortimer. "What do you think? Your nose is better than mine."

Mortimer hesitated. It hadn't *looked* like a reflection. He could still see the way the man's slippers had sunk into the grass, and his bewildered look as he stared down at them. "He seemed real."

DI Adams tucked her chin into her coat, looking across the field to the retreat. "So how does this happen? Someone appearing and disappearing like that?"

"It doesn't," Beaufort said.

"It doesn't?"

"It shouldn't be possible. I've never heard of it."

She nodded. "Great. So now we've got something even dragons haven't heard of. What *is* it with this place?"

Mortimer figured that didn't need an answer, although he gave Beaufort a sideways glance, just in case the High Lord thought he should be saying something. He was just watching the inspector, though, waiting.

DI Adams looked down at her feet, rocking on her heels thoughtfully. "Sinkhole?"

"That wouldn't just close up again," Beaufort said.

"Well, yes," DI Adams agreed. "Unlikely. Wormhole?"

"It'd have to be a very big worm."

The inspector snorted. "Mortimer, those scents you get from people – traces, whatever – what was Dom like?"

"Just a bit angry and sad. Frustrated, I suppose."

"Hardly damning. What about Lachlan there?"

Mortimer moved slightly as one of the sheep leaned on him, soaking up his warmth. "I haven't been close enough to get anything clearly. It's just money and curiosity and … and seaweed for some reason."

Beaufort and DI Adams gave him matching puzzled looks.

"Is that suspicious?" the inspector asked.

"I don't know. Maybe he likes seaweed."

"Not even mermaids like seaweed," Beaufort said.

"I do," DI Adams said, and shrugged when the dragons stared at her. "It's tasty. But I take it you don't mean he was eating it."

"Hard to tell," Mortimer said.

They all looked at the retreat, as if waiting for someone to pop out and explain the seaweed situation. DI Adams folded her arms across her chest, and as the moment stretched, Mortimer could feel the High Lord getting restless with inaction.

He was almost expecting Beaufort to announce that they should launch a joint raid on the retreat when the sheep started to bleat and shift in alarm, and a party of a dozen geese and almost as many swans came marching across the field from the woods. They ignored the little group and their woolly escorts, and instead headed straight to the wall where the dragons had triggered the alarm that morning, their necks snaking and their wings fluttering in fury. Mortimer almost fancied he could hear the regimented stomp of their webbed feet across the soft, muddy ground, and they didn't falter or pause, just leaped to the top of the wall, where they settled, setting up a honking chorus.

"*Huh*," DI Adams said. Dandy, who'd been watching, looked back at her and gave one short, sharp bark, and she dropped into a crouch, the movement instant and smooth with instinct. "Get down. Someone's coming." She looked at her bright jacket, and sighed, straightening up again as the sheep clustered around them more closely. "Well, I've got reason to be here, I suppose."

Mortimer, who was trying to hang onto his grassy tones, had the mournful thought that hiding in a pack of sheep was possibly a new personal low, but he flattened himself to the grass as Dandy walked forward a few paces, his head low and his eyes luminous. DI Adams stayed where she was, arms crossed, and Mortimer peered through the sheep at the gate in the wall, which gave a view to the garden and the retreat beyond.

The geese were still trumpeting as Lachlan stalked through the flower-beds, a rifle broken over one arm. A younger man scurried after him, holding another rifle, both of them bareheaded and jacketless in the rain. Lachlan snapped the barrels into place and sighted along it at the birds, but they scattered before he could pull the trigger. He jerked the gun upward, aiming higher, and fired. Mortimer swallowed a screech of fright, and over the angry bleating of the sheep he heard the man yell, "Bloody menaces!"

Mortimer watched, wide-eyed, as Lachlan lowered the gun and stared out at them. DI Adams didn't move, and the man didn't acknowledge her. They just looked at each other for a long moment, then he turned and stormed back inside. The young man scrambled to follow him, and a moment later they were lost to sight.

"Interesting," DI Adams said.

"Can you arrest him for that?" Mortimer asked her. His ears were ringing, far too much for it to be just the sound of the shot.

"Not if he's got a licence, and I imagine he has. Might be able to issue a fine for discharging a firearm over land he doesn't own, but that would be about it." She looked around at the woolly backs surrounding the dragons. "Guard sheep. Why not, I guess."

Mortimer rose to all fours, watching the geese warily. They were returning to the field one by one, all looking disgruntled and a bit rumpled. One of them put its head down, making a half-hearted charge at the little group. A sheep stamped its hoof, and the goose stopped. They stared each other down, and Mortimer eased himself behind Beaufort, trying to keep out of sight.

"Easy, lad," Beaufort said. "They're not dangerous."

"They are," Mortimer replied. "They're going to take my scales."

Beaufort made a dubious sound, but didn't argue. He looked at the goose instead. "Where's Nellie then?" he asked. "Go on, find us Nellie. Get Nellie!"

The goose reared up, beating its wings and hissing, and the other geese turned to see what was going on, stalking across the field to join the standoff with the sheep.

"D'you think they do know where she is?" DI Adams asked, raising her voice to be heard over the birds.

"If anyone does, they do," Beaufort said.

DI Adams nodded, squinting at the retreat, then shook her head. "I'm not hanging about to get yelled at by a damn goose. I've requested some dog handlers to help on the search, but no word on when they get here. You might want to make yourselves scarce when they're around, though."

"Of course," Beaufort said. "We're quite capable of being subtle."

"I'd rather you be invisible. But …" She hesitated, then sighed. "From what you're saying, I don't think the dogs are going to help. So keep me updated, alright? See if you get … oh, bloody hell." She pinched the bridge of her nose. "See if you get anything out of the geese."

"Will do," the High Lord said.

"And keep the W.I. out of it."

"That may be harder."

"It always is," she said, not moving, her fingers resuming a restless tapping on her legs. "What about the flooding?"

"We need to find Nellie," Beaufort said. "She may just be the key to everything."

DI Adams nodded. "I had that feeling. Let me know if you need help." She turned back to the farm, breaking into a jog without a backward glance, her head bowed against the rain.

"What now?" Mortimer said.

"Now we see how Margery got on with Daphne." Beaufort turned and headed for the wall and the forest beyond, and Mortimer followed, not without a shiver of relief. At least they'd avoided storming the retreat.

16
DI ADAMS

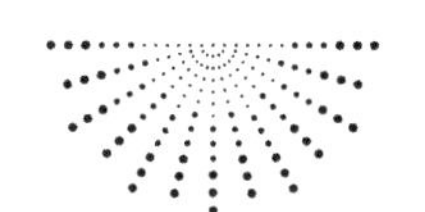

DI Adams didn't think she'd ever been quite so drenched. The rain felt like it had soaked all the way through to her bones, leaving her fingertips wrinkled and her nose running with both her lingering cold and the actual cold of the day. Hoods annoyed her, limiting her field of vision and making her feel too enclosed, so she kept pushing the one on her jacket back, and now her hair was sodden, and rain was seeping around her neck and sneaking further and further down her back. Her boots, which she'd thought were entirely waterproof, had become overwhelmed and admitted defeat at some stage, or the water had come in over the top – she wasn't entirely sure which, but the end result was the same. Her socks were sodden, and she sloshed with every step. Rashid and Jayne, the two officers helping her, appeared to be in much the same state, all three of them bedraggled and veering between dejected and infuriated, depending on the moment.

Only Dandy was enjoying himself, galloping across the fields and the farmyard with his dreadlocks flying dark and long, chasing the ducks and dancing around a handful of stoic-looking cows. She hated to think what he was going to do to her car, and she found herself wondering if she could just leave him to make his own way home. It wasn't as if he couldn't, and probably quicker than she could herself.

She straightened up, stretching with her hands in the small of her back. One handkerchief really wasn't enough to turn this into a full-scale search, not with most evidence still suggesting Toot Hansell was the most logical place for the missing people to still be located. *People.* Three of them, and other than the hanky, the only lead was what the dragons had seen. She gazed across the fields at the retreat, wishing she had something more concrete. Very quickly after she'd seen Lachlan shooting at the birds – astonishingly quickly, in fact, she'd barely made it back to Dom's – she'd received a call from her DCI, in which it was stated in no uncertain terms she was to stay away from the man.

"Unless you see one of your missing persons trussed up at his bloody kitchen table, you do not go over there again, got it?" Maud had said. She'd sounded infuriated, but DI Adams had a feeling that was less directed at her than at whatever phone calls the DCI herself had been fielding. "You've got nothing concrete that points at him, do you?"

"No. Two possible sightings of missing persons near his property—"

"Possible. Near."

"Yes."

"Back off him, Adams. You only get one run at someone like that, and you don't have enough to try it. You'll wind up with both of us transferred to the bloody Shetlands, and I hate ponies."

DI Adams wondered if ponies would be less problematic than W.I.s and dragons, but with her luck the Shetlands would have selkies and Viking clubs or something like that instead. "Got it," she said, because there was nothing else she *could* say. Maud had to tell her to back off, and she had to say okay, and then she had to work out how to disregard everything her DCI said, because those birds pointed to Nellie being in the retreat. They *had* to. And she had to find Nellie, because it seemed the sprite was the thread that could unravel everything.

But she didn't know how to get hold of that thread when she had no access to the retreat. She had an idea a dodgier copper would know just how to create access when there weren't strictly grounds for it, but that wasn't her. So for now she just had to keep looking, until she found another way in.

She was poking rather dispiritedly around the back of a flooded chicken coop, hissing at Dandy that he should make himself useful and find her some clues when her phone rang, and she fished it out of her pocket, checking the screen. *PC Harrison, Skipton,* it read, and she pulled her hood up to protect it from the worst of the damp.

"Harrison," she said.

"Graham," he reminded her, and she made a frustrated noise.

"I don't have *time*."

"You don't have time to be civil?"

"Do you have any idea how wet I am?" DI Adams asked, squinting at the grey fields. Dimly, on the phone, she could hear what sounded like … She frowned. "Is that a fruit machine? Are you in the *pub?*"

"New search headquarters. W.I. have been exiled, apparently, and have taken their baked goods with them. New catering options are not quite up to scratch, if I'm being honest."

"What d'you mean, they've been exiled?"

"Tech Boy's declared he's not providing water anymore because the W.I. have hurt his feelings. Locals are not happy, and according to the pub landlord, who's been sampling his own wares rather intensively, there was very nearly a street battle just before Ben and I got to the pub, but it was broken up by geese. To hear him tell it, it was a good thing too, as there were going to be witch trials." He considered it. "My money would be on the W.I., to be honest."

"Mine too," she said. "Have they settled down?"

"The W.I. or the locals?"

"Either."

"Not sure about the W.I. General unrest is afoot, however. We've lost another one."

"What?"

"Edward Wiggan. Friends with the previous one. Or enemies, I'm not sure."

DI Adams squeezed the bridge of her nose. "He's the shopkeeper. Vera's the tea-shop owner."

"Look at you, knowing people's names."

"No indication of where Wiggan might've gone?"

"No, but rumour has it he had a bit of a run-in with the W.I. yesterday, and that Vera wasn't their favourite, either."

DI Adams said something that made Graham whistle through his teeth, then she said, "They're blaming the W.I."

"People need to blame someone."

"Are we going to have a problem?"

"I think we've got too many other problems for that to get out of hand yet," he said, his tone changing. "The flooding's getting worse."

"How bad?"

"There's a sinkhole in the village square where the well was, and it's spreading. It's not the only one, either. Place is more water than land at this point."

Of course it was. With the tunnels that honeycombed the earth beneath Toot Hansell, running from church to pub to village centre and everywhere else besides, the wonder was that nothing had caved in before. All this water would be destabilising the whole place, rapidly. DI Adams turned to look toward the retreat, half-hidden behind shifting sheets of rain, and rubbed the back of her neck through the hood. "We're not losing these people into sinkholes, are we?"

"Not so far as I can tell," Graham replied. "Look, we've been taping off hazards as we go, helping with sandbagging where needed, checking on everyone, but we can't search properly and do that. Plus there aren't enough of us to clear the place if it gets worse. *When* it gets worse. I think we need to call it now so we can get things moving before dark."

"Get things moving? Are we talking evacuation?"

He was silent for a moment, and she could hear the fruit machine dinging behind him, and someone laughing. "We're not far off, boss.

But I'd rather you made that call. Don't fancy getting read the riot act by Maud for overreacting."

"Alright. I'll head your way. Can you line up some hot drinks and food? I'll bring Jayne and Rashid with me. We're all bloody freezing."

"On it. Won't be W.I.-standard, but it'll be something."

"Good enough." She was about to hang up, then paused. "What about the birds?"

"Seem to have thinned out a bit," he said. "Word has it they're working for the W.I."

"What?"

"Told you, the birds broke up the street battle so the ladies could get away. With their swords."

"*What?*"

"Wooden ones. Although I think that's already changing in the telling. Give it a couple more pints and they'll be wearing armour and lugging siege machines."

"I wouldn't put it past them." She hung up, flicking through to Maud's number as she turned back to the farmyard.

Maud answered after only a few rings. "Tell me you're not calling because you've accidentally fallen into Lachlan Jameson's property."

"No. We do have a problem, though."

"If it's the birds, the RSPB sent a team out to take a look yesterday, and have now found themselves unaccountably busy. Graham's already had me try them four times, and I think they're screening my calls."

"Right. I've just got off the phone with him, and apparently we may need to evacuate the village."

"Because of *birds?*"

"No, flooding."

There was a pause, then Maud said, "Really? There's nothing on the weather about it."

"The ground's completely waterlogged, and the rain hasn't stopped since I've been here. We've got sinkholes."

There was the sound of clicking on the other end of the line, and Maud said, "There's no weather alerts, nothing."

"Okay, sure, but I'm telling you, it's sodden," DI Adams said, trying to keep her voice level. "I think I've got trench foot."

"I don't think it can happen that quickly."

DI Adams made a doubtful noise, and waved to Jayne, pointing at the cars. "My brother went to Glastonbury and came back with it after a weekend."

"*Huh.* Perhaps your family's simply prone to it."

"That's a lovely thought. But the village is *drowning*. We don't have the bodies to shift everyone out, not fast enough. We need support."

Maud was silent for a moment, then she said, "Are you in the village?"

"No. Graham just called me."

Another pause, while DI Adams watched Rashid plod through the gate from the field, looking as drenched as she felt. Then Maud said, "Get yourself in there, take some footage, and send it to me. I'll get the request in, but with no weather alerts we're going to have to prove we really need the assistance."

"On the way." DI Adams hung up, and looked at the two officers who were waiting by their car, both dripping water and mud. Jayne looked unimpressed, and the inspector had a pang of guilt over the way she'd talked to the younger woman in the barn. All because of bloody dragons, too. Rashid had mud up to his knees and looked as if he'd rolled in a cowpat at some point, but he seemed cheery enough.

"You got something, boss?" he asked.

"We're heading for the village," she said. "Hot drinks and a bite to eat, then we'll regroup."

"Sweet." He grinned at Jayne, who frowned.

"What about Blackwood?"

"I'm going to have a word with him now."

"We're not arresting him?"

"On the basis of a handkerchief? Not right now. Get yourselves into the pub in the middle of the village, warm up, and I'll be right behind you."

"The *pub?*" Jayne asked, sounding horrified. "Why the *pub?*"

DI Adams bit the inside of her cheek to hide a smile, and

wondered what the young woman's feelings on first names were. "The pub. Graham's there, and he'll brief you." She didn't wait for them to answer, just slogged through the mud to the kitchen door of the farmhouse, pushing her hood back again as she banged briskly on the door. There was no answer from inside. She tried again, but there was still no response, so she pushed the door open onto a kitchen that was empty other than the goat watching her with baleful eyes. "Dom? Mr Blackwood?"

Nothing. She looked back into the yard. The police car was already bumping down the drive, leaving her car sitting alone. An old Land Rover was just visible inside one of the barn doors, nestled next to a tractor, but that didn't necessarily mean anything. She stepped into the kitchen, calling Dom's name again, and the goat bleated at her, stomping its hooves. "To you, too," she said, heading into the hall. She checked the downstairs fast, trailed by the goat as she pushed open one door after the other to peer inside the silent rooms, calling out periodically. No one in the cosy living room, scented with woodsmoke, or in the empty, dusty dining room; no one in the well-used utility room or the surprisingly clean downstairs loo.

"Bollocks," she muttered, then gave a yelp as the goat head-butted her leg without a lot of force, but with a certain intent. "Stop that." She pushed it away as it tried again, then ran up the stairs. It took her no more time to check the rooms up here that it had downstairs, and she found exactly what she expected to. Nothing. She stood in the upstairs hallway with the palms of her hands pressed to her forehead, and swore. This was ridiculous. People were vanishing everywhere, and she didn't even know if Dom was the next missing person or a suspect on the run. She didn't have the bodies to cover this sort of area at the best of times, and now she had to organise an evacuation on top, and the rain just *wouldn't bloody stop.* She swore again, loudly and roundly, then dropped her hands and looked at the goat, which had followed her upstairs. "Sorry." She clicked the shoulder mic on her radio. "Rashid, Adams."

"Ay-up," he replied, which was hardly proper radio protocol, but she wasn't going to argue about that now. She could hear car noises around the words.

"Did either of you see Dominic Blackwood leaving?"

There was a pause, presumably while he conferred with Jayne, then he came back and said, "No, nothing."

"Copy," she said, heading for the stairs.

"Adams, Westin."

DI Adams' mouth twitched. That proved her theory about Jayne and last names. "Go ahead."

"Is Blackwood missing?"

"He's not in the house."

"Do you want us to come back and help search?"

"No—" She stopped as the house gave a shuddering groan, and she froze halfway down the stairs, one hand on the wall. The goat fled past her with a panicked bleat.

"Adams, Westin."

The house juddered again, dust drifting down from the ceiling and tiny bits of plaster cracking on the walls. Her stomach flopped over, the world suddenly unaccountably treacherous. Those thick stone walls that had weathered centuries, and now they were *trembling?*

"Adams, Adams, this is Westin, copy?"

She forced herself to move as the shivering faded away, making it to the bottom of the stairs and running for the kitchen. The goat was standing in the sink with its front hooves up on the window frame, bleating pitifully, and she tried to haul the door open, but it wouldn't move.

"Adams, Adams, do you copy, over?"

She jiggled the lock, but it wasn't engaged, and another one of those shudders ran through the house, like a beast rolling over in its sleep, sending a vast crack snapping across the ceiling and down one of the walls. Mugs rattled in the sink, and the goat gave something that was uncomfortably close to a scream. DI Adams braced one hand on the wall and heaved on the handle with the other, and this time the door flew open. "Come on!" she shouted to the goat, but it was already launching itself off the worktop and straight out the door, almost bowling her over. "You're welcome," she muttered, following it out into the churned mud of the yard. The ground gave one final shiver then stilled, and she realised her phone was ringing. She pulled it out and hit answer almost mechanically, staring around the yard, still braced for the ground to betray her again.

"Adams," she said.

"What the hell's going on now?" Maud demanded.

"Um, earthquake?" she offered, bewildered as to how Maud knew.

"What? No, I mean Lachlan Jameson calling to complain about his property being invaded by a pack of women of a certain age, *in costume*, apparently. He's calling it disturbing the peace, trespassing, harassment, *and* assault. He wants the whole lot arrested."

"Oh, bloody hell," DI Adams muttered. "I'm on it."

"Adams—"

"Jayne and Rashid are already on the way to the village, and I'm still near Jameson's. Graham can handle the flood for now. It's got to be the bloody W.I., and I think it's better I deal with that on my own." She hesitated, then added, "There's probably some Toot Hansell stuff involved."

There was a pause as she heard Maud take a deep breath, then the DCI said, "You couldn't wait for Colin to get back to go all Toot Hansell on me?"

"I promise it's not by choice," she said, as her phone vibrated with another incoming call.

"*Fine.* Only because I really don't want to know about anything W.I.-related." Maud paused. "Hang about. Earthquake?"

"Felt like it."

"Toot sodding Hansell," the DCI said, and hung up.

DI Adams hit accept on the other call, frowning at the yard.

"Bloody *hell,*" Rashid said. "Jayne here was just about having conniptions."

"I was not," DI Adams heard Jayne – Westin – say faintly. "Tell her it wasn't proper radio protocol to just cut off like that."

"She says—"

"I heard. I'm fine. Get yourself to the village, and Graham'll take it from there."

"You're not following?"

"Not just yet."

"You want us to come back?"

"No," she said. "You go on." She hit disconnect and walked to her car. Or rather, to where her car had been when she went inside. Now there was simply a hole, and she stood well back from the edge, peering into the depths. Her car was nestled neatly into the bottom, looking more as if it had slid down on a Golf-shaped lift than fallen anywhere. "Well, bollocks,," she said, and was rewarded by a huff. She looked around and found Dandy standing next to her, tail wagging gently. "Now what?" she asked him. She could find some keys and help herself to the Land Rover, she supposed, but that only helped if she was intending to head for the village, and she didn't think she was. Not anytime soon, anyway.

The problem wasn't in the village, after all. The problem was out here. Not just the W.I. and their protest – and, more importantly, whatever the hell sort of shenanigans their protest was meant to cover up – but Esther had been seen out here, and so had one of the other missing persons. The damn *geese* were out here, and now Dom had taken himself off. And everything was centred on the retreat. She took a step back from the sinkhole, giving her car a final, regretful look, and headed for the farmhouse.

She paused on the threshold, looking around distrustfully and waiting for another of those tremors. Nothing came, and she sidled inside to the table, where the laptop was still sitting, covered in a gentle dusting of plaster dust. She grabbed it and retreated to the doorway, so she could run if she needed to, poking the mousepad to wake the screen up. It lit, the cursor flashing in the passcode field, and she frowned at it. *0000.* No. *1234.* Not that either. She sighed, looking around, then back at the laptop. It was very new. She put in the year, and the screen cleared immediately. "Nice," she murmured, and clicked on the same icon Dom had used before, finding the feed to the camera that was pointed at the retreat. She rewound it, skipping through the frames until movement flashed into the picture, and she stopped, hitting play. A quad bike puttered across the screen, towing an enclosed trailer that could've had sheep in it, but she had an idea didn't. It paused at the gates to the retreat, then vanished inside, with two brown dogs ranging alongside it.

"Dammit," she said softly. He must've had the bike stashed somewhere far enough away that they hadn't heard it. She checked the time. Dom had a good half hour's lead, and she looked at Dandy. "Want to go and sort out some ladies of a certain age? See if we can find a sprite? Some missing persons? Any or all of the above you feel like being useful about?"

He huffed, and shoved his nose against her pocket. She sighed, took the rubber duck from her coat, and gave it to him. He snatched it, backing away and squeaking it enthusiastically.

"Wonderful," she muttered. "Great help." She set the laptop back on the table and stepped outside again. At least she *definitely* had an excuse for poking around Lachlan Jameson now. The only downside was the fact that the whole place was likely infested by the W.I. That was fairly situation normal, though. She headed for the gate to the fields, Dandy loping ahead of her and the goat trailing behind, bleating insistently.

It was hardly the team she'd have chosen, but it seemed to be the team she'd got.

17

MIRIAM

"No," Miriam said. Or, rather, that was what she said in her mind, and she was willing herself to say it aloud as well, but the nine other ladies of the Toot Hansell Women's Institute were all looking at her expectantly. They were sitting around the long table in the village hall, still wearing dripping trousers and soaking boots. Mugs of tea sat in front of them, and the apple cake and jammy dodgers had been broken into, as a little fortification against the cold. For those in need of additional fortification, Gert had poured generous measures of cordial for them all. Carlotta had produced a flask from her handbag, but it had been unanimously decided that it was too early for that particular degree of fortification. Well, unanimously by everyone except Carlotta, who looked mildly put out.

"Miriam?" Alice said.

Miriam thought *no* again, very firmly, then said, "Why me?"

"Because you have a history of such things," Priya said.

"I do not," Miriam said, a little more sharply than she'd intended. "Or not for *ages,* anyway."

"But you do have a history," Rosemary said. "I still remember that time you were arrested for paint-bombing a visiting dignitary."

"It was flour and water and a bit of food colouring, not paint, and he wasn't a dignitary, he was some nasty old politician who liked fur coats," Miriam said, her cheeks pink. "And I wasn't *really* arrested. Just got a good telling off."

"See, you *do* have a history," Jasmine said.

"*Scandalous,*" Rose said with a chuckle, helping herself to a little more cordial.

"I was seventeen, and I didn't last much longer after that. Protests were always more Rainbow's thing." Even when her sister had still been Judith, rather than Rainbow, she had been much more militant than Miriam. Miriam could never decide if she admired or despaired of her sister. She had an idea it was a little of both.

"The point is, you're the most likely person to stage a protest, especially against polluting the waters," Jasmine said. "And I suspect that someone like Lachlan will have done at least a little bit of research on the people he's dealing with. So if *I* were to suddenly start protesting, for instance, he'd think it very suspicious."

"What about Gert? Or Rose?"

"No," Rose said, taking a piece of Battenberg and peeling the marzipan off. "I'm not one for protests. Too busy looking for beasties."

"Protests aren't how I get things done," Gert said, folding her arms and leaning back in her chair.

Miriam gave Alice a despairing look. "But I'm not ... I don't even know *how!*"

"You don't have to do anything much," Alice said. "You simply set everything in motion."

"Then we take over," Pearl said, stealing the marzipan off Rose's plate. "And you two sneak off and find us a sprite."

Miriam stared at her glass, which just had plain cordial in it, rather than Gert's. She looked at Rose. "Did you get anything from testing the water?"

She shook her head. "Nothing immediate. My friend's doing some more tests today. But you can see from the way the plants are dying it's not harmless. Plus there's some sort of white deposit, salt or chalk or something, where the rain isn't washing it away. There's definitely something in it."

"It's a very legitimate reason to protest," Alice said.

Miriam felt it rather unfair that she had to lead a protest *and* hunt a sprite, but the village was crumbling at the edges, and the longer she argued, the more time things had to fall apart. So she leaned over and helped herself to Gert's cordial, adding it to her glass and drinking the whole thing in one gulp. She gasped, and said in a strangled voice, "Okay."

WHICH WAS HOW, an hour and an assortment of hastily-made placards later, a small procession of five cars proceeded down the last stretch of lane to Lachlan Jameson's retreat, all of them with their horns blaring in dignified fury. The gate was shut, which was actually much more convenient than expected, and they parked in the road, blocking it entirely to traffic.

"That's good protest technique, really," Miriam said to Alice as they got out. "Maximum disruption. Gives it a touch of authenticity."

"Stops him leaving, too," she said, and smiled.

Miriam thought Alice was much better suited to protest than she was. Or possibly to something rather more devious. She hurried to Gert's van, where Priya had opened the back doors and was handing out signs reading *Save Our Waters!* and *Water Rights Matter!* They weren't very imaginative, but that was hardly the point. She took one of the bright yellow ponchos, of the sort that came in little plastic packets and are always sold at the seaside, for when one forgets one's jacket in the ever-fickle British summer, and pulled it on. Priya handed her a large purple cowboy hat and she set it on her head, taking a deep breath to settle herself. Then she looked at the others, all decked out in their own yellow ponchos and a mishmash of hats and headdresses – Rose was wearing some sort of Little Bo Peep bonnet, and Gert had a towering, pale blue wig that was in danger of flying off every time she turned her head.

"Alright," Miriam said. "Here we go." She took a deep breath and marched up to the gate, pushing the intercom button. It was answered almost immediately, making her sure they'd already been seen on the ever-present security cameras somewhere.

"Hello?" an unfamiliar woman's voice said.

"We'd like to speak to Lachlan Jameson," Miriam said, as firmly as she could.

"He's not available."

"We're not going anywhere until he speaks to us. We know it's him destroying our waters, and we're not standing for it!" Miriam was startled to find her voice raising entirely of its own accord. "He can't just come in here and devastate our village just because he wants to! Damaging wildlife habitats! I have a hedgehog hibernating in my airing cupboard!"

"Good for you," the woman said. "He's still not available."

"Well, we gave you a chance," Miriam said.

"We've called the police," the woman replied. "So this is *your* chance. Off you toddle."

Miriam thought she probably could have been scared off by the threat of the police if it hadn't been for that condescending *off you toddle*. Instead she turned around, lifting a megaphone to shout, "We want water! *We want water!*"

"*We want water!*" the W.I. roared back. "*We want water!*" They began to march in a circle, around the cars parked in the road, up to the gate and back, bouncing their placards and blowing plastic party horns and metal whistles between their shouts. "*We want water!*"

Ten minutes later they were still circling, and Rose swung close enough to Miriam to say, "Have we been going long enough yet? My arms are starting to hurt."

"Time for shifts," Alice said from behind them, and raised her voice. "Three at a time in the back of the van for a break."

"Finally!" Pearl said. "I think I have a stone in my shoe."

"Hot drinks!" Rosemary called. "Everyone hydrate!"

"Is this going to work?" Miriam asked, as they kept walking. Everyone's enthusiasm for the horns had faded somewhat, although Rose was keeping up a steady rhythm of whistling on every second step, which Angelus replied to with a watery howl.

"It's a good distraction," Alice said. "They'll be watching this rather than anything else."

"We can't be sure of that," Miriam said. "And if the wall's alarmed, how do we get over it?"

"Distraction," Alice replied, and walked on.

Miriam had to admit that the next step really was quite simple. No one came to the gate to observe them or move them on, Lachlan apparently assuming that if he ignored them for long enough, they'd go away. That, or he was waiting for either the police or his own personal army to turn up. Miriam thought the latter was quite possible. But by the time she and Alice took a break in the van, no armed heavies or exasperated police had arrived to chase them off.

In the cover of the van, she struggled out of her poncho and handed her cowboy hat to Priya, who settled the hat on her own head, handing over a heavy, unfamiliar jacket that smelled faintly of fish. It had a camouflage pattern on it, and was so large Miriam had to roll the sleeves up twice. Alice was already dressed in a rather better-fitting jacket in a nondescript green, her cane in her hand.

"Ready?" she asked, doing up the chest strap on a compact black backpack.

"I suppose," Miriam said.

"Come on, then." Alice slid open the van's side door, which faced away from the retreat, and Miriam followed her as she slipped out, the day ringing with horns and whistles and the cheery shouts of the ladies, which had changed to simply, "*Wa-ter! Wa-ter!*" Rose sounded like she might be shouting something slightly different and possibly directed at Lachlan, though.

They'd stopped in such a way that the two cars parked ahead of the van gave them enough cover to get to the big wall that encircled the garden, cutting off the retreat building's view of the road. They hurried toward it, heads down, Miriam's heart beating far too fast. And they hadn't even *done* anything yet. They were still on a public road. She suddenly wished she'd had a little more cordial.

Once they were in the shelter of the high wall, new trees blooming above the stone, Alice led the way down the lane toward where the forest took over from the retreat's garden, walking fast with her cane tapping the tarmac lightly. Miriam hurried after her, wondering if they'd been seen. She supposed it didn't matter too much. There was no way they were going to get away with this entirely. They were going to be seen at *some* point, it was just a question of when.

Not far from the lay-by where they'd met the dragons the day before – and didn't that seem like so much longer ago! – Alice found a narrow stone stile on the forest side of the road. It wasn't much more than a couple of longer slabs of slate trapped in the stone, sticking out to either side of the wall and offering a rudimentary step to clamber over. It was broken and unused, and Miriam had the sense it begrudged allowing anyone to pass.

Alice looked at her. "You'll have to go over first. I may need a hand to get down on the other side."

She spoke cheerily, but Miriam could feel the frustration on her, that she could no longer trust her body to do what she expected of it. So she didn't argue, even though she wasn't sure she wanted to be first into the forest, dark and dripping beyond the wall, and pressing so close to it she wondered how there'd even be space on the other side. She could feel the unfriendliness of the repelling charms in a way she never had before, like a glowering stranger or a *Beware of the Dog* sign, and she wondered if they'd changed somehow, or it was just knowing that the dryad regarded them with such enmity. This was the edges still, the places where old paths lingered, for all they were overgrown and unused. It shouldn't have felt so *hostile*. As if branches were waiting to fall, or the ground to yawn underfoot, the way the sink-holes had in the village.

But Alice was looking at her expectantly, so she put a hand on the cold stone, half expecting it to throw her back. It didn't, though, and she clambered up the stile, a little clumsy in her spare wellies that were a size too big, and the constriction of her borrowed waterproof trousers, the same colour as the jacket and just as baggy, but terribly un-stretchy. She stopped at the top, peering into the shadows, and said, "I rather hoped the dragons would be here."

"We really must come up with a decent way to communicate with them at some stage," Alice said. "One evidently can't rely on the cat to be around to carry messages when one needs him."

"Mortimer and I did talk about mobile phones," Miriam said. "But talons and screens seemed like a bad combination."

"No pockets to carry them, either," Alice said thoughtfully, then shook her head. "We can worry about such things later. Shall we go?"

"Yes," Miriam said, but still didn't move.

"Miriam?"

"It feels very unfriendly," she said softly. "It doesn't want us to go in."

"I imagine not. But we're not going to get to the bottom of things otherwise."

"But can we even do that? Are we going to be able to get anywhere near the retreat? There must be cameras everywhere."

Alice nodded. "Undoubtedly. But Lachlan won't be keen to take on all of us, and we're definitely not going to find out anything from here."

"But *Nellie.* How could he have captured a sprite? How would he *know* about a sprite?"

"I don't know," Alice admitted. "And it may well not be the truth of the matter. But either way we need to figure it out."

"Lachlan didn't feel like he'd know about this sort of thing," Miriam said.

Alice regarded her curiously. "And you can always tell?"

Miriam thought about it, then shook her head. "No. I mean, DI Adams just feels sort of scary and efficient, and not at all perceptive, except in that awful police way where you know she notices *everything*. But she can see Dandy. *I* can't even see Dandy."

"Well, there we go, then," Alice said. "Evidently it takes all sorts. But I leave it to you as to whether we go into the woods. You're much better at these things than I am."

"What? At breaking into places? I'm *terrible* at breaking into places."

Alice smiled. "Not breaking into places, dear. Feeling things. How unfriendly is the forest? Is it safe?"

Miriam hesitated for a moment, peering into the damp, dripping tangle of trees with its scents of moss and loss, then finally nodded. "I think we can. We probably shouldn't go too far, though. And definitely not off the path."

"Well, then," Alice said. "Let's try it."

So Miriam did. The stile was very skinny at the top, nothing more than a gap where a couple of the vertical topping stones had been removed. It was barely wide enough to squeeze her calves through, and so high she got her hair tangled in an overhanging branch as she clambered over it in an uncomfortable crouch. The stones were slippery with rain and encroached on by a bramble that snagged her hand, making her yelp. She stared at the blood beading on the surface of her skin, then looked at the forest almost fearfully.

"I'm sorry," she said. "We're trying to help. Honest." There was no response, although the shadows felt deeper, if that were possible, the whispers of the branches more ominous. There wasn't much wind, the rain falling more and more insistently, and as she clambered down on the other side the ground was treacherous underfoot. "Sorry," she said again. "We really do want to help. We're trying to make sure you don't end up with people just popping up about the place, because that would be terrible. Nobody needs people appearing and disappearing all over. It'd be like having fleas or something, only worse."

"Miriam," Alice said from the top of the stile.

Miriam swallowed. "Sorry. I'm a bit nervous."

"Yes, I noticed." Alice reached out a hand, and Miriam grabbed it quickly. The older woman barely put any weight on her as she climbed down, but Miriam thought that was the way support worked best. It was always about being there in case one was needed, not because the need was already there.

Alice tapped the ground with her cane, looking along the wall in the direction of the retreat. "Off we go, then."

They followed a vestigial trail at the base of the wall which looked more as if it had been made by foxes and rabbits than by human feet, and Miriam wondered when the last time was that anyone had walked along here who wasn't animal or Folk. The trees pressed more and more tightly over the path, until they found themselves having to duck and wriggle through tight spots, more brambles clutching and tugging at their raincoats and trousers, while unseasonably persistent nettles slapped insolently at their hands. It was slow going, but they made steady enough progress until Alice made a small noise and stopped abruptly, taking a step back and bumping into Miriam.

"What is it?" Miriam demanded. "*Who* is it?" Her heart thrummed in her ears, and she couldn't stop peering into the trees, as if expecting something to come charging out at them. She wasn't sure what she thought that might be, of course. It wasn't like there were going to be bears, or wolves, or wild boar, or even emus in here. The worst there might be was a badger, and she felt fairly confident that a badger wasn't going to come rushing out and attack them. Although one never knew, of course. She hadn't expected attack ducks, either.

"It's just a stream," Alice said. "It's rather slippery, though."

"Do be careful."

Alice picked her way forward, taking her time and testing each step with her cane. The steam that barred their way wasn't big, emerging from under the wall and swelling out across the rocks and roots in a shallow, swift-flowing sheet. The ground around it was wet and deeply soggy, and Alice's practical hiking boots were sinking almost up to the ankle. She started out as close to the wall as she could, but rather than finding rocks and harder ground there, her feet sank in deeper with every step. She stopped again and stepped back, using the wall for support and pulling her front foot free with some effort. She tried again a little further from the wall, but she only got bogged down more quickly, and this time Miriam had to grab her arm to help her back to firmer land.

"Let me try," she said, edging around Alice.

"Maybe a little further into the trees," Alice suggested.

Miriam gave the woods a dubious look. "I don't think they're going to like that," she said, but she shuffled a little further in anyway, and took a careful step over the muddy, rushing waters. Her welly sank in deeply, all the way up to the ankle, then found fairly solid ground. "That seems okay," she said, and gingerly took another step.

For a moment she thought she was stable, then whatever she'd stood on simply melted away, leaving her foot moving inexorably deeper. She squeaked and pulled back, and her front foot popped straight out of the welly. She wobbled on the edge of balance, one socked foot waving in the air, and, with all her weight now on it, her back foot started sinking too.

"Careful, Miriam!" Alice said. "Grab my cane." She was standing well back, where she was sure the ground was trustworthy, and Miriam tried to sway toward her, but the soft mud had her off balance. Her wobbles grew more pronounced, and she flailed with both hands and her free foot, then pitched sideways. She managed to get her foot down, but it plunged straight in until she was up to her knee, and she simply kept toppling. Her standing foot flew free of her surviving welly, and she splashed into the mud on her side, one outstretched hand plunging past tangled roots and scratchy little rocks, on and on as if it'd never stop. Water rushed up her trousers and into her jacket, and her yelp turned into a splutter of muddy water.

"Miriam!" Alice exclaimed.

"Stay back!" Miriam yelled. *"Don't get caught! It's quicksand!"* She rolled violently away from her submerged arm, flinging her free arm and leg wide and starfish-ing herself in the frigid water. Her heart pounded wildly, black dots swinging in her vision, and water lapped at her thighs and around her neck as the ground sank away beneath her. She stared at the winter sky where it met the reaching limbs of the trees, and wondered if she'd end up like those prehistoric bodies people found entombed in bogs, where researchers could look at them and discover things about lost civilisations. She hoped she'd be useful to science, at least. Although what the scientists would make of her waterproof trousers and the crocheted flower she still had pinned to the jumper underneath her jacket, she didn't know.

Alice shouted something, but Miriam had mud in her ears due to the inescapable grip of the quicksand, and she lifted her head to wave a sorrowful farewell. Three large goose heads, attached to three large geese with churning wings and pounding feet, filled her vision, and she exploded out of the mud like a geyser had erupted beneath her, trying to break into a run. Her hearing cleared, and now she could hear Alice shouting, "*Get out of it! Out!*" as she swiped at the geese with her cane. But Miriam barely registered that, because her surge to get up had sent her pitching forward, legs too slow to free themselves. She hit the muddy ground on her belly with both arms outstretched, slick jacket turning her into a missile as she shot down a gentle slope into the trees under her own momentum, adding a shriek of alarm to the commotion, and not even having time to appreciate not needing to donate herself to science just yet.

18
ALICE

Alice had been hard-pressed to keep her laughter in check when Miriam ended up spreadeagled in the mud, apparently so overcome with the idea of quicksand that she'd given up all hope of survival. Once she realised Miriam was alright, of course. She wasn't so harsh as to laugh at someone who had actually hurt themselves. Not if she liked the someone in question, at least. But then the geese came swooping down from the wall, aiming straight for the beatifically awash Miriam, and she waved at them furiously.

"Shoo! No! *No!*"

The birds ignored her entirely, crashing to the ground and splashing toward Miriam in a chorus of wild hissing, necks snaking furiously. Miriam's gaze, trained peacefully on the trees, jerked toward the geese, and she surged up and out of the mud like a monster in a very cheap horror movie, showering water and debris everywhere as Alice shouted, "*Get out of it! Out!*"

Miriam's feet were still mired in the mud, and she belly-flopped back to the ground with a screech of alarm, arms outstretched as if she were channelling superman. There was a slope here, more so than Alice had realised, and she watched in astonishment as Miriam slid straight through the trees and out of sight, still shrieking. The geese were screaming too, and had been joined by half a dozen others that had alighted on the wall. There were a few swans as well, all of them eyeing up Alice hungrily.

She ignored them. "*Miriam!* Miriam, are you alright?"

The shrieking had trailed off, and now there was only the cacophony of the birds.

"*Hush,*" she said, shaking her cane at them pointedly. "Behave." To her astonishment, they quieted, and in the near-silence she couldn't hear anything from the trees. "Miriam!" She picked her way toward where the other woman had disappeared, testing the ground ahead of her with as much patience as she could muster. It was no good both of them falling. "Miriam, answer me!"

The ground was slippery, but the further she got from the wall the firmer it seemed, and she was able to work her way carefully along Miriam's path, checking on the birds from time to time. They'd crashed down to the ground and were following her, but the cane seemed to be persuading them they were better to keep their distance.

Alice arrived at a row of oddly uniform trees, the trunks slim and the ground below them tangled with undergrowth. She frowned. Some of the trees looked a little precarious, leaning unsteadily, but the scrubby brush at their bases seemed to be stuck firmly in place. A slick path of water and mud ran between two trunks, and there was a Miriam-shaped gap torn through the undergrowth.

"Miriam!" Alice shouted again. "Can you hear me?"

"I'm here," a shout came back. "I'm okay."

Alice pressed her free hand to her chest just briefly, then bent to peer through the gap. She couldn't see anything but more mud and trees, and the slope carrying on. "Are you stuck?"

"Not exactly." Miriam sounded distracted, and Alice frowned.

"Do you need help?"

"It's a bit slippery, but if you can get through, I think you should see this."

Well, that sounded promising. Or ominous, but Alice preferred the former. She stuck her cane in the mud so that it stood up on its own and tugged at the bushes where Miriam had vanished. It looked terribly slick and even more steep on the other side, and she called, "Is there a better way down? I don't fancy your technique."

There was some splashing below, then Miriam shouted, "Go to the left of the gap. My left, I mean. Your right. It looks a little more gentle there."

Alice retrieved her cane and worked her way along the trees, which carried on in that strangely uniform line, the undergrowth still filling the gaps between their trunks, and where the ground seemed fairly stable she stopped, inspecting the odd growths of bush. She hesitated, then reached down and grabbed a branch, giving it a brisk tug. An entire clump of wood and leaves the size of a goose (since that seemed to be a good unit of reference at the moment) came away in her hand, and she stared at it suspiciously. It was organic, as far as she could tell, but it hadn't been attached to anything. She supposed it could be debris that had caught among the trunks, but when another clump of almost exactly the same size and shape came loose, she dismissed that idea. She poked one of the trees, but again, it was wood. It swayed slightly when she touched it, though, so either it hadn't been planted here for long enough to get a good grip on the earth, or there were no roots under it at all.

But it was hardly important right now. Watched by the birds, who were still tailing her, she pulled some more of the filler away then climbed carefully through the gap, finding herself on a bank above a large, dirty pond. It extended away to either side of the trees Alice had come through, and she spied more of the same regimented plantings on the bank to the far side, and circling all the way around it. There was no mistaking the mix of trunks and brush for what it was, once one was on this side. It was a hide, but a dreadfully oversized one, and rather than concealing a hunter or two, it was the pond it was hiding.

Not that she could see anything special about it. It was rectangular and brutally symmetrical, and a couple of good-sized cars could have fit in it quite easily, nose to tail. The sides were fresh, dark earth, the sheared ends of roots visible like bones in the raw walls. The water was a murky shade of brown, with bits of broken branches and twigs and old leaves bobbing in it serenely, but there were no reeds at the edges, no water plants at all. A faintly noisome scent rose from the surface, as of old water left rotting in buckets. It scratched at the back of her throat.

Miriam was still in the water, which was up to her waist, and was circling the edge with her head down, raising a trail of darker sediment which rolled in her wake, intensifying the smell. Her face wrinkled with distaste as she looked at Alice. "Isn't it awful?"

"It is. Do you not want to get out? You might catch something."

"I was hoping I might stumble on something on the bottom. A ... a shoe, or something."

Alice looked at Miriam's set, pale face and at the murky water, and said, "Come out, Miriam."

'But there might be—"

"I know. But you don't want to stumble on that."

Miriam looked down. "I don't. But ..."

"We shall tell DI Adams. Come on." She edged her way carefully around the pond as Miriam peered dubiously at the bank. It was higher than her head, and there was nothing to help her climb out. Alice got to the closest point, hooked one arm around a tree, and extended the cane to Miriam. "Here we go."

"I'll pull you in."

"You won't."

Miriam made a doubtful noise, but she grabbed the end of the cane in both hands, clutching it to help her walk her feet up the wall, bottom sticking out as she tried to get traction on the fragile earth. She was barely halfway up when her feet lost their grip and her hands slipped, sending her splashing back into the water with a yelp. She vanished under the surface before bobbing back up. *"Ew!"* she gasped, spluttering stale water. "Oh, I *swallowed* some!"

"You had some of Gert's cordial. That'll kill anything," Alice said, as reassuringly as she could. The cane wasn't going to work, and she could already see Miriam shivering, her teeth chattering in the cold. She swung her pack off her shoulders, opening it quickly. The coil of rope was at the bottom, not heavy, just a useful weight and length for everything from tethering rogue livestock to strapping Christmas trees to cars. And also for impromptu climbs. She looped it around the base of a more solid tree beyond the hide, then threw one end to Miriam. She grabbed it, looking at Alice dubiously.

"It's very thin."

"It's more than strong enough." Alice sat down on the ground with her back to the pond, her feet braced against the tree trunk and the rope running from Miriam, around the tree, and back to her in a U. "Tie it under your shoulders."

"I'm not very good with knots—"

"Quickly, Miriam."

Miriam was silent for a moment, concentrating, then she said, "Okay?"

"Start climbing. Help me as much as you can." Alice leaned back, pulling the rope in smoothly hand over hand, the friction on the trunk making progress slow and difficult, but the angle meaning she had more purchase to take Miriam's weight. The rope jerked and bounced a couple of times, accompanied by some startled squeals from the younger woman, then Miriam called, "I made it! I'm here!"

The weight came off the rope entirely, and Alice eased her grip, turning to see Miriam sprawled on her belly on the bank, clawing her way to more secure ground as the edge crumbled under her legs. She made it clear and rolled to a seated position, grinning at Alice with purple lips. "We did it!"

Alice grabbed the pack and found a survival blanket in a packet. "Jacket off," she said, ripping it open.

"I don't feel—"

"Jacket off."

Miriam subsided, fumbling at the zip with clumsy fingers until Alice helped her, pushing the coat off and wrapping her in the blanket. "Wool?" she asked, nodding at the jumper.

"Yes. And my undershirt, too."

"Well done." She found a flask in a side pocket of the pack and took the lid off, handing it to Miriam. "Have a swig."

Miriam did, then promptly burst out coughing and wheezing. Alice patted her on the back gently.

"There we go. Now let's get back to the van and get you warmed up."

"No, we need to—"

"We don't. You'll freeze. And did you see the pipes?" Alice pointed at the set of fat, ugly plastic tubes that emerged from a large drainage pipe, spilling more dirty water into the pond. "I'll take a couple of photos and we can send them to DI Adams. Lachlan won't have permission for this, and in combination with the flooding, the police will have to do something." Not that it was going to be quick enough to help their missing people, but Miriam was her concern right now. The rest would have to wait. Alice stepped a little closer to the bank, taking out her phone.

She had it aimed at the pipes, zooming in to take a more detailed shot, when the geese burst off the far side of the pond, where they'd been waiting while the two women extricated themselves. They circled the water in tight, enraged turns, barely avoiding crashing into each other, and Miriam choked on another mouthful of the whisky. One bird plunged straight at Alice, and she stumbled back, almost falling. She dropped the phone, and it spun across the wet grass.

"No—" she started, grabbing for it, but it flipped neatly off the edge into the water. "Oh, *damn.*" She turned to the birds, raising a hand to protect herself, but they were surging back to the other side of the pond, where they crashed to the bank and charged through the fence of trees, heading toward the wall. Someone swore, and Alice hurried back to Miriam. "Someone's coming."

Miriam scrambled to her feet, face pale, and Alice snatched the pack in one hand and her cane in the other, hurrying out of the hide and into the trees, dragging the rope with them. The undergrowth was heavy, making it hard to move quickly and quietly at the same time, but the birds were setting up such a cacophony it hardly mattered. They didn't go far, the old growth clustering around them once the hide was left behind, and Alice pulled Miriam into the shelter of a fallen, twisted trunk, helping her tuck her jacket over the survival blanket. Then they were still, waiting, the clamour of the birds still ringing beyond the pond.

A gunshot went off, a snarl of sound, and Miriam clapped a hand over her mouth, staring at Alice fearfully. Alice put a finger to her lips, peering toward the hide as the sound of the birds retreated rapidly. The forest fell into silence again, other than the chatter of tumbling water.

Then underbrush crackled on the far side of the pond, carrying easily to them in the rain-spattered stillness, and someone swore, the startled exclamation of a slip or a stumble. It was quiet for a moment before someone said, "Niall?"

That was Lachlan, Alice was sure of it. She crept out of shelter, shaking Miriam off gently when the younger woman caught her arm, and sidled close enough to the hide that she could glimpse someone through a gap in the undergrowth. Sure enough, Lachlan was on the other side of the pond, his phone in his hand.

"Someone's been here," he said. "Did you see them on the cameras?"

Niall's voice came from the phone's speaker, low but clear. "Sorry, no. They must've come around from the road."

"Is it the W.I. lot? It must be, right?"

"I suppose? There were ten here at the start, but they're taking breaks in the van and swapping around. We can't get a proper count on them."

"Well, try. This is the last thing we need. The bank here's all kicked up, so they've been in the water, maybe taken samples. How the hell did they even find it?"

"They can't know—"

"They don't need to know the details, do they? If they drag some bloody independent environmental expert out here it's going to blow the whole thing up."

Niall didn't answer straight away, and Lachlan clicked his tongue irritably.

"*Well?*" he demanded.

"Um ..." Niall rallied, his voice coming back firmer. "We go on the attack. The water bottling plant's been damaged, and the protesters are likely the culprits. We're prepared to be generous and not press charges, but only if they drop everything. We even take out restraining orders, and in the meantime we clear out everything but the bottling machinery. Stash it until this all blows over. Any run-off is down to the rain."

"*Hmm.* Doesn't help us right now, though. We're still short. The whole point was not having to buy any in from overseas."

"We can delay production."

"We can't. First batch of electric cars with all components built in the UK? We can't afford to have it behind schedule."

"We top up from overseas suppliers on the quiet?"

"No." Lachlan's voice was flat. "Someone'll sniff it out. If I can track down this other spring from the map we should be able to get running again with clean water, and we'll still make the schedule. Call our contact again, ask what the hell we're paying her for if we can't get police out here when we need them, then see if you can track down whoever's out here."

"Got it."

Alice glanced back at Miriam, who stared at her with wide eyes.

"Bloody mess," Lachlan said to his phone. "You said you could handle this."

"It'll be fine," Niall said, his voice slightly breathless. "The W.I. are on the outs in the village already. We'll start supplying water again tomorrow, once everyone's had a chance to get a bit twitchy. Contingent on them keeping their noses out, of course. I'll sort it."

"You'd bloody better. I'm paying you to stop these issues before they happen." Lachlan tapped the phone, squinting at it as he swiped through a couple of screens, then nodded and put it back in his pocket, turning to clamber back up toward the wall. A moment later Alice heard him yell, and the clamour of the birds.

She went back to Miriam, taking the whisky from her and having a sip before passing it back again. "One more."

Miriam grimaced, but had a sip anyway, not shuddering as much this time. "What do we do? Follow him?"

"No," Alice said thoughtfully. "He's out of the way for now. We need to get in and find out what they're actually doing, what's been causing the damage, before they clear away all the evidence."

"We're just going to walk in?"

She looked at her watch. "Gert'll be starting the diversion any moment."

"That's a yes, then, isn't it?"

"Yes," Alice agreed, and Miriam took a final swig of whisky before handing the flask back.

"Alright," she said. "At least it didn't sound like he knew about Nellie."

Alice wasn't sure if that was a good thing or not, since it meant they might now have two issues – Lachlan's mysterious water-based project, and Nellie's backlash against it. Either of them could be responsible for the vanishing people, and there was no telling which. But right now they needed to move before Miriam got any colder. For the moment the blueness had left the younger woman's lips, leaving behind a hectic flush in her cheeks, which was an improvement. The whisky on top of the elderflower cordial was probably not going to be a good combination later, but a little liquid courage could be surprisingly useful.

The woods seemed to be empty again, and Alice said, "Off we go, then." She led the way around the hide, skirting its borders and climbing the bank toward the wall that bordered the retreat's garden. It was harder work climbing back up than the adrenaline-spiked scramble down had been, but they clung to the trees and each other, slipping and sliding but never quite falling, and eventually fought their way to the wall a little further along from where they'd left it.

Alice had been expecting to have to keep walking, to find a stile, or an overhanging tree that she could employ with her rope to give them a helping hand, but when they struggled through the last of the undergrowth they found a smart aluminium ladder straddling the wall.

"How considerate," Alice said, giving it a little shake. Locking cross-bars held it firmly in its A-frame, and while its feet were sunk deeply into the sodden ground, it seemed stable.

Miriam looked at it suspiciously. "Is it a trap?"

Alice managed not to say *it's a ladder,* but only just. She was spending too much time around the currently missing cat. He was a terrible influence, and now these little comments would insist on jumping out. Plus his taste for organic fish was doing equally terrible things to her grocery bill. She gave the ladder another shake, then carefully climbed it far enough to peek into the garden beyond, the wall to the field on their right and the one to the road on the left, both of them visible only as glimpses beyond the sculpted, multilevel flower-beds and decorative shrubs. Directly ahead, the main building was almost hidden behind the vegetation. She had a strong suspicion she was likely already on camera, even if the alarms for the wall had been disengaged to allow Lachlan to leave, but there was no helping that. From the front of the building she could hear a persistent chorus of whistles and horns, so evidently the W.I. were still in full swing.

She manoeuvred herself carefully over the top of the ladder and down the other side, the metal cold under her fingers, and Miriam followed a little more quickly, the survival blanket rustling under her jacket. She glared at the garden. "Terrible planting, too. Who puts cosmos with roses?"

"Come on," Alice said. "Let's go."

They were halfway up the rain-drenched garden with its wilting edges when Niall came running toward them, his hair dishevelled and his well-fitted jumper stretched at the neck. "What're you *doing?*" he demanded. "What's happening here?"

"We could ask you the same thing," Miriam said, and before Alice could step in Teresa came charging across the garden, waving a bright green top hat in one hand.

"Free the waters!" she yelled. *"Water waters!"*

Only it wasn't quite *water waters,* as Rose's changes had evidently stuck. Niall swung around to look at her, and Teresa hurled an egg and cress sandwich at him. He ducked, and it hit Miriam.

"Hey!"

"Sorry! *Run!*" She galloped off at an easy pace, and Miriam and Alice looked at each other.

"I can't run," Alice said.

"Don't you *dare* run!" Niall shouted, jabbing a finger at her. "The police are on their way!"

"I shall walk," Alice said, heading for the main building.

"*Stop,*" Niall said, grabbing her shoulder, and Miriam pulled him away.

"Don't you touch her! That's assault!"

He looked horrified, then glanced from Miriam's face to her hand. "So's that!"

Alice ignored them both and kept going, thinking she should encourage Miriam to drink more whisky. She wasn't worried about Niall trying to physically stop her. He might be a fixer for Lachlan, but she doubted he was the sort of person who'd attack a woman of a certain age. The security guards she wasn't so sure about, but as long as the rest of the W.I. were keeping them occupied, she should have time to get inside and make herself scarce.

And from the sounds of the shouting, the W.I. were doing an excellent job of that.

19
MORTIMER

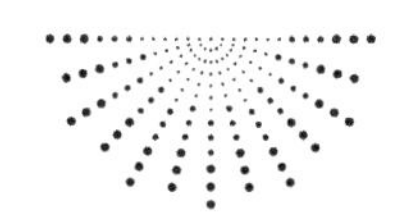

"No," Daphne said, her gnarled arms folded and the mossy strands of her hair swinging softly.

"But the waters are affecting your trees," Beaufort pointed out.

"Beaufort, Margery has already discussed this with me," Daphne said. "The water situation's unfortunate, yes, but the heart of the forest is safe for now. The humans have been nibbling at the edges, little worms that they are, but the true old woods remain. I'm not risking that by letting you paw around, disturbing the waters."

"The heart won't stay safe forever," the High Lord said. "Not if the Source is affected. If we don't fix this, the pollution will spread. Roots will rot. Trees will fall. It will be the end for all of us. You told us that yourself."

Daphne looked at Lord Margery, who was sitting in the clearing with her head high and her wings angled to keep the rain off her head. Her scales gleamed purple and copper, and every line of her was so deeply *dragon* that Mortimer tucked his patchy tail out of sight under his paws. Not that it helped with the fact that he was a dull, stressed grey, and his talons were chipped and scarred from the workshop.

"Daphne is free to protect her woods as she sees fit, Beaufort,"

Margery said. "You're talking about diverting the water to protect the *village*. That's nothing to do with the Source."

"All waters are connected," Beaufort said, and Margery snorted.

"Sure. Not everyone's priority is your little human pets, you know. Some of us have bigger things to worry about."

"Bigger things than the whole valley sinking?" Amelia demanded. "The land's *crumbling.* It's not just the humans that are going to lose their homes. This will affect *all* of us."

"Life has its rhythms," Daphne said. "Spring follows winter. Storms follow drought. Little dragons without the perspective to see might not understand this, but some of us have been around long enough to know nothing is permanent. All ground is shaky. All foundations fall. Even the strongest tree rots eventually." There was a soft, sing-song tone to her words that would've been soothing if not for the resignation that accompanied it. "Maybe the time of Toot Hansell is done. Maybe something new will rise in its place, or maybe all will sink beneath the waters, and we will move on."

"Absolutely not," Amelia snapped. "You think we're so powerless? Even dormice protect themselves against the winter, and birds fly south, and squirrels hide nuts, and trees put out new shoots. Nothing just *gives up*."

Daphne waved vaguely, and scratched her arm, where the peeling patch of bark had spread, revealing more raw skin underneath. "You're too young to understand that sometimes we must just let things happen. Go and play with your baubles, little dragon. Dance with your humans while you can."

Amelia looked as if she were about to choke on the tumble of words that tried to come out all at once, flushing an infuriated puce that was so deep she was flashing with stripes of purple like an alarm. She started toward the dryad. "You— You're just— How can— *You mossy little half-rotten stump of lichen-encrusted—"*

Mortimer flung himself forward and wrapped both forelegs around Amelia's neck, cutting her off and clutching her tightly in place as he babbled, "She doesn't mean it, she's just upset, it's the stress—"

"I do mean it and yes I'm upset and if you don't get your paws off me I'll take your talons and—"

"Gods, control your groupies, can't you, Beaufort?" Margery demanded, and Amelia threw Mortimer off.

"You sour old human-phobic, species-ist, posing—"

"Amelia," Beaufort said, not raising his voice, but his tone sharp. "That's enough."

The young dragon jabbed a paw at Margery and Daphne. "They don't *care.* Margery just wants to be High Lord, and she's politicking about the place, pandering to all the old, scared dragons who don't want anything to ever change, even though it *has,* and it *has to.* Daphne's got tree rot that's gone to her brain or something—"

"How rude. This is an allergic reaction."

Amelia ignored her. "—and we're all standing here pretending to care, when if we *really* cared, not just about Toot Hansell, but about Nellie and everything, we'd *do* something!"

"Another one spending too much time around humans," Margery said. "Her and her strange little brother both."

Amelia spun toward her, and Mortimer surprised himself by stepping forward and saying, "He's not *strange."*

Margery raised her eyebrow ridges. "The little grey shadow has an opinion of his own? A voice? Shocking."

"You're the one being shocking," he said, wondering who on *earth* was talking like this to *Lord Margery,* because it couldn't possibly be him. "What's wrong with you, that rather than stepping up to make things better you'll sit here picking on Amelia for actually caring about something other than old ways and old Folk? And being rude about Gilbert who cares so much it's *impossible,* but it's also wonderful, and I don't understand him at all, I mean *ever,* but he's going to do more to help dragons and Folk survive in this world than all your hiding and stubbornness ever will. This is *not* five hundred years ago, or even a hundred. *Everything's* different, and you're just scared because you don't understand it." He pointed at Amelia. "She and Gilbert do. So stop being so ... so *old."*

Margery's chest had been slowly brightening to a volcanic red, a vast heat building in it, her wings dropping toward her back as her head lowered. Raindrops steamed on her neck and chest, and her voice rumbled with fury as she rose to all fours with a terrible, slow deliberation. "You two cubs best make your apologies to me *and* Daphne. Don't think I can't take you apart. I'll take *pleasure* in it. Though you can't even *fight,*" she added, almost spitting the word at Mortimer.

He managed not to collapse in fright, still standing between her and Amelia with his joints feeling like they'd been replaced with mashed potatoes. And not the nice sort, either. He tried to say something, and the words failed in his suddenly dry mouth.

"I'll fight you," Amelia said, her wings pulled back and her teeth bared. "I'll fight any one of you old bullies."

"No one's fighting anyone," Beaufort said, and Margery rounded on him, actually taking a couple of steps forward as if she were going to attack him then and there.

"No? Why not? Maybe it's time we had it out, Beaufort. Settle things the old way, without your ridiculous *democracy*."

"No one's fighting," he repeated, and she snarled at him, her teeth long and raw and flame licking around her jaws.

"You don't get to just *decide*." Her muscles were coiled springs, her tail twisting and curling behind her like a creature in its own right, her chest incandescent with heat. Beaufort merely regarded her with an odd mix of sorrow and interest, his scales his usual rich, emerald greens and golds, still sitting back on his haunches and making no move to defend himself. Margery gathered herself, and Mortimer stumbled forward.

"Don't!" he managed, and Margery turned on him, rearing up. He braced himself for the onslaught of her flame, for teeth and talons and fury, half-raising one paw as if that was going to protect him, and something wet and solid hit the other dragon in the face with a furious hiss of steam, sending her staggering backward, spluttering little bursts of flame.

"I say," Beaufort said. "Good shot, Walter."

Walter bounced another sandbag in his paws, sitting at the edge of the spring with his scruffy scales slick with rain. "Still got one left, too. You done, Margie?"

"*Walter.* Don't tell me you've gone all soft and—"

"Don't tell me you really think this is a good time to start scrapping for leadership, when the damn county's sinking."

She huffed, touching her snout gingerly. "That *hurt.*"

"Serves you right. The hatchlings are an odd lot, but they've got the right of it." He nodded at Beaufort. "I found a way we might be able to slow the waters."

"Outside my woods, I hope," Daphne said, her arms folded. "I haven't given you permission, and I'm not going to. You're a threat to us all."

Walter huffed. "You've got humans scurrying away on your edges like mites. You can stand a few dragons. But no, I've found somewhere else."

Daphne scowled, looking at Margery and scratching the raw spot on her arm again. "Suit yourselves. Bloody bleeding-heart dragons. Never thought *that* would be a problem."

"Shouldn't be," Margery muttered.

"Can you send her home now?" Amelia asked Beaufort. "She'll probably bite someone just to spite us."

"Nice not to be accused for a change," Walter said, puffing his chest out.

Margery looked at Beaufort. "This is your choice, is it? Endanger your clan to save your pets? I thought Walter was the one going senile."

"Not so senile I can't still throw a good sandbag." Walter sounded inordinately proud.

"Save the village that saved us," Beaufort said. "And let's not forget the waters feed our tarn, and the woods. The waters die, everything dies. No waters means nothing to protect any of us, sprite or dragon or pixie or fox. We'll be exposed. One has to take a wider perspective, Margery, regardless of one's personal feelings on the matter."

She growled softly, and Walter said, "Never mind, Margie, you'll understand when you grow up a bit." He was grinning widely, his worn-down teeth yellow and jagged.

"Do it yourself, then," she said. "I'm not getting involved. And I *will* be telling everyone what's going on. See how popular your little human rescue mission is when I tell the clan you're running around in the open in the daylight, just begging to be seen."

"Oh, good, *Margie,*" Amelia spat. "Start a panic, why don't you? Some High Lord *you'd* be."

"Amelia," Beaufort said, and she shrugged.

"Just because she's old doesn't mean I have to grovel to her."

Walter huffed creaking laughter. "Come on. Waters are coming up fast in the village. If we don't do something now it'll be a moot point anyway."

Beaufort nodded at Daphne. "We will do our best to keep the waters out of your woods, too."

"*You* stay out of them," she said. "There are still places dragons are best not treading, you know."

The High Lord inclined his head, then took flight, spiralling up and out of the trees. Mortimer followed, then Amelia, and when Mortimer looked back he could see Walter lumbering after them. Margery stayed where she was, and he wondered if she really would raise the Cloverlies against them. Beaufort didn't have unequivocal support, after all. But, on the other hand, almost all the clan benefited from the bauble trade and the comforts it brought them, so she might have less support than she imagined.

They'd have to deal with that later, though. Walter had gained creaking height, and he led the way north, his tatty wings ragged at the edges and his belly hanging low and ungainly from his swayback.

"That was unexpected," Amelia called, rolling toward Mortimer until they were flying wingtip to wingtip.

"Walter? I know. I thought he'd be in Margery's camp."

"Not him. That wasn't unexpected at all. He'd raze the Houses of Parliament if it meant protecting Rose and her truffles. You."

"*Me?*"

"Absolutely," she said. "You even stopped being grey." She rolled away again, and he looked down at his chest. She was right. He was a luxuriously deep royal blue, edged with gold. Which was all very well, but it was quite an inconvenient time for it, when one was flying between green trees and grey clouds, and on the way to deal with humans. He was better off being anxious and grey, really.

❧

WALTER DROPPED LOWER and lower as they approached the edge of the forest, giving the retreat a wide berth and leading them to a field on the far side of the road. Toot Hansell's valley was losing its grip here, the road tracing the furthest limits of the lush (and currently water-logged) fields that rolled toward the village, along with the woods which swirled across part of the valley to ascend to the dragon's mount.

On the other side of the road the old forest was replaced with younger, more civilised plantings, presenting a friendlier face to walkers, but the land itself took a tougher stance, scattered with rocky outcroppings and jumbled boulders that marched up to the fells. The footpaths here were well-travelled, but even Mortimer couldn't manage to worry about it too much on a day like today.

Walter swung into the shelter of a copse and thudded heavily to the ground, his talons tearing divots out of the earth. The others followed, landing with rather more grace, and Beaufort looked around with interest.

"Even I can smell the difference here."

Mortimer didn't answer. He was too busy breathing in the scent of fresh, cold water bubbling up from a distant spring, purified by rock and age and stone. He licked his chops, abruptly thirsty.

"The water's still good," he said, and looked at Walter. "What is this place?"

The old dragon shrugged. "Harriet says if it's not the Source, it's close enough."

"*Wonderful,*" Beaufort said. "Well done, you two."

Walter shook his wings out. "She has an eye for these things."

"And for intruders," someone said, and everyone except Walter jumped. He just chuckled.

Amelia craned her neck to peer up into the trees. "Harriet? What're you doing up there?"

"Keeping watch," she said, looking down at them. She was almost as well-camouflaged as a dryad, her scales dappled and delicate.

"How's the water diversion going?" Walter asked. "Did you find a way to send it away from the village?"

"No," she said.

He made a disappointed noise. "What're you doing up there, then? Why aren't you working on it?"

"The tiddy 'uns are working on it," she said.

"Oh, that's very handy," Beaufort said. "What about Nellie?"

"They haven't seen her. Said she'd been gone for a while."

"But they were happy to help?" Beaufort asked. "Even though they left the village?"

Harriet made a thoughtful noise. "They had some strange ideas about Toot Hansell needing drowning, and not wanting to do anything to stop it. It was quite hard getting them to focus."

"So why aren't you supervising them?" Walter demanded.

"I said I'd eat them if they didn't shift their mindset. That seemed to do the trick."

"Ah," Beaufort said, while Walter stared up at Harriet with his jaw hanging open.

After a moment Harriet added, "You said it was urgent."

"I want to be her when I grow up," Amelia whispered to Mortimer.

Walter padded past Harriet's tree, muttering about loose interpretations of instructions and people thinking for themselves far too much, but Mortimer found himself marginally less alarmed by the old dragon than usual. Harriet was another matter, but she stayed behind as the rest of them followed Walter.

Not far from the copse they came to the edge of a gaping hole slashed into the land. It looked as though someone had driven a knife through the rock and twisted it when they pulled it back out, leaving a misshapen gash that was at least thirty metres deep and twice as long, its sides sheer and decorated with small plants and determined grass. A waterfall tumbled out of the rocks not far from the top of one wall, frothing to the distant bottom, and Mortimer had an idea it would normally vanish back into the earth through some secret way. Now, though, the entire yawning gap was awash in a couple of metres of desperately clear water. He could see the jumbles of hefty boulders through it, screes of smaller stone and the old bones of a luckless sheep – more than one – which gleamed on the submerged, grassy bottom, as if it were a giant fishbowl.

There was no way down that Mortimer could see, although a foot-path with a sign warning walkers of unstable ground skirted the edge, and metal rings were driven into the sides in a few places. He wondered if they were for getting sheep back up, or if humans climbed down for the fun of it. He had an idea it might be the latter. Humans were odd.

And also evidently regular visitors. This was a public place, a *human* place, and he looked around uneasily. "This can't really be the Source, can it?"

"Sometimes the best hiding places aren't hiding at all," Beaufort said, peering into the depths. "It's filling up fast."

It was, the water lapping eagerly at the sides, and faint flashes of movement marked the tiddy 'uns, shifting boulders at the bottom to block the outlet.

"We can't hold it here forever," Walter said. "What's the plan?"

Beaufort *hmm*ed. "It seems we're no closer to Nellie."

"The tiddy 'uns would know if she were anywhere in the waters," Walter said. "She has to be stuck somewhere else."

"Or hiding out," Amelia said darkly.

"Possibly," Beaufort agreed. "So we resume the search."

"Where do we start?" Walter asked.

"We'll see if we can find some scents around the retreat," the High Lord said. "It all starts from there."

"We're going *into* the retreat?" Mortimer said, thinking of the men with their guns, shooting at the geese as if they were nothing but toys.

Beaufort looked like he was considering the answer with more care than usual, then a soft, musical bird call drifted through the trees. They looked at each other, puzzled.

"Was that a blackbird?" Beaufort asked. "They don't usually sing at this time of year."

The call came again.

"It does sound like one," Mortimer said. "How odd."

This time, instead of a call, there was an exasperated, *"Incoming,"* from the path, and Amelia said, *"Ohhh."*

The dragons scattered, slipping into the undergrowth. Mortimer hunkered down behind a handy boulder, wrapping himself around it so he could peer out and see who was coming.

They didn't have long to wait. A man in sleek waterproofs appeared, staring at his phone. Lachlan, with his horrible gun broken over his arm. "This is a public footpath," he said. "We can't do much on a public bloody footpath."

Mortimer tried to peer around without moving, to see who he was speaking to, then realised it was the phone. He could almost smell the scent of plastic and money rising off the man even through the rain.

"Do you want me to call our contact on the council again?" someone on the other end of the phone said, sounding faintly breathless.

"Yes— What's happening, Niall? Is there a problem?"

"No," Niall said. "We've located the two people who were in the woods. It's that Alice and Miriam."

Mortimer's stomach rolled over, a horrible, sickening lurch.

"Good. You've contained the situation?"

"Um. Pretty much, yes."

Lachlan crouched down at the edge of the gap, hands dangling between his knees as he peered into the depths, and Harriet leaned out of the cover of a bush, seeming to simply materialise among the leaves. She mimed pushing, and Mortimer shook his head violently, until Lachlan's gaze flicked to him. Mortimer froze, pressing himself to the rock again, and the man frowned, then stood up.

"Pretty much better mean yes. This water looks good. It's got to be

the main spring – that bloody Dom lied through his teeth about our land being over the primary source."

"Do you want me to come up with a sample kit?"

"No, I've got one." Lachlan swung a pack off his back, fishing a wide-necked glass jar and some thin rope out. He tied the rope to the jar's neck a little precariously, talking as he worked. "If this is the same supply, we can bunker the water over by truck after dark until we can figure out a way to run pipes. A couple of tanks'll be enough to get what we need for now."

"I'll get a tanker booked."

"Soon as you can, Niall. Are the police on the way?" He walked to where the waterfall tumbled from the rocks and lowered the jar on its rope until it swung into the stream.

"Apparently."

"They better be. I didn't gift holidays to half the authorities in the place for nothing." He reclaimed the jar and stood up, screwing a lid onto it. "Alright, I'm on the way back." He tucked the jar into his bag, and headed for the path.

The dragons waited until they were sure the little patch of woods was empty again before emerging, and Amelia said, "It's not enough they've drowned half the village, they're going to take this too?"

"They've got Alice and Miriam," Mortimer said, ignoring Amelia. "They've *contained the situation?* What does that even mean?"

"I don't know," Beaufort said. "But we need to go. This is enough now."

"Should've let me push him," Harriet said. "Much simpler."

Mortimer was horrified to find himself half in agreement.

20
DI ADAMS

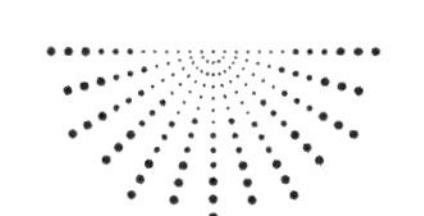

DI Adams followed Dandy as he ran across the field from Dom's land to Lachlan's, the ground wet underfoot and treacherous with soft spots and rabbit holes. There was no sign of Dom's path, the grass so wet it had just sprung up again behind him. Not that it mattered, as she knew where he'd gone, and according to the camera he hadn't come back. The only question was if he'd left a different way, or if the missing people (because she had to assume they'd been crammed into the sheep trailer) were now stashed in the retreat somewhere. In the shifting rain and the slick grass, everything was featureless, and she felt again that she was chasing ghosts. Shivers ran through the land under her now and then, not as big as the ones in the house, but enough to be unsettling.

A cluster of geese and swans milled about in the field, white smears on green grass, with the sheep eyeing them distrustfully. None moved toward her, just watched her pass with hostile eyes, like a gang waiting for a signal. She picked up the pace as Dandy looked back at her, giving the toy duck a pointed squeeze as he did so. "Yes, I'm coming."

As she drew closer to the wall that divided the farm from the retreat, a chorus of horns and whistles drifted to her, undoubtedly the peace-disturbing activities of the Toot Hansell W.I. She headed for the gate, stopping with one hand on its top to listen to the chants rising from the front of the building, a ragged chorus that seemed to be mostly built around demanding the water back. There was no one in sight, so she let herself through the gate and jogged to the outbuildings, skirting the side of the big *Sourced* barn to the back, where there was a reassuringly normal jumble of old pallets and unused bits of wood and broken tiles piled up near a garden shed. The steady rumble of machinery had quieted, so evidently Lachlan wasn't bottling today.

She hurried along the back of the building, where a white van and a few cars were parked, politely out of sight of the main retreat. No quad bike and trailer, though. The van had *Sourced* stencilled on the side, but the rest were unmarked. No one was around, so she kept going, stopping at the corner where she could see the sweep of the drive to the front of the retreat, the gate shut and a row of cars blocking the road entirely. Well. No one had got off the property that way.

Plus they'd have been hard-pushed to get past the W.I. themselves. DI Adams had expected to find the ladies parading around with signs, making a nuisance of themselves, but they'd taken it one step further. They'd invaded the property.

The gate was still shut, but that hadn't stopped anyone. Armed with the expected placards, and clad in an astonishing array of hats and headdresses, blowing whistles and wielding carrier bags, the ladies of the Toot Hansell Women's Institute had scaled the gate and taken the battle to the enemy. Gert was shouting at a startled-looking Niall, and when he tried to back away she grabbed the front of his jumper in one hand, pulling him to a halt.

"Sort this water out *now,*" she bellowed, shaking him with one hand. Given the young man's muscular shoulders, he probably could've thrown her off easily, but he merely shrank away.

"It's not … I haven't …"

A burly man with a big beard stepped forward, then yelped as he took a sandwich to the face. "*Oi!* Who threw that?"

"Not me," Pearl said, looking around innocently, despite the carrier bag dangling from one arm and the sandwich in her other hand. Martha ambled forward to eat the evidence.

"You need to get out," a woman in the same all black gear said as the bearded man said. "You're trespassing. Police are on the way."

"Water!" Priya shouted, waving a sign at them. *"Give us back our water!"*

The woman grabbed the sign, trying to wrest it off Priya. Carlotta and Rosemary promptly started bombarding her with unwrapped sandwiches and miniature pork pies.

"We have a right to protest!" Rose shouted, and when a lean man in more black gear tried to take hold of her arm Angelus surged forward, barking in great furious bellows. The man leaped back, grabbing a baton from his belt and snapping it out.

"He's armed!" Teresa yelled. *"Run!"*

"No, *stop!*" Niall shouted, but the W.I. were already scattering. Not back to the gate, of course, because that would've been sensible. No, they bolted deeper into the property, some going to the right of the retreat and some to the left, abandoning their signs but taking their bags of edible missiles, Angelus and Primrose barking in utter abandon. Gert shoved Niall away from her so hard he tripped and went down into the gravel, then she charged the bearded man. He jumped out of the way, turning to watch her barrel toward the garden with a bewildered look on his face.

"Ah – what do we do?" he asked.

"Catch them," the black-clad woman said, already running down the right side of the retreat, the lean man taking the left. *"Hey! You're trespassing!"*

"I dunno," the bearded man said to Niall as he helped him up. "That big one looks like my mum."

"She's not, though, is she?" he demanded. "Come on, before Lachlan gets back and fires us all."

They ran off, leaving Martha still munching her way happily through the debris, and DI Adams decided she didn't see much point in intervening right now. The W.I. had things in some sort of control, and she couldn't take the time to do this officially. She needed to find

Esther and the others now, or she might be too late. She looked at Dandy. "Where's Dom? Where's he put these people, then?"

Dandy squeaked the duck pointedly, then looked at the big *Sourced* outbuilding.

"You'd better not be looking for another flapjack," she told him.

He headed for the door Niall had used earlier, and she followed, spotting a phalanx of geese sneaking over the wall and into the garden. A moment later a distinctly masculine shout of alarm went up, making her wonder if Graham had been onto something with his sexist geese.

At the door she tried a quick knock and a "DI Adams, North Yorkshire Police," to give herself an air of respectability, then tested the handle. It was locked, and she scowled at the keypad. She couldn't break into that, and the big garage doors were no more helpful. She stepped back to survey the building, frowning, and the ground shuddered again. "Dandy?"

He was gone, perhaps vanished inside by his own methods, so she hurried around the back, to the van with the *Sourced* logo on it. It was open, and she dug into the console, looking for a card or a pass of some sort, but came up with nothing. She slammed the door, swearing, and the ground juddered underfoot, a more muscular shudder than previously. She braced herself against it in a sudden swell of fright, feeling as if the earth might simply melt away beneath her. A dog started barking, and a second joined in. For a moment she thought it must be Martha and Angelus, but it was coming from the wrong direction.

The barking stopped again almost immediately, and she scanned the yard, trying to pinpoint where it had come from. Lachlan had his personal quarters in a small outbuilding huddled right against the boundary wall, an all but windowless, squat structure of old stone. The roof had been recently replaced, and the door was new, all dark wood and metal.

DI Adams hurried to it, pausing to check the one window on the front, but it was tinted glass and she couldn't see in. The door was locked, and she hesitated as she stepped back, considering, then circled the building to the far side, where a large garden shed stood, the double doors not quite closed. She pulled one open, revealing a large quad bike parked on top of bags of fertiliser, which had split in places and were disgorging their contents onto the ground. She nodded, and looked at the compost heap next to the shed. It had a fancy rustic wooden enclosure, and was divided into three sections with wooden lids. She knocked on the nearest one, setting off an explosion of barking.

"Dom? Out you come."

There was a pause, then the next lid over opened, and Dom stood up, scowling. "Bloody mutts," he said to the dogs, who looked up at him, somewhat bewildered.

"Get out," she said.

He sighed. "Look, I wasn't under arrest, right? You never said I had to stay home."

She nodded. "Just enjoy hanging out in compost bins, do you?"

"This one's empty," he pointed out, still not moving.

"Where's Esther and the others?'

"No idea."

"I saw you on the camera," she said, leaving out the bit where she'd only seen the trailer, and not who or what was in it.

Dom ran a hand over his face, evidently thinking about it, then said, "*Fine*. Look, Lachlan asked me to look after them. But I knew if you found them on my property you'd blame me."

"Can't imagine why."

"But I didn't *do* anything." Dom hesitated, then the words came out in a tumble. "Okay, I mean, I looked after them, but they were *safe,* and Lachlan said he'd make it worth my while if I helped, and that it fell under my NDA anyway, so if I said anything he'd sue me and take the whole farm, and I think he might anyway, and—"

"Kidnapping was *under the NDA?*"

"Anything to do with operations on his property is covered, apparently. And it's not like I could fight his lawyers. And—"

"Okay, okay. Just get out of the bin and show me where they are."

Dom nodded, pulling his hat down more firmly over his ears and scrambled out, followed by the dogs. He led the way to the back of the *Sourced* building, to a spot on the wall where the new panels of the extension were exposed, and lifted a small flap DI Adams hadn't even seen. It revealed another of the keypads, and Dom took a card from his wallet. "I didn't kidnap anyone, though. You have to believe that. I was keeping them safe."

"Sure."

He gave her a dubious look, then pressed the card to the screen. There was a pause, a beep, and the click of a latch. A larger, door-shaped panel popped ajar, and Dom hooked the edge with his fingers, pulling it wide. There was a set of stairs behind it, heading down below the building, the walls plastered in concrete that still smelled fresh. Industrial bulbs in protective cages punctuated the walls, washing everything in cold white light, and DI Adams could see the concrete sweating, hairline cracks and larger fissures spiderwebbing across the dull grey surface. Muddy water pooled on the steps, and in places had accumulated enough to dribble down to the next. Dandy appeared next to her, panting, and Dom's dogs backed away with their teeth bared.

"Not looking too good," Dom said, nodding at the walls. "He threw it up too fast, I reckon. Kind of a sneaky build."

"Not on the planning permission, then?"

"Don't know. He tried to cover up building it by saying he was reinforcing the foundations of the barn for his equipment. I spotted it one night, though."

"One night?"

"They were working all hours, so I was keeping an eye on things." He grimaced. "Until Lachlan busted me. Again, NDA. So I couldn't tell anyone about it, even if there was anything to tell."

"What's down here?"

"Just a couple of storage rooms and some stuff to do with the bottling plant. I thought it'd be a safe spot to leave Esther and the others for now."

Looking at the cracking walls, and with the earth still shivering, DI Adams wasn't sure she agreed. She nodded at the stairs. "Let's go."

Dom clicked his fingers at the dogs, who sat immediately, then he started down the steps. DI Adams hesitated as another tremor ran through the ground. One of the cracks opened a little wider, the drips of water becoming a dribble. She didn't fancy being underground at the moment, but she couldn't just stand around out here. She headed after Dom, Dandy running ahead of her.

The stairs were wide and well-spaced, the passageway broad enough that DI Adams couldn't really call it claustrophobic. She was still happy when they reached the bottom, though, and Dom unbolted a second door, opening it onto a brightly-lit space mostly taken up with a rounded, enclosed tank. Pipes ran into it from the ceiling, and others ran out of its base into a large tunnel-like opening at the bottom of one wall, blocked off with heavy mesh. If her sense of direction was right – and she didn't feel as if she'd been turned around by the stairs – it was pointed to the woods.

She stopped on the bottom step and looked around, frowning. There were no people, no other rooms, no other doors, *nothing.* She started to retreat, grabbing for her baton, and Dom whistled, sharp and low. Fast paws skittered on the stairs directly behind her, and she didn't even have time to spin to face the dogs before they hit her, silent and solid, not snapping, simply using their weight to send her to the floor.

"Dom!" she shouted. The dogs were already bolting back up the stairs, Dandy charging in pursuit, and she rolled to her feet, lunging after them. Dom was ahead of her, though, slamming the inner door in her face. She grabbed the handle, fighting to open it, but he'd already shot the bolt to. "Dom! What the hell are you playing at?"

"I'm sorry," he said, and DI Adams wondered if she could set Dandy on him. It was tempting, but she wasn't sure how, and it wasn't going to help her get out. Invisible dogs weren't great at the Lassie routine, she'd found.

"Don't be sorry," she said. "Just open the door."

"I will. Just not yet. Lachlan needs a bit of time, right?"

"What are you, his gofer?" He didn't answer, and she softened her tone. "Look, you've assaulted a police officer, and unlawfully detained me. That's serious, Dom. But you can still come back from it. Let me out, and we can sort this."

He sighed deeply. "But then Lachlan'll sue me. He's already threatening to sue me for misrepresenting the sale, just because the land wasn't *exactly* on top of the main spring. I thought it was, or near enough."

"That seems unfair."

"It *is* unfair. But if I help him, he'll set me up for life. Buy the whole farm, give me an actual salary."

"He already went back on your deals for water, and the sheep. Do you think this'll be any different?"

"Well, I know things now. I worked out what he's doing, so I can make him stick to the deal."

DI Adams had been examining the chamber, looking for something to attack the door with, but now she paused. "What's he doing?"

"It's his run-off poisoning everything and causing the flooding."

"Run-off from what?"

He hesitated. "I can't say. Look, I'll come back. We just need some time to clean up, then you can come out and everyone can go home."

His voice was already retreating, and DI Adams shouted, "*Stop!* Dom, you do *not* want to do this."

There was no response, and she kicked the door with her sodden boot, scowling, then turned around to examine the chamber again. No new doors had materialised, but she hadn't seen the one at the top of the stairs, either. She circled the walls, patting them hopefully, but found nothing except more damp concrete. Every now and then another tremble passed through the room, and muddy water spilled from crumbling cracks and splits, small but significant. The floor was already puddled with it.

She walked over to the tunnel that carried the pipes toward the woods, taking her torch from her jacket pocket and shining the beam down it. It wasn't big enough for anyone to crawl along, unless they were skinny, determined, and happy to wriggle on their belly for as long as it took. And got past the mesh, of course. The pipes took up most of the space, the tunnel itself clearly just there to provide them passage. She prodded the mesh, but it was solid, and she was interrupted by a deep rumble from upstairs. The vibration shook the walls, and water sloshed and rushed in the pipes and tank. She looked at it mistrustfully, then flinched as a chunk of concrete fell from the ceiling. Bloody place was going to come down around her ears, but what could she do? She had no phone signal, and the radio definitely wouldn't work down here.

She tried it anyway but got no reply, so she just stood there, fingers tapping against her thighs as she wondered what to do next. Dandy whined, and she shifted her attention to him. He was standing on top of the tank, peering down between his paws.

"There you are. Fancy getting a dragon for me?"

He huffed, and pawed the tank. She stood on her tiptoes, spotting a panel standing a little proud from the tank itself. An inspection hatch, maybe? He looked at her, then pawed it again, using both front paws this time, as if he thought he could dig his way through.

"Okay, okay." She clambered onto one of the pipes so she could heft herself onto the tank next to him, hunkered down under the low ceiling.

"What?" she asked, and he whined again. She peered at the inspection hatch. It was secured with six wing nuts, and she tried one. It was tightly wound down, but she fished her multitool out of her jacket and hit it a couple of times, which got it moving. She moved from one to the other methodically, loosening each one before starting to take them off completely, doing it as much to be doing *something* as in any hope that it might lead somewhere. By the time she was on the last three nuts the seal had well and truly broken, and water was dribbling onto the top of the tank, the sloshing louder than ever beneath and the smell swampy and unpleasant. She looked at Dandy. "Sure?"

He huffed, and she looked down, then gave a yelp and scrambled backward, slipping on the rounded top and nearly tumbling off. Three pale, wrinkled fingers had emerged in the gap, clawing weakly at the edge before vanishing again.

"Bloody *hell*— Nellie?" DI Adams lunged back to attack the remaining nuts, until, with only one left, she was able to spin the hatch open, revealing nothing but murky, stinking water. For one horrifying moment she thought it wasn't even the sprite, that she'd found someone – or some*thing* – else entirely, and was about to unleash some monstrosity into her prison, then she recovered herself and plunged her arm into the tank, pawing through the water. Nothing, and nothing.

She sat up, swearing roundly and loudly as she stripped her jacket and its cargo off, then swung her legs into the tank. She had to wriggle a little to get her hips in, then she was through, the water cold enough to make her gasp, Dandy staring at her in consternation. She ducked under the surface, eyes squeezed shut, and felt her way along the underside of the top, the water gritty and harsh against her skin. Nothing. She worked her way back to the hatch by feel, took a breath of air, and tried again.

This time, her hand tangled into someone's hair, and she flinched back as her fingers slid over still skin. She grabbed what felt like a shoulder and heaved, then a current swirled out of nowhere, tumbling her over. The maybe-shoulder was pulled out of her grip, and she paddled frantically, suddenly unsure where the hatch was, or even which way was up. She forced herself to stop and drift, and bobbed in a direction that was apparently up, bumping into a hard surface, and scrabbling her way along it, trying to ignore her straining lungs. Her hand encountered air, and she grabbed the edge of the hatch, pulling herself to the surface with a gasp, staring at Dandy with wide eyes. He stared back, and this time when she ducked under she kept hold of the hatch with one hand. She reached out for where she'd lost her quarry, and found the same drifting tangle of hair. She gave up on niceties, wrapped her hand in it, and heaved.

A moment later she was working her way out of the hatch again, trying to keep hold of the unmoving sprite. She managed to get herself sat on the edge, lined Nellie's shoulders up with the gap, and heaved. The sprite was slight, and DI Adams was able to lift her out fairly easily, then slide her off the side of the tank to the floor. She jumped down and crouched next to her to check for a pulse. There was nothing, but surely those had been her fingers before? They hadn't *floated* there. Maybe sprites' pulses were in different places. She rocked back on her heels, looking around the room and wondering about that current in the water. It hadn't been Nellie, evidently.

She turned back to the sprite regretfully, wondering if it would help to put her in the recovery position, and was just in time to see Nellie uncurl like a cat, grab the inspector's hand in both of her own, and sink her teeth deep into the edge of it.

"*Ow!* Dammit, Nellie!" DI Adams wrenched her hand away, falling back onto her bum, and the sprite hissed, scuttling away into a corner. Dandy started barking, the noise deafening in the small space, and both sprite and inspector yelled, "*Shut up!*"

Dandy shut up, looking put out, and DI Adams examined her bleeding hand. "Ungrateful monster."

"*I'm* not a monster! *They're* monsters! They trapped me!" Nellie was shivering, and DI Adams looked at her more closely. The sprite's scales were dull and rough, scummed with an odd mould, and her bulbous eyes were even more staring than usual.

"Didn't have to bite me, though," DI Adams said.

"No," Nellie admitted, then turned away and retched. Dandy barked again. It was just once, short and businesslike, and he jumped off the tank, backing away from it.

"What's happening?" DI Adams asked, as the pipes started to groan, and the rumbling from above grew louder. "What the hell's that?" She looked at the hatch, still hanging from one bolt, as water started to swirl audibly in the tank. "Oh, *no*—" She launched herself forward, grabbing the hatch and trying to jam it back in place, but the water was already surging out of the gap, a thundering flood of filthy overflow, throwing the panel back and sending DI Adams staggering away as it poured onto the floor.

"Well, you're wet already," Nellie said, her voice still wobbly. "Could be worse."

The inspector wasn't sure how.

21

MIRIAM

Miriam started after Alice, and Niall grabbed her arm. "You can't," he said.

She pulled her arm away. "You're ruining our village," she said, frowning at him. "We're going to do whatever we need to."

"We're not ruining anything," he said. "We're supplying water, and supporting the local economy, and—"

"And drowning the whole place, and kidnapping people," she snapped. He flinched, and she gasped, grabbing his arm. "You know where they are!"

"I don't know what you're talking about." Niall was the one trying to pull away now, looking around the garden desperately. "You need to leave. I'll get security!"

Miriam kept hold of his arm, even though she was shaking, from cold and fright and worry all at once. "Please. You can't be happy about all this."

He wrenched his arm out of her grip. "It doesn't matter if I'm happy or not," he hissed. "It's my *job*."

"That's the most ridiculous excuse I've ever heard."

"You don't know what it's like! This is the best job *ever*. Everyone wants it!"

Miriam sniffed. "Then everyone's very misguided. He's destroying our village."

"It's the rain."

"It's *not*. What are you *really* doing? And what have you done with Esther and everyone else?"

He shook his head. "I've called the cops, and we're going to press charges."

"Good. I want to talk to the police myself," she replied, and turned to march resolutely after Alice. She almost bumped straight into a broad, black-clad chest decorated with a large beard. "Excuse me," she said, trying to sidestep it.

"No," the beard's owner said, taking her arm.

"Would everyone stop *touching* me," she snapped, trying to pull away, but she couldn't even move in his grip. "Let go!"

"Up to the house," he said, steering her in the very direction she'd been intending on going anyway, and she dug her heels in.

"Absolutely not."

"Please don't make me carry you." He propelled her forward, her feet stumbling along against her will, and she let herself collapse to the ground, turning into a deadweight. The bearded man stopped, looking down at her. "Stop that."

"No. This is a non-violent protest."

"Tell that to your friends," he said, sounding aggrieved. "I'm vegan, and one of them threw a ham sandwich at me."

Miriam winced. "Sorry."

"I'll forgive you if you get up."

"No." She crossed her legs, wondering where Alice was. Hopefully finding something to use against Lachlan when they did get arrested.

"Niall, give me a hand," the bearded man said.

"What?"

"Take her other arm."

"I'm not dragging some old lady across the garden!"

"*Excuse me,*" Miriam said. "Just because you're about twelve."

The bearded man sighed, crouched down, and grabbed Miriam under the arms. He lifted her to standing, and she hung there like a kitten dangling from its mother's mouth. "Put your feet down," he said.

"No."

"Grab her feet," he said to Niall.

"Scott, I'm not—"

"Grab her feet."

Niall made an infuriated sound, and grabbed Miriam's ankles. "Sorry," he said, then frowned. "Why don't you have any shoes?"

"Not forgiven, and I lost them in your horrible run-off." She wriggled her toes, and he gagged, letting go of her.

"Bloody *hell.*" Scott lowered Miriam back to the ground. She tried to let herself puddle into a sitting position, but he shifted his grip and hefted her up in a fireman's carry. "I'm sending you my physio bill," he said to Niall as he headed for the house.

"You've got it on the private insurance," Niall replied, trotting after him.

"Metaphorically."

Scott carted Miriam to the house and into a gym equipped with beige weights and white straps hanging from pale wood frames. Miriam watched it pass from her head-down position, looking mostly at the floor, which was padded with beige matting. Her head throbbed with the jouncing and from being upside down, and she said, "I think I might be sick."

"Hold it in," Scott said, heading for the back of the room. There was an agreeable beep ahead of them, then the whisper of a door sliding open. A roar greeted them, and Niall squawked. Miriam found herself whirled around and dumped unceremoniously just over the threshold, and Scott jumped back through the already closing door. "Feral bloody meat-eaters!" he shouted through the gap.

Priya hurdled Miriam and grabbed the door, Teresa right behind her, both of them hooking their fingers around the edge and trying to stop it closing. "Gert!" Teresa shouted. "Help!"

"Hold on!" Gert charged toward them, but the door was closing too fast.

"Get your hands out!" Miriam shouted. "It's not going to stop!"

"It has to—" Priya strained against the door, but Teresa let go, pulling the shorter woman away as it snapped shut. "*Dammit!*" Priya banged on the panelling with both fists. "Hey! *Hey! It's flooding!*"

Gert pulled Miriam to her feet. "Alright?"

"Fine," she said, then realised Gert was looking at the survival blanket sticking out from under her jacket, and her bare feet. "Oh. Yes. I fell down a bank and into some run-off."

"Did you see the dogs?" Pearl asked, her fingers twisting together anxiously.

"No, sorry. Is everyone alright?"

"Mostly." Gert pointed at her own face. "Got a black eye, though."

"*What?*"

"She ran into an apple tree," Rose said. "Knocked her right over and two of the security guards jumped her."

"I was just going to go with being jumped by two security guards," Gert observed.

Rose shrugged, and looked at Miriam. "Where's Alice?"

"I'm not sure. How did you all end up in here?"

Carlotta looked slightly embarrassed. "Rosemary and I saw a door open and decided to look for Esther and co, but we got shut in. Priya and Teresa tried to get the door open and one of those hefty security lots threw them in with us, then picked off the others."

"Searching the retreat wasn't part of the plan," Miriam said.

"No, but it was raining," Carlotta replied. "And not all of us can happily do laps all day like Teresa. Plus we ran out of cake to throw."

"I don't think even I could outrun that lot forever," Teresa said.

"Did you find anyone?" Miriam asked.

"We've not really had time to look," Gert said, dusting her hands over her trousers. "Shall we?"

Miriam nodded, looking around. "Where's Jasmine?"

"Last I saw Primrose was trying to savage that security woman," Rosemary said.

"She does have her uses," Priya said.

Miriam started to say something, then stopped as the whole house shivered. It was gentle, almost slow motion, but something toppled over in the coffee cart with a crash, and they all froze. The glass panels that enclosed the courtyard groaned, and beyond them the pool slopped and rolled, swamping the grass that surrounded it and lapping up the walls. Water crept across the floor of the transition room, coming in around the frames.

"The whole damn place is going to come down," Rose said.

"Then let's get moving," Gert said, clapping her hands together. "There *must* be a way out. Check the bookshelves, look for remotes, anything. We might still find our missing people, too."

Miriam shivered, a chill working through her as she looked at the pool. The water was still moving even though the tremors had died away, as if it were full of furtive life. She hurried to the glass and peered out, but there was no sign of Nellie, or anything else for that matter. She tried the remote Lachlan had used, but it was dead, the doors unresponsive. Behind her the ladies spread out, banging on walls and kicking shelving units, pulling figurines off plinths and moving furniture.

She hesitated a moment longer, then turned and circled the transition room to where the guest rooms were. They all had loos, so it'd be the best place to put someone. She thought it far more likely the missing people were stashed in some outbuilding, though, so when she knocked on the first door and called, "Esther, are you in there?" she actually gave a little scream when someone replied.

"Who's that?" a woman's voice asked. "Tati, is that you? I can't get out of my room."

"Esther?"

"Of course it's Esther. Who else would it be?"

"Gert!" Miriam shouted, and an answering yell went up from further around the transition room. "I've found them!" She went back to the door. "Esther, can you see a keypad in there?"

"A what?"

"Like a little panel by the door, with a screen? Or maybe with little numbers on it?"

There was a pause, and Miriam stepped back as the rest of the W.I. hurried to join her. The rooms were marked with small plaques. *Suite Source,* one read, and *Suite Springs.* A third was *Suite Streams,* which made her wrinkle her nose.

Miriam turned back to the door. "Esther?" she asked. "Have you found the keypad?"

"I have it," a new voice said.

"Vera?"

"Yes." She sounded peevish. "Why are we here?"

"You don't know?"

"*No.* Have you dragged us into some W.I. nonsense?"

"No! We've been looking for you," Miriam said, as the building shuddered. One of the glass wall panels gave a sickening snap, cracks spidering across it, and the women turned to look at the pool. The water was rising higher across the courtyard.

"We need to hurry," Rosemary said.

Teresa had been tapping on one of the other doors, talking in a low voice, and now she shouted, "*Ha!*"

The door slid open, revealing Ed and Ambrose. Ed was wearing grey joggers and a large blue fleece, and he scowled at them. "What're we doing here?"

"I'm checking the outside door," Gert said, pushing past the men into the room. Teresa hurried to Miriam's door, and she stepped back.

"Ambrose?" Miriam said. "Do you remember anything?"

"No," he said absently. "But I've been trying a new varietal, and it may be a bit strong. Got the seeds from a friend in Amsterdam."

Gert reappeared. "The keypads on the outside doors aren't working."

That made sense, Miriam supposed. Not much point putting anyone in here if they could just walk out.

"The little arrows that point away from each other," Teresa was saying. "Like on a lift." There was a click, and the door slid open. "Two from two!" she shouted.

"Well done," Pearl said, and Carlotta stepped forward to help

Esther. Miriam watched them head for the seating areas, Esther weaving slightly, and Vera looked at her.

"It was the voices," she said.

"The voices?"

"And the faces in the water. I thought I heard something, and went to look. And then I don't know what happened." She rubbed her forehead, frowning. "I'd like to go home. The cats need feeding."

Miriam nodded, and watched her potter after Esther. Rosemary was holding Ed up, and Ambrose had a hand on Pearl's shoulder. She looked at Rose, who was staring at the growing pool with her arms crossed. "They're not right," she said.

Rose glanced at her, and shook her head. "No. Ed's being positively nice."

"Do you think they were sedated?"

"Seems likely."

The building juddered again. It seemed to go on longer this time, the aftershocks lingering. The broken glass in one of the panes crazed over further, but didn't shatter. There was a more distant crack, another panel snapping on the far side of the pool. The sloshing water was building up momentum, setting up a steady surge that crashed from one glass wall panel to the next. It looked to be climbing with every swell, and Miriam wondered if they were more likely to get swept away in a flood or buried under a collapsing roof.

"We need to get out of here," Gert said, joining them.

Miriam nodded. "Any of the other doors working?"

"Not so far. There's no bloody handles. They're all on those electronic locks, and even when we can find the keypads we can't make them work."

And the only other way out was into the pool area. Miriam wasn't looking forward to all that glass breaking. Not only because the filthy water was going to come rushing in, but she was still barefoot. Not that any of them should be paddling in that. They'd have to get Esther and the others up onto the furniture or the coffee cart, and hope the water didn't come too high. She examined the ceiling, wondering if there was a crawl space up there, some way onto the roof. If nothing else, it couldn't fall on them then. She rubbed her face, wishing Alice were there. Gert was looking at her expectantly, as if thinking she was going to come up with a plan, but what was she meant to do? Even her phone was soaking—

"*Phones,*" she said, dropping her hand. "Why're we all standing around in here when we've got *phones?* Call DI Adams!"

Gert shook her head. "No signal. There's Wi-Fi, but we don't know what the password is. Priya tried."

Miriam unzipped her jacket, suddenly far too hot. "We never should've come here. What were we *thinking?* We've lost Alice, and we've lost Jasmine, and it doesn't even matter that we've found Esther and everyone, because we can't get them out!" She struggled out of her jacket and dropped it on the floor, letting the survival blanket fall with it. "Why do we keep thinking we can *do* these things!"

"Because we usually can," Rose said, offering her a bottle of very fancy-looking whisky.

Miriam waved it away. "Where did you get that?"

"There's a cocktail cart on the other side of the pool. Carlotta and Rosemary were talking about margaritas."

Miriam shuddered. Her one experience with tequila was many years behind her, but she had no desire to repeat it. "Pity we can't just drive the carts out," she said.

"If we can get the doors open, we can," Gert said. "We'll figure it out." She took the bottle from Rose and swigged it.

Miriam would have liked Gert's confidence. She looked at the pool, wishing the dragons would just pop into the gap in the centre of the building and pluck them neatly out, or Alice throw open the door and give them her small smile and say, "Well, come on, then."

But no dragons appeared, and no Alice, and she was wondering if a little of Rose's stolen whisky might actually be a good idea when Priya cried out. Miriam turned to see Ambrose keel gently out of his chair and slide to the ground, Priya steadying him as well as she could. "*Ambrose!*"

Gert was already running across the room, lowering herself to her knees next to the older man and rolling him onto his back.

"Ambrose?" she said, her voice imperious. "Ambrose, can you hear me?"

Nothing. She tapped his collarbone briskly, but there was still no response. His face was pale, lips faintly blue, and Gert lowered her ear near his mouth. "He's still breathing," she said, looking at Miriam.

"Silly man," Esther said affectionately. "He's always messing about."

Gert tapped his collarbone again, and this time Ambrose flinched. "There we go," Gert said, patting his face. "Come on, old boy."

Ambrose eyes fluttered open a tiny bit. "Who're you calling old?" he whispered.

Miriam pressed her hands to her chest. "You're okay?"

"Pacemaker," he said, licking his lips. "Gets a bit dicky sometimes."

Gert was checking his pulse, eyes on her watch. "Not surprising, in this."

Vera had been watching Ambrose. "Is he at it again?"

"Again?"

"Being dramatic. Fainting about the place."

Miriam looked at Gert, who grimaced.

"She exaggerates," Ambrose said, his voice low as he tried to rise onto his elbows. "Help me up."

"She doesn't," Ed said. He was pale, but seemed a bit steadier than the others. He waved away the bottle of whisky Rose offered to him. "He had a turn earlier."

Gert pushed Ambrose back down casually. "We can't hang around in here."

Miriam nodded, looking at the pool and its crazed glass panels. "Alright. Esther, can I use your slippers?"

"Of course." Esther stuck her legs out in front of her, and Miriam took her slippers, shuffling into them. They were a little small, but they'd work.

She hurried to the coffee cart and peered around the back, spotting power cables running to plugs in the wall. She pulled them out, then put her shoulder to the cart. It rocked gently, but didn't move.

Carlotta had joined her, and she said, "Wait a moment." She fiddled with the tow bar attachment, then stood up. "Brake was on."

"Thanks." Miriam tried again. The tow bar was already pointed at the glass doors, and the cart rolled forward gently. "We need to get it going faster."

Rosemary joined her and Carlotta, and they put their shoulders to the cart. It was only little, lightweight despite the big coffee machine nestled into it, and they soon had it moving, aiming the tow bar straight at the cracked glass door.

"Fire in the *hole!*" Rosemary shouted cheerily as they picked up speed. But there wasn't much room, and they were still barely above a fast walk when they collided with the glass. It shivered but remained whole, and the cart bumped gently back.

"Oh," Miriam said. "I thought that'd work."

"It will," Rose said, joining them and hurrying to the front of the cart. "We need a better run-up."

"Let me help," Priya said, Teresa and Pearl crowding around with her, everyone trying to get their hands on the cart.

"No, wait," Miriam said. "It's too many people. Teresa and Priya, help me. Everyone else make sure no one's going to end up with glass on them or anything."

They scattered without argument, and she, Priya, and Teresa pushed the cart all the way to the far wall. Ambrose had already been helped onto a sofa, where he reclined rather elegantly, while Rose was persuading Vera to move out of her chair and to another at the back wall. Ed and Esther followed docilely, and by the time they had the cart in position, the path to the glass wall was clear.

"Ready?" Miriam asked.

"Ready," Priya and Teresa chorused.

They pushed, slowly at first, but gradually picking up speed, until, by the time they were closing on the glass, they were all running, driving the cart ahead of them fast enough that Miriam was having trouble keeping up. They aimed dead centre at the giant pane of already crazed glass, and as they reached the last couple of metres she shouted, "Stop!"

They let go and the cart charged on, the tow bar smashing into the panel, not rebounding this time. Instead the glass bowed, and for one horrible moment Miriam thought it must be some super-strength new material, then the whole thing collapsed, showering the cart in great chunks of safety glass as it carried on through to bog down in the water before it reached the pool.

The courtyard, which had become a knee-deep lake, spilled rapidly into the transition room, swirling around everyone's ankles and rising steadily, and Miriam waded out after the cart.

"Miriam? What're you doing?" Rose asked, following her.

"Can I borrow your phone?"

Rose dug in her jacket pocket and handed her mobile to Miriam. "I don't think you'll get signal."

"Then I'll shout really loudly." She tried to smile, but she wasn't sure this was one of her better ideas. She climbed into the coffee cart then boosted herself up to sit on the counter, not sure if the shakes she was feeling were her, the cart, or the earth beneath them.

Teresa called, "Miriam, wait!" She splashed through the water, stepped into the cart and held both hands up. "Here."

"Thanks." Miriam stood carefully, her fingers linked into Teresa's for support, then waited for the taller woman to clamber onto the counter next to her. Carlotta hurried over to steady Teresa in turn, and the cart trembled beneath them. The pool spat and surged, and Miriam tried not to look at it or the ground, keeping her eyes instead on the gentle slope of the roof. She took Teresa's hand again, and stepped up onto the coffee machine, feeling both very high up and very, very unsteady.

"Do you want me to do it?" Teresa asked.

"I can manage," Miriam said, with more confidence than she felt. The cart had stopped in just the right spot, and all she had to do was lean forward slightly to touch the tiles. The roof didn't rise to a ridge the way a normal one would, but instead the highest point was here, where it stopped at the courtyard. It slid gently down to the eaves on the outside of the hexagon, as if the peak had been scooped away by a giant melon-baller, along with the centre of the building. She couldn't see the grounds from here, though, so she needed to get still higher, and she swallowed, her throat clicking. The tiles felt horribly slick under her fingertips, but what else could she do? If she could get up there, at the very least she could yell that Ambrose was having a heart attack. Surely even Lachlan couldn't be so brutal as to ignore that.

"Boost me up," she said to Teresa, scuffing out of the borrowed slippers, and the other woman braced herself on the cart's counter, lacing her hands together to give Miriam a step up. She heaved upward with surprising strength, spilling Miriam onto the roof, and there was one teetering moment where she thought she was going to pitch head first down the tiles. But she grabbed the edge of the roof with both hands and swung around, scrabbling with her bare feet until she got some purchase, then suddenly she was *climbing a roof* for the first time since she was a teenager. In the rain. With the whole place still shaking from time to time. She decided it was best not to think about it too much.

"Careful, Miriam!" Priya called, and Teresa hushed her.

"Don't distract her!"

"I'm *encouraging* her!"

"You're reminding her she could fall."

"I'm telling her not to!"

Miriam didn't need any reminders about falling, but rather than responding she just shuffled on her bottom toward the far edge of the roof, shaking with cold and effort, wishing she hadn't forgotten her jacket inside, and wondering why she hadn't asked if anyone else wanted to do this. But then, finally and impossibly, she was far enough down the tiles that the fountain mired in its fresh grass was visible below her, and beyond it the gravel drive and the outbuildings, drowning in the rain.

And all of it was empty. There was no one to shout to, no one to call for help. The entire place was devoid of life, not even sheep visible in the field. She'd climbed all the way up here, and they were as trapped as they'd been before. No Alice, no DI Adams, no dragons, and no way to help Ambrose. She swallowed, throat clicking, then remembered Rose's phone. She settled her bare heels more firmly against the tiles, making sure she wasn't going to slide anywhere, and took it from her pocket, holding it high above her and muttering, “Please, please,” under her breath.

Nothing. Just an *x* where the signal should be. She stared at it, then back at the yard, and finally put the phone away. She’d just have to see if there was a way down herself. She started to shuffle sideways along the roof, and that was when the worst yet of the tremors hit. Miriam gave a screech of fright as her heels slipped, and flung herself back against the roof, scrabbling for grip as she started to slide.

22
ALICE

Alice left Miriam and Niall arguing in the garden and headed around the retreat in the direction of the outbuildings, keeping a wary eye out for the security guards. She spotted Pearl engaged in a tug of war with a muscular female guard over a carrier bag, which split and spilled muffins and shortbread over the grass.

"Now look what you've done," Pearl exclaimed. "That's just a waste, that is!"

"You were *throwing* them at me."

"Well, they don't hurt, do they?" Pearl asked, grabbing a muffin off the ground and flinging it at the woman. She knocked it away irritably.

"*Stop it.* The water in this place should come with a bloody warning label, if this is what it does to you." She caught Pearl's arm and pushed her toward the house.

"Martha!" Pearl shouted, struggling to pull away. "*Martha!*"

Alice considered intervening, but she harboured no illusions about her abilities in a physical confrontation. It'd only end up with both of them caught. The whole point of the diversion had been to give Miriam and herself time to find some answers. She couldn't go changing the plan now.

She skirted a couple of flower-beds, crouching briefly behind a rhododendron bush to allow the bearded security guard to overtake her, his hand hooked through Angelus's collar. The big dog seemed confused rather than scared, whining in a questioning way as they met the leaner man coming from the other direction.

"Is that the last of them?" the lean man asked.

"I got the Lab," the bearded man said, rubbing Angelus behind the ears.

"Oh, that must've been a challenge. What'd you do, give her a biscuit?"

"Cheese sandwich. The sugar's not good for them."

The lean man sighed. "What about the yappy mutt?"

"Thought the bloody thing was going to go for my throat when I tried to grab that PCSO woman. They're still in the garden somewhere."

"Alright. Get rid of that one, then we'll go after them."

"Great," the bearded man said, without much enthusiasm, and nudged Angelus. "Come on, boy. Walk on."

Angelus whined again, but he walked on, and Alice hesitated, then followed. She wasn't a dog person. They were always slobbery, often smelly, and generally untidy. But she didn't *dis*like them, as they seemed like decent creatures (other than Primrose, but she was fairly sure that was a personality issue rather than a species one), and she hadn't liked *get rid of that one*. Not that she could exactly tackle the bearded man, who was at least twice her size, but if he was leaving the dogs somewhere, she could free them. And he was going in the same direction as her anyway.

The bearded man led Angelus through the garden with Alice keeping to the cover of the bushes behind him, then crunched across the waterlogged gravel to the outbuildings. Alice couldn't follow, not without being immediately heard, so she checked for other unfriendly eyes, then followed the wall that divided the yard from the field. A small stretch of grass and hesitant flower-beds bordered the wall, and she could move more quietly here, even if the cover was non-existent.

By the time she reached the first of the outbuildings the bearded man still hadn't re-emerged, and her stomach was tight with apprehension. It wouldn't take him this long if he was just tying the dogs up somewhere, and the idea that he might *do something* to them was somehow worse than the simmering threat to the W.I. itself.

Alice reached the *Sourced* building without anyone shouting at her, or rushing out to grab her. The stone was stained with rain, and the new structure that had been erected inside the shell of the old barn made it seem like a creature breaking out of a chrysalis. The walls rumbled with the sound of machinery inside, evidently buffered by some heavy-duty sound insulation, but this close she could feel the vibrations in the stone as much as hear it. Its smattering of tinted windows revealed nothing, no sign as to whether she were observed, but at least getting around its corner meant she was no longer visible from the garden or the retreat. There was a second, smaller building out here, pressed up to the drystone wall, but she ignored it as she hurried to the old barn's corner and peered around it. A parking area held a handful of cars, and Scott, the bearded security guard, had the back of a shiny Range Rover open, Angelus peering out of it anxiously.

"There you go," Scott was saying, scratching the big dog under the chin. "You stay in there all nice and dry with your little friend. Quietly, okay?" He tried to close the door, and Angelus set up a pitiful howl. Scott sighed. "Now, that's not helping, is it?" He gave Angelus another scratch behind the ears and said, "I really do have to go this time." He shut the door, wincing as the Great Dane howled again, then headed off at a jog, not even looking around. Alice watched him go, then slipped around to the back of the building. She didn't bother with releasing the dogs – they were probably safer in the car than out here, and evidently Scott wasn't about to throw them in a sinkhole or anything similar.

The ground shuddered as she examined the outside of the *Sourced* building, looking for a window or a back door, some way in that wasn't through the keycard-locked main entrance. But there was nothing she could see, and she was wasting time. At some point, probably sooner rather than later, the W.I. would be forced off the property, Lachlan would return, the police would come, and any chance she had to determine exactly what was going on here would be gone. She looked at the small building huddled against the wall to the field. The door was slightly ajar, and she headed for it, suddenly hopeful. The tinted glass and keypad lock suggested it was more than a garden shed.

She pushed the door gently, and it swung soundlessly open into a single large room with a mezzanine above it. It was painfully tidy, and in contrast to the pale wood and nondescript beige of the retreat everything was dark wood and rich, deep tones. A brown leather sofa with dusky red throw cushions faced an oversized TV, and black and chrome bar stools snuggled up to a breakfast bar that separated the living area from a compact kitchen beneath the mezzanine. A couple of closed doors behind the stairs suggested a bathroom and toilet, and to the right, beyond the TV area, a large wooden table held four computer screens, a variety of keyboards, one mouse, and a chair. Low lights gave the whole place the air of a gentlemen's lounge, and Alice hesitated on the threshold until she heard a toilet flush behind one of the closed doors. She almost fled back outside again, but she wasn't going to get access in here again if she did so. And she was all but certain that the answers she wanted were on that desk.

She hurried across the bare wood floors into the kitchen area, walking as quietly as she could, and ducked down behind the breakfast bar as she heard the toilet door open. She'd been hoping to make it to a tall corner cupboard that looked like it might be a pantry, but there was no time for that now, so she just stayed where she was and hoped whoever was out there didn't decide to make a cuppa.

Footsteps crossed the room, paused, and the desk chair creaked. Keys clicked, and someone sighed. More clicks, although, oddly, they seemed to be coming closer. *Tappity-tappity-tap,* and Alice suddenly recognised the sound. Hard claws on hard wood, and she looked up as a small form emerged around the breakfast bar, nose twitching. She and the dog stared at each other, then Primrose braced her front paws and burst into a volley of yapping.

"*Shhh!*" Alice hissed, and the person on the computer gave a little shriek.

"Who's there?"

"*Jasmine?*" By the time Alice had got to her feet, the younger woman was already across the room, staring down at her. "How did you get in here?"

"Um," Jasmine said, her cheeks pink. "How did *you* get in here?"

"You left the door open."

Jasmine grimaced. "I was scared I might not be able to get out again."

"Close it," Alice said. "If someone else sees it open we'll be in all sorts of trouble."

The younger woman hurried to the door and peeked outside, then shut it gently, coming back to look at Alice. "Have you felt all the tremors?"

"Yes." They were ongoing, some so small Alice wasn't sure if she was really feeling them or just imagining them, others making the ground feel as if she were standing on a moving train. "Something very odd's going on. Miriam and I found an entire pond of polluted water in the woods. They're not just bottling water here."

"I know. I came to see if the missing persons might be being held here, but look." Jasmine went to the desk and picked up a piece of paper that had been propped behind the keyboard. "I found this. You don't use this stuff for *water.* And with what Rose said about the run-off…"

Alice joined her and took the paper, examining it. It was an invoice from an industrial supply company, listing quantities and a delivery date, and, while she didn't know much about the process of bottling water, she doubted it used what was on the sheet. "Sodium carbonate. Potassium hydroxide. Sulphuric acid. Lots of all of it. What would one use that for?"

"I don't know. I can't see any other paper files, and I've been trying to get into the computer, but I can't figure out the password." She leaned over the keyboard again. "I'm honestly just guessing. I did the numbers from the postcode, all the usual ones like 0000 and 1234—"

"I think it might be more tricky than that."

"It was worth trying," Jasmine said with a sigh.

"It was," Alice agreed. "But we don't have much time. We need to see if we can find what he's using the chemicals for."

"We need Rose," Jasmine said. "She might know."

Alice nodded, handing the paper back to the younger woman. "Have you taken a photo of it?" She watched Jasmine take her phone out, then added, "How did you get in here?"

The younger woman's cheeks flushed visibly, even in the mellow light, as she clicked a photo of the invoice. "I sort of broke in."

"How?"

"Well, I mean, I didn't *break* in, break in. I used a keycard. That I stole. Well, sort of stole."

"*Jasmine,*" Alice said. "I'm very impressed."

She made a small noise. "It's not that impressive. Gert knocked one of the security guards over, and he must've had his card in his pocket. It fell out and I picked it up."

"And then you used your initiative." Alice wasn't pretending to be impressed. This was excellent thinking, and all after she'd thought Jasmine was becoming far too stuck on the rules.

"It hasn't helped, though," Jasmine said, putting her phone away again. "I haven't found much."

"It's more than we had before. Do you have any signal? I lost my phone."

"No signal, but I found the router and got my phone on the Wi-Fi. I've already called DI Adams."

"And?"

"No answer. I tried Ben, and he wouldn't listen. He said they're evacuating the village, and we need to stop making nuisances of ourselves."

Alice nodded. "I see."

"I was going to try the station, but then I thought, well. The only person who'll probably help is DI Adams, so there was no point." She tucked the invoice under one corner of the keyboard, presumably where it had been before. "So we should go and look at the bottling plant while we wait for her to answer. If I'm breaking into one place, I may as well break into all of them."

Alice supposed she shouldn't feel *quite* as proud of that as she did.

NO ONE WAS in view outside, and despite the recurring shivers of the destabilised land, no great crevasses had opened around them. Jasmine led the way to the door of the *Sourced* shed, since there didn't appear to be any other way in, and pressed the keycard to the panel. There was a pause, while Alice wondered if they were maybe coded for different places, then the lock clicked obligingly. Jasmine pulled the door open and they both slipped inside, a grumbling Primrose trotting after them with her ears back and her teeth bared. She barked at a coat hanging from a hook on the wall, and Jasmine picked her up, shushing her.

The inner door just had a normal handle, and when Alice tried it, it turned easily. The door itself was heavy and soundproof, and as it opened onto the main floor of the plant a roar of sound greeted them, rumbling and angry. The machinery that filled the room shook like a beast preparing itself for battle. The walls were flat, bright white, and metal fittings gleamed everywhere, but muddy water pooled on the floor and dribbled steadily from seams on the machinery and tanks. A metal table equipped with a neat clipboard and tidily aligned boxes of gloves and cleaning cloths and little collections of stationery also held a dirty bucket that had fallen on its side, revealing a muddy sponge and crumpled rags, and a tool bag was open on the floor, spilling its contents onto the ground.

"This doesn't sound right," Alice said, raising her voice as they ventured further in. The overhead lights were blinding on the white walls.

"The dirt in the water clogging things up, perhaps?" Jasmine asked.

"Quite likely." Alice picked up the clipboard, but all it held was a checklist for setting up the bottling machine, which was on one wall. She crossed to it, examining the racks of bottles waiting to be filled. It all seemed very simple, and while she supposed there must be a lot of filtration and so on involved, the machinery in here felt excessive. There had to be something else to this.

"Alice," Jasmine shouted.

"Yes?" She touched some of the grimy water leaking from one of the joints, rubbing it between her fingertips and sniffing it. It told her nothing, and she looked back at the bottles, following the pipes with her gaze as she tried to figure out how everything connected. She couldn't see where the water would run from the great tanks and complicated-looking bits of machinery to the bottles, nothing seeming to connect in logical sequence. And why was it so *noisy?* She went to join Jasmine, who was peering behind the bottling plant.

"Sulphuric acid," Jasmine said, pointing at a row of drums lined up against the wall, bright yellow warning labels blaring on them. "Potassium hydroxide. They were on the invoice, weren't they?"

"They were," Alice replied, looking back at the bottle-filling station. From this angle she'd spotted something new. "Oh. I see."

"What?"

"They're just filling the bottles from a tap."

"*What?*" Jasmine followed her gaze, and they both stared at the tap sticking out of the wall, a simple garden hose attached to it and feeding into a tank that fed directly to the filling nozzles for the bottles, bypassing everything else in the room completely. "But what's the rest of the equipment for?"

"I don't know. Something that creates a lot of run-off, though. They're not after the water."

Jasmine took her phone from her pocket and squinted at it, then nodded. "I'm still on the Wi-Fi." She tapped the screen hurriedly while Alice walked around the machinery. She didn't understand how the run-off was flooding the village's land while not filling the waterways, but what was clear was that it was poisoning everything. They needed to shut this down, but she couldn't see any controls from here, so she turned toward the entryway, leaving Jasmine to her research.

As if on cue, the machinery vibrated into silence, and Lachlan appeared in the door, a tablet in one hand. Primrose exploded into yapping fury, racing across the floor to confront him.

"Prim!" Jasmine shouted, starting forward. Lachlan fended off the little dog with one boot, and she bounced away before he could make contact, almost frothing with rage. *"Don't hurt her!"*

"Control her, then," he said. "What're you doing in here?" His voice was cool as he examined Alice.

"Just having a little look around," she said. "I've never been in a bottling plant before."

"How did you get in?"

"The door was open."

He smiled slightly, glancing at Jasmine as she scurried forward to pick up Primrose, trying to calm the snarling dog. "That seems unlikely. I think you've gone straight past trespassing and into breaking and entering."

"What are you doing with all this?" Alice asked. "The damage you're causing the village is unacceptable."

"So's your campaign of harassment," he said, his tone sharpening.

"You're *destroying* Toot Hansell," Jasmine snapped, hugging Primrose to her. "All the flooding and run-off – no one's even going to be able to farm anymore!"

"That's rather an exaggeration."

"The village is being evacuated as we speak," Alice said.

"That's the rain."

"And all your chemicals? Your fake bottling plant?"

Lachlan's face remained neutral, but Alice saw his jaw twitch. "It's not fake."

"You're filling the bottles from a garden hose." She pointed at the machinery looming above them. "All this is for some sort of extraction, and the run-off's killing the waters. That's wholesale environmental destruction. We have laws about that."

"I have no idea what you're talking about."

"Then you won't mind us getting the Environment Agency in to take a look."

He smiled. "You might have trouble with that. I've made sure I'm very well-liked in government departments."

Alice shook her head. "You can't have any sort of licence for this."

Lachlan shrugged. "Industry moves much faster than government. There *is* no licence for what I'm doing yet, not in this country. Things will catch up eventually, but so much progress would be lost if I waited. And this is for the benefit of the environment in the long run."

The environment. Electric cars. Extraction. Something clicked, and Alice said, "Batteries."

Next to her, Jasmine gasped. "The stuff! The stuff in car batteries ... lithium! It was on the news! It *devastates* places when it's done wrong!"

"Oh, well done," Lachlan said. "Clever girl."

Jasmine scowled at him, and Alice said, "It was never about the retreat, was it?"

"No. There's not much money in them. Or not enough for it be worthwhile by my standards."

Alice frowned. "How did you even find out about the lithium? I've never heard of it in the UK."

"Neither has anyone else. And it did start with the wellness. I read about the waters here, and I thought if I could buy some in bulk it'd be good for my treatments. There's no point putting in the work I do only to use substandard water."

"I imagine."

He smiled slightly. "I bought a small tanker's worth from Dom, and when I tested it for purity some of the properties were a bit unusual. A little more investigation, and there it was. The UK's first source of lithium brine."

"So you decided to destroy an entire village over it?"

He puffed air over his lower lip. "That wasn't the intention. The flooding's been rather excessive, and I'm not sure why. Combination of the rain and some unanticipated diversion in the groundwaters, I suppose."

"But you don't even care!" Jasmine said. "The village is *drowning.*"

"That's rather dramatic."

"It's true! There's sinkholes and quicksand and half the streets are washed out, and everything's dying!"

"Progress demands sacrifice."

"Not yours, though, right?" Jasmine demanded.

"I don't know," Alice said. "Things aren't looking too good in here, either." As if to illustrate, the building shivered, groaning, and more water dribbled from some of the joints in the machinery.

"I can fairly confidently say it'll be declared a natural disaster," Lachlan replied. "And if your insurance doesn't pay up, I'll help out. I'm quite the philanthropist."

"That's not the word I'd use," Jasmine said, glaring at him, and just then someone banged through the outside door behind him.

"Lachlan! Lachlan, I've been trying to call—"

"Not now, Dom," he said sharply.

"It's urgent." Dom stopped, staring at Alice and Jasmine. "Oh, bloody hell."

"Exactly. Wait for me outside."

"No, look. I caught that copper sneaking around. But it's okay. I've sorted it."

"You *what?*" Lachlan demanded, half turning, his attention shifting off the women.

Alice stooped to the tool bag, grabbed a hefty wrench, and hurled it as hard as she could, even as Jasmine dropped Primrose to the ground and yelled, "*Get them!*"

The wrench smacked into Lachlan's shoulder with an audible, bony thud, and he cried out, dropping the tablet. Dom grabbed for it, his fingers grazing the screen, and the machinery roared, grinding into furious life. Jasmine sprinted after Primrose, rushing the door, Alice following with her cane at the ready. But Dom had already pulled Lachlan into the locker room and slammed the inner door closed, and by the time Jasmine reached it all she could do was jiggle the handle furiously.

"They've locked it," she said, then raised her voice to a shout. "Let us out! *Let us out!*"

Alice picked up the tablet. Its screen was shattered, the image pixellated, but she poked it hopefully. Nothing responded, and the pipes shook with the assault of debris-laden water, the noise grinding up and up with the pressure, vibrations intensifying, feeding into the tremors in the earth itself.

"Ah," she said.

23
MORTIMER

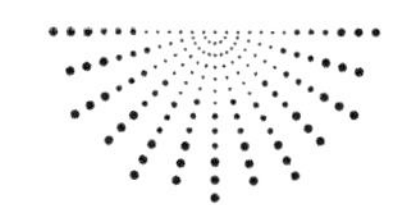

By the time the dragons emerged warily from the trees, there was no one in sight on the footpath that wound back downhill toward the road and the retreat beyond. With the spring behind them, Mortimer could once again taste the odd, metallic tang of stale water soaking the land. The rain was heavier, and his talons sank into the sodden earth with every step.

"This is no good," Amelia said, staring down at her paws. "The village must be just about underwater by now."

Beaufort looked out across the valley, toward where Toot Hansell was visible in the distance, beyond the farmland and a curve of the forest. "There's nothing more we can do," he said. "Our focus now has to be finding Nellie. Anything else is going to leave us exposed, and the clan were clear on that."

"*Margery* was clear on that," Amelia said. "It's just that she's so loud, it makes it seem like everyone's agreeing."

Beaufort gave her an amused look. "Margery has always acted in the interest of the Cloverlies. She's justified in her insistence on keeping us hidden, and I have to admit I have not been as diligent about that as I could've been in recent years."

Mortimer flinched at a sudden surge of guilt. He'd been the one to bring them into the village to start with, after all. If it hadn't been for his ideas about barbecues, and subsequent encounter with Miriam when he'd been looking for gas bottles to borrow, they'd never have risked exposure at all. Perhaps this awful man with his *extraction* would never have even heard about Toot Hansell's waters, and none of this would've happened. "Should we be going to the retreat?" he asked.

Beaufort hesitated, just slightly, but it was noticeable, and Amelia and Mortimer exchanged glances. "We need to avoid it if we can," he said. "We're still not sure how perceptive this Lachlan might be. Hopefully we can find Nellie outside the property rather than inside." He checked the slope below them again, then took a couple of loping strides before launching himself off the nearest rocky outcropping, colour bleeding from his scales and leaving him as mere suggestion of movement against the sky. Walter followed, lumbering and graceless yet efficient, and Mortimer looked at Amelia. She still had infuriated puce patches on her snout that hadn't quite faded.

"After you," he said.

"I'm going to become a Lord," she told him. "And then I'm going to outlaw all Lords. We'll have senior dragons or something, but not all this rubbish about having authority because you got yourself a title by doing one useful thing five hundred years ago." She thought about it. "We'll have *elect* dragons. That we vote for."

"Voting didn't go that well for Beaufort."

She sniffed. "People like to cling to old ways just because it's easy. I'll *make* them change their minds."

Mortimer had no doubt she would, and he watched her take flight after the older dragons, her angry patches washing away as if caught in her slipstream.

"I'll vote for her," Harriet said, far too close to Mortimer's ear, and he yelped, staggering sideways.

"*Please* stop doing that."

"No," she said, giving him a toothy grin, and he stumbled into the air, momentarily clumsy until he got going, arrowing after the other three dragons with his heart going too fast. Not that he could entirely blame Harriet for that. He was glad she was staying behind to keep an eye on the tiddy 'uns, though. He had more than enough to worry about without sneaky dragons as well.

He caught up to the others as they circled over the woods, scribing a graceful arc around the retreat to avoid being seen. Beaufort angled into a gap in the trees, tucking his wings close so he didn't graze the branches. Walter and Amelia followed in quick succession, and Mortimer lingered for a moment, his gaze on the retreat, separated from them by the last of the woods and a field. A line of cars was visible on the road, and the gravel in front of the building was scattered with debris, placards and hats and other things he couldn't identify. At least two of the cars were familiar, Alice's little 4x4 and Gert's big van, but he couldn't see the ladies themselves anywhere, and it sent a shiver of alarm through his belly. What were they *doing?*

Beaufort watched him land and said, "See anything, lad?"

"No. Nothing at all. But I think the W.I. are there. Their cars are on the road."

"Oh dear."

"And it's very quiet."

"That seems rather out of character."

Walter was casting around the little clearing, his wings twitching, and now he said, "That man came through here earlier."

"Here?" Beaufort asked. "Why here? He could've just walked from the retreat over the road, and it's rather muddy."

It was a lot more than *rather.* It was even more waterlogged here than it had been near the spring, and Mortimer wondered uneasily how long the tiddy 'uns would be able to hold back the water, and what would happen when it broke its restraints.

"Let's find out," Walter said, and slouched off through the trees, following an indistinct path that meandered through the frayed edges of woods where the charms were lighter. It headed more or less directly toward the retreat, and it wasn't long before they reached the border of the garden. A ladder was set over the wall like a makeshift stile, metallic and incongruous.

"Alice and Miriam were here," Mortimer said, catching the twin threads of their traces on the treads of the ladder, Miriam scattering anxiety and cheesy puffs, and Alice altogether cooler and quieter, deep shadows on hot days. There was no panic in the scents, at least. Worry, yes, and a little fear, but nothing more.

Amelia examined the garden. "There's no one here."

"There must be. Their cars are outside the gate."

"Can you see anyone?"

The dragons lined up along the wall, front paws on the stone, searching for movement in the flower-beds or among the shrubs, but there was nothing to be seen.

"What do we do?" Mortimer asked. "Go after the ladies or find Nellie?"

"Same thing, isn't it?" Amelia said. "They'll all be in there."

"Perhaps we check outside the wall more carefully," Beaufort said. "We don't know Nellie's being held *in* the retreat." He sounded uncharacteristically doubtful, and Mortimer looked at him curiously. Beaufort would normally be the first to charge straight in, the first to take that risk not only for Nellie, but for their friends. Margery must've shaken him more than Mortimer had realised. The old dragon was still the High Lord after all, and there was more than just himself to worry about. It was broad daylight, and he could expose their entire clan to this man and his questionable motives, who might know about Folk and might not. And there wasn't even a cat around to help clean up the aftermath.

There was a long silence, then the ground juddered, hard enough that a stone slipped from the top of the wall and landed on Amelia's hind paw. "*Ow,*" she said, and bared her teeth at the building. "I bet he's doing that too."

"It has to be connected," Beaufort agreed, but he still didn't move. "We need to come back after dark. This isn't any good, rushing in."

"But anything could've happened to the ladies," Mortimer blurted out. "And we've checked the woods before. Nellie's not here."

"And we need to stop fancy man with his *tankers,*" Amelia said. "Even if we find Nellie, she can't fix anything if he's still pumping his poison water about the place. As it is, she's going to struggle to heal all this."

"Let's keep an eye on things for a bit, then," Beaufort said. "See who's moving about in there so we have a better idea what we're up against." He dropped his forepaws off the wall and looked around. "And we've hardly searched out here."

"I'm too old for all this *faffing*," Walter declared, and launched himself over the wall in a slither of loose scales.

"*Walter!*" Mortimer hissed. "What're you *doing?*"

"*Yes, Walter,*" Amelia said, and scampered after the old dragon, who was already padding into the garden, his saggy skin and patchy scales blending effortlessly with the bedraggled undergrowth.

"Walter," Beaufort called, putting his paws up on the wall again. "We don't have a plan."

"I do," Walter said, peering around a hydrangea at the building. A crevasse had opened in the new turf, tearing it in unnaturally straight lines along its seams, and a rock garden was sliding slowly into the gap, clumps of heather looking unperturbed by their new angles. "Go in, roar a bit, maybe bite someone, and get the sprite out."

Amelia peeked into the hole in the grass, then scuttled back as the edges trembled and crumbled, and it yawned a little wider. A new apple tree lurched drunkenly sideways. "We best be quick about it."

Mortimer looked at Beaufort, and he gave a sudden, toothy, and much more familiar grin. "Well. No going back now, is there?"

"It's out of your paws," Mortimer agreed. "Walter fell in a sinkhole and we had to go after him. Amelia and I both saw it."

"I didn't fall in *anything*," Walter said. "Just because I'm old—"

"Look, *I* fell in," Amelia said, her tail twitching with irritation. "*Eek, ooh,* female in distress, please save me, etcetera. Can we just get on, or do we want to give this lot time to figure out how to throw us all in a trap with Nellie?"

"I do agree that age doesn't automatically warrant respect," Beaufort said, scaling the wall effortlessly. "But I am still High Lord, Amelia."

"I'm *helping,*" she protested.

Mortimer supposed she was, at that. He looked along the wall, where Miriam and Alice's path vanished into the woods, and wondered again what *contained the situation* had meant. But the only answers were ahead of them, so he climbed the wall and dropped into the garden, smelling the odd scents of new turf and transplanted plants, not quite part of the land yet, still finding ways to sink their roots in. If they got the chance, of course.

The grass was a mess of scent traces, dropped cake and sparkling adrenaline, crushed pork pies and pops of surprise. Evidently the W.I. had been running about in here with a certain wild abandon. There wasn't much fear in evidence, which Mortimer thought rather in keeping with the ladies as a whole. The dragons worked their way across the garden carefully, keeping a screen of bushes and trees between them and the main building, the ladies' traces muddled in with the frustrated, hot tarmac smudges of strangers.

It was impossible to follow any one scent, and Mortimer couldn't quite work out what had happened. The hairiness of dogs and a drifting whisper of feathers overlaid the commotion, and everyone seemed to be going in every direction at once. The only thing he was sure of was that no one was left in the garden anymore, and as the cover ran out they regrouped behind a large, tiered planter full of drowning herbs.

"What now?" Amelia asked. Ahead was the main building, or they could sneak past it toward the outbuildings behind the retreat.

"We split up," Beaufort said. "Walter, you and Amelia check the retreat, but do try not to be seen. Find out what the situation is, how many people Lachlan has inside, that sort of thing. Mortimer and I will take the outbuildings, and you can join us once you've scouted things out a bit."

Walter gave a grunt of agreement, and he and Amelia slipped away through the last stands of the shivering garden, even as another tremor in the earth claimed a pretty trellis and its roses, pitching them to the ground.

Beaufort looked at Mortimer. "Ready, lad?"

"Yes," Mortimer said, although he wasn't, really. He didn't think he was the sort of dragon who'd ever be ready for raiding a human retreat. But he followed the High Lord and they crept out of the garden. Mortimer's scales twitched as he waited for a net or a gun, shouts or screams. None came, though, and they circuited the bare gravel at the back of the building, keeping to the grass border. Mortimer kept catching little flashes of Alice, which seemed promising.

Everything seemed desperately quiet, though. They'd seen no one outside the retreat or in the garden. No one at the door to the *Sourced* building as they approached, or hurrying along the gravel drive to the road. The fountain at the back of the retreat had stopped, and near-silence hung above them, not even birdsong or the mutter of livestock to lift the sense that the clouds were crushing the land, smothering every scrap of life and rendering the fields a drenched wasteland. The only noise was an artificial one, the muffled rumble of machinery, heard as if from deep underground. It seemed to be exacerbating the judders of the earth, or causing them. The shivers ran through Mortimer's paws, all but constant now.

He didn't want to get any closer to that sound, but the vibration grew as they approached the outbuildings, swelling until he felt he should be shouting over it, even though the volume was barely any higher than when he'd first heard it. He followed Beaufort around to the back of the *Sourced* building, his scales itching, and found a tangle of scents and traces, criss-crossing and overlaid, and all leading to the same place – that throb of machinery.

"What have you got, lad?" Beaufort asked, as Mortimer sniffed around carefully, searching for a clear note through the rain and the heavy metallic tang of machinery.

"DI Adams was here," he said. "Alice and Jasmine, too."

"Where exactly?"

"I think they went inside," Mortimer said, and looked mistrustfully at the big building. It seemed to loom too high, and the stink of unfamiliar things leached from it, sharp-edged and unfriendly, the scent of the waters stripped and distilled to a terrible intensity.

"Then we have to go in as well," Beaufort said.

Mortimer opened his mouth to agree, however reluctantly, and gravel crunched on the drive. The dragons ducked out of sight, and watched Lachlan stride toward the *Sourced* building, Niall hurrying after him.

"Why's the equipment running?" Lachlan demanded. "The water's too dirty. It's blocking up the filters and putting too much strain on the pumps."

"I don't know," Niall said. "We were dealing with the W.I."

"Where are they?"

"In the transition room."

"You couldn't just pack them off?"

"They were really aggressive," Niall said, plucking at the front of his jumper.

"Right." Lachlan paused as the ground gave a particularly violent shudder. "Where the hell are the coppers?"

"They should be here," Niall said. "I'll try them again. Only they're really busy with the village, I think. Evacuation, it says on the Facebook group."

Lachlan swore. "Is it the flooding? I thought you said that was under control."

"It's probably just a precaution."

Lachlan sighed, running a hand back over his hair. "It wasn't meant to get this bad."

"It's the rain," Niall said.

"I suppose. Alright. Let me shut the plant down, then we'll sort out this bloody W.I. situation. *Nightmares*."

Lachlan hurried around the back of the *Sourced* building, heading to another, smaller outbuilding, then paused at a muffled bark. He looked around, frowning, and stared at one of the parked cars as the bark came again. "Why are there *dogs* in Scott's car?"

Niall shook his head. "No idea."

"Right." Lachlan flashed a keycard at the door of the smaller building and vanished inside, then came out a moment later with a tablet in his hand, his frown even deeper. "Have you been in there?"

"No."

"Odd. Chair was in the wrong place." He strode to the door of the *Sourced* building and opened it, the sound rising slightly before it closed behind him. Niall stayed where he was, looking around dubiously, until someone called, "Oi, Niall!"

Mortimer spotted someone peering out of the garden shed, perched on a quad bike, and had a moment of dislocation before he recognised Dom, the farmer.

"What?" Niall asked, scanning the yard as if afraid they'd be overheard. "What're you doing here?"

"I had to bring your guests over. The police were searching my place, and they'd have found them at that shepherd's hut before long."

"So you bought them *here?*"

"They're your responsibility."

Niall rubbed a hand over his face, checking for Lachlan as the machinery quieted. "Where are they?"

"Put them in the guest rooms with a cuppa. They're locked in."

"Alright. Great. One more thing to bloody well clean up." He frowned at Dom. "Did you start the plant?"

"Yeah." He hesitated, and Niall narrowed his eyes.

"Why? What did you do that for?"

"It was that copper. She saw me bringing the trailer over, so I took her down to the treatment tanks. Said everyone was down there and ... well, I shut her in."

"You *what?*"

"It keeps her out of the way, and no one'll hear her if the pumps are running."

Niall stared at him. "That is so far over the line, Dom. We're not bloody gangsters. Get her out."

"Should we? She's the only one who's proper suspicious. You need this project to work. *I* need it to. She could blow the whole thing up."

"*No.* Paying a few people off is one thing—"

"So figure out how to pay *her* off." Dom headed for the *Sourced* building.

"What're you doing?" Niall asked, grabbing his arm.

"Talking to Lachlan."

"You can't. He doesn't need to know about this."

"I'm not letting you dump everything on me," Dom snapped, pulling away, and when Niall tried to step in front of him he shoved the younger man aside, whistling sharply as he did so. Two dogs came sprinting toward them, lean and silent, and stationed themselves at his sides. "Guard," Dom said, and went to the door. Niall tried to follow and the dogs lunged at him, snarling. He backed up, hands raised, then turned and ran for the retreat.

Mortimer stared at Beaufort. "What's a treatment tank? He doesn't mean he's *drowning* her, does he?"

"I don't know," Beaufort said. "Can you find her?"

Mortimer didn't bother answering, just loped out of their dubious shelter and rushed to where he'd caught the inspector's scent before, cool and sharp-edged and spun with lightning. It led straight to the side of the building, then stopped. No sign of a door, or a handle, or anything at all. But she hadn't just fallen into the earth. He reared back, his chest burning, and spat fire at the side of the building. It was the new portion here, wood panelling rather than stone, and whatever else it might've been built to resist, dragon fire wasn't included. It charred fast, the material crumbling away to reveal a metal door set flush to the wall, a melted patch of plastic and electronics showing where the lock had been.

"Easy, lad," Beaufort said, joining Mortimer as he scrabbled at the seam. "Let me try."

The High Lord tapped the door, gave a *hmm,* then exhaled on one patch, his fire focused and intense. The metal resisted, glowing red then white-hot, and while it still glowed, Beaufort gave it a little poke. The entire edge of the door crumbled away, and it popped ajar.

"There we go," he said, sounding slightly smug. That only lasted until he opened the door, though, and the two dragons peered down into a stairwell as the machinery next door started up again, shaking the walls and setting the ground trembling under their paws. "Oh," Beaufort said.

The stairwell was flooded. The water sat not far below ground level, stinking and filthy, and there was no DI Adams paddling in it, no Dandy with his squeaky toy. There was nothing but gently swirling currents.

"He drowned her," Mortimer whispered. "He *drowned* her."

"We don't know that," Beaufort said, but his voice was almost as quiet. "Maybe there's another way out."

"That wasn't what Dom was saying." Mortimer backed away from the door, his chest tight and hot with rage as he turned toward voices at the other end of the building.

"What the hell sort of business do you think this is?" Lachlan was demanding.

"A profitable one," Dom said. "You were happy enough to drown the village. *Justifiable cost of progress,* wasn't it?"

"That's not on my own bloody property, is it? Plausible deniability is a thing, you numpty. This could ruin *everything,* and not just what we're doing here. *Everything!*"

Mortimer prowled forward, his head low, and Beaufort said, "Stop."

"We can't let them just get away with it!"

"So what are you going to do, lad? Devour them? Scorch them? I know you want to, but this isn't how we act. Some things we have to let go, so the clan survives. And so *we* survive in ourselves."

Mortimer wanted to scream at the old dragon that he didn't *care,* that he'd prefer one moment of glorious vengeance over centuries of safety, but he knew Beaufort was right, on both counts. He'd never forgive himself, no matter how many hedgehogs he saved. He swallowed hard against the fire in his chest and said, "So what *do* we do?"

"Find Nellie."

"How? Even the geese have gone. They've probably drowned everyone!" He stared at Lachlan and Dom as they headed for the smaller building, Dom grabbing the other man's arm to slow him down.

"Let go," Lachlan said grimly. "You're a bloody liability."

Dom started to say something else, and in that moment another tremor passed through the ground, heavier than previously. A scream rang out from the house, and the two men spun to look just as one of the doors burst open, and the big, bearded security guard sprinted through it, still yelling. A man and a woman in matching black coats were hard on his heels, and behind them romped Walter, his wings wrapped tightly to his back.

"*Crocodile!*" the bearded man screamed. "There's crocodiles in the water!"

Lachlan took a hesitant step forward, looking bewildered, and a cacophony of sound surged up from the field. It swept toward them, a babbling, honking, infuriated clamour, and the geese and swans rolled into the yard in a feathery, raging tide.

"What the *hell,*" Lachlan started, and the first two geese reached him, lashing out in a fury of beaks and feet. He cried out, covering his head, and ran for the cars. Dom fled for the quad bike and Mortimer threw himself forward, doing his best crocodile impression. He used his tail to sweep the man off his feet, and he went down with a scream. At the house the three security guards had done a hard about face under the onslaught of the birds and were sprinting back to the door, avoiding a snapping Walter. They made it to the steps before Amelia bounded out, teeth bared, and they spun again, facing the waterfowl who were crowding the garden in impossible numbers, pecking and ripping at the plants, splashing across the sodden gravel, and destroying everything they touched.

And behind the birds, swinging over the wall and marching toward the house with her head up and a very large stick in one hand, dripping with mud and filthy water, came DI Adams, the dandy bounding ahead of her to join the fight.

"Oh no," Dom said, rolling to his feet, and abandoned his bike, sprinting for the wall instead.

Mortimer looked at Beaufort.

"No scorching," the High Lord said, and Mortimer bolted after Dom, teeth bared.

24
DI ADAMS

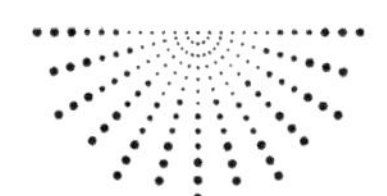

DI Adams had discovered that, while earlier in the day she had *believed* she'd never been quite so waterlogged, there were other, previously unsuspected heights of drenched-ness which one could attain. And being dragged through an underwater, underground tunnel by a weak but furious sprite, with nowhere to surface and nowhere to take a breath, had enabled her to fully appreciate just how much filthy water she could accumulate on her person, and also ingest, as a round of heavy retching had proved when they finally, finally surfaced in a muddy, obviously human-made pond in the forest.

They hadn't had much time to talk things through beforehand. The water belching out of the tank was rising far faster than the exit pipe could handle, and Nellie, still too wobbly to even stand, had pointed at the mesh and said, "Get it out."

DI Adams hadn't argued. She couldn't get through the door, and the water wasn't slowing. There were no other options. She'd attacked the mesh with her multitool, having to work with her hands underwater initially, then rapidly with the rest of her submerged too. Dandy had watched, offering a squeak with his rubber duck from time to time in encouragement, although by the time she finished he was standing on top of the tank so he could keep his snout clear.

"Done," she'd said to Nellie.

"Grab some air."

"What?"

"Breathe."

And before she could more than gasp a couple of lungfuls of stale air the sprite had her by the back of her fleece, dragging her into the tunnel. DI Adams had a moment of near-panic, terror bubbling up in her chest as her back scraped the pipes and her nose bumped the raw concrete of the tunnel wall, and she'd thought she wasn't going to fit, she was going to be wedged down here, decomposing beneath the land, or if she did fit she wouldn't be able to hold her breath long enough, and Nellie would simply drag her corpse to the surface, but at least her mum would have something to bury, there was that, and of course it had been bloody Toot Hansell that had got her, not a decent city case— And then she simply let herself go limp, because it was drown out there or drown in here, and at least this way she was trying.

Nellie may have been sick and weakened, but she moved through the water like another current, swift and liquid. DI Adams had no reference as to how fast they might be going, or how far, but when she bumped off something it *felt* fast, like tumbling through unseen rapids in deep night. Even so, it seemed like only a moment before her chest tightened, becoming painful, the need to breathe clawing at her throat and threatening to betray her. She held on, counting to herself in the tumbling dark, imagining each number exploding over her head then vanishing in her wake like a firework, over and over again, until there were so many stars behind her eyes that she couldn't see the numbers anymore. She *had* to breathe. *Had* to.

She was actually opening her mouth, on the way to sucking in water just because she couldn't *not,* her body so convinced there had to be air out there that she simply couldn't resist it, when she broke the surface with an undramatic *sploosh*. She gasped, a great whooping slurp of air, getting water with it too, but mostly glorious, wonderful, *incomparable* air, and then she burst out coughing, sinking under the surface again. She flailed, touched bottom, and managed to stabilise herself enough that she could finish coughing without drowning. That would've been embarrassing at this stage.

A *whuff* greeted her, and she looked around with streaming eyes to see Dandy standing on a bank above her. He dropped his rubber duck off the edge to bob next to her then sat down, waiting.

Nellie was drifting next to her, and the inspector managed a "Thanks."

"Likewise."

"Are you alright?"

"No," the sprite said, inspecting her arms and scratching at the mould collected on her scales. "I went to figure out what the hell was going on and got sucked into some bloody tank. They put all these damn additives in, and I just about suffocated right there and then. I found a way out, but all it did was put me in the tank where you found me. It was just a slower way to suffocate."

"Sorry we didn't find you earlier," DI Adams said, and the sprite waved irritably.

"As if you could, in there. I was trying to get the sodding birds to find the W.I. for me, but who knows what happened with that."

DI Adams frowned, trying not to feel offended that the sprite had more faith in the Women's Institute than a detective inspector. "Why the W.I.?"

"I was hoping they'd get the dragons and burn the whole place down, but I suppose the message never got through."

"It might've got intercepted," DI Adams said, thinking of faces in the water and the missing people. "The waters have gone a bit wrong."

"Of course they bloody have. What d'you think I am, a mermaid sitting about combing her damn hair and plucking off sailors? I *work* to keep these waters running smoothly. They get upset if I'm not around."

DI Adams didn't much fancy the idea that the waters were so alive that they'd sink a village if they were having a bad day – it was even worse than shy duck ponds that were sometimes bottomless – but she had more urgent things to deal with. "Can you stop the flooding?"

Nellie sank into the water slightly, then bobbed up, nose wrinkled. "Can I strip the flesh from the bones of those who've wronged me and my waters, and keep eels in their ribcages?"

"No."

"Feed their toes to the pike and let their livers be nibbled by minnows, and allow frogs to spawn in their eye sockets?"

"Also no."

Nellie pouted. "So … what— I just fix everything and they skip happily off and do it all over again?"

"I'll arrest them."

"Oh, I'm sure *that'll* help."

DI Adams had to admit she felt a bit the same. "How about you destroy their machinery, flatten their buildings, sink their cars, and make sure they're so scared of water they'll never put a toe in so much as a paddling pool for the rest of their lives?"

Nellie stared at her for a moment, then said, "I'd probably have accepted a little localised flood damage, but yes."

The inspector winced. "Can we just do that, then?"

"No, you suggested all the rest." Nellie put her fingers in her mouth and whistled, a shrill, sweet sound that carried far better than it should have, echoing around the trees in strange ways, amplifying among the branches. "I suggest you go and arrest as many as you can before I get started."

An ominous sound swelled in the trees, a rumbling, rustling noise as of fast water on mossy rocks, or high winds in tall trees, and DI Adams said, "What're you doing?"

"Giving you a bit of backup," the sprite said, and slithered up the bank, quick and lithe. "I'm taking one of the old waterways. Meet you in there." She vanished into the trees, and DI Adams stared after her, listening to the sound still boiling through the woods, then waded to the bank, looking up at Dandy.

"This should be fun," she said.

It *was* fun, if one termed fun to be something akin to vertical mud-wrestling while so cold her fingers were almost refusing to bend. Eventually, though, she got her hands tangled in Dandy's thick dread-locks, and with him backing away from the edge and her kicking wildly at it, she finally ended up on the bank, panting and marginally warmer simply from the exertion. She got up, patted her pockets as if the contents of her jacket might have magically shifted themselves across to her, and came up with nothing but the keys for her car, which was of zero use, considering its current location. Dandy whined.

"What?"

He whined again, and lifted his chin at the far bank. She turned to look, and took a step backward, only to set off muttering in the trees all around her. She spun, and found herself surrounded. Beady avian eyes stared back at her, every scrap of ground crowded with ducks and geese and swans. None of them moved to rush her, and after a moment she said, "Right. Backup."

And then, because there was nothing else to do, she headed in the general direction of where she thought the retreat must be, only stopping when Dandy offered her a large stick. "Thanks," she said, taking it, and kept going. Whatever the W.I. were up to at the retreat, she needed to get them out before Nellie brought the whole place down. The ground was trembling underfoot, shudders running up her legs, and the wet earth felt like it was more liquid than dirt. Nothing was going to hold for much longer.

She clambered over the wall into the field that adjoined Lachlan's property, heading across it directly toward the outbuildings and the back of the retreat. The tremors continued, the birds hustling and fussing as if desperate to overtake her but waiting for a signal, and the sense of urgency grew and grew around her. By the time she reached the garden wall she was running, her feathery army pouring across the grass, quacking and honking and hissing, Dandy loping easily at her side. Shouts and screams started up from the retreat, and the birds broke, sweeping past her and surging over the wall.

The ground was shuddering constantly now, great convulsions that threatened to trip her up, pushing her faster. She spotted a stile to her left and sprinted to it, scrambling over the wall after the birds. Her view was obscured by them for a moment, then she spotted two dragons chasing the security guards across the yard, their wings tight to their backs while the guards yelled about crocodiles. Niall was running for the front of the house, and Beaufort was attacking the door to the *Sourced* building, which was vibrating so severely tiles were coming off the new roof, and she could hear machinery screaming under pressure. Dom sprinted past followed by Mortimer, who was yelling at the two dogs that he wasn't going to hurt *them*, while the dogs chased him as determinedly as he was chasing Dom.

And, to her utter astonishment, Miriam was sitting on the roof of the retreat, waving frantically. "*It's flooding!*" she yelled. "*We can't get out!*"

"Oh, bollocks," DI Adams said, thinking of Nellie and her furious waters, and the pool in the centre of the house. She sprinted for the retreat as the birds swamped the guards, and yelled to the world in general as she went, "*No one eat anyone!*"

Niall had made it to the house and was trying to get in the door, but a flood of geese descended on him, beating him about the head with their wings. He screamed, staggering back with both arms raised to protect himself, and DI Adams grabbed him by the scruff of his sweater.

"Keycard," she said, shaking him brusquely.

"Let me go!"

"Keycard, or I feed you to the crocodiles."

"You can't do that," he gasped. "You're *police.*"

"Want to try me?"

He flinched as a swan belted him on the leg, and scrabbled a keycard out of his pocket, thrusting it at her. She grabbed it and shoved him aside, running through the open door and into one of the desperately beige workout rooms, then on to the door panel at the back. She waved the keycard at the little screen next to it, but nothing happened. "*Hey,*" she shouted at Niall, who'd stumbled in after her and backed himself into a corner with a foam roller in each hand, trying to fend off the geese. "Why's this not working?"

He took a swipe at the nearest goose and the bird reared up, beating its wings wildly. "Power's gone down. Must be the water."

"And it defaults to *locked?*"

He gave her a frantic look as more birds waddled into the room. "It's a security feature!"

DI Adams abandoned him to the geese and ran back outside. "*Beaufort!*" she yelled. "I need this door opening!"

He didn't move from the *Sourced* building, just called back, "The machinery's making a terrible noise, and Alice and Jasmine are still in there."

"Go on, then." She spun as Walter galloped cheerily past. "Walter! Give me a hand."

He bounded over to her, and she pointed at the inner door. "Can you get that open?"

"Of course." He padded across the floor, pausing to snarl at the terrified Niall, who screamed, "Why are there *crocodiles?*"

"Escaped from the zoo," DI Adams said shortly. Walter reared up on his hindquarters, drawing in a deep breath, but even as he went to exhale on the panel, the building started to shake. It wasn't a shudder, or a tremble. This was a bone-felt shaking, starting from deep beneath them and rushing to the surface. "Oh, *no*—" DI Adams dropped her stick and ran across the room, grabbing Niall and hauling him to his feet. "Walter, *out!*" she shouted, and dragged the young man toward the door. The ground heaved, betraying her, and she stumbled, losing her grip on Niall and sprawling across the floor. She tried to get her feet under her, but everything was moving with the nightmarish sensation of a world become liquid, treacherous and unfamiliar, making it impossible to even stand, let alone run.

Sloshing echoed from behind the inner doors, the building gave one final shudder, and the inside walls exploded outward under the weight of some unimaginable amount of water. DI Adams grabbed the doorframe as the flood swept her up, clutching it desperately as she reached for Niall, but there was no holding on. The sheer weight of the inundation tore her away, and she covered her head with her hands, trying to draw her knees up to protect herself as she tumbled out into the garden, everything water and shouts and screams and the blaring birds, and she really, really wished she hadn't given Nellie ideas.

The water wasn't never-ending, though, as much as it felt like it was going to be, and it finally deposited her on the grass beyond the fountain, where she rolled unsteadily to a crouch, staring fearfully back at the building. Great gaps yawned in it, where windows had been busted out and taken parts of the walls with them, and at one corner the roof had taken on a dramatic angle, lurching toward the garden. Water was still washing out, not a flood anymore, but a steady river, and her stomach rolled over as she imagined the W.I. trapped in the transition room, pinned against the walls or jammed under the furniture, crushed and obliterated by the sheer weight of the water.

Except …

Except movement caught her eye and she turned to look at the largest gap in the walls. Rose floated out of it on a sofa cushion, holding onto Esther, who was belly-down on her own cushion, kicking her feet in delight.

"*Wheee!*" she shrieked, and Rose laughed. Behind them drifted Teresa and Pearl, each with a hand on another cushion that carried Ambrose. Gert waded through one of the doors, looking as if she hadn't enjoyed it half as much as the others, carting Vera in a piggyback and demanding that she stop trying to choke her. Rosemary and Carlotta were already grounded on the grass near the doors with Ed, and even he was giggling as all three of them rolled on the ground, trying to get to their feet. Priya was the last to emerge, sitting in a life ring that must have come from the pool, her long dark hair loose around her, looking as if she should have a cocktail in one hand.

DI Adams just stared at them, too startled to even feel relieved, until she heard a crash from behind her. She spun in time to see a large, soundproofed door come spinning out of the *Sourced* building, and a scaly tail vanishing inside. The whole structure was visibly shaking, and one end of the roof had already crumbled. She scrambled up, torn between checking on the ladies, helping Beaufort get Alice and Jasmine out, or arresting someone. She *really* wanted to arrest someone, and not everyone had stopped to look at the flooding. The three security guards were running for the cars, the birds still in honking pursuit, and they got halfway there before another battalion swept around the outbuildings from the opposite direction. The bearded man gave up and hunkered down in place, arms over his head, screaming, *"I surrender! I surrender!"*

The other two were made of sterner stuff, putting their backs to each other, and brandishing batons at the birds. They weren't going anywhere just yet. Walter had Niall face down on the gravel, one large paw resting casually on his back, and Mortimer had been chasing Dom, so that just left Lachlan still lurking somewhere, and—

"Where's Miriam?" she shouted. *"Miriam!"*

She was rewarded by a screech of brakes and the hideous, unmistakable crunch of a windscreen breaking from the front of the building, and she bounced to her feet, breaking into a sprint.

"Miriam!" Gert yelled, and the cry was taken up by the rest of the W.I., so that by the time DI Adams raced around the front of the retreat she had the full force of the Toot Hansell Women's Institute thundering after her.

A car had stopped with its nose almost touching the retreat building, a skidding path etched in the gravel behind it. The windscreen was a haze of shattered glass, and Miriam stood on the edge of the newly flat roof, her bare feet planted wide and her curly hair drenched and wild, clutching a roof tile in both hands.

"I've got more where that came from!" she yelled, as Lachlan clambered out of the car.

"You're *insane!*" he shouted back at her. "You could've killed me! You and your damn dog!"

"I don't *have* a dog!"

DI Adams looked at the path in the gravel, then at Dandy, standing in front of the gate in his usual Labrador size. He tipped his head at her and squeaked his duck, and she had an idea that he might've been a little larger and rather more visible a few moments ago, which would explain the car veering close enough to Miriam to allow her to hit it with her tile.

"This is property destruction!" Lachlan bellowed.

"You locked us in a collapsing building!" Priya shouted, and he swung around, suddenly aware he had an audience.

"You're trespassers! You've been harassing me since I got here!" He spotted DI Adams and jabbed a finger at her. "*Finally*. Arrest them *all*."

DI Adams nodded. "Yeah, a bit of trespassing does not justify abduction, false imprisonment, recklessness, and wholesale environmental damage."

"I didn't do any of those!"

"If you didn't, you told someone to," she said, and looked at Miriam. "Would you like to come down?"

"Ooh, yes please. It's making me quite dizzy," she said, and dropped the tile. It bounced off the edge of the roof and spun toward Lachlan, making him jump back.

"*Hey*," he said, and looked at DI Adams. "That's assault! You all saw it!"

"I didn't," Teresa said, to a murmur of agreement.

"And I don't *care*," Miriam said. "Plus there was sugar in that last cake. *Lots* of it."

"And gluten," Alice called. She was limping up the drive with Jasmine, her hair uncharacteristically dishevelled, but her back still straight.

"You ... but ..." Lachlan glared from one of them to the other, then at DI Adams. "*Arrest them!*"

"For cake? Not bloody likely." She looked around. "I need to use a phone, though. Anyone's work?"

"Mine," Jasmine said, hurrying forward. She looked at Lachlan as she handed the mobile to DI Adams. "Thanks for the Wi-Fi. I don't think you'll have a lot of support in the village now."

"What?"

DI Adams looked at the phone. It was open on the Toot Hansell Facebook group, where a Live broadcast had very recently ended, and the comments section was already flooding with angry emojis and all caps text. "What's this?" she asked Jasmine.

"You may want a copy," Alice said. "Jasmine recorded everything Lachlan told us."

"That's inadmissible," Lachlan said, planting his legs wide. "It's been faked."

DI Adams nodded. "Well, I'm arresting you for false imprisonment."

"Rubbish. This lot stormed in *entirely* on their own."

"And locked themselves in a flooding building? That's just a start, anyway. I'll have a few more charges by this afternoon." She waved him ahead of her, back toward the outbuildings. "Come on. My car's in a sinkhole, so you'll have to sit tight for a bit."

"Bloody country coppers," Lachlan muttered, marching forward with his arms crossed. "You've no idea what you're dealing with."

"I don't think you do, either," DI Adams said, and wondered how to handle the whole crocodile/dragon situation, as well as the attack birds. She could sort that out later, though. Right now she got to arrest a very rich man who thought nothing could catch up to him, as well as his minions, and she called that a good day.

The best sort, in fact.

She started back toward where the dragons were blocking the security guards' cars from leaving, the ground already steadier underfoot. The rain had stopped, too.

"Um, DI Adams?" Miriam called from behind her. "I'm still stuck."

"Oh, *right.* Sorry."

25
MIRIAM

Miriam put one final wreath into the big cardboard box and shut the lid, sliding it a little further back on the stage so she could pull an empty one to the front in its place.

"Rose," she called. "Are you *still* putting bones on the wreaths? I'm not sure we're going to sell a lot of them."

"Of course we will," Rose said. "Not everyone wants chocolate and hearts for Valentine's, you know."

"We can sell them as a set with Gilbert's earrings," Gert said, holding up a pair. They were incredibly delicate, skeletal fish worked from dragon scales and wire, and when they caught the light they seemed to move. Miriam had an idea they *did* move, and had already decided she wouldn't be buying any. The last thing she needed was earrings biting her neck in the middle of her Morrison's shop.

"Sorry," Mortimer said. "But he was so proud of them. Maybe we can keep them for Halloween?"

"They are exceptionally good," Beaufort said. "From a technical point of view." He had a plate of cheese scones in front of him that were an alarming orange colour and topped with so much of what Miriam suspected to be cayenne pepper that no one else had been able to touch them. He seemed to be enjoying them, though.

The dragons both seemed very relaxed, sprawled on the hall's scarred floor with large mugs of tea next to them. During the floods, to hear Mortimer tell it, they'd been on the brink of civil war, but Beaufort had been rather more sanguine when Miriam asked him about it. "Everyone needs to be heard," he had said. "I've been listening. We may make a few changes, but mostly people just need to know their concerns are taken into consideration. I think it's less likely to be civil war and more likely to be an Amelia-led revolution, to be honest. And that would be rather interesting, in my mind."

"We shall put the earrings on the stall," Alice said now, wrapping ribbon around the top of a jar of cherry jam and tying it off neatly. "Rose is quite right. It breaks up the monotony a little."

"Monotony?" Carlotta said. "It's *Valentine's.* Love! Hearts! Flowers! What could be monotonous about that?"

"It's a very single-minded theme," Alice said, putting the jar in a box and moving on to another. "One needs a little variety."

"You have no sense of romance," Rosemary said. "No wonder your husband vanished."

"He was a criminal," Alice protested, but she was smiling.

"Vanished," Teresa said, making air quotes, and the ladies laughed. The question of Alice's twice-missing husband wasn't one that would ever have an answer, but everyone needed their secrets.

Miriam picked up another willow wreath, taking a sip of tea as she did so. She was personally in favour of any sort of variety over the usual Valentine's saccharine tones of pastel pinks and luminous reds, but she also thought the W.I. walked that line rather well, as they did many things. She remained unconvinced by the bones, though.

The hall was warm, the boiler thrumming away in the cupboard with dragon-tuned efficiency, and the whole place smelled of cake and jam and sugar, and the gentle scents of wicker and willow and dried flowers. Outside, the sun was out, the sky a pale, high blue that Miriam had greeted with something close to wonder every day for the last two weeks. The flood-waters were gone, drawn back into the earth, and the duck pond had returned to its usual dimensions. The waterways that encircled the village and blossomed in side streets and squares and back gardens were clear and cool again, sharp with the memory of old snows and deep ice, and she hadn't seen faces in any of them.

The village square did still have a cavernous hole in the middle of it, admittedly, and some history students were currently arguing heatedly with the council, who were trying to fill it in, about the importance of the tunnels and the relevance of some of the items found at the bottom. That had somehow spilled over into the archaeology departments of at least two major universities, resulting in some fairly entertaining disputes over who got to dig up what, as well as brisk business for both the deli and the pub as they came out for day trips.

The mud and debris had been cleared from the streets and the traumatised gardens, and Miriam thought most of them would recover. There were some nasty crevasses and holes still dotted around the village, strung about with increasingly tatty warning tape, but other than a couple of incidents with drinkers returning home from the pubs, no one had come to any harm over them (and that had been less harm than embarrassment at having to be pulled out of an ex-koi pond at 11 p.m. by one's neighbours).

Otherwise, Toot Hansell had slowly slid back toward normality, other than the fact that there were still too many geese and swans about the place. They weren't as aggressive, though, and Miriam did understand Nellie wanting to keep them close for now. She was likely very unsettled. The only other lasting effect seemed to be that almost everyone had acquired extra boarders. She currently had Mortimer's hedgehog plus two others hibernating in one of her kitchen cupboards, and a family of shrews had taken over her favourite wellies.

She got up, stretching, and said, "More tea?"

A murmur of agreement went up around the table, and she wandered through to the kitchen, taking a moment to revel in the clear water running from the tap. It was such a *luxury,* when one thought about it, just like the blue sky and the sun and not having to struggle into a waterproof jacket every time one stepped outside. She sighed, a little exhalation of happiness, and muddled about with the big teapots, humming to herself quietly.

When she walked back into the hall, straining under the weight of the two full pots, she almost dropped them. DI Colin Collins, also known as her nephew, jumped up from the end of the table and came to take them from her.

"One at a time, Aunty," he said, giving her a quick peck on the cheek.

"I can manage," she protested, although, admittedly, the sight of DI Adams sitting at the table had shaken her somewhat. "Um … coffee?" she offered, and DI Adams held up a mug.

"I brought my own."

"Our coffee's excellent," Priya protested.

"I didn't say it wasn't. But we were at the deli, so I got one there."

"Careful, Adams. You're offending the locals," Colin said, sitting down and helping himself to a mince pie, then offering two to Mortimer. "Get them while you can, lad."

"Thanks," Mortimer said. He'd been a rather lovely deep blue earlier, but he seemed to have faded somewhat since the inspectors had arrived.

"Why are you even here?" DI Adams demanded of Colin. "You had nothing to do with this case."

He held up a neatly chequered piece of Battenburg cake in answer, then added, "Also, floods? Secret mining operations? Abductions? Street battles? Attack geese? I miss all the good stuff."

"It didn't feel very good at the time," Pearl said. "Our poor village. It just about sank."

"It's looking alright now," DI Adams said, taking a piece of apple cake from the plate Rosemary was offering her. "It must've been a big clean-up."

"Well, the rain stopped almost immediately," Alice said. "I assume that was to do with Nellie?"

"It was," Beaufort said, a little indistinctly. He swallowed hard and let out a small belch of flame. "Excuse me."

"Excused," Priya said.

"As soon as Nellie was back, the waters settled," the old dragon said. "A sprite can't survive if her waters die, but that goes both ways."

"Symbiotic relationship," Rose observed.

"So that's why the waters weren't running properly?" DI Adams asked. "They couldn't without her?"

"Oh, she was alive, so they *could*," Beaufort said. "They just didn't want to, and took it on themselves to flood everything until the culprit gave Nellie back."

There was a long pause, and Miriam shivered. She'd always respected water in the same vague way she respected trees and weather and the natural world in general, but it had never occurred to her that any of it might go on the attack in quite such a deliberate manner.

"Great," DI Adams muttered, and took a large swig of coffee. "But fine. The water stopped flooding as soon as it got Nellie back."

"They," Beaufort said. "I mean, it's a small detail, but..."

"They," DI Adams agreed, and Colin took a careful bite of his cake and munched on it slowly, not taking his eyes off the High Lord as he continued.

"The waters went back to normal, filled the streams and took all the excess groundwater with them. They also let the rain go."

"They let the rain go," Colin whispered, and had a mouthful of tea.

"The rain was part of the water trying to drown everything?" Teresa asked.

"Maybe, or maybe they were trying to clean the run-off away. There is a certain amount of guesswork involved with these theories. I'm not sure even Nellie understands how things work completely."

"So rain stopped, water went back to normal, and that was it?" DI Adams asked.

"Somewhat," Alice said. "There was rather a lot of cleaning up to do, but everyone got stuck in."

"She means *we* got stuck in," Gert said. "Plus I got my niece's partner's cousin's brother-in-law to round up a few young folk and get them over here for a weekend. Food and a few quid in exchange for some sweeping and shovelling and clearing the drains."

Colin leaned toward Miriam. "Is she just making these relatives up at this point?" he whispered.

"I really don't know," she whispered back. "I've never asked."

Colin nodded, and straightened up again, handing Mortimer another mince pie.

"Once we started, everyone else did, too," Alice said. "Cleaning up, making runs for water until we were sure ours was drinkable, all that sort of thing. Jasmine's video rather brought everyone together. Common enemy, I imagine."

"The video was good thinking," DI Adams said, passing a piece of tea loaf to the empty air next to her chair. It vanished. "Well done."

"Thanks," Jasmine said. She was very pink, and Miriam didn't think it was from the heating. "I was just lucky I got onto the Wi-Fi. I was actually already on Facebook Live when Lachlan came in, because I wanted to show everyone what was really going on, the chemicals and the fake bottling plant and so on. I didn't think he'd *tell* us what he was doing."

"Did it help you?" Pearl asked DI Adams. "What's happened with him?"

DI Adams made a frustrated noise, and Colin said, "Her coffee intake is truly alarming right now. I think she went to the deli here because Skipton's run out."

The inspector scowled at him, then shrugged. "Lachlan's not just rich. He's *filthy* rich, and has absolutely no qualms with throwing people under the bus. He's still pushing the idea the Live was faked, and Niall will probably take the fall for anything we can actually get to stick, which so far isn't much. Lachlan's name isn't on anything. I still think we *could* trace some stuff to him, but it means getting the Serious Fraud Office involved, and they're not interested because there's not enough evidence. So then there's the Environment Agency, but so far we haven't been able to find any of the lithium brine he extracted. No one's sure if he somehow got rid of all traces of it, or if it was never there in the first place. Testing's not turned up anything in the spring water at all so …" She raised her hands and dropped them again. "Maybe it was just a Toot Hansell thing?"

"Which means she's drinking a lot of coffee and getting a lot of people's backs up while she tries to get something to stick," Colin said, leaning over the table and pushing the plate of Battenberg toward her. "Have some cake, Adams."

She frowned at it. "I have heard he's having a lot of trouble with water wherever he stays, though. Burst pipes and rain getting in ceilings and cars falling into potholes."

"Well, that's something," Pearl said.

"Also he's filed a load of complaints about harassment."

"Harassment?" Alice asked, frowning. "Against us, do you mean?"

"No, random people keep running up and throwing milkshakes and eggs at him. His security guards have caught a couple of them, but they don't seem to have any particular affiliations, and as soon as they're bailed out they vanish on us."

"Fancy that," Gert said, and reached for the teapot. DI Adams narrowed her eyes, but didn't say anything.

"Are we going to get charged with anything?" Jasmine asked. "I mean, I know we *did* trespass—"

"No," DI Adams said, holding up both hands. "You were exercising your legal right to protest, on public property. I didn't see anything else. Plus, if he does that, you can go after him for false imprisonment, and he knows it."

"What about the security people?" Carlotta asked.

"Weirdly nervous about crocodiles and geese, and unwilling to admit they were bested by a Women's Institute."

"Well," Alice said, picking up her tea. "That's nothing to be ashamed of, really."

"What about Dom?" Miriam asked. "What's happening with him?"

"He and Lachlan are both still charged with kidnapping and false imprisonment for Esther and the others, and I'm doing what I can with that. I've told Dom he gets a pass on shutting me into that bloody room if he can give up enough information for me to get Lachlan, but we're not there yet."

"You'll give him a *pass?*" Mortimer blurted. "You almost drowned!"

DI Adams grimaced. "Only because I took the lid of the tank off.

He just intended to keep me in there while they cleared out the extraction equipment and made a plan for the missing people." She looked at the space by her chair. "The whole tank thing was your fault, you know." A squeak came from the space, and Angelus lumbered to his feet with an anxious whine. DI Adams sighed. "Anyone know how to get an invisible dog to give up on a chew toy?"

"Training," Rose said firmly. "I keep saying."

Priya snorted. "Rubbish. You just hide Angelus's toys when you don't like them."

"That works too."

"Opening the tank meant you saved Nellie, and therefore the village," Beaufort said to the inspector, and she shrugged.

"*Did* Dom and Lachlan kidnap Esther and the rest?" Pearl asked, leaning forward. "What happened there?"

DI Adams shook her head. "They both have the same story – they found them wandering around the fields, and took them in. Obviously they're then claiming different things happened after. Dom says Lachlan coerced him into hiding all four on his property, in case they'd seen anything that might give away what Lachlan was up to. Lachlan says he asked Dom to take them back to the village and assumed he had."

"Mortimer had an idea about the vanishing," Miriam said, and Mortimer choked on his mince pie, his scales fading even further.

He swallowed hard and said, "Um, yes. So Nellie was sending messages through the waters, trying to get to the W.I., but basically just attracting anyone sensitive enough to notice them. And if anyone went to investigate the messages the birds would chase them, and drive them through the forest to the farm in the hope they'd save Nellie. But when that didn't work, and the people were taken in by Dom or whoever, the waters got a bit frustrated and started showing reflections of them and imitating their voices. Maybe hoping that anyone who saw them would come to the rescue. And I guess those reflections turned into projections, if one were *really* perceptive. They were never actually there at all, although they looked very real, which is why I couldn't get any scents, and we couldn't find Ambrose's toothbrush."

There was silence for a moment, then Gert said, "No wonder Ambrose's pacemaker was a bit dicky, after all that walking to get to the farm."

"How did Esther do that *at all?*" DI Adams asked. "And in the rain?"

"Tunnels," Beaufort said. "That's our theory, anyway. Either they weren't all flooded, so people could still walk, or the waters simply picked people up and floated them along. There are hot springs out there, you know. It wouldn't have been cold at all."

Colin sipped his tea and grinned. "How could I miss all this? Really?"

"Well, you come and get muddy and have your car fall in a sinkhole next time," DI Adams said. "My insurance premiums are going to be *ridiculous* next year."

Rose tapped the table. "Well, other than a few milkshakes"—she arched her eyebrows at Gert, who tipped her head slightly—"Lachlan sounds like he's going to get away with this."

"He won't," DI Adams and Beaufort said together, and the inspector leaned back in her chair to frown at the High Lord. He grinned at her, toothy and cheerful, and after a moment she straightened up. "I need more coffee," she said to her mug.

"Have this," Priya said, pushing an already buttered slice of tea loaf toward her. "There's some caffeine in it, at least. And dates."

DI Adams took it with a sigh, had a large bite, and looked along the table at the wreaths and jars. "What is all this? Did you raid a Laura Ashley?"

"Valentine's market on Saturday, Inspector," Alice said. "The wreaths are a little unusual, admittedly, but we like to try something new every year. All proceeds go to the village clean-up and helping fix the damage in people's houses. Will you be coming? We can keep a wreath for you." DI Adams gave her a horrified look, and Alice smiled, her eyes crinkling at the corners as she held up one of Carlotta's creations, exploding with pink ribbons, flowers, and wooden heart shapes. "Maybe this one?"

"I'll buy it," Colin declared. "I'll pay double if you put it on your desk, Adams. *Please.*"

DI Adams managed to swallow her cake, and Miriam thought she'd refuse outright, but instead she pointed at another wreath. This one was Rosemary's, and Miriam was almost sure she and Carlotta had done their best to out-do each other with the sheer amount of hearts and glitter. It had pink lollipops on it, and the word *love* shaped in shiny red metal studded it in about five different places. "I'll take that one," the inspector said. "If I have to have one, he does too."

A ripple of laughter ran around the table, and Miriam leaned back in her chair, looking at the windows. A sliver of blue sky was visible, and while the afternoon light was already low, it was rich with sun. Birdsong filtered in even through the closed door, and if she squinted she could just see the duck pond. She could imagine Nellie there, her hair swirling around her as she chased the fish with pale, snapping fingers, her bulbous eyes luminous in the murky water. Murky, but not dirty, the waters that fed it clear and muscular, embracing the village once more.

It was all so desperately fragile, the balance they all walked, Folk and humans alike. Each trying to find their way in a world that was constantly changing, constantly offering up new challenges and new threats and new wonders, and sometimes one was hard-pressed to know the difference. And they were all so deeply entwined, whether they knew it or not, human magic and Folk magic and the everyday enchantment of both. One couldn't survive without the other; there was no way to divide the world into factions and believe it still worked. It was a dance of parts, as beautiful as it was delicate, and the very thought of it filled her heart, like spring mists and autumn moons, heartbreaking and beautiful all at once.

She took a deep, gentle breath, and a rasping yet oddly cultured voice said, "Ay-up. What've you done to my village? There's a hole in it!"

"Thompson, get off the table," Alice said, flicking a piece of willow at the ragged tabby tomcat who had just appeared next to the milk jug, one paw in a plate of Scotch eggs.

"Some welcome that is. Take a break from the rain and come back to find the place trashed and people poking you with sticks." But he jumped off the table onto a spare chair and said, "Seriously. What happened here?"

"We fixed it, no thanks to you," Rose said.

He narrowed his eyes at her. "Bet you broke it in the first place, too."

"Where were you?" Beaufort asked. "We could've used a little help."

"You're not my only responsibility, you know. I had business to attend to in Leeds."

"More important than the village sinking?" Priya demanded.

"A lot more."

"We almost lost the whole place," Gert said, frowning at him.

"You'd have lost more than that if I hadn't gone to Leeds." Thompson yawned. He had raw, painful-looking patches on one shoulder and some new notches in his ears, and he added, "Any salmon?"

"You've hardly earned it," Alice said, but she got up and walked to the kitchen, and Miriam watched her go with a smile. Love had so many shapes, and so many forms, and she couldn't think of a greater joy than seeing so many of them gathered in one small hall, in one small village, in one small corner of the world. And how many others must be out there, each as strange and complicated and messy and beautiful as the other! It made her heart hurt in the best possible way.

"Mince pie?" she said to Mortimer.

"I think I've finished them."

"I've got more," she said, and he gave her his big, toothy grin and she was quite sure she couldn't possibly feel any more joy than this. Nor did she need to.

This moment, right here, was enough. Small, and inexplicable, and wild with the most strange and wonderful magic. And that was all one needed in the end.

For things to be enough.

A BEAUFORT SCALES MYSTERY

THANK YOU

Thank you once again for joining me on another cake-fuelled romp across the Yorkshire Dales, lovely people. Well, possibly less a romp and more a splash this time, but either way, thank you.

Thank you for your patience in waiting for this next Beaufort, thank you for your messages and emails and chats, thank you for your title ideas and suggestions and enthusiasm. Thank you so, so much for believing there's space in the world for tea-drinking dragons and resourceful ladies of a certain age, and thank you for *creating* that space. Yorkshire isn't the only place magic can be found, that's quite clear.

I hope very much you've enjoyed this latest, somewhat damp instalment, and that you were able to keep your cake out of the water and the shrews out of your wellies. It's always such a pleasure to share these tales with you, and it means such a lot that you're willing to invest your time and energy in coming along with me on some very strange adventures. You are *amazing.*

But before I let you go and check on the ducks, of course, I need to make my usual request. I'd appreciate it immensely if you could take the time to pop a quick review up at your favourite retailer, or on Goodreads. It doesn't have to be long – "has anyone checked on the sheep," or "those herons were definitely up to no good" will more than suffice. More reviews mean the retailers decide people really are interested in rogue geese, so they show my books to other readers who might also harbour an interest in rogue geese, and in this way we shall build our kingdom of cake-based escapism! *Muahaha!*

Wait, no. I mean in this way we shall introduce more people to the importance of small dragons and large cakes, which means I can write more books and eat more cake, and you can read more books and eat more cake, and ... actually, yes, the end of the last paragraph was kind of accurate, I guess? *Anyhow.* Reviews are as vital as cake for authors, so if you are able to leave one, it would be the most wonderful help. Thank you so much!

And if you'd like to send me a copy of your review, to chat about dragons and baked goods, or ask about anything, drop me a message at kim@kmwatt.com. I'd love to hear from you!

Until next time - read on!

Kim

BEWARE THE SNAP-SNAP-SNAP ...

Baton. Light. Chocolate. Duck.

This is not DS Adams' usual kit. This is not DS Adams' usual case. She doesn't think it's *anyone's* usual case, not with the vanishing children and the looming bridge and the hungry river. Not with the *snap-snap-snap*.

But six kids are missing, and she's not going to let there be a seventh. Not on her watch. And she knows how to handle human monsters, after all. How different can this really be?

So: Baton. Light. Chocolate. And the bloody duck.

Let's be having you, then.

Scan above to find What Happened in London, or use the link below:
https://readerlinks.com/l/3699721/b8

PS: This is a darker story. There's precious little cake and a whole lot of peril, and not a single dragon. So it may not be for everyone. Just so you're prepared!

TREATS TO TAME THE COLD

Your free recipe collection awaits!

And cakes to soothe the geese. Possibly the swans. Not sure about the ducks, though. They were unexpected.

Ducks aside, though, having some treats to hand can help in all sorts of investigations. No one can be up to much if they arrive bearing cake, can they …?

Grab your free collection at the link, plus, if this is your first visit to Toot Hansell and my newsletter, I'm also going to send you some story collections – including one about how that whole barbecue thing started …

Happy baking!

Scan above or head to https://readerlinks.com/l/4454085/rm to get your free recipe collection!

ABOUT THE AUTHOR

Hello, lovely person. I'm Kim, and in addition to the Beaufort Scales stories I write other funny, magical books that offer a little escape from the serious stuff in the world and hopefully leave you a wee bit happier than you were when you started. Because happiness, like friendship, matters.

I write about baking-obsessed reapers setting up baby ghoul petting cafes, and ladies of a certain age joining the Apocalypse on their Vespas. I write about friendship, and loyalty, and lifting each other up, and the importance of tea and cake.

But mostly I write about how wonderful people (of all species) can really be.

If you'd like to find out the latest on new books in *The Beaufort Scales* series, as well as discover other books and series, giveaways, extra reading, and more, jump on over to www.kmwatt.com and check everything out there.

Read on!

amazon.com/Kim-M-Watt/e/B07JMHRBMC
goodreads.com/kimmwatt
bookbub.com/authors/kim-m-watt
facebook.com/KimMWatt
instagram.com/kimmwatt

ACKNOWLEDGEMENTS

A snail has 14,000 teeth.

Entirely irrelevant, I know (I tried to find out fun facts about ducks, but they were less fun and more horrifying, and now I fear them more than the geese, and anatidaephobia makes a *lot* more sense), but if you've made it this far I figured the least you deserved was a fun fact that you can casually drop into conversation later.

And if you ask how snail teeth would ever come up in conversation, well. Come and sit next to me. *Many* things come up that one would not expect.

But fun facts are not the point of this section. The point of this section is to say a little thank you to the many, many people who helped make this book a reality. And they are, in no particular order whatsoever, and likely forgetting a great many wonderful people (I am *sorry,* you know I love you, I just can't fit you all in now I've brought up toothy snails):

You, of course, lovely reader. For reading, supporting, and believing in the power of dragons, cake, and ladies of a certain age. Without you, none of these books would exist.

My wonderful friends, who rarely question my strange diversions into snail-related trivia, who remind me to take days off and eat and go outside, and are patient with me when I vanish for weeks at a time into a story.

The fabulous Lynda at Easy Reader Editing, who has worked her magic on every one of my books. They would be much lesser without her (and I wouldn't have a fraction as much fun editing). All good grammar praise goes to her. All mistakes are mine.

Jon, who has beta read every single one of my books, and been a critique partner for many. Thank you for knowing how to soothe a writer's fragile ego at the same time as challenge them to do better. That's an art, and I appreciate it so much.

My utterly wonderful beta readers, who squeeze in the time to read my surprise books at all sorts of unpredictable intervals, and give me invaluable feedback on everything from dormice distribution to the differentiation between aquifers and springs. (Naomi, I'm sorry I disregarded your advice on the dormice. I just needed a dormouse for some reason ...)

Every writer needs a support network. We don't exist in glorious solitude, no matter what movies might tell us. And I have the best network possible. Thank you all.

Onward to the next adventure, lovely people. May your world be full of all the best and most beautiful loves and magics.

Kim x

ALSO BY KIM M. WATT

The Beaufort Scales Series (cozy mysteries with dragons)

"The addition of covert dragons to a cozy mystery is perfect ... and the dragons are as quirky and entertaining as the rest of the slightly eccentric residents of Toot Hansell."

– Goodreads reviewer

The Gobbelino London, PI series

"This series is a wonderful combination of humor and suspense that won't let you stop until you've finished the book. Fair warning, don't plan on doing anything else until you're done ..."

– Goodreads reviewer

The DI Adams Mysteries

"... will grip you within its story and not let go so be prepared going in with snacks and caffeine because you won't want to put it down."

– Goodreads reviewer

The Hollowbeck Paranormal Cozy Mysteries

(With Amelia Ash)

"It's a no-brainer to recommend this one to anyone who enjoys cozies. Or laughing. Or paranormal stuff. Or sarcastic wit. Or great writing in any form."

- Amazon reviewer

Other Tales

Oddly Enough: Tales of the Unordinary, Volume One

"The stories are quirky, charming, hilarious, and some are all of the above without a dud amongst the bunch …"

– Goodreads reviewer

Need more stories?

Join the Ko-fi membership site for monthly, member-exclusive short stories, behind-the scenes content, early access to ebooks, and more!

Free stories!

The Cat Did It

Of course the cat did it. Sneaky, snarky, and up to no good – that's the cats in this feline collection, which you can grab free by signing up to the newsletter. Just remember – if the cat winks, always wink back …

The Tales of Beaufort Scales

Modern dragons are a little different these days. There's the barbecue fixation, for starters … You'll get these tales free once you've signed up for the newsletter!

Printed in Great Britain
by Amazon